FAR CRY

A NOVEL

FAR CRY

Sigrid Heath

EPIGRAPH BOOKS
RHINEBECK, NEW YORK

Paperback ISBN 978-1-951937-01-0
Hardcover ISBN 978-1-951937-02-7
eBook ISBN 978-1-951937-03-4

Library of Congress Control Number 2020903571

Ilustrations by Carol Zaloom
Book design by Colin Rolfe

Epigraph Books
22 East Market Street, Suite 304
Rhinebeck, NY 12572
(845) 876-4861
epigraphps.com

For my daughter, Siri Crane,
whose presence in my life is an endless joy

'...we must suffer, suffer into truth.'
Aeschylus, *The Oresteia*,
translator Robert Fagles

'I imagine one of the reasons
people cling to their hates so
stubbornly is because they sense,
once hate is gone, they will be
forced to deal with pain.'
James Baldwin

PART ONE
INDIAN COUNTRY

CHAPTER 1

I was sitting on the ground, straight up against something rigid, my head was hanging, my chin on my chest. I smelled smoke and heard the snap and hiss of a fire. I'd been asleep and didn't want to wake up but had to know where the fire was, so I opened my eyes. I saw my hands lying loosely in my lap. My legs were sticking straight out in front of me like a doll's and my ankles were tied. I saw that I was wearing Jake's boots and a pair of his thick woollen socks.

I raised my head, it hurt terribly to do it, and saw that, yes, there was a fire in front of me, not too close, but not that far away. It was a small, tame fire, quietly burning on the ground. People were standing around it. They seemed unnaturally tall, and for a moment I thought I was dreaming and was relieved. I then realised they seemed large because I was on the ground and they were standing. A few were moving about slowly, almost lazily, spreading things on the ground by the fire. Someone tossed in a small branch, sparks rose.

The people didn't seem to know I was there. I was thirsty. I tried to say something, but couldn't. Something bitter came into my throat and I had to cough it up. Coughing made a pain rise in my head like a demon pounding on my skull from the inside. When I held myself still, it subsided somewhat.

The people were settling themselves around the fire. I tried to count them, but was unable to. There weren't that many, as far as I could tell, fewer than ten. I was *very* thirsty. I tried to lift my arm to gesture to them, but found that both arms were tied against my body. Then I realised that my body was tied to a tree, my back rammed up against the trunk, with ropes going around and around my torso. The people sitting around that fire had to be the ones who'd tied me to the tree.

My breathing got fast and my heart felt strange in my chest. At least I believe this is how it was. I'm struggling now to recall as much as I can of these events, as I struggled then to stay conscious and make sense of it all. I was determined to put together, piece by piece, the particulars of my situation. I had to wake up.

I had to keep my eyes on those people. The fire's light didn't spread far and it was night. I saw colours moving the way water moves, in and out of deep shadows, punctuated by the articulation of an arm, a head turning, someone rising, going into the dark, someone returning from the dark. But I could see nothing that told me who those people were. Something was wrong with my eyes. I blinked and squinted, blinked and squinted harder though it hurt like hell. I forced myself to stare through the murk and distortions. I kept at it until, bit by bit, I understood that those people around the fire, those people who'd tied me to that tree, were Indians. I'd seen Indians, and those were Indians. I'd been captured by Indians.

I don't remember exactly how I felt. Knowing myself as I do now, I imagine I was stunned, yet removed. *Is this what's happened to me? Truly?* It was like something out of someone else's story, I'd heard many. But here I was, tied to a tree, and there were the Indians, sitting around the fire. I was a captive, those people were my captors, and there was no escape.

They're going to kill me. I won't let them, I told myself. I'll make myself die before they do it in some hideous way. I was certain they were waiting for a larger audience to do the unspeakable things I'd heard of. I'd stop my breath, stop my heart. I'd *will* myself dead. But I thought of my mother. I had to see my mother again. *I will stay alive. One way or another. I will keep my wits about me and I will stay alive.*

Then one of them stood. I watched him walk towards me, silhouetted against the firelight, coming closer and closer, until he was right in front of me and I could see nothing else. He was holding something metal. *He's going to cut my throat.* I pushed my spine into the tree trunk, turned my head sharply away and forced a howl out of my mouth. He put his hand on my jaw and began to turn my face front. I tried to bite him. He laughed and spoke to me as if I were a skittish horse. I made myself look. There was the hand at the end of a red sleeve, but no knife. He was urging me to drink from a metal cup. I felt the cool edge of it against my lower lip. Water. He slowly tipped the cup and I finished it. He turned back to the others. I watched as they arranged their blankets and then lay down by the dwindling fire. *What happened? How did I get here?*

I was lying on my horse with my arm hanging down, stroking him. I thought I'd been hurt and he was taking me home. Then I realised it wasn't Pegasus, I was on some other horse, was tied to it. The shock of this was awful, I feared for my horse. *But what came before this? Before the horse?* Plums. *What? Stupid! Think harder.* A bright sky. The smell of smoke. *Yes.* The sound of something shattering close by my ear. *Yes. Yes. Go deeper.*

The sound of shattering came back over and over. I wanted to shut it out, it stirred up such fear in me that I couldn't breathe properly. But I had to know what it was, it seemed somehow the key, so I let it come and come and come, with greater and greater intensity, until I was so terrified by it that I pissed myself. Oddly, the letting go, the warmth of it between my legs, feeling it seep through my skirts, sitting there in the cooling wetness of my piss eliminated any remaining confusion about my condition. It brought back the thing that explained the sound, that told me how I'd gotten there.

The wild plums were ripe. I'd walked out of the dugout, around behind it, up over the crest of the hill and then down the long slope to the creek where there the plums grew thick. I heard my skirt swishing in the grass, the crunch of my husband's boots, the ping of my wedding ring striking grass seeds. The sun was going down behind the hill in back of me and it was already shadowy along the creek. The creek water didn't move fast, but it moved and made a pleasant sound.

The air buzzed with cicadas. A red-winged blackbird called. I filled the basket with plums, stood for a bit among the trees watching the water. Then I turned and began walking back up the hill with the basket of fruit in the crook of my left arm, my carbine in my right.

The sun had just dropped behind the ridge and tall spears of grass were sharp black against the yellow sky. I thought I smelled smoke on the breeze, and as I was wondering about this, thin black swirls started rising from the other side of the hill. I stood transfixed as the swirls thickened, the smell became unmistakeable, it was smoke, more and more of it. The dugout! *Pegasus!* I began to run, tripping on my skirts, I grabbed them up and ran harder.

Just short of the crest, at the steepest part of the hill, they sprang up out of the grass right in front of me. Four of them — black against the sky — as if the earth had just spit them up from its bowels. I raised the gun but one of them wrenched it from my hand. I saw his hair flying, the arc of his arm as it rose and rose and then came down.

That shattering was the sound of bones breaking. Mine, the bones of my face.

I'd been a girl gathering plums. Demeter's daughter was a girl gathering flowers when Hades rose up from a crack in the earth and took her. That's what happened. They rose up in front of me, cracked my head, and took me. They dragged me away face down through the grass as I reached for the plums.

These are my first memories of captivity. The men around the fire — a small band of Lakota, as I later learned — took me just after sunset on a September afternoon in 1866. I was nineteen years old.

CHAPTER 2

I woke up, still sitting, still tied to a tree. The same tree? No. They'd taken me to a different place. I was pretty sure of that. It seemed a good sign that I could tell, though I'm not sure how. Time had passed. Hours? *Days?* How many? Not knowing disturbed me, but there was nothing I could do about it.

I was not in such awful pain as before, but my vision was still murky. There were trees, the Indians, a fire. But it was like trying to see underwater in the pond back home in Virginia. That water was the colour of tea and nearly opaque. The air between me and the Indians around the fire was like that. I could barely see through it, no matter how hard I tried.

I closed my eyes. I assessed my injuries, moving my parts one by one. Toes, ankles, calves, knees, thighs, hips; fingers, wrists, elbows, shoulders. My limbs worked, as far as I could tell. I could take a deep breath with no terrible pain, and could swell and contract my belly. My body was not badly hurt.

The ropes held my upper arms to my body but I lifted my hands as far as I could and slowly lowered my head to touch my face. *Ah! Good god! Here it is! Here's where the pain lives. In these bones.* I felt my face with my fingers, gently, gently.

The entire left side seemed pretty well ruined. I could barely feel the shape of my left eye, everything was swollen, it was stuck shut. All around the eye, up to my forehead and into my hair, across my spongy cheek and over to my ear, down to that side of my mouth was what I guessed was crusted blood. I could open my mouth a bit, so the hinge worked, but the act made me stupid with pain. My teeth on that side felt poorly anchored. But the right side of my head was not damaged.

So this is how it is, I said to myself. I lifted my head again, letting the pain roar on, waiting for it to stop. It didn't stop. I lowered my head, thinking to put my cool fingers on my face. Vertigo. I began to vomit and nearly choked. Someone brought me water.

I slept.

I woke later the same day. Or perhaps a different day. Maddening not to know. I saw that my skirt was streaked with dried blood and there were Jake's boots emerging from the hems. I hadn't imagined it. Why was I wearing his boots? Then I saw that my ankles were no longer bound. They'd bound my hands instead. I leaned forward, I was no longer tied to the tree.

'*I could run!*'

I said this out loud and laughed. One of the Indians turned to look at me. Did he know what I'd said? He turned away. I tried again to count them and came up with eleven, but couldn't be sure. The images would drift and I had to fight to bring them back. The one who'd looked at me wore a red European-style shirt that made him stand out. He was the one who'd brought me water. I focused my attention on him.

My captors were having an argument. The one in the red shirt and a large man with a top-knot stuck through with feathers were snarling at one another. Guttural sounds careened around like ordnance, getting sharper and louder until they both sprang up. I pressed my back hard against the tree as if I could increase my distance from them.

The big one held up what appeared to be a small dead animal, shaking it for emphasis. It was a bag made of fur. From it, he grabbed a kitten-sized pelt with pale, feathery hair and was poking it at the other's face. The hair was so pale, it was almost transparent. I squinted to see it more clearly and my veins went hollow. It was a child's scalp. It must have been a very young child, and that man was proud of his trophy. Grasping it in his fist, he stood and held it up in the air, declaiming forcefully. This infuriated the man in the red shirt who also stood, challenging him. They stared into one another's faces. The air was charged, everyone was silent, on edge, watching.

Holding his body erect and still, the red-shirted one stabbed at the big man with his voice. This time, the other had no answer. He'd lost. Disgusted with this outcome, he thrust the pale scalp back into the fur bag and looked at the faces around the fire. Two of the others stood up, then one more. He pivoted and, grabbing up his blanket and a larger sack, pointed his chin at the others and they grabbed their things.

The big man, the loser, was about to throw a blanket on one of the nearby horses, then changed his mind and went to fetch a horse I couldn't see. In a minute, they rode off and the man with the scalps was on my horse. *My horse! My Pegasus!* He must have been taken along with me and this man had just ridden off on him. The bastard knew a good horse. I began to sob and couldn't stop for a long while.

Red Shirt stood for a bit, watching them leave, then turned and sat down. Someone lit and then handed him a long pipe. He inhaled, exhaled and waved the smoke over his face and head several times, saying something very softly. He passed the pipe to the man next to him, and it went round the circle.

When the pipe was put down, they began to talk, quietly but with intensity and much nodding of heads. They seemed to agree that what had just happened was a good thing, or so it appeared to me. My horse was gone, but at least he was alive. And I was still alive. The angry man with scalps and his comrades were gone.

I slept.

Waking after what seemed a long time, I noticed I could see a bit more clearly — out of my only open eye — so I looked closely at my captors. I counted six now. Their hair was loose or braided or in some combination. One or two of them had twisted ornaments in with the braids. Most wore shirts or pants any white man might, but these were paired with garments made of hide, fringed, and some were decorated with beads. Red Shirt wore a sash pulling in the fullness of the shirt, fringed breeches and moccasins. His hair hung straight under a band around his head, and he wore a tight necklace that looked as if it was made of some sort of shells.

The fire had dwindled. The breeze shifted and I could smell a smell like something I did not want to get on my hands, like something I'd want to wash off with a strong soap in clear flowing water. Revulsion and something like hatred rose in me. Then I realised the stench was from my own body and clothes.

Why I was wearing Jake's boots? Where was he? Had they killed him? No, no. I'd been alone when they came, I was sure of this. I hadn't seen him for some time. We'd been at Fort Laramie, but something had happened and we'd left. I lay down and made myself as comfortable as possible. My head on tufted grass growing in the tree's root, my bound hands in front of me. I had just begun to fall asleep when I remembered I'd been living in the dugout. Maybe it was the smell of dirt.

There'd been trouble at Fort Laramie, Jake had gotten into some sort of trouble, so he'd taken me to a dugout. He was there and gone, there and gone. And then he was gone. He'd left his old boots. I remember being glad of that as my shoes were destroyed.

And he'd left the carbine. More details began to come. A shooting. Scandal. They'd wanted to court martial him. Then something about Colorado, a gold mine, we fought about the stupidity. He left with a woman who was holding a parasol.

There were still far too many lacunae. Thinking, and the pain in my head, exhausted me. I slept.

I woke and slowly pushed and pulled myself to a sitting position against the tree. Carefully, as if my skull were fragile as a porcelain doll's, I lifted my head and tilted it until I could see the sky through the tops of the trees. It was without brightness, impossible to tell the time of day. The swaying branches made me dizzy. I carefully lowered my head to a normal position and tried to settle it between protrusions of bark on the tree trunk.

Someone brought me water to drink, and then a bowl of thin gruel. My hands shook, but I managed to take it in. I kept it down. I looked around me. The Indians seemed calmer. Those who'd left must have been troublesome, and these were glad they'd gone. My captors were sitting around conversing, as anyone would.

The thing all white women feared most had happened to me. I'd rarely even seen an Indian, except those in an encampment just outside Fort Laramie. Once on our way west, a small band of Indians had kept pace with the wagon train on a ridge some distance away. The men took out their rifles and carried them across their legs, passing the word: 'Don't do anything that might rile 'em. Most likely just a hunting party, wanting to make their presence known.'

The Indians shadowed our progress all day in a line on the ridge. Jake checked again and again to make sure there was shot in both chambers of the rifle. He checked his revolver, demanded I check mine even if I'd just done so. They dropped out of sight in the late afternoon and we saw no more Indians until we got to Fort Laramie.

Long after the Indians had disappeared, people were still shaken up and talking about it. We'd all heard stories of the massacre four years earlier, in 1862, when Sioux raided the Minnesota countryside because their annuities were late. They'd killed hundreds of settlers, women and children as well as men. Other incidents were recalled, murders and scalpings, rapes, bodies cut up grotesquely. The men doubled the usual watch.

I told Jake it had thrilled me to see them. It had been like two packs of predators sizing one another up and choosing not to fight. He laughed, 'Yeah. This time!' But he'd liked it too. After all, that's why we'd come west.

I was recalling more about my husband, Jake. Lieutenant Jackson Lee Byrd, formerly a cavalry officer for the Confederacy. He had a variety of skills, of inclinations, that he didn't want to put down just because that war in the east was over. He wanted to kill Indians, and it was worth the irony of putting on the blue uniform of the Union Army to do it. I came west with him because that's what wives do.

I wonder about memory. What is it, after all? Stories we tell ourselves often enough that we come to believe in them. We might choose among recollections in order to build upon who we think we are, or should be, or wish we were, or hope we will become, or want others to believe we have always been. Maybe we choose in the very moment of things happening, maybe later.

But, thinking of all this, as I do often, I trust my memory for what's important, for the details. These stay with me and are precise. I make nothing up, I soften no hard truths, and I don't care what anyone thinks of me.

I slept and woke, slept and woke, and stayed awake a bit longer each time. On one particular waking, it seemed dusk, not yet dark night, I'd been awakened by soft laughter. The men were joking with one another. I lifted my hands to feel my eye and the pain made me groan. Heads turned, eyes fastened briefly on me, then turned away.

But one pair of eyes stayed with me. Someone was looking at me steadily from the other side of the fire, but the fire was directly between us, making the air shiver. I scooted over a bit. Squinted. Good god! *A white woman!* She had dark hair falling around her face. She was still tied, as I had been at first, in a sitting position against a tree. She was looking in my direction, but I could not tell if she could see me.

'Hello! *Hello!*'

A couple of the men looked at me, at the other woman, and went back to their conversation. They seemed not to care, so I raised my voice.

'*Hello! Can you hear me? Can you speak?*'

She continued to stare but did not seem to recognise me as one of her own kind. She looked away into the trees, first on one side and then slowly around to the other. Her mouth was open and I could see she was either struggling to breathe or sobbing.

'Hold on,' I said, speaking loudly, hoping she could hear. 'You must hold on.'

She didn't respond.

'You are not alone. I'm here, too. I...'

I stopped because Red Shirt was looking at me. He got up carrying a cup and a bladder under his arm. He poured me a cup of water from the bladder. I drank it and he took the cup and refilled it. I drank again. He waited for the cup, then left me and walked around the fire and over to the other woman. On the way, he said something to one of the others, and that one brought a bowl of gruel that he put in my hands. The other woman turned her head away from the bowl she was offered. Silently, I urged her: *Eat, eat. Live.*

The Indians pulled blankets around themselves and resumed talking. I shivered with cold, but slept for a bit in spite of it.

When I woke again, it was night. A little flame still licked at some pieces of wood in the pit, coals glowed beneath. The men were stretched out here and there on the ground, rolled in blankets. We were all fairly close to one another. I could hear the small sounds of the fire, I could hear them breathing. I looked over at the woman. In what little light came from the fire, it looked as if her eyes were open. I *felt* they were, I believed I could feel her *seeing* me.

'Can you hear me? Can you speak?'

I whispered hoarsely, enunciating as clearly as I could. I saw a man close to me, lying with his face in my direction, open his eyes and close them again. The woman took a shuddering breath and answered.

'Yes.'

'Are you badly hurt?'

The woman's mouth moved as she struggled to form words.

'Never mind, don't try to speak now.'

'The month...'

'What?'

'*What is the month?*'

'September.'

'*Where am I?*'

'We, we're...'

'*What happened?*'

'We're captives of these Indians...'

An animal sound came out of the woman's chest as if it had been coiled in there, waiting to escape. She dropped her head. Her shoulders moved convulsively but she made no noise. After a bit, she was still. She did not raise her head again. I was afraid she'd died, but then she sighed deeply. I watched her. Every few breaths she shuddered and sighed, but did not wake again.

The fire had burned down to embers and I was shivering, the rattling of my teeth hurt my face. Had the other woman been here all the time? How could I not have seen her? Can I have been so dim from my injuries that I'd failed to see another captive? *A white woman!* I'd counted the men, or tried to, watched their movements, made note of their clothing, their hair. *How could I not have seen her?*

I reminded myself of how badly I'd been hurt, how my vision was so affected I was nearly blind and it was only now beginning to get a bit better. I slid down and curled myself into a ball, drawing my knees up against my belly. Sleep took me over in spite of the cold.

I woke in pain a bit worse than usual. The Indians were readying the horses. It was a chilly damp dawn, fog moved among the trees. Suddenly I remembered the other woman and looked for her, half expecting not to see her, afraid I would not, thinking it might have been a dream or fabrication, or, worse, that she had died during the night. I hoped with all my heart that she had not died. But there she was. She was just then being lifted onto a horse and tied, she gasped and moaned. She lay against the horse and I could see her body moving. They came for me, helped me up, did not tie me lying down but only tied my hands to ropes around the horse's girth. I could sit the horse reasonably.

The journey continued, but I was no longer alone.

CHAPTER 3

Our captors followed a meandering trail or series of trails through grasslands. I could barely see these passages and the tough grass seemed to recover quickly, as if we'd never passed there. I was unsure of the direction in which we were going, the days were heavily clouded, but the ground was rising gradually. Looking behind me, I could see that we were moving steadily into higher country.

Occasionally, we descended into a hollow that I hadn't seen until we started down into it. Usually, there would be a stream at the bottom. The horses would drink and the Indians filled their skins and gave us water as well. I began to slowly, very gingerly, rinse the crusted blood from my face. My left eye would not open, I would not force it. The trees along the banks were nearly all turned yellow, brown, or dull red.

In the line of six Indians and their two captives, the other woman was always a few horses ahead of me. At the end of this line, there was a small string of horses, stolen, I assumed, as my Pegasus had been. The other woman seemed to have been very badly hurt. Sometimes she cried out in pain. I did not want her to die and leave me.

When we stopped to make camp, they would now take us to a single tree where we'd spend the night together. After eating and drinking water we lay close as animals for warmth. Somehow, we slept.

Everyone who has learned of what happened to us has assumed we were violated. So many of the stories told of this, but we were not molested in any way. I kept waiting for it to happen, but it didn't. Our captors rarely made eye contact with us and when they did, it was brief and expressionless.

We did not move fast. They didn't act like people who were being pursued. Yet, each took turns at night keeping watch, sitting a bit away from the fire that they let fall to mere embers.

In the morning and again in the evening they gave us a single bowl of gruel to share, and sometimes, when we stopped for water, a bit of dried pemmican. I couldn't chew it, it hurt to move my jaw. I would suck on it until it softened enough to tear into small pieces and swallow. It was delicious. The other woman and I smiled about the taste. We were getting stronger, and had begun to talk a bit.

One evening, after bringing us to the tree where we would sleep, they untied our hands and from then on we traveled unbound. We were both rubbing our wrists and she took mine and rubbed them for me one by one. Her attentiveness that came so naturally, moved me. I wondered if she had children. I asked her name.

'Mrs. Elizabeth Brown. Yours?'

'Mrs. Sarah Byrd. Sarah Blair Randolph Byrd. You seem better. Are you in much pain?'

She didn't acknowledge the question, but asked,

'Mrs. Byrd, do you have any idea where we might be?'

'Not really. West from where we started out. When the sky clears and I can see the sun, that's what I think. And perhaps north. Now, please, considering our circumstances, let us not be formal with one another. I would like it if you were to call me Sarah.'

'Thank you. I feel the same way. Please call me Elizabeth.'

After eating, Elizabeth caught Red Shirt's eye and rubbed her arms with her hands, shivering theatrically. She addressed him emphatically. 'We're *cold!* We need *blankets!*' He signalled with a nod and a word, and one of the men brought us a single blanket that we spread over our legs. We slept more comfortably that night.

I was clumsy, my balance was poor, but improving. I could now walk a bit without stumbling, though the effort often made me dizzy. Elizabeth must have had ribs broken and perhaps damage done inside as well. She walked gingerly, keeping her arms tight against her body, wincing in pain or even crying out from time to time, a brief yelp for which she'd apologise. They let us walk a few steps behind our tree to relieve ourselves, but one of them would follow, standing nearby. I helped her when it looked as if she needed it, but she never complained. We were becoming more attached, treating one another with delicacy and concern. I imagined it must be something like this to have a sister.

I admired her stoicism and was careful not to whine about my eye. It hurt. The entire front of my head on the left side hurt and I still had headaches that seemed to involve my entire scull. But the pain around my eye was most disturbing as I had come to realise that I couldn't see out of it. I could feel what I thought was a slight opening at the outer corner, but when trying to move my eye in that direction under the lid, the stupid thing seemed to have forgotten how it was done. No light came in through the opening, but fluid seeped out. It wasn't bloody. I didn't know what it was and tried not think about it.

One evening after we ate, while there was still light, she looked at my face critically. When she raised her hand towards my eye, I pulled back.

'I will not hurt you, Sarah.'

She examined my wounds, touching me very lightly here and there around my brow bone and below my eye, and more lightly still on the eye itself.

'Be careful, please, it hurts all around my eye.'

'They must have hit you very hard with something. Do you remember?'

'They took my carbine and hit me with it. I know my eye is badly hurt and the bones of my face on that side. I think I've also lost a tooth.'

'Yes. But it's on the side, not in front, which is fortunate. I hope you do not lose that eye. Let me take a closer look.'

Lose my eye? At first the phrase made no sense. *Lose it? Put it down somewhere and forget about it?* I had not considered that possibility and wished she hadn't said it. I thought her rather rude to have done so. I pulled back sharply.

'Let me look, Sarah, perhaps it is not so bad as it seems and there might be something I can do.'

She did not hurt me with her gentle exploration, but, *Lose my eye?* If it was as bad as that, I could not imagine what she could possibly do. I pulled away from her fingers.

'It will heal. It just needs time.'

She smiled indulgently. I asked her where she was injured.

'I am hurt badly here. Even to breathe is painful.'

She ran her hands over her mid-section.

'We should wrap you, wrap your ribs and below with something, tear strips of our clothing, perhaps...'

'There's nothing to do. And it's getting better, thank our good Lord.'

We had not spoken of how we'd come to be captives, but one night, once settled against the tree, she asked me, tentatively.

'Were you... Were you with family when they came?'

'No. I was alone.'

'That was a blessing, in a way. You lost no one.'

She looked away. I wanted to ask about her family, clearly something horrible had happened. I would not have broached it, but she began to tell me without my asking.

'I lost a dear friend and all three of his children.'

'I am so very sorry, Elizabeth.'

'My husband William was at the fort with our two boys. They'd left me with our friend and gone on to the sutler's store for supplies. I was to make supper for him, help him tidy up a bit, and they'd pick me up on the way home. Our friend — Robert was his name — had lost his wife only a few months before while giving birth to another boy. The baby died with her. He was left with his two boys, a couple of years younger than mine, and a little girl just over a year old.

'I'd cooked a nice meal and we'd just sat down when the dog started up a wild racket of barking. Suddenly, the door banged open, and Indians burst in. They stood staring for a moment. Robert offered them food. The dog was still barking. One of the Indians turned, looked at the dog, lifted his rifle and shot it making its body fly across the room and slam into a wall. That seemed to set it all off. They killed Robert, and then the three children. I thank God over and over that my boys decided to go with their father to the fort. I'd asked if they didn't want to stay and play with those little boys, but they didn't. They didn't stay. Thank God, thank God.'

'I am *so* sorry.'

'The worst part is *how* they did it, the pleasure they took in it.'

She was stifling sobs.

'No more, Elizabeth…'

'They seemed to be in a *lust* of…'

She made a violent sweep with her hands. She was shaking.

'Elizabeth, no more now…'

But the words rolled out of her.

'They set fire to the house and I was running, but one of them caught me from behind. He threw me down, put his knee in my back, pulled back my hair and put his knife to my head. Here, can you see it?'

I had seen the wound at her hairline.

'I was praying and praying, but someone shouted and he stopped. He kicked me in the body, kicked me hard, rolled me over and kicked me again before throwing me on a horse. But, oh dear God, I will never forget… Those children. That baby girl, little blond angel child, just walking…'

'Little blond angel child.' It must have been this child's scalp that hideous bastard had been lifting like a prize. And Elizabeth had seen him take it.

'God will punish them. They will burn in the fires of Hell. Heathen! *Savages!*'

She'd spoken those last words loudly, punctuated by sobs. I put my fingers on her lips, leaned close to her face.

'You *must* stop, dear.'

I shifted my eyes towards the men and back, hoping to make her understand. The atmosphere in the clearing had changed. They were no longer talking among themselves, they were listening to us, watching us. What did they understand? I spoke simply, smiling as if I were telling a nice story.

'Elizabeth. Dear friend. You must calm yourself. You *must.*'

She gathered her wits. I took her hands and held them as her violence subsided.

'We must be careful,' I told her. 'We don't know what might set something off.'

She nodded. In a moment she looked at me and spoke, this time keeping her voice low.

'I cannot imagine why God chose to spare me and let those innocent children be murdered. So much blood... And why spare me just to remember it until I too am killed? As I'm sure I will be. *We* will be. He must have a plan. We cannot know God's mind, though, can we. Of course, we cannot. There must be a reason, a plan for me, for us both...'

She went on like this as if it were an incantation. Suddenly Red Shirt was there with a cup of water and she went silent. I took it from him and gave it to Elizabeth.

CHAPTER 4

'I can't do it with him standing there,' Elizabeth hissed.

'This is better than before. He's not so close.'

'I still can't.'

'We'd better try or we'll become sick from constipation.'

'I need to grunt. That's how I help my boys and I cannot grunt with that man there!'

We laughed.

'I'll grunt with you. We'll both grunt.'

So we grunted voluptuously, laughing like children. We looked at our guard. Nothing. He remained with his back to us. This made us laugh so hard we nearly fell over and Elizabeth had to clutch her body for the pain.

I could not recall the last time I'd laughed so naturally. Ironic, I thought, that it should be as a gravely injured captive in the company of another gravely injured captive who'd endured horrors, lost in this trackless country, facing what would most likely be a hideous, ritualised death, that I remembered how to laugh.

We'd been moving through a rough terrain of rocks, with gold and rust coloured trees and dark evergreens that we hadn't seen before, when we rode into a small, well hidden encampment of perhaps ten tipis. Elizabeth looked back and we exchanged our fear in glances.

The men seemed pleased to have arrived at the place, and these people, old ones and children among them, seemed happy to see them. Red Shirt was greeted with affection. They helped us down from the horses. We were given water. One of the men in our bunch pointed to a tree and we went there to sit like good dogs.

We watched the Indians. After a bit Elizabeth looked at me and leaned her head close.

'Do you have any idea which of these might be the ones who murdered my friend and his children?'

'I don't believe any of these people did it. Early on — I don't know when, I haven't been able to keep track of the days — there was an argument. That one, the one who wears the red shirt, sent some men away. Three or four left with my horse and some other horses. One of them seemed to be an especially violent man.'

'The one in the red shirt appears to be the leader. The others defer to him.'

'Yes, I think so. And I think he's a reasonable man. I believe the ones he sent away must have been the murderers.'

I did not tell her about the scalps.

We watched the men eat and talk, and the women tend to the cooking and to the children. The little ones were curious about us and would sneak peeks. One of the women brought us each a bowl of stew. We nodded our thanks and she acknowledged it with a smile. This surprised me. The men had barely recognised our presence. Red Shirt had been the exception, but his expression never changed, it revealed absolutely nothing.

After a few words about how good the stew was, though somewhat greasy, Elizabeth asked me about the details of my capture.

'You said you were alone when they came. Your husband was not with you?'

'No. He wasn't. He wasn't there that day.'

'Where were you living?'

My first inclination with people is to tell the truth. It's simpler. But if the situation calls for a lie, I am perfectly able to lie convincingly. Elizabeth was waiting for me to answer her question.

'Not far from Fort Laramie. My husband had been assigned there, and I'd come west with him. We're both from Virginia. Jackson, Jake, had been a Lieutenant in the Confederacy and when that war was over he wanted to join in the Indian Wars, so he signed up with the Union Army. But he and the fort commander didn't get along, so he moved us out. Then he resigned his commission. He'd made a business connection in… San Francisco. He'd go out there first and, once he'd gotten us a house, he'd arrange for me to follow.'

This was a lie. Here is what really happened before the Indians came.

We'd arrived at Fort Laramie around April, about six months before I was taken. The fort commander found Jake morally objectionable from the beginning and wasn't subtle about it. He'd learned of his leadership in the atrocious treatment of a family of Yankee sympathisers and the handful of Union soldiers, including an officer, they'd sheltered in the mountains of North Carolina. The soldiers were tortured before they were hung. The women in the family, including a young girl, were raped then eviscerated with bayonets.

I'd overheard Jake and Jake's father talking with my father about how to manage it. They were confident they could call in enough political favours to save Jake's military career. Enough of Jake's men spoke for him — I wonder what they were paid or how they were threatened — so he kept his commission. He was formally reprimanded, though, and passed over for Captain, which vexed him.

With The War in the east over and the Indian War heating up, and as more and more settlers arrived and wanted protection, the western forts were desperate for trained military personnel. Jake had been to West Point.

At first, he seemed to enjoy himself in spite of the commander's disapprobation. He'd joke about it with a small group of men with whom he'd drink and play cards almost every night after dinner. I'd go back up to our room. I'd brought my good mattress and a small dressing table with a mirror from home. Departing soldiers had left books and magazines, I was comfortable in that room. I'd get into bed and read until I fell asleep.

It was always very late and Jake was always very drunk when he slid into bed beside me, rummaging in my nightdress. I'd pretend to be asleep, but he'd slam into me anyway. If he passed out on top of me, I'd roll him off. If he fell to the floor, there he'd stay. He'd always considered himself quite a cocksman and had perfected a grin that was his flag. I'd found it exciting, at first. But at this point, he'd taken me against my wishes too many times, and he'd done it sloppily, he'd sometimes hurt me, so when he'd flash that grin as if he'd earned the right no matter what, it infuriated me.

I had little to do during the day. I could walk on the parade ground, but found it boring. I tried to converse with a couple of the other wives, but we had little to say to one another. Mostly, I stayed in the room, reading. One day, Jake came slamming in, ripping off his uniform. As he changed his clothes, he said the commander had called him in that morning and drilled him down hard about his '*unbecoming behaviour*' since arriving at Laramie, warning that he'd better shape up fast. 'Who the fuck does he think he is!'

He said that if he didn't 'get away from that fucking, moralistic, self-righteous Yankee son-of-a-bitch', he'd have to kill him. Not long after this, a friend told him of a dugout cabin that a married couple he'd known had only recently left, and he moved us there in a wagon with my mattress and dressing table.

I went to the fort with him once or twice over the next few weeks to pick up supplies at the sutler's store while he met with various officers, one of whom was a solicitor with the Army. He told me he was in the process of resigning his commission, negotiating a reasonable severance. I didn't know one could do that. Once, sitting by the stove, reading a *Harper's* while waiting for him, I heard someone whisper, '*Byrd's wife.*' There was a hushed conversation about a shooting down in the Indian camp, a possible court martial, a woman. I couldn't hear details.

He was drunk when I asked him about it. He told me the fort was peopled by miscreants, I should know better than to listen to their yammering. When I pressed him about the shooting and the woman, he told me to shut up. I wouldn't, so he slammed me up against the wall. I was his *wife, goddamnit!* If I questioned him again, he'd leave marks to remind me of how to behave.

It was not unusual for him to leave me alone in the dugout for a few nights, it was a long ride. I had no idea whether or not he was still reporting for duty. He could have been doing anything. I didn't care.

Sometime around the middle of June, however, I was alone for more than a week and that was too long. I wondered if I should pack my things and take Pegasus to the fort looking for him. I was having the last of the coffee one morning, when I heard someone coming. I went to the window. It was Jake on a rig with a woman at his side. He was in civilian clothes.

He jumped down, called my name, opened the door and came into the dugout moving fast, flashing his grin, smelling of liquor. While throwing his clothing in my good carpetbag, told me a story about having won an interest in a Colorado gold mine. He'd arrange for a house and would soon be back for me or send word about when I could join him.

'That fucker finally got me kicked out of this piss-ant Army. Hallelujah!'

I looked at the woman — she'd put up a parasol and was gazing over the prairie as if on a Sunday outing — and back at him. He snorted. 'Her? No, no, no!' He grabbed my face and kissed me hard on the mouth. 'She's to meet her husband, another partner in this deal.'

He told me he'd arranged for a couple of soldiers to come by the following day. I should return with them to the fort and wait for him there. I told him I would not, I'd wait for him right where I stood. 'Well, it's likely to be a while.' I repeated my intention to wait in the dugout.

He said he'd planned for my pig-headedness. The boys would have some supplies when they arrived tomorrow and he'd given the sutler enough money to keep me provisioned until I got over being stupid, but warned that it had better be soon.

'Then you'd better come back soon. We'll go home to Virginia together. Start a reasonable life.'

He guffawed, threw his hands in the air, and still laughing, turned and left with the woman.

I stood at the door and watched until there was nothing to see. The grass sprang back quickly after the wheels passed, so I could not even see their tracks. I hoped they'd get attacked by Indians, shot full of arrows. I hoped they'd get scalped. I hoped they'd still be alive when the carrion birds pecked at their eyes. I hoped they'd still have at least a thin veil of consciousness when the wolves came.

'You were at Fort Laramie?'

'Yes. Then we moved to a place just west of there.'

'How far?'

'Several hours' ride.'

'That's not far from our home! We're west and north from Laramie about the same distance. It's strange I never saw you at the fort.'

'After we moved into the dugout, I rarely went there.'

'*Dugout?* Oh, you poor dear! Were you building your house?'

She made a face like that of a little girl imagining having to live in a hole in the ground. Dirt, spiders, droppings, darkness! I nearly laughed. Of course, at times, bits of sod or creatures would fall from the ceiling. The floor was earth and though I kept it swept of whatever dropped from above or blew in from outside, it never felt clean. But the walls had been whitewashed, and the door and single window faced west, so the afternoon light was pleasant. I told her I'd developed an odd affection for it.

'It was only partially underground. I didn't mind it.'

'How long were you there?'

'Oh… a couple of months, I think, before he left.'

'And then how long was it before the Indians came?'

'Three months, I think.'

'Oh! Alone all that time! Weren't you terribly frightened?

'Not really. I didn't mind being alone. I rather liked it, I did a lot of riding. I've always enjoyed my own company.'

In fact, I'd never really been alone before. At home in Virginia, I could go upstairs to my room, shut the door and imagine myself 'alone', but I could still hear and feel the hum of life in the house and just outside it, off a bit to the slave's cabins, and off a bit more to the barns and other structures and then the fields. People were always around, talking, calling out to one another, laughing, singing, working. Making things clatter and bump.

Alone in the dugout, there was no clatter and bump. Nothing to distract me from a mental state that swung between avoidance of how things were, to terror, to furious anger.

I fed myself. I kept myself clean. I tended to my horse and took long rides. I gathered kindling and wood for the small stove that I broke up with a hatchet I found in the lean-to where I kept Pegasus' tack. I wrote letters to my mother, fictions about Frontier Life, that I gave to the boys to post when they came to deliver staples. They came about once a week and each time they'd try to get me to go back with them.

Evenings, when it was nice, I'd pull a chair outside and sit for a while before sunset and a bit after, when the stars began to show. I'd pour some whiskey into a cut glass tumbler I'd brought from home and sip it as the night slid up around me like slow rising water, smooth and silent.

The days were warm still, but the nights were getting chilly. On one visit, I asked the boys the date and was shocked to learn it was late August, almost September. The look on my face prompted a more energetic attempt than usual to get me to return with them.

'Indians been acting up, ma'am. It ain't safe. The colonel's real worried. You don't got much, why don't you pack up your horse right now and come back with us.'

'Tell the colonel to stop worrying and don't you two worry either. Go on back now, boys. See you next week. And bring some more of that canned fruit.'

Later, in bed, I wasn't so sure. Almost September. I *should* go back. But how would that look? Disgraced officer's wife abandoned in a dugout. And at home? My father would assume it was my fault. My mother would say she'd warned me.

If I chose to stay?

Death was already coming around. I'd look in the mirror and there he'd be, right behind me, raising an eyebrow as if to say, '*Now?*' Fear oozed from my skin in a slick of sweat. Sometimes, I could not take a deep breath without a pain in my chest. Days of bad weather I stayed in bed. Covers up over my head, I sank into the familiar topography of my body, the dry swells and damp hollows, each with its own smell. But if the weather was good, I'd splash water on my face and saddle up Pegasus — better companion than any damn husband! — and I'd ride.

My two guns began to flirt with me. The carbine was not as seductive as the Colt. Once, I sat down at my dressing table and took it from the drawer where I kept it loaded and primed. I kept both guns primed and loaded.

Watching myself in the mirror, I held it with the muzzle pressing my skull just above my right ear. The gun was heavy. I had to lean my elbow on the table, tilt my head a bit and press the thing hard against the bone to keep it steady. I studied this geometry of hand, forearm, angle of elbow, upper arm, shoulder, neck, head... gun. I imagined there'd be a *flash!* and then nothing. I put it back fast. Some days, I had to be careful not to open that drawer.

Some days, I could not look at the knife Jake had left. A heavy thing in its black leather sheath decorated with silver. The blade was the length of my hand plus a few inches and the point had been cut in a curve, both sides razor sharp. It had a guard where the blade met the handle. It was terribly beautiful, that knife. I was often sorely tempted by its beauty.

I was terrified of what my life had become, but didn't have the guts to end it myself. I did, however, enjoy imagining how it would be if Jake actually came back. I'd hear the rig, take the carbine, sit up in the bed. He'd call my name and I'd say, 'Come on in, darlin'. I've been waiting for you.'

Elizabeth asked me why I hadn't gone to the fort to wait for my husband.

'You would have had a good safe place to stay until he returned. And we'd have met! We'd have become friends. I'd have taken you home to our house and you would not have had to wait alone. Oh, it's too bad! But your husband must have learned by now what's happened to you, and is on his way back from San Francisco — isn't that where you said he'd gone? — to join in the search. I'm sure you'll be reunited before too long.'

I could think of no reasonable way to respond to this. I turned the conversation to Elizabeth.

'How long have you been in the west? Where did you come from?'

'Near Albany, New York. We had a dairy farm there. It was close by both families, our home. But my husband was in love with the idea of going west. The east was filling up and he wanted to spread out, do something different, something of his own. He talked of little else. After a while, I began to see it as he did.'

'How long have you been out here?'

'Almost two and a half years. Joey was a baby when we came.'

'Is it all you'd hoped it would be?'

'Yes and no. It's been hard, to be honest. People say rain follows the plow, but I don't know where that might be. This grass will break your plow. New York is cold in the winter and it snows, but nothing like this. When the snow blows, you can't see beyond your hand. Last winter, before the snows came down hard, I had William drive in poles and tie a rope from the house to the barn so I wouldn't lose my way.'

'Do you miss your home in New York?'

'Oh, yes. I miss my family.'

'A large family?'

'Quite a big family. And happy. Blessed by God.'

'Do you think that if we are rescued, you and your husband and boys will go back to New York?'

'"*If* we are rescued"? Oh, Sarah! We *will* be rescued! Even now we are being tracked, I'm sure of it. When William and the boys came to fetch me and found that horror, I am certain he went directly to the fort. They're on our trail. I *know* this. I know this as surely as I know God is watching over us now. *We will be rescued.*'

'Forgive me. I didn't mean to suggest...'

'And about staying or going, this is our home now. I will be returned to my family and we'll make our farm a good farm. There must be a crop that will do well here — look at the grass! The flowers! — and we'll find it. We'll buy more land, maybe have beef cattle, William's been thinking about it. Bring up our boys in this place.'

27

She was looking far into the future but I was unable to go with her.

'Sometimes I think we should not be here at all,' I said. 'Sometimes I think we should leave this country to the Indians. Let them keep it.'

She looked at me as I were a child who'd made a simple mistake.

'That's your loneliness speaking. Also, you haven't *seen* it yet, Sarah, dear, not really. No matter how hard the winter is, when spring comes and everything begins anew…You'll learn to love this country. It will get better and better. You'll never want to leave.'

She said their home was not yet finished, but that William never stopped working on it. Though their house was now in the middle of emptiness, she could *see* new farms appearing within sight of theirs, fields and pastures laid out like quilts at a bee. Houses, stores, churches. Towns! 'The railroad is coming!' she exclaimed, 'everyone knows this!' The continent will soon be bridged coast to coast.

'It is destined. More of us are coming all the time and the more who come, who work the land, make it produce, the better it will be for all of us.'

She told me this was straight from God, a promise and a directive. Her brown eyes shone with passion.

I'd never heard anyone talk this way. Religion in my home had been a brief Sunday service at a church with a pastor my mother liked. During The War, the pastor would come to the house when he was able to, and often he was not. The slaves were 'invited' to services to keep up morale. But it was never a part of everyday conversation. I was used to cynicism and irony. To the clever, foul humour tossed about by my father and Jake and his father.

Elizabeth's zeal irritated me. But we needed one another, lost as we were on the dark side of her dream of the west.

CHAPTER 5

'A tipi? What do you think this means, Sarah?'

'It will be good not to get rained on.'

A couple of women had brought poles and hides and brusquely moved us out of the way as they set it up. It was a bit smaller than the others, as if it had been made for a child.

'I wonder if this means we'll be here for a while. What do you think?'

'I don't know, Elizabeth.'

'I hope so. The less we move, the faster they will find us.'

I was distracted. My eye was seeping more than usual and wiping it had made a sticky mess on my cheek. Elizabeth looked at it closely, frowning. She tore a strip from her petticoat and went over to a woman who had just put a pot of water over a fire. She tried to dip the cloth in it, but the woman waved her away.

'I must clean her eye,' Elizabeth said loudly, as if volume would help, while wiping at her own eye and pointing at me. Red Shirt said something to the woman and she let Elizabeth dampen the cloth in the hot water. He said something else and the woman went off purposefully.

'Now, be very careful, Elizabeth, it still...'

'Of course. Move your hand, Sarah.'

Elizabeth wiped at my eye gently but the entire area was extremely sensitive. *I* was sensitive. My squeamishness probably had more to do with its being my *eye* than anything else.

'I'm trying to remove some of this crust to see if we can open it a bit. It's dried blood and pus. It needs cleaning. This entire wound needs cleaning.'

'Don't bother trying to open it, Elizabeth. I think it will open when...'

'When it *feels* like opening? Let's help it a bit.'

Elizabeth went over to the woman with the pot to re-wet the cloth when a much older woman, carrying a small bag, came up to them. Red Shirt joined them and warmly embraced the old woman. He turned to Elizabeth, making sure he also had my attention, then pointed from the bag she carried to his eye to the old woman and nodded as if to say, this is what your eye needs and this is the person who will administer it.

The old woman emptied twigs and leaves out of the bag into the hot water. She stirred this tea for a bit then said something to the other woman. That one folded a piece of blanket that had been on a rock by the fire and lifted the pot. The two came towards me.

They put the pot on the ground right outside our tipi. A pleasant smell came from it. The old woman took a folded piece of pale cloth from the bag, perhaps it had once been white and was now slightly tanned but it appeared clean, and dipped it into the tea. She moved towards me. Elizabeth, flustered, put up her hand.

'Wait! We don't know what this is. I think perhaps plain water would be best.'

'It smells soothing.'

'I'm not sure we should trust it. These people... I don't know Sarah.'

I looked at this old woman. I recalled that Red Shirt had embraced her like an auntie when we first rode in. Her round face was scored from top to bottom with deep folds of soft skin. She smiled at us as one smiles to reassure children. She brought the cloth close to her nose and breathed the steam in deeply, smiling and nodding, then put it to my nose. The scent was pleasant, there was nothing acrid in it.

She offered it to Elizabeth to smell. Elizabeth sniffed, sniffed again, nodded, then reached for it, but the woman said something, speaking mildly, and held on to what I could now see was a piece of smooth hide. Doeskin, I guessed. She had me sit, then settled herself in front of me. Elizabeth stood by her, bending down to watch. The woman's friend, the one who'd been boiling the water, came over to observe as well. I was very nervous, but the old woman's sweet demeanour was calming. She began to blot my wounds gently over and over with the hot tea until she had cleansed my entire face.

Then she took a fresh piece of doeskin, folded it to a point, and went to work on my eye. While wetting it generously and removing a lot of crusted stuff, she gently tried to spread my lids with her fingers. In thinking of it, I'm not sure if any of this actually hurt or if I expected it to and so became tense and backed away. She'd stop and wait patiently a bit before resuming. She never stopped smiling and cooing at me.

'Can you see anything out of it?'

I closed my other eye.

'No. Is it open?'

'A little. Can you see any light?'

'I'm not sure. I don't think so.'

Then the woman took another clean square of skin, dipped it in the tea, squeezed out the excess, folded it, placed it gently over my eye, and guided my hand to hold it in place. Then she took a long strap of soft cotton fabric from the bag, and while I held the doeskin in place over my eye, she bound it so it would stay.

I touched the old woman's hand and thanked her. She smiled and patted my hand. When they turned away, I asked Elizabeth.

'How did it look to you?'

'The outside wounds seem to have healed well.'

'How did the eye itself look?'

'Well, I could only see a bit of it, so I can't...'

'You're a terrible liar. Tell me the truth, Elizabeth.'

She told me that what ought to have been white was dark red. Like a dyed egg. As children make for Easter.

'*A dyed egg?*'

'I'm sorry, dearest, but that doesn't mean...'

'Could you see *none* of the blue of my eye?'

'No. But perhaps it was not open far enough. How does it feel?'

'My head aches. I'm going to lie down.'

I stood up shakily. Elizabeth helped me into the tipi and I lay down. The women had spread hides on the ground and placed blankets for us.

'I'll get you some water,' she said. 'Your eye will heal, Sarah. But you must be patient. It was a bad injury.'

I had turned my back and pretended to be asleep when she returned. I heard her drink water and then lie down. When one of the women came by later with food, Elizabeth called to me softly, but I continued to feign sleep.

I had lost the sight in my eye. Elizabeth was trying to preserve me, but I knew I was blind in that eye. Blind in my left eye. Lost all sight in it. Lost my eye. The phrases came one upon the other. I have lost this eye. I said it over and over. I've lost my eye. Lost it with that horrible crash, that shattering sound when he slammed the butt of the carbine into my face. With that sound, I lost my eye. I would have to get used to it.

Several days after the woman had cleaned my eye, or maybe longer, we woke before dawn hearing the men pack up the horses. We were leaving. I'd come to like the place and our simple routines. We'd both benefited from the rest. We'd eaten well and we'd slept. The old woman liked me and I'd made efforts to let her know how much I liked her. The children had come closer and Elizabeth flirted with them. They'd all been kind to us.

When the men were bringing the horses around, the two old women came up to us. The old woman with the pot gave us a burlap bag filled with pemmican and dried berries. My old woman handed me a small pouch. She opened it, showing me some folded pieces of doeskin, and beneath these, I saw leaves and twigs, the tea for my eye. She held my hand as she gave me the pouch, then touched my face gently. I squeezed her hand and spoke my thanks.

I didn't want to leave. I wanted to go lie down in the little tipi, but as I looked over there, it was being taken apart. I looked at Elizabeth and could see that she, too, was emotional, but with her it did not seem to be sentimentality. She was obviously terrified of what might come next. They helped us onto horses. Four young men from the group with which we'd been staying joined us. Now we were ten men, two captives, and a string of about a dozen horses.

CHAPTER 6

We'd left the prairie behind, having crossed one wide river and many creeks, and were now traversing a tortuous trail up through cliffs and gorges, with many small, fast streams. The cliff edges were softened by foliage and dappled sun. After the expanse of the prairie, this was intimate terrain. We could reach out to touch lichen on a rock face. The men would reach down to pluck berries from a shrub, so did we. The rolling walk of the horses, the relaxed mien of our captors, the absence of event, the diminution of pain, all brought a comforting dullness. I moved through that part of the journey, as I recall, in a pleasant stupor.

Then we were out of the trees and moving along a high ridge. The air had changed and the light was dramatically different. An open country spread out wide below us, undulating, sere, all the shades of brown and ochre, darkened here and there by evergreens, brightened by yellow and deep crimson where trees clustered along the edges of streams. The pelt of this broad land changed colour as wind-driven clouds sped over it. Rising from the horizon a long distance away, the great sky arced up and up and up and over us and down.

My parents' house was quite beautiful. Not as large or grand as those of some of their friends, but we had columns and verandas and everything was painted white to stand out against the green around it. Lilac trees, magnolias, myrtle, laurel, Rose of Sharon, grew all around the house, and there were also my mother's flower gardens that she designed and tended with a handful of Negroes who had the feel for it. She prized her roses above all the other flowers. They were extraordinary.

In what my mother called her 'grand hall' was a painting I'd always loved. Framed in heavy, gilded wood, it contained a world: a landscape in a moody, rather dark palette, of fields and low hills rolling off beyond the right-hand edge of the canvas. A brook coursed over and around rocks in the middle of the painting. The bank that was on the left rose to thick bushes at the top and tall trees with thin, bare, black branches arching over, stroking a pale sky. A few black silhouettes of birds in flight followed the direction of the branches towards an emptiness that also seemed to extend beyond the limits of the frame. As a child, I would stand in front of it and make up stories.

I will build a tiny cabin there, by the water. I'll cut down small trees for its walls, tie them with rope and put mud between them, roof it with woven evergreen branches. I'll gather berries, set a rabbit trap as Jewell had showed me. He was our half-Cherokee, half-black slave who taught me tracking, and how to tell direction by the sun and stars. I'll shoot birds with the bow and arrows he made for me and cook my meat on a green stick over a fire. Make warm things from the pelts. No one will ever find me.

33

Once, lost in this fantasy, I suddenly felt my mother's hands on my shoulders. I'd had no idea she'd slipped up behind me. She was looking over my head at the painting.

She said, 'My friend sent me that from Paris a few years ago, she thought the artist would become famous, I wonder if he has. I've watched you standing in front of it for the longest time. Wouldn't you just love to go there?'

'Not really,' I told her and shrugged out from under her hands and ran upstairs. I could be a cruel child.

My fantasies grew as I did. I'd begun to imagine that I could will the painting to grow until it filled the wall where it hung. Then I'd take a knife, slash it, pull aside the canvas, and there, on the other side, the world of the painting would have expanded and become a great, wild country. I'd step through the canvas, escape a life that had become thick with foreboding, and never look back.

As I looked out over that valley, I thought, *Here it is*. I've entered it. I could see no evidence of human habitation, no filament of rising smoke, no wheel ruts, no ground broken for planting, no fences. This country was alive with strange gods who did not have the slightest interest in me. I was intoxicated with excitement. I looked at Elizabeth to see what she might be feeling.

The wind whipped my hair into my good eye making it water. Elizabeth's mouth was moving. From the look on her face, I knew she was praying, but the wind grabbed the words from her mouth and blew them away.

We stayed on that high plateau for a couple of days, camping in places protected by trees. Sometimes we moved within sight of the valley, sometimes not. Elizabeth and I talked little. She'd ask about my eye, make tea with the herbs, cleanse it a bit and re-tie the skin. The light pressure was comforting, as was the simple ritual of tending to it.

That ritual brought us both comfort, gave us something to do. And it brought us closer together. I felt indebted to Elizabeth.

One morning, the men were up very early and bustling about rather excitedly. Many took out small pouches and began to paint their faces and chests. They re-braided their hair and adjusted the feathers and ornaments, using small mirrors. Some decorated their horses, too. Red Shirt remained apart from these preparations, drinking coffee and talking, urgently, I thought, with a few of his men. I believed these were his closest confederates from the beginning.

Through the course of our journey, we'd begun to actually *see* these men. They'd become familiar. Red Shirt was conspicuous not only for his shirt, but because of how he held himself and how the others behaved towards him. I knew his face rather well by this time. Elizabeth and I had spoken of this, of how the Indians were now no longer just *Indians*, but distinct individuals. We'd begun to get a sense of their different personalities, the hierarchy within the group, the relationships among them.

I told her I'd begun to trust that these men would not harm us. She'd said this was probably not a good way to think; we must always be on our guard. Nevertheless, though under watch, we were no longer tied down and I felt that was a good sign. Looking back, I suppose they knew we were smart enough, or still weak enough, not to try to run.

Now, painted and excited in some way we could not understand, they were strange again.

'They look like savages,' Elizabeth whispered.

This time, after we mounted, they tied our hands in front of us and tied us to our horses. None of them looked us in the eye. Everything had changed. Something was about to happen.

'*Yea, though I walk through the valley of the shadow of Death...*' Elizabeth intoned as we set off.

All that day we moved across a high plateau gouged by ravines. Just as the sun was about to drop into the earth ahead of us, we were again in dense trees. We were riding along the edge of what seemed a steep drop, though trees obscured most of the view. The horses picked their way carefully down and down until we came to a place where the trees thinned and we saw below us another valley, not so wide as the other, and this one ringed by hills with a broad river meandering through it.

On the far side of that river was a strip of dense forest that worked its way up a high hill with higher hills behind it. Covering the plain on our side of the river were tipis. The skins of the tipis were gold in the late light, and the river was bronze. There were tipis in rough circles tangent to one another, circle after circle spiralling. Too many tipis to count; perhaps hundreds, perhaps a thousand. It was a city of tipis along a burning river.

Blue smoke from innumerable cook fires joined in a haze that drifted close to the ground. There was a great herd of horses grazing beyond the nearest of the circles of tipis and horses standing in the river near the bank. I could see people moving back and forth, in and out of the tipis, around the fires. We moved down from the ridge, following a trail cut in the slope, the horses stepping smartly, with every now and then their hooves starting a small tumble of stones.

When we reached the floor of the valley they began to gallop the horses. It was hard to stay seated, we gripped our horses' manes with our tied hands. Red Shirt and a few of his men were in front. They sang and hollered and shook their bows. We galloped towards the river until we neared a group of tipis on the outer edge of that encampment. Men had jumped on horses and galloped up to greet us with great whoops. Boys rode up then peeled off with the string of horses. More Indians — men, women and even children — had come running. Our captors slowed their horses to a trot and the people ran alongside us cheering and shouting, women were making the tremolo as more and more people joined the crowd.

We came to the centre of a circle and pranced around and around a big fire. He's showing us off, I thought, like trophies. I tried to catch Elizabeth's eye but kept missing her what with the fire and smoke and the horses' prancing and the Indians crowding. Small boys threw things; women jeered, some struck at us with sticks amid a din of shouting and laughing. The air quivered and twisting currents of dust and fume swirled so the shapes rising and pulsing in the fire's flare were like something legendary.

Then Red Shirt directed a couple of women who'd crowded close to pull us down from the horses. They unbound our hands and re-tied them behind our backs. Ropes went around our necks. The women held the ends and acted gleefully, theatrically, enraged. With Red Shirt at the fore, the women jerked us away from the fire and led us through a pressing crowd of bodies and faces, all shining with triumphant hatred. I kept throwing myself towards Red Shirt with the woman yanking me back hard, nearly strangling me. '*You! You!*' I had to get his attention, make him look at me. I had to look him in the eyes and have him look back into mine. I would know then, know by his look, if we were about to be killed. '*YOU!*' I shouted over and over.

But he did not turn to look at us, and the women pulled us roughly through the crowd of Indians.

CHAPTER 7

The women pushed us into a tipi and threw us down. They kicked us in our legs and backs, shouting and jeering, then they opened the flap and went outside. They did not kick us hard enough to do harm, though they could have. They could have beaten our brains out or cut our throats. They must have been instructed not to kill us or injure us too badly. Yet. Whatever would be done would be done ritualistically, I thought, with an audience, to make a point. My insides wrenched themselves into a hard bolus of fear.

Our hands were still tied behind our backs. We shifted around so that Elizabeth faced me. Her face was a mask of fear, as I'm sure mine was. I could look past her towards the flap of the tipi. I could see the shadows of two men standing in front. The band that had protected my eye now hung around my neck, the tea-soaked padding was lost. I was worried for my eye. It was all I could think about. That and thirst. We both licked our lips over and over but neither of us had any spit left, it had been scared out of us.

Two old women came in with a bowl of water, a bowl of food, and some straw. As they were leaving, another came in with a pair of blankets. The water and blankets were on one side of the tipi, the straw on the opposite.

'I need water,' I said.

We got to our knees and crawled, fell, then moved like sidewinders over to where it was and took turns putting our mouths on the lip of the horn bowl and tipping it enough to drink. Neither of us could eat.

We lay down where we were, face to face. I had not realised I'd fallen asleep and Elizabeth as well, until we were both startled awake by loud voices outside the tipi. The flap slapped open and suddenly there was brightness and smoke from a fire right outside, noise from all around, and a young woman entered. She stood just inside the flap and addressed us in a clear, bright voice.

'I speak English.'

Her voice and her words were like the sweetest music. I remember every detail of our first meeting with Mary Small Wing and especially the sweetness of her voice. She wore a calico dress with a beaded sash from which hung a small beaded sack and a knife in a sheath. Her moccasins were fringed, dainty. She was silhouetted against the open flap so we couldn't see her features clearly.

She said something to the man holding open the flap and he closed it, resuming his position outside. She walked over and knelt down close to us.

'Are you bad hurt?'

'No,' I told her, 'thank you.'

I began to struggle to a sitting position. The girl helped us both to sit up and then settled herself in front of us.

Elizabeth said, 'You speak English?'

'Yes. Some English,' said the girl, smiling. Elizabeth clapped her hands and exclaimed,

'You have been sent by God!'

The girl laughed gently.

'I do not know this, but I will try to help you, if I can.'

Elizabeth immediately began to question her.

'Can you tell us anything about the man who brought us here? About why he took us? We call him Red Shirt. Do you know the one I mean?'

'Yes. That shirt is strong medicine for him. His name is...'

And she pronounced a name of several syllables with sounds that I could not visualise in English letters. When she saw our faces, she laughed.

'It means he is one who even if he calls from far away, we will hear his voice. Like the cry of an eagle, very far away, and yet very clear. I have heard his name said as "Far Cry" in English.'

Elizabeth and I repeated the name. Elizabeth continued.

'Where are we? How far are we from Fort Laramie?'

'Far, I think, from the fort of Laramie, but maybe some other fort, not so far...'

'What other fort?'

'I do not know the name... '

'What do they want with us?'

'I will try to tell this. This is why I came to you, to tell this.'

The girl closed her eyes for a moment as if she were gathering together the words to explain, wanting to recite it accurately.

'The white soldier chiefs have two Lakota boys in one of the soldier forts as prisoner. Far Cry has you. He thinks if he gives you to the white soldier chiefs, they will give back these boys. This is why he keeps you.'

Elizabeth said, 'Where are the boys held? Which fort?'

'I do not know. The boys are relations of a woman who was sister to, what did you call his name? Far Cry? Whites killed her and the boys got taken. He promises her relatives he will get back these boys. So he takes you to trade for them.'

I turned to Elizabeth.

'That's why they've kept us alive. We're hostages. We will not be killed.'

Elizabeth asked, 'Will this trade happen now? Is that why all these Indians have come here?'

'No. This is big pow-pow, very big, many Lakota — Oglala, Hunkpapa, Mniconjou — and Cheyenne and some others. White soldier chiefs want to make new treaty about Powder River Road, Immigrant Road — I do not know your name for it — tell where Lakota and other tribes should stay, other things. We are told the white soldier chiefs want all our chiefs to come together soon to make their marks, and...'

'To sign this new treaty?'

'Yes. At Fort Laramie...'

Elizabeth interrupted again.

'The treaty is to be signed at Laramie? When?'

'I do not know. First, all these chiefs must talk. If they decide they will sign, all chiefs will go. If Far Cry goes with the Old Man Chiefs to sign this paper, he will bring you with him to Laramie. Or this is what I think. My husband tells me little, but I listen when the men talk.'

Elizabeth continued.

'Are there white soldiers here at this pow-wow?'

'Some whites are here, I have seen them. Not soldiers, but I hear these are white chiefs. I think they are here to speak for the White Father in Washington. Other whites are traders, with new guns. Better guns.'

She looked at us, at our parched mouths, and around the tipi.

'Here. I will help you.'

The girl reached for the bowl of water and held it so we could drink.

'Are you hungry? I can help you...'

But neither Elizabeth nor I could think of food. The girl looked at my face.

'Your eye...'

'The cloth around my neck, it was covering my eye. Could you put it back in place? Tie it around my head?'

'This is dirty...'

'Here, rip some cloth from my underskirt.'

She tore a strip and dipped an end of it in our water, came back and gently stroked it over my eye.

'Are these your people?' I asked her.

'These are mostly Lakota, many clans. I am not Lakota. The Lakota call my people Sahiyela, whites say Cheyenne, so I say Cheyenne to you. Many Cheyenne are here, too. I am married to a Lakota man and I stay with his family. My family are all dead.'

'Where did you learn to speak English?' Elizabeth asked her. 'You speak very well.'

She beamed with pride.

'Missionary! When I was little, the Father was with us for a long time. He could talk our language, and many children learn English from him. I talk it in my head to remember, and it is not so good now. I am very, very happy to talk to you!'

Elizabeth asked, 'You are married to a Lakota man?'

As she tied the cloth around my head, the girl explained that the Cheyenne and Lakota had always been friends, sharing several common enemies, the Crow and the Snakes, and, I assumed — the girl was too polite to say so — the whites.

'What is your name?' I asked.

'The Father named me Mary when he... I don't know what it is called. I have lessons, then eat little bread that is Jesus' body?'

'Communion!' said Elizabeth. 'You took communion?'

'Yes. My name in his religion is Mary, but my Cheyenne name in English is Small Wing, so he called me Mary Small Wing.'

'Mary Small Wing. What a pretty name. I am Sarah.'

'And I am Elizabeth. *Mary.* A lovely Christian name, a sign of hope.'

'What is your husband's name?' I asked.

'This I can tell you. His name in English is Quick To See.'

Elizabeth asked if Far Cry was a man of importance. Mary nodded.

'He is a strong chief even though he is young. My husband is friend to him. There are many chiefs here from many bands of those tribes, young chiefs and Old Man chiefs. This man, Far Cry, his father was of great importance, a medicine man. Far Cry has strong medicine too, though not so much as his father. Far Cry and some others think to go far away from whites, to live as always and have no trouble with them. But the Old Man chiefs say we must all sign the paper and do what it says, go to live where they...'

Elizabeth interrupted her.

'Mary, if Far Cry decides he does not want to sign the treaty, does that mean he will not go to Fort Laramie? What would happen to us?'

At that moment, one of the guards put his face in the opening and spoke sharply to the girl.

'I have been here too long. Do not be worried. Far Cry will trade you back to your people. He has promised he will do this. Good bye, Sarah, and...'

'Elizabeth.'

'E-liz-bet?'

'Yes! Please come back as soon as you can. We thank God for sending you.'

We were both quiet. Elizabeth was staring at the back wall. Then she turned to me suddenly. There was a strange excitement in her look.

'When Mary comes back, we must ask her to cut our bonds part way so we look as if we are still tied but can break out of them when... the time comes. When we're ready.'

'Ready for what?'

'Ready to run. To escape.'

'*What?* You saw the size of this camp, the number of Indians. And we're under constant guard. Besides, where would we go?'

'Mary can tell us the direction in which we should go. When she says "the Immigrant Road" she surely means the Oregon Trail, I'm quite certain of it. While they're all distracted with this pow-wow, we can slip away. I've been looking at the bottom of that back wall, where the hide meets the ground, I'm sure we can get under it, the stakes are far enough apart. We're right by the river. There's very little between us and the river, I looked closely at it as we rode in. It's wide, but I saw horses out towards the middle of it and the water only came to their knees. We'll get to the woods on the other side of the river and head in the direction of the Trail.'

Her words came at me in a rush. I did not like this plan at all. I did not think either of us could move fast enough, it seemed suicidal to try.

'Why not wait? Far Cry will probably choose to sign this thing, and besides, as the girl said, he promised to make the exchange, so he will bring us to Laramie. We must wait. We'll be returned...'

'I have no faith in any of that, Sarah. Who knows when or if this signing will happen. I've heard too much about how hard it is to get Indians to sign these things and then to abide by the agreements. What if Far Cry decides *not* to sign? No. We must get away from this camp, get closer to the Trail. Word of our escape will travel...'

'And I have no faith in *that*.'

'Someone will hear of it. Whatever whites are here will learn of our escape, word will get to the forts, they'll assume...'

'Elizabeth, please stop. This is... It's too much *if this* and *if that*... No more. I can't hear any more.'

I crawled over to the blankets on my knees, managed to roll up in one and partially cover myself.

'Sarah! Stay with me, please!'

'I will talk it out with you, but not now. I can't. I'm in pain and can't think.'

I turned my back to her and closed my eyes. This idea of running off into the wilderness with me half blind, both of us still in pain and barely able to move, guided by vaguest hopes seemed not only utterly ridiculous but like a sure way to be killed. The Indians could have killed us, but hadn't. They needed us whole. Could she not see this? But Elizabeth was ablaze with her idea. Outside there was drumming and the sound of voices, sometimes rising in anger. I curled more tightly into myself.

CHAPTER 8

My head's in Mama's lap and she strokes my hair as she reads to me. I can't quite make out the words but her voice is like gently running water. I want to remain on her lap, cocooned in her warmth but something intrudes.

I struggle to stay in the dream. I'm aware of the fetid smell of the tipi and noise from outside, yet I can still hear the susurration of Mama's voice. She's saying something over and over.

What are you saying, Mama?

I'm afraid. I'm afraid, sweet girl. I'm afraid.

I'm fully awake, now, lying on my side with Elizabeth spooned up against me. I can tell by her breathing that she's asleep. The drumming and shouting have stopped outside and it's quiet. I hear water rushing. The stream. Elizabeth is right, it's very close by.

I'm afraid.

The tipi stank from our shit and piss. It had been three days since Mary Small Wing had left saying she'd be back. The life of the camp passed back and forth on the other side of our prison's flap all day and into the night. Sometimes our guards' friends would keep them company, they'd talk and laugh. Children called to one another. Dogs barked. Someone might pass on horseback. We'd hear the crackle of kindling being broken to build the fire nearby, then the hiss of flames, the dull clunk of wooden utensils on heavy cooking pots.

But in the hot, stinking tipi, the only people we saw were the women who came to feed and water us and to muck out our waste, replacing it with fresh straw and never enough of that. They did not once look at us.

At night, we heard drumming and sometimes singing. Occasionally there was shouting. We slept poorly, and during the day, we were listless. Both of us were sick. The first meal had been chunks of meat that tasted like venison. Now we got a greasy, rancid stew we could barely swallow. Our bowels rebelled.

'They're poisoning us,' Elizabeth said. 'Feeding us bad food to keep us weak.'

Elizabeth would blurt something like this, then she'd be silent until her next declaration.

'They must have made a decision by now. I believe they *must* have done so. Soon we'll be on our way to Laramie. I'll see my boys. Please, God, let it be so, oh, please.'

Elizabeth *knew* it would be soon, they were talking *now*, she could *feel* it. Every time a group of men walked past the tipi talking, she'd sit up, come to attention, as if she might miraculously understand their language if she listened hard enough. When they passed by, she'd pray.

Her constant praying annoyed me thoroughly. Every time I heard her begin, I wanted to press her face into the dirty straw. If god were bothering to watch us, I imagined he was as curious as we were to see how things turned out. I was certain that he didn't care about us any more than he cared about any other thing on this earth that lives and dies.

I remained in a state of torpor. I heard Elizabeth's rants, her sighs, knew when she sat, lay down, turned over, slept. I heard the river. Dreams came and went. I wanted my mother to come again, but she didn't. Watching the colour deepen on the hide, I remembered sitting outside the dugout in the late afternoon sun. How I wanted a drink.

If this treaty actually were to happen, and if Far Cry decided to sign it, if he took us to Laramie, and if the negotiations went well and if the two boys, Far Cry's nephews or whatever they were, were given back to his family, and *if* we were given back...

What would I be returning to at Laramie? I would have no choice but to go back to Virginia. Then what?

The air in the tipi seemed to be getting hotter, thicker, and more foul. Our wrists were chafed from being tied. We both slept off and on, sweating and in discomfort from our bowels. Elizabeth counted three days since we'd last seen Mary Small Wing.

'We must drink as much water as we can,' I told Elizabeth.

I remembered one of the doctors talking to my mother about a sickness that was running through the slave cabins, people were vomiting and shitting liquid. The doctor said to keep them drinking as much water as they could get down.

'Where in God's name is she!' Elizabeth cried out while trying to wipe her leg clean of her loose stool by pulling up her skirts and rubbing it with dirt from the floor. I answered as I always did.

'She'll come when she has something to tell us.'

'They're keeping her from us, otherwise she'd have come by now.'

'We don't know...'

'No, we don't! We don't know anything and I can't bear it!'

She sobbed and I let her. I lay where I'd taken to lying as I watched the light move across the hides.

Sometime in the afternoon, I pulled myself up and made my way towards the flap. Our guards were standing a bit apart and to the side, talking with some other men. I wanted a breath of fresh air. I wanted it badly and I wanted it right then.

'Elizabeth. Let's step outside.'

Elizabeth looked at me as if I'd just spoken in Greek.

'Let's open the flap and go outside. I want a breath of fresh air. And, who knows, maybe we could just... walk away.'

She grinned. We leaned down, pressed against the flap and, surprisingly — I'd assumed it was tied or fastened somehow — it opened. In two steps we were standing outside the tipi, hands still tied behind us. At first, no one noticed. There we were, two pale white women, one dark-haired, one fair, dressed in unspeakably filthy, stinking ragged clothes, standing in the yellow light, heads lifted like animals sniffing the air.

Then a woman stirring a pot at a fire just across from us shouted to some men off to the side, two of whom were our guards, and they turned to look. It was as if the entire population of the camp, or at least that particular circle, stopped and stared at us. Even a dog I'd noticed chewing on a stick, lifted its head and stared. Without waiting for the order, we ducked back inside. The laugh was worth it. As was a moment or two of air.

CHAPTER 9

That night, the din from the pow-wow was louder and angrier. The drumming would begin then stop then begin again. We did not talk. From time to time, we turned to look at one another and then look away. A crisis was coming. We both felt it.

After a time, the rising and falling waves of voices lessened in pitch and volume and then — and this seemed to happen suddenly — broke up, dispersed, and, for the most part, stopped. We pulled ourselves up to sit facing the flap. Men walked past talking, not arguing. Elizabeth put her head down and prayed. Then we heard that sweet voice:

'Sarah! Leez-bet!'

'Oh, thank God! You've come! Come inside! Quickly, quickly, please! What has happened? Tell us!'

Mary seemed out of breath, agitated.

'Much! Much. Big Chiefs cannot agree. This treaty talk, it breaks us, clan from clan, even families...'

'What does this mean?'

'I will tell you, Lizbet. It is hard. Far Cry has said his plan. He will *not* touch the pen. He will take his people to a place, far west, near the Shining Mountains. We go too, my husband and me. And Far Cry takes you. Both of you.'

Elizabeth and I were stunned. Elizabeth demanded,

'What about the trade? How will that happen if he takes us so far away?'

'I do not know...'

'*What?*'

I stopped Elizabeth with a gesture and turned to the girl, who was obviously very upset.

'Mary Small Wing, sit down with us, please. Elizabeth let the girl tell us what she can, but slowly. Let us all sit down and speak softly.'

'Please forgive me, my English... I am sorry.'

I reassured her, 'Your English is very good, Mary Small Wing. Tell us as much as you can, as well as you can tell it. We will not rush you, but we need to know as much as you can tell us. I know you understand.'

'I understand well,' she said.

A disagreement among the chiefs of the different clans centred on whether or not the whites could be trusted to keep to the terms of their own treaty. Many chiefs had put pen to many papers, signed many treaties, and all had been broken. Mary was unable to make clear the particulars, but at the up-coming meeting with the white chiefs, now maybe not until the spring, the Indians would be told they must remain on certain lands where whites would not go, and these would include places holy to the Lakota. This was good.

But the Indians would have to agree not to attack whites living in settlements or traveling on the immigrant roads ever again. If the Indians adhered to the agreement, they'd receive annuities — food and tools, guns and ammunition for hunting, blankets, various items including farming implements. These latter the Indians found insulting, as they were not farmers and looked down upon it.

Mary explained that some of the older chiefs who had seen too much death wanted to make peace, even under poor terms, even knowing those terms would probably be broken. They had seen the numbers of whites, always more coming, and believed it was the only hope to preserve the lives of their children's children. Even if they lost much else, they would keep their holy places, and that was vital. Others, mostly among the younger men, were angry and wanted to kill all the whites in the forts, on farms, and traveling on the trails. If they killed enough whites, they argued, they would stop coming.

'They are wrong about that,' Elizabeth interrupted her. 'Our soldiers will stop any such thing. We are here and more will come, the railroad will be finished, and then...'

'Elizabeth! Let the girl speak. What does Far Cry say about all this?'

'He says, and these are his words, he will not be "made into a white man". But he said that for Lakota warriors to fight the endless numbers of *wasichus,* whites, is to open their bodies to their guns, leaving our weak ones to be killed or die of hunger. He will have nothing more to do with whites. He said he will take his people and all who wish to go with him far from the roads and forts...'

'*What about us?* What will he do with us?'

'Elizabeth, my husband asked this question. He told my husband that when we all come to this new place, there will be time. He will think.'

'*Think?* But his promise! How will this trade happen if we are in some impossible place?'

Mary held her hands tight in her lap when she answered Elizabeth.

'This thing, *I* asked him. Far Cry answered me. I think he knew I would tell you. He says he will bring you to this winter camp, that he must talk with his men and think about these many things in quiet. He will keep you safe. Then maybe in the spring, if he thinks it is good, he will...'

'*Maybe?* Everything with you people is '*maybe*', or '*if*', or '*perhaps*'! Except the killing! You'll do that with no hesitation, women, children, anyone!'

Elizabeth struggled to stand, walked away and turned her back to us. Mary and I were both a bit stunned. We sat in silence. I wondered if Far Cry regretted having taken us. But now he had us. We were apparently pieces in a complicated game.

'When does he plan to begin this journey?' Elizabeth asked.

'Tomorrow. At first light.'

The flap opened and the woman came in with bowls of food and water. The guard came with her and looked at Mary severely. Before he could say anything, Mary stood and spoke to him. They exchanged a few sentences and he went out. The woman followed him. The girl explained.

'I told him Far Cry and my husband told me to let you know about tomorrow. I must go now and prepare. Far Cry is a good man. He will keep his promise about the boys, and you will be given back to your people. You will be safe.'

As she turned to go, Elizabeth stopped her.

'Mary, take your knife and cut part way through the ties around our wrists so if that woman comes again or anyone else, it will look as if we are still bound. But we must be able to break out easily.'

Mary looked at her in horror.

'Lizbet! Do not try to run away. They will kill you. Far Cry may not, but others already want to. There was talk of this, that it was bad medicine to keep you. Far Cry spoke for you, said it would be worse medicine to kill you. But if...'

'They will kill us anyway. I do not intend to wait.'

'No, Lizbet! Far Cry said...'

'*Enough about him.* Please just do what I asked, Mary.'

'They will know that I...'

I stepped forward.

'Elizabeth, no. We can't do this. We can not do this to Mary.'

Elizabeth dismissed me with a gesture, and moving close to Mary, looked into her eyes and spoke, her face sweet and soft, her words coming fast, urgent, precisely aimed.

'Mary, listen to me. I know you believe in God. You do, don't you?'

'Yes. I am Christian.'

'Then you know that God is always watching, that he sees everything his children do. God loves you and He loves Sarah and me. He knows that we, His children, are in great danger but I have prayed, and Sarah has, too, and He will help us. And you — *you!* — are surely His instrument for helping us. Do you understand? God has brought you to us for this purpose. He will reward you, He will *bless* you...'

'But they will kill you...'

'Oh, no, dear child, they will not. Listen to me. I am a very devout Christian. God *knows* me. I believe with all my heart that God wants me to return to my little children, that this is His will, and because this is true, it *will* happen. I believe this. Look at my face. Do you see how I believe this?'

'Yes, Lizbet, I see...'

'We will pray for you, for God to protect you and bless you. Help us, Mary. Help us to do God's will. Do it quickly now. Cut us loose.'

Mary cut one loop of our ties so they hung loosely but it appeared we were still bound.

'God bless you child!'

Just as she'd returned her knife to its sheath, the guard pushed open the flap. Mary looked from Elizabeth's face to mine, clearly frightened by what she'd done.

'God will bless you, Mary,' Elizabeth said again.

The man gestured impatiently for Mary to come. She went out quickly.

CHAPTER 10

'*How could you do that!* You used that child's faith! You could get us all killed! Her too!'

'Because it was the only way. God inspired me, and...'

'No! You *used* her and, god help me... No, god *damn* me, I let you do it.'

'God will forgive your lack of faith.'

'I am not asking for anyone's forgiveness! What you did was cruel. And evil! Evil to put that girl in danger.'

'Well, you might consider that, as a result of my "cruelty" and the rest of it, if we leave now, we may just survive this...'

'*We will not! Think!* How far do you think we can get? Neither of us is healed from our injuries, and now there's this sickness in our guts, we're too weak!'

'Did you not hear her? He's leaving at first light and plans to take us *far away from whites.* Do you really think he'll feed us and keep us through a long journey, the two of us? With winter coming on? We are a burden and a danger. "*Bad medicine*"!'

'Mary said he intends to keep the promise...'

'And you believe this? He's one of *them!* And so is the girl. They're not like us, Sarah. We can't fool ourselves into thinking we will be told the truth.'

'I don't believe Mary would lie to us...'

'*Mary is an Indian!* For all her missionary English and sweet ways, she could be telling us only what she was *told* to tell us. Did that never occur to you? Trade us? Oh, I believe he will trade us. We're valuable property. *But to whom and for what?* He could trade us for horses, for guns! To those traders she said were here with the latest models. He could be completing the deal right now. No. We must get away from these savages. Tonight. Do not forget that this is a war and they are the enemy. You of all people, having lived through the horrors of that other war, should understand that.'

I stared at her standing in front of me, blazing her faith, her certainty. How different she was from the woman weeping against a tree, so severely hurt in body and spirit, so nearly destroyed by grief and so needing of my care. I did not see that damaged soul in the woman standing there looking hard at me. This was Elizabeth's true self. She would do anything, *anything*, to return to her children.

Perhaps, lacking that ferocious mother-instinct, I was the weaker of us two in this instance. Perhaps I had been a sentimental fool to put faith in a young, sweet-faced *Indian* bride eager to show off her English. Perhaps — and this seemed worse — I'd been a romantic fool to put faith in the word of an Indian whose looks and manner I liked. Perhaps Elizabeth was right.

'How do you imagine we do this thing? What about the guards? They're always there.'

'Yes, *there*. Out front. Come here.'

She pulled her hands free with a snap, reached around and loosed my ties. Then she pulled me to the back wall and we lay down on our bellies. She lifted the skin between a couple of stakes and we looked outside. It was not yet fully dark. The tipis to our left were barely visible, those to our right were not visible at all. Ours was closest to the river. Upriver, to our left, towards the west where the sky was still pinkish, we could see horses on the bank, but downriver there was nothing.

The river was wide. From our perspective it was hard to tell how wide, but if it was shallow all the way across, we would be able to do it easily. Farther downstream it seemed to narrow a bit as it curved away from the camp.

As if she read my thoughts, Elizabeth whispered,

'I think it's shallow. Look how the water moves around those rocks sticking up.'

'I see that. And I remember seeing the horses standing in it, but that was upstream.'

The water rushed around rocks near where we'd enter it, but there were fewer rocks in the middle. In front of us, grass grew right to the edge of the water. From what we could see of it through the grass, the riverbank on this side seemed to be pretty much on a level with the ground. But the opposite bank looked steep and rocky, about twelve or fifteen feet high with a dense tangle of shrubs and trees at the top. Darkness already filled those woods. It would have been a hard climb in daylight, but in the dark? How would we ever find a path in the dark?

'Please, Elizabeth, consider carefully. If we make it up that bank, how far do you really think we would get in those woods at night? We would not only be fighting our way in complete dark, but as I said before, neither of us is strong...'

'Tell me. In the last days of the journey to this place, I believe we were traveling west. What do you think? Am I right?'

'Yes. We were traveling west. And somewhat northerly, too. I've been watching the path the sun makes on the hides, west is that way, upstream.'

'So, when we get to the other side, we'll turn right and go east. We'll keep following the river east.'

I got up and walked away from her to the other side of the tipi. I turned to her, raised my hands, a gesture of supplication, to try again to dissuade her, but could think of nothing to say and dropped my hands to my sides. She sat for a moment looking at me in the fast waning light. Her face softened.

'How do you want to die, Sarah? Do you want to wait for them to kill us or shall we take our chances together? I believe we will get away.'

'When would you have us do this?'

'After dark. After the camp is bedded down.'

'What if there's a moon?'

'We will pray for clouds to cover it.'

'The dogs will bark. We have no food! I still don't see how we will make our way...'

She waved her hands in front of her face as if my words were insects she was swatting away. But her voice remained gentle.

'God helps those who help themselves. If you are afraid to go, dearest, then stay. I'm going tonight.'

I was defeated. I answered as I'm sure she knew I would:

'I'll come with you.'

'Oh, my dear friend! We shall pray on it.'

She got up onto her knees and waved me over.

'Pray with me. You must pray'.

'Elizabeth, I...'

'Lizzie, call me Lizzie. My family all calls me Lizzie.'

CHAPTER 11

'The moon...'

'Not so bright. Barely at the quarter.'

'Let's wait, Lizzie. It might cloud over a little, there were some clouds earlier...'

'Ah! There's a bit of cloud. See it? See how it covers those stars?'

'Shhh! Yes.'

'It's coming fast, it will move over the moon.'

'It looks thin.'

'Just the edges. In a minute... Get ready...'

'Too thin.'

'There'll be another. Besides, there's no one to see us. Everyone's at their fires, doing what they do.'

'Yes. It's quiet back here. Except for the river.'

'And the river is louder than I imagined. That's good.'

'Yes.'

'Remember, make for the centre and we'll work our way down a bit before we go up that other bank.'

'Yes.'

'This may be the best we are to have it. Are you ready, Sarah?'

'No. But let's do this now or not at all.'

Through the grass and into the water. Mud, then slick round rocks that slip and roll from under foot. Striding through the water, Lizzie just behind and to my left, it's faster than I'd thought, making for the centre, and here it is, I think, it must be, and it's faster here and cold! Water to the knee, over the knee. Current getting faster, we're moving fast, pulled hard. Water to my hip. Skirts float, fill up and swirl, drag. Where is she? Behind me. I reach out. *Grab my hand!* Slipping on rocks.

We're moving downstream fast in the centre of the stream, feet pushing off something below and looking for some other thing with sudden wild stretches of feet paddling free before another rock to push off from. We'll know when to cross, we'll see it. I can feel I'm grinning. I look back at her. Big, bright eyes, she's grinning too, yells something I hear as, *We can do this!*

Yes! I'm nodding and nodding and I slip and the stream bed's gone. Deep water, sucking eddies, so damn fast, sudden boulders but I can't grab and keep hold, too slick. Skirts going round my legs like dogs playing. I've lost her hand. *Your hand! Lizzie! Take my hand!* I shout but the water's louder. I anchor myself, legs spread between two big rocks and reach, she lunges and we grab forearms, fists at elbows, holding tight.

The river pushes, pulls, throws, slams. The beast would kill us and it wouldn't care. It wants to pull us down, tries to pull us apart, but we hold, we hold, we pull each other forward, first one is ahead and then the other. Sometimes there's a stone both feet can step on, a breath, maybe two before the current pushes me off and I'm swimming, pulling her along or she's pulling me.

And, suddenly, we're close, we're within reach of it, but the bank's too high here, steep and hanging over. Impossible. Cold, teeth clatter, muscles jerk. There'll be a place farther down, no choice, and the water grabs, though at least now there's a bottom... Aaaaah! Snag got my leg! And now it's deep again, swimming, trying to kick. That crown of rock just there... there... *there!* No! Too slick! Please, God... Big gnarl of driftwood sticking out, coming, coming, *now!* Grab, hold, please, hold, can't breathe, please... I wrap my free arm tight around it. Lizzie's got my other arm, our fists like bird claws tight on one another's arms. *You okay? Yes, you? Yes!* We say these things with eyes and nods. I stare downstream and see how narrow, how fast. The water's so loud I have to shout to get her attention, she's looking up towards the top of the bank. *Lizzie!* I shake my head, *No!* and nod downstream, but she lifts her chin to have me look up at the embankment. Not so high as before and no overhang. And it's all we've got, and I'm so tired, and she's just as tired.

We let go of one another, push off. It's close, *but the water!* The water pulls us downstream and, hard as we try, the bank is no closer and no closer. Keep at it, keep at it, keep at it! Ribboned moonlight and the noise of water, the whole universe is a roar of mad water, and suddenly it's shallow and there are rocks beneath our feet and pebbles and sand, and we are crawling up, scrambling on all fours, sucking hard for air, coughing, shaking cold. I want to stop for a moment, but we can't. We drag one another up, pulling at small branches, up and over rocks and, finally, we're lying on the ground. Oh, the good ground! We're gasping and spitting river water from our lungs.

'Sarah?'

'I'm here.'

We are on our bellies where we fell, side by side, looking at each other. Her face is streaked mud and bloody scratches. Mine must be the same. It hurts where that snag gouged the calf of my leg.

It hurts to breathe. We lie gasping among roots and leaves and rocks, in a clear place right at the top of the bank. The river roars on below.

'A few minutes,' she says, 'no more.'

But we don't even have that before we hear them.

Branches crashing, hooves pounding the ground, horses coming towards us fast. I scramble up and throw my body forward. I turn my head to see, and she's right behind me, then I thrust myself into the thickest growth, where it's dark, I'm grabbing, whipping myself forward, swinging myself around, leaping over, stumbling, grabbing, beating at branches in my face. Elizabeth screams. Don't look back, run faster, harder. Now there's a horse behind me, close behind, then so close I can hear its hard breathing, its hooves at my heels. If I slip I'm trampled. I dart to the side but the hooves, the hooves, and now it's beside me, there's its hot breath, there's its wild eye, the shoulder muscle, a man's leg, the red-sleeved arm that pulls me up. I thrash against that flank like a hooked fish.

CHAPTER 12

I woke lying on my side in the tipi, I recognised the smell. Elizabeth was lying beside me. Light from the open flap. Legs, there are people standing right by us. Then a familiar voice,

'You are awake? You can hear me?'

Mary Small Wing. A man was standing close behind her, I could see his moccasins. Another man was farther back, in the shadows, shifting his feet. I was lying on my belly, my hands tied behind me. Mary was kneeling beside me, leaning down, talking urgently into my face.

'Sarah! *You can hear me?*'

'Yes.'

I had a second's panic for Elizabeth and tried to turn to see her, but I heard her say *Yes* and was relieved. Mary spoke in a manner obviously tuned for the men, but her voice shook.

'I am told to tell you that Far Cry will leave in the morning as he has said. He will take you both. If you try to escape again, you will be killed. Do you understand me?'

We both said, Yes.

Mary stood and the three walked to the flap. The man who'd been farther away was first out of the tipi. The other turned to Mary and hissed something then he wheeled and went out. Mary turned to us.

'Far Cry says to tell you that you have no ears. You do not know how to listen. I am telling you that you must obey him or die.'

And she left us.

I was wet all over and cold to the bone, shivering so hard I was afraid I'd lose more teeth. My calf hurt and remembering the snag I wanted to see it. I rolled over on to my side, but my skirts had been pulled down over my legs and it seemed too difficult to pull them up with my hands tied behind me. Moving my leg, though, I could feel it was not so bad and that it had been bandaged. Mary must have done it. I turned to face Elizabeth who was facing me. She had a mean-looking knot rising on the side of her forehead. She asked about me.

'Are you hurt?'

'Not badly.'

She scooted sideways, grabbed an edge of the blanket we were lying on, I did the same and then we rolled to face one another, nose to nose. With some adjusting, our backs were at least partially covered and we could share the warmth of our breath and our bodies. Elizabeth whispered into my face.

'We must never stop trying to escape.'

A laugh tried to rise but when it hit my throat, became a cough.

'Do you hear me? We must not give up.'

'Since you seem on intimate terms, does god's plan for you involve much more of this sort of thing?'

'God's plan for *us*.'

'God's plan for our *clothing*. We don't stink as badly.'

'Sarah, please...'

'Don't speak.'

Before dawn, we were put on horses, but our tied hands were in front so we could hold on to ropes around the horses' girths. About thirty Indians, some on horses pulling travois, many women with children, the two of us captives, and a large string of horses left the city of tipis behind. After a day or two, our hands were untied. Several riders separated me from Elizabeth, and Mary Small Wing was kept well removed from us. From time to time I'd see her, always in the company of her husband. When we made camp for the night, she did not come to speak with us and rarely even made eye contact.

Elizabeth and I were allowed to be together at night. They never again tied our hands. We each had a blanket roll, but no shelter and were cold at night. My leg hurt where I had to press it against the horse, but not badly, and I also had knot on my head, in the back. Both of us were bruised all over our bodies, and our faces, arms and legs were scored with cuts and scratches.

I can't remember how many days we traveled. Not knowing where we were going, it seemed a long time. We were moving west and south, as well as I could determine. Sometimes there was no sun. We traveled into the foothills of mountains, moving slowly. We would come to the top of a ridge and see a higher ridge beyond it. On the higher peaks, there was snow. The trees were different at this altitude. Even the quality of light was different and it was colder at night. We were given an extra blanket.

Late one afternoon, we saw smoke from fires and came down into a valley through which ran a stream — fairly wide but quite shallow — with trees and shrubs along the banks. Riding into this camp was a significantly quieter affair than the last. It was much smaller than the great gathering of clans, but a good deal larger than the camp in the woods where we'd been given a tipi and the old woman had helped me. I couldn't get a count of the tipis as many were deeper into the trees all along the stream. Again, people came forward to greet Far Cry and his people with pleasure. Children looked at us with curiosity; the adults barely regarded us.

We were shown where to sit and Mary brought us blankets. She smiled and it was as if she'd stroked my face. But she didn't talk and didn't stay. A good number of men gathered in and around a large tipi not far away. Men walked in and out, and a few women chatted while watching a large pot suspended above a fire right nearby. It was as if we were invisible. Only the occasional dog trotting past looked at us.

At dusk, that seemed to fall fast, Mary brought bowls of soup. The talking continued. Elizabeth and I huddled together and fell asleep. I woke once to a quiet camp. The weather had cleared and there were stars scattered all over the black sky. The blanket wasn't nearly warm enough, but we'd known worse. I cuddled closer to Elizabeth and, in her sleep, she did the same. I did not feel threatened, but couldn't say why. Maybe I was simply too tired for the drama of fear. No matter what had happened and what might yet happen, nothing bad was happening at that moment and that was a good thing.

In the morning, a woman brought two bowls of mush. I searched her face, but she betrayed nothing. Later, Mary brought us tin cups full of steaming liquid, smiled and said, 'Coffee!' Then she left us. The brew was not coffee but it had the look of coffee and enough pleasant aroma and flavour of its own to feel good going down. It was good and hot.

We were emptying the last drops when a small group of women, including a smiling Mary, came for us. Mary gestured and said, 'Come.' We walked a short way with this troop before stopping in front of two tipis, rather close together. Mary called and an old woman stepped out of one of the lodges. Mary said a few words, indicated me and the old woman looked me over. Elizabeth was given the same examination by a woman who came out of the other tipi. Mary explained that these two had lost husbands and sons in battles with white soldiers. They had no other children. We were to live with them and take care of them. Neither of us quite understood and Mary explained in a sentence.

'Things taken are given to those who need them. You belong to these women now.'

Before we could ask questions, the old women, with the encouragement and participation of their friends, began herding us into the woods amid much prodding with sticks and barking of orders and laughter.

So our new routine began. Our first task that day and every day, was to gather sticks and branches to build a fire that we were to keep going all day. The women hit us with switches for no discernible reasons, jeered at us, cackled about us with the others, making exaggerated expressions of impatience.

More jobs were added in the ensuing days. We were apparently hilariously incompetent at all of them. We were whipped until we did things correctly, and then we were whipped because it seemed to entertain these old women. Yet we weren't whipped terribly hard and after a while, not at all.

The work began at dawn and continued through the day, so sleep came easily. We slept in the tipis across the floor from our old women. We slept on skins with warm blankets. We ate regularly. We did not spend the day on horseback. We could relieve ourselves whenever the need arose with no guard.

We were able to talk while gathering firewood, picking berries, digging for roots, tending the fires, cooking, while at the river to wash clothing and blankets or to bathe, which we did in our undergarments to the amusement of the Indian women. Mary Small Wing was a regular visitor at both our fires. I don't know how much time passed, possibly weeks.

'How long will we stay with these old women?'

Mary looked at us quizzically, as if Elizabeth had asked a silly, obvious question.

'Until they are dead.'

We were both dumfounded. But I had a sudden realisation. I asked her,

'What are we to these women?'

'You are given to these women, Sarah, I told you. You belong to these women now.'

'So, we are slaves!'

It made me laugh.

'How can you laugh? This is anything but funny,' said Elizabeth. 'We're Christian women and we're held as slaves by heathen. It's like the Bible story about...'

'I don't think it's funny. I don't know what it is. It's... interesting, ironic.'

'Your family must have had slaves, did you not?'

'Yes, of course we had servants. Everyone did.'

'So how can you possibly laugh?'

'This is good news, Lizzie. They won't injure us. If we were to become damaged goods, we would no longer have the same value in a trade. Don't you see? He plans to keep that promise and make the trade.'

'I pray you're right.'

'I know I am. My parents treated our servants well so they would stay healthy, do their work properly, and wouldn't have any desire to run away. My father used to say it was just good business. But it was more than that in my home. There was great affection. Our cook, Ruth, who also ran the house and kept the girls in line, was a remarkable woman. We loved her, and she loved us. Other families we knew had some difficulties with their servants, but our home was harmonious. We will not be injured, Lizzie. He needs us whole and healthy.'

One day, while we three were sipping something at the fire in front of my tipi while both old women napped, I asked Mary about Far Cry. Although there were older men who by their demeanour and his deference to them, I assumed had greater status, he seemed to be widely respected.

'Why does he not have a wife?'

'He had a wife,' Mary said. 'She was killed and he has not wanted to love another. When he was a boy, his mother and a young sister died of the... I don't what you call it, the spotted disease. His father died not long ago, but a good death. He was well enough to begin singing his Death song before he slept.'

'When did he lose his wife?'

'Maybe two years, maybe a little longer. In a bad way. She was Cheyenne. She was visiting relatives and went to a village where Moketavato, your word is Black Kettle, a chief who was trying to make peace with whites, was. A place where a Big Chief of the whites told the people to gather. Black Kettle's people put up a white flag. They believed this would let the soldiers know they were what you call friendlies. But the soldiers fired a big gun into the camp and killed many, then shot more for no reason. Hundreds of the people were killed or torn up by bullets. Then they were cut with knives. Most of the dead were women and children, the men had gone hunting. Far Cry has a hole where his heart used to live.'

'Good god. I can see why he would hate whites,' I said.

'After that happened, Cheyenne friends came and he rode with them to carry the war pipe to other Lakota, to make allies against these soldiers. Then he went away into a holy place to be alone, to heal his heart and to think how he wanted his people to live. Before this thing happened, he wanted to be like an Oglala called... Man Whose Horse is Crazy...'

'Crazy Horse!'

Elizabeth and I said the name at the same time. We'd both heard of him. Everyone had heard of him, every white person in the west was terrified of Crazy Horse, and a bit in awe.

'Yes, this is the one, a warrior with very strong medicine. Far Cry had wanted to go on the warpath with him. But when he came down from the mountains he told his people he would make his own path, far away from whites' settlements and roads. This is what he told again at the pow wow.'

Elizabeth asked the name of the Cheyenne chief again, and then said she had heard of this battle.

'Yes, Black Kettle. I heard all about it when we first came, it had recently happened at Sand Creek, in the Colorado Territory. But I'm afraid you're mistaken, Mary, in much of your story. Colonel Chivington was only doing what had to be done. The Indians, those *particular* Indians, had become very dangerous and unpredictable, stealing livestock and killing settlers and immigrants. They had been warned to stay in a certain place but they would not, and would not stop killing whites. They had to be taught a harsh lesson. And not that many were killed and most of these were warriors. Only a few of the dead were Indian women and children, not as many as you say, and that was mostly by accident. '

Mary's face, that had been so open to us, closed. She stood straight, and composed herself before speaking directly to Elizabeth.

'*You* are the one who is wrong, Lizbet. You are *very* wrong. My husband told me everything. Far Cry saw the body of his wife and the body of the baby that was cut out of her. He saw the others lying along the bank. The soldiers were drunk and they… I cannot speak of what they did. But I *know*, everyone knows who knows the truth. I am Cheyenne. I had friends and relations in that camp. It was as I told it to you.'

And she left us. Elizabeth was shaken and she too walked away, saying there was something she had to do for her old woman. We never spoke of it again, but I could see that she had, perhaps for the first time, seen how we whites did not always hear the truth of what actually happened in the field of battle.

Our relations with Mary repaired, but she and Elizabeth were tentative with one another for some time. I was thankful for her friendship. One evening Elizabeth asked her,

'How long will we stay here? In this camp?'

'Here? Here is winter camp. We are *here* now.'

'*Winter camp?* So, we will be here until the spring?'

'Yes. We will move a little, for the horses to eat fresh grass, but never far. It is a pretty place. Don't you think yes?'

Mary looked around at the protective range of high mountains to the north, the lower hills cradling our small meadow that was open to the south, the wide eastward flowing creek that sang over its bed of stones. It *was* a pretty place. But Elizabeth's brow was dark. She leaned in close to the girl's face.

'We must find a way to get word to one of the forts, Mary. I can't imagine how it might be done, but you must help us.'

Mary stared at her, incredulous.

'*Lizbet!* You do not remember what I told you?'

'Of course, but…'

I interrupted, hoping to mediate and trying by my expression to communicate to Elizabeth that we should not appear to be speaking urgently. We were being watched. We were always being watched.

'Of course, we remember. But Elizabeth has two little children, little boys, whom she misses terribly, and a husband she loves. We both hope to return to our own people, as I am sure you understand.'

Mary stiffened.

'I can promise you this one thing, and only this. I can promise you that if you try to escape, no matter what Far Cry wants to do, his men will shoot you. Some of his men think you will draw the soldiers to us and...'

'Mary, dear. I promise that Sarah and I will not involve you in any plans we make...'

'*Do not make these plans!* Please be patient. Far Cry has said he will find a way to make the trade this spring. Nothing can happen now, with winter coming. We must all wait.'

To soften this, Mary reached out to touch Elizabeth's arm.

'It is a good place. You will see. I will have my baby here.'

Elizabeth's entire aspect changed abruptly.

'Your *baby?* You're to have a child? But, Mary, this is wonderful! When will the baby be born?'

'There will still be snow when the baby comes, but it will be melting. I forget your name. We call it the Moon of Snowblindness.'

CHAPTER 13

Our injuries were healing. We began to reacquaint ourselves with our bodies. Coming out of the tipis in the early morning, we arched our backs like cats. Sitting at the banks of the stream, we took off our shoes — Jake's old boots were still good enough, but Mary's buckled shoes were falling apart. Our mad fight with the river had all but destroyed them. She shoved soft pieces of skin into the toes and tied the soles on with rawhide cord. We stretched out our legs and looked at our pale feet. We spread our toes. We lay back and when the sun was out, it rested gently on us.

We were getting strong with the chores, and our faces and arms had taken on colour from being outside so much. Elizabeth was especially brown. She had been accustomed to the hard work of farming, and pushed herself with a kind of enthusiasm, though I could see from time to time she still had pains in her body. I was not at all prepared for this sort of exertion but managed to keep up. I was still dizzy from time to time, but it was good to feel strength coming in my arms and legs. I hadn't felt this strong since girlhood.

Every now and then, a sharp pain would come from behind my dead eye. I tried to notice if certain movements caused it, but there was no consistency. Elizabeth and Mary both would inspect the eye from time to time to make certain it was healing. Mary offered a mirror, but I didn't want to look at it, not yet. Lizzie told me that while the scars around it were still colourful, the eye itself was no longer red. It was now a cloudy, yellow-white. That seemed an improvement, but I didn't want to see it and didn't let myself think about it.

It was getting colder. The trees along the stream banks had all turned gold, brown and russet. The tops of some trees were almost bare. When the wind blew, leaves showered down and were caught in the current and carried east towards the Missouri. I imagined their journey from the Missouri to the Mississippi and south, all the way to the Gulf of Mexico.

On clear days, the sky was cerulean. I knew the colour from my paint box. Other days it was dark as slate and the wind-whipped rain beat hard against the hides of the tipis. But there were more brilliant days than dark days and when the sun shone, the rich light, especially in the afternoons, deepened the colours of meadow, woods and mountains. The air was cool and smelled like something nice to drink. Lizzie and I decided it must be October. It *looked* like October.

One day, Mary told us the autumn hunt would happen the following day. The women set about preparing a feast, we captives were given our orders. All the fires in the village had food cooking over them, and in the evening people gathered in the main circle. The old ones sat propped against wicker chair-backs. People came out of their tipis in fancy clothes and wearing more jewellery. There were more feathers on display. People visited from fire to fire, and the children were excited. Even the dogs seemed exuberant. At night there was drumming and singing, a lot of laughter.

Mary explained that the feasting was to give the hunters a good send-off. The songs asked help from certain spirits. The autumn hunt was a most important hunt, she said. The hunters might be gone for a long time but would return with meat for the winter and hides to repair the walls and floors of tipis, to provide warm skins for sleeping under, and to make winter robes. There'd be other skins, as well, for winter moccasins and other clothing. And maybe they'd come back with horses, if they happened to raid a Crow camp while they were at it. Elizabeth's eyes widened. Mary had added this to the list in such a way that suggested this was nothing extraordinary, simply part of life.

'What is a long time?' asked Elizabeth.

'Many, many days and nights. As long as they need for a good hunt. Sometimes now, the buffalo are hard to find. Not like before.'

Just after dawn, the women prepared the horses their men liked for hunting, and waited by them. Boys pulled packhorses from the herd and brought them around. Everyone was out wishing the hunters luck, hugging them, kissing them. Some of the older boys, still children though they didn't believe themselves to be, were sullen that they weren't allowed to join the party. The medicine man went to each hunter, blowing smoke over their heads and their horses' heads and murmuring prayers. Mary Small Wing, visibly pregnant now, hugged Quick To See and caressed his face. They were a loving, sweet couple. I noticed the men only had a few guns among them, old carbines, but they had good bows — many of the men carried two — and full quivers. I recalled watching them make new bows and arrows in the past few weeks. As they rode off, the women did the tremolo.

With the men gone, the women behaved as if on holiday. They smiled at us more. Even our old ones chattered at us in pleasant tones without seeming to care that we had no idea what they were saying. The older boys strutted about with new importance — they were the men of the camp now. They made a big thing of going off with their short bows to shoot birds or, if they were lucky, a rabbit for the cook pots.

The old men smoked and snoozed. The old women kept warm by the fires, chatting, and the younger women gossiped and laughed as they worked, as we all worked, doing what needed to be done to keep life going.

I began to ask Mary the names of things.

'What do you call this beautiful blue flower? I see them everywhere.'

Mary would tell me and I'd struggle to repeat the sounds. She'd laugh and I'd beg her to say it again. I'd repeat it back to her until I got it right. Elizabeth would not try. I didn't think anything of this until one day when Mary's efforts to teach me, and my efforts to learn, seemed to annoy her rather a lot. She interrupted one of our 'lessons' to question Mary.

'Are you really the only one of these people who speaks *any* English?'

'A few know some little words, Lizbet. Medicine Crow and his wife know a little. Far Cry knows a little. Like me, he learned from missionaries, but not as much as me.'

Occasionally, it had seemed he understood a word or two but I decided he was just particularly astute at interpreting a tone of voice and reading gestures.

'How much English does he speak?'

'I do not know. What he knows, he will not speak.'

'Why not?'

Mary ducked her head slightly, an apologetic gesture.

'It is the language of the whites and the whites are killing his people.'

'Ah. Of course. How stupid of me not to guess. But, I do want to learn at least a little of the Lakota language. Will you help me?'

'Yes. I will be happy for this. I can teach you every day, and you too Lizbet.'

'No, thank you. I don't want to learn it. I understand Far Cry's choice.'

'I understand his choice, as well, Lizzie, but don't you think it will make our lives here easier?'

Elizabeth's face turned hard, but she kept her voice even.

'It is not important that our lives here be *easier*. And *this* is not "our lives". This is something we must endure until we are rescued from it. Far Cry is right. We must not forget that we are enemies.'

Mary sat looking down at her hands. I could not let this pass unquestioned.

'But do you not think our ability to "endure" this, might be helped by being able to understand some of what is being said around us? *About* us?'

'I pray that we will be far away from this place and these people long before either of us has time to learn this heathen language.'

I hated that Mary had to hear this and turned to the girl, speaking gently.

'Well, I would like to try, with your help, Mary, to understand a few words of your beautiful language.'

Elizabeth got up and walked away. I was angry. She had been rude, ungrateful, mean-spirited. There was no reason to speak that way in front of that sweet child. 'Heathen language.' Good god. I caught up with her.

'Elizabeth. We must talk about your feelings regarding the language. I should think...'

She turned around and levelled her gaze at me like the barrel of a gun.

'You constantly forget that these people are our enemies, Sarah, no matter how pleasant some may seem. I do not want a single syllable of their language in my mouth or in my mind. I have no choice but to hear it, but I pay as little attention to it as possible.'

'But do you not understand that it would be wiser if we...'

'*Understand? You* are the one who lacks understanding. When we pray to God, the words themselves, even the *sounds* of the words, help to bring Him into our minds and hearts. The *words*, Sarah! Words have this power. If I learn and repeat the words of a Godless people, who knows what might enter my heart.'

'Do you really believe that?'

'*Yes! Of course I do!* When you started asking the names of things, it was fun at first to try to say them. But, as I thought about it, I understood that speaking the name of a flower in that language would be a door opening a bit. Then there would be more words and the door would open further. If we were to learn it, this language would alter the shape of our thoughts. It would change us.'

'Lizzie, this makes no sense. I learned to speak French fairly well. I learned to sing a few songs in Italian. I can read a tiny bit of Greek. I am still who I've always been.'

She ignored this. I reminded her that Mary Small Wing had put herself in danger to help us. She was a sweet, good soul. I reminded her of the laughter we enjoyed with the other women even without vocabulary, the oddly affectionate harassment dealt out by our funny old keepers. I brought up the children's voices at play...

She interrupted me.

'All that is what it is. But those savages — those men from the same tribe as that Far Cry — slit our dear friend Robert's throat as he offered them food. His blood spurted over the table and onto the floor. Then they did the two little boys the same. Someone held me by the hair and jerked my head so I couldn't turn away when they pulled the baby from her cradle by the feet and dashed her brains out on the hearth. They made jokes as they did it *in this language that you are so eager to learn!* As God is my witness, I will not learn it. I will not forget who I am. Do not forget who *you* are.

'And that blue flower you love so much is an aster. *An aster.*'

The men returned after a bit more than a week with abundant meat and hides draped over the packhorses. They were welcomed exuberantly, meat was cooked and the hunters were celebrated with singing and dancing, with stories. Elizabeth and I — having forgiven one another as we always did, as we needed one another too much to hold on to differences — watched from the periphery. Their joy was infectious. I'd look over to see Elizabeth smiling.

The following morning the men sat outside the tipis to smoke and talk, to relax after their exertions. The women — including Elizabeth and I — and the older girls cut the red muscle meat into thin strips and hung them on wooden frames we'd built while the men were gone. These would dry in the sun or over fires to be put away in sacks for the winter. The skins were stretched and pinned to the ground. Elizabeth and I were shown how to scrape them clean with scapular bones and rub them with brain to soften them.

At the end of the day, we went to the stream with the other women to bathe.

'What a nasty mess!' said Elizabeth.

'I agree! This mess by any name — *in any language!* — would be just as nasty!'

We lay down in the stream and let the shallow cold water run over and all around us and soak the stink out of our clothing.

Often at night, now, the moon shone through a high thin scrim of cloud, and during the day a haze seemed to filter the sunlight. Wild geese and ducks flew over in chevrons. One morning it was strangely quiet, as if all the songbirds had departed at once. Mary told us the old people said certain signs had come early. Beaver had been busy at the willows for weeks; we'd seen them. Muskrats were building unusually tall lodges in the reeds along the creek-beds. The old people were shaking their heads.

Yet the days were still mild and the village atmosphere was easy and pleasant. Plenty of meat was drying on the racks. The men smoked and talked. Boys practiced shooting arrows at flying grasshoppers. Girls tied their dolls into papoose boards and sang to them. Girls and boys together played running games and games with hoops. The women gossiped as they sewed winter clothing for their families. We patched our own clothing as best we could and, with Mary's supervision and one or two of the other women, worked on making warm things for our old crones.

Some of the women were particularly good at decorating these items and would show us how to do it. We'd trade hair pins, or strips of ribbon or open-work from what was left of our petticoats, for quills or beads. They enjoyed showing us these things, and Elizabeth was quite adept. The cooking pots were full and the village at dusk, with the people eating together, was a good place to be.

What had been so strange and unnerving a short time before, had become so familiar to me as to feel pleasant. But even as I noted this, I felt guilty. As if I were betraying Elizabeth, somehow. As if I were beginning to fulfil her fears of forgetting.

CHAPTER 14

We had given up trying to count the days. Without the help of numbered days and a new month beginning with 'one' — which seems arbitrary and almost silly, when I think about it — and without knowledge of the stars or other markers, I relied on simpler things. I observed the natural signs of the advancing season. I also observed the pace at which the fabric of my old clothing disintegrated. Both progressions were inexorable. Both had their own kind of eloquence.

The cold came down hard when it came, and, no matter who we were or had been, we all shared the cold. It was a deeper cold than I had ever experienced. Elizabeth, who'd known severe cold from time to time in New York, said she'd known nothing like it. Even Mary said it was unusual.

Elizabeth and I emerged from our tipis in the morning with the rest of the camp. We fixed food for our old women, joined one another for tea or coffee if either of us had any. Mary visited if she could, and then we all went about doing what needed doing: gathering wood, preparing skins, making and mending clothes, washing up, digging tubers, gathering berries. We laughed, we complained, we watched the children at play, the men talking, smoking and cleaning their weapons, departing for or returning from a hunt or a raid. We stood well back from the dancing when they came back, especially when they were showing scalps they'd taken, though that was rare and Mary would explain: 'Snakes. Bad people.'

We prepared food, served it up, ate it. We did our work. We washed, we pissed, we shat, we slept near our old women with buffalo robes piled on top of us. We helped our old women who felt the cold. For a while, neither of us thought or spoke about rescue. I need to correct that statement. *I* never thought of it. Elizabeth never *spoke* of it, but I doubt it ever left her mind.

One day a party of warriors rode into the village. They came in fast and I was gut-struck with fear but Far Cry and other men greeted them as comrades and they all went immediately into the lodge of one of the Old Man Chiefs.

The women exchanged looks. Presently, Mary came to tell us with some excitement that the strangers were Cheyenne. We had learned from her that her people generally ranged farther south and east, but these were northern Cheyenne. Both were allied with the Lakota. They shared enemies, mostly Crow and white soldiers.

Crow scouts often worked with the US Army, which further embittered the Lakota and Cheyenne against them. This group had come with big news.

'Does it have to do with us?'

'No, Lizbet. Something big has happened, big battle. I will tell you when I find out.'

The meal was shared and then the children were put to sleep early. We took care of our old women and then came outside, standing silently together, listening, watching. We put our arms around each other's waists. A few of the wives went to the open door of the big lodge and stood listening to the men. From time to time, the group inside erupted in shouts — triumph? anger? — it was hard to tell. The fires were kept burning high. Later, drumming and singing commenced and continued late into the night. It was impossible to sleep. The Cheyenne left in the early morning.

Elizabeth and I went about our morning chores distracted and anxious. Waiting for Mary. The men spoke quietly in twos and threes; the women's faces displayed nothing unusual. Finally Mary came to sit with us.

'It has been a very big thing,' she said. 'A big killing has happened. They are calling it The Battle of One Hundred Slain.'

'One hundred Indians?'

'No, Lizbet. Whites. Soldiers at a fort.'

'Oh, my dear God...'

'A dreamer, a Lakota, a Big Chief, I don't know of what clan, dreamed it by that name and it happened as he said it would. The *wasichus,* whites, had started to build a road from a fort to a place west of that place, a place where whites are finding gold, so many are coming. They are coming into Indian country where they were told not to go. This new road will be joined by others and, like streams flowing into rivers, will soon be a road deep into country promised to us in a big treaty many years ago. The treaty said we would have this country forever and no whites would come into it. Now the whites are making this road and will build new forts on it. All is against the treaty...'

Elizabeth and I interrupted simultaneously,

'Where was this battle? Which fort?'

'A new-built fort... I do not know the name.'

'Smith? Fort C. F. Smith?' asked Elizabeth. 'That's recently built, I think.'

'I do not know.'

'Never mind. What else can you tell us?'

'When the dream came to this chief he sent his men against the white soldier chief at this fort. This *wasichu* chief is hated by all the people. He has done many bad things and has said he will kill every Indian he sees. So Crazy Horse made this battle and he and his warriors killed this *wasichu* soldier chief and all his men.'

'*All* his men? *All* the men at this fort?'

'All, Lizbet. And the warriors took their guns. Many new guns. These Cheyenne gave some to Far Cry.'

'What does Far Cry plan to do?' I asked.

'Some of the young chiefs want to ride off to join Crazy Horse. He is making war on the *wasichus* wherever he can. These Cheyenne who came here are going to smoke the war pipe with him.'

'What about Far Cry?' I asked again. 'Will Far Cry and his men go?'

'Two of the young chiefs of this clan rode away this morning with the Cheyenne. Men with no wives to take care of, no children.'

'But what does Far Cry think of this?' asked Elizabeth. 'He must know the whites will not let this go unanswered.'

'Far Cry has said many times that he will have nothing to do with the *wasichu*, and he will keep to this path. This country is very big, he says.'

'Are we in danger?'

'No, Lizbet, this camp is good. We stay here.'

'Does Far Cry still plan to make a trade for us?'

'Yes. I tell you this many times. He made this promise and he will keep it. When this thing is done and he has all his friends and relations with him, we will go far away, maybe into Grandmother Country.'

I had not heard of this place.

'It's their name for Canada,' said Elizabeth.

'Yes. Now, I must get back to my work. Quick To See is tired today. And angry.'

'Did he want to join with Crazy Horse?'

'I think yes, but he will stay with Far Cry. He is glad about the killing. And he is angry.'

Mary walked away, her head lowered. I looked at Elizabeth. Her eyes were wide and alive. I didn't like it.

'Please, do not suggest what I know you are thinking of.'

'I am always thinking of it. As you should be as well.'

'He still plans to trade us. You heard her say it. And it sounds as if there might be reason to hope he will want to do it sooner rather than later.'

'I have yet to see evidence of effort in that direction. When he rides off, it's to hunt or to kill Crow and steal their horses. How long are we to wait? And now with winter closing in…'

'We must be patient, Elizabeth…'

'Be *patient*? *My little boys, Sarah!* Would you tell them to "be patient"? They must think their mother is dead! Can you not understand how that makes me feel? No, of course you cannot. You have no children, you do not know what this love is like. *It tears my heart!* to imagine what they must be feeling. Oh, I miss them so, their little faces, their bodies, their hands and feet… *Can you not even imagine how I feel? What is wrong with you?*'

She put her head in her hands and sobbed, choking, as if she would truly cry her heart out. All I could do was hold her.

Perhaps there was something wrong with me. I had nothing in my heart to match her pain either in degree or nature. I thought of my own mother. By now, the young soldiers from Laramie would have found the ruins of the dugout. The commander would have had an address from Jake's records. He would have written a letter of condolence.

The news might have killed her. She was fragile enough. It made me horribly sad, but I was not shattered as my friend seemed to be. All these people — my mother, Elizabeth, most likely her husband, as well, and her boys, Mary Small Wing, and Far Cry, too, who was apparently devoted to his family, those dead and those living — I suspected *most* human beings were built with a capacity to feel that I lacked. Had I always been like this? Had I always been so involved with my own tiny life that I could not fully understand another person's pain?

CHAPTER 15

My old woman tugged at my sleeve early one morning and pointed to a small white-feathered owl watching us from a nearby branch. She shook her head and mimed trembling with cold, holding her arms close around her body. Later Mary Small Wing said someone else had seen another. These birds came from far away north, she told us, and the people were surprised to see them in this country so soon.

A few young men, Far Cry was not among them, left one morning without ceremony on what Mary explained was a short hunting excursion to bring back more animals with pelts suitable for warm robes and bedding, especially for the children and old ones.

One morning, we looked up to see large flakes of snow drifting across the camp. Flurries had come and gone in the last few weeks, but the air was different this day. Within moments, it was thick with flakes like scraps of paper torn and wind tossed. Soon we could not see across the camp. The people went into their lodges early and closed the flaps. Smoke came up through the holes at the tops and disappeared in the blowing white.

The blizzard lasted two days. Elizabeth and I worried about the hunters, but on the morning of the third day there was pale sun and the hunters came back with furs that we women set to work on right away. We were racing to do it before the next snow and feared that we did not have much time. We did not. Within days another blizzard struck with howling and blowing snow that got whipped into high drifts. This lasted three days.

This time, when the snow stopped, the sun came out with surprising force as if to reassert its power. Soon the ice-crusted banks on either side of the paths where people walked between the lodges melted and the pathways turned to mud. Everything dripped. It was good to be out of the stifling air inside the tipis, and the mild air was a relief. But the harsh weather had made some of our oldest and youngest sick. Both of our old women had been visibly weakened.

Mary came to visit. She was getting large, with a deep rosy colour in her cheeks. Elizabeth grinned at her.

'You look so pretty Mary! I think being with child agrees with you as it did with me. Do you feel well?'

'Yes. I feel well. Thank you.'

'When is this Moon of Snowblindness?' I asked her, looking at her belly.

Mary counted on her fingers.

'Four moons from now. Springtime. Early springtime.'

'Ah. What is this month called? This one, now.'

'This is the Moon of Popping Trees — December, as we learned to say it in your counting. This I know from the missionary father. It is the month of your Christmas.'

Elizabeth and I looked at one another in shock.

December? I hadn't thought it had been so long since we were first taken.

'*Have we missed Christmas?*'

Somehow, this seemed an awful thing.

'I know about Christmas,' Mary said. 'It is a very pretty story, your Jesus' birthday story.'

Elizabeth and I were still staring at one another in a confused dismay. We seemed to amuse Mary.

'Do not be sorry if you have missed the day of Christmas. Pretend it is today and be happy!'

She turned from us and went about whatever she'd been doing. Lizzie and I looked at one another. It was sage advice. We called after her,

'Happy Christmas, Mary Small Wing!'

She turned and laughed and continued on her way.

My old woman had been suffering from a head and chest cold for some time and was sleeping fitfully. I'd helped her sip some hot tea and put a warm wet cloth on her head and she had just fallen to sleep when Elizabeth whispered my name and slipped into the tipi. I ladled some of the tea into a bowl for her and we sat down on skins close to the small fire.

'I am actually very sad we missed Christmas, Sarah. Silly, I know, considering...'

'It's not silly. Christmas always makes one think of home and family.'

'This would have been our second Christmas together out west. Last year, William and the boys cut a tree and we spent a whole day decorating it with the few pretty things we'd brought from home. We also strung it with popcorn and ribbons that I'd twisted into garlands. The boys hung their stockings from the mantel William carved for the hearth. When they finally fell asleep, we filled them with gifts. William and a neighbour of ours had spent weeks carving little carriages and farm animals. I painted them. And I'd been busy knitting socks, sweaters, caps.'

'I'm sure they loved everything you made for them.'

'They did, God bless them! Woke before dawn to see! '

'Lizzie! What are their names, your boys? If you've told me, I've forgotten and I'm terribly sorry'.

'I don't know if I have told you. My first born, now eight years old — and, oh, he looks so much like his father! — is Charles. William's full name is William Charles Brown, Charles was his father's name. We call our boy Charlie, though he's lately begun to ask to be called simply "Charles". And my baby, though he, too, has William's long legs — they will both be tall, I think — is Joseph, after my father. Our Joey. He is six. They are such good boys, Sarah.'

'I'm sure they are. Did you cook them a wonderful Christmas dinner?'

'Oh, yes! A big hen and roasted potatoes, bread of Indian meal and molasses, a tinned pudding from the sutler's store at the fort — what a treat *that* was! And things my family sent. Canned pears, Sarah! I baked two pies, and there was cream for the dried berries.'

'It sounds wonderful, Lizzie.'

'It was. How did you keep Christmas in Virginia?'

'Oh, well! It was quite the event with a house-full of people. Reduced a bit during The War, but my mother insisted that we always keep the holiday and make it festive as was possible. We had swags of evergreens hung all over the place. And there were big silk bows in red, green and gold all down the banister. Candles everywhere. There could never be too many candles for my mother. An enormous decorated tree! Up to the ceiling, with a crystal star from Vienna on top.'

'Virginia ham?'

'Yes, ma'am! Indeed! When I think of the table! We put together two or three to make a great long one that my mother covered in white linen damask from her trousseau and set with her good bone china from England. You should have seen the silver candelabras, cut crystal goblets, silver platters, white china bowls filled with every good thing to eat. Our Ruth is a brilliant cook. The men came in full dress uniform or formal clothes, and all the ladies wore jewel-coloured gowns — garnets, emeralds, sapphires! — and wore jewels to go with them. I always had a new dress made just for Christmas.'

'You were rich!'

'Well, what I just described was all before The War. During it, things were not quite so grand. But, yes. I suppose we were rich.'

'We weren't at all rich, but we had enough, thank the good Lord. We had plenty. And I know my family here, we Browns, will do well.'

'I am sure you will. You have determination and your William sounds like a good man.'

'He is. He is.'

She was quiet for a moment and then, softly,

'I wonder what they are doing now, how they are keeping Christmas this year without me...'

I opened my arms and she rested her head on my shoulder. After a bit, my face in her hair, I began to sing very softly so only she could hear.

God rest ye, merry gentlemen...

I felt her smile.

Let nothing you dismay...

Remember Christ our Sa-a-vior...

Here, her voice joined mine...

Was born upon this day...

She was with me in the song now but we sang very softly, so as not to wake the sick old thing sleeping so near us.

To save us all from Satan's pow'r...

When we were gone astray...

O – oh, tidings of co-om-fort and joy,

Comfort and joy...

Here we gave a good long pause...

Oh – oh...

Ti-i-dings...

Of...

Still softly, we held that note a long sweet time before relaxing into...

Co-om-fort... And...

We finished with a major chord in harmony:

Joy!

We were facing one another, singing through smiles and tears, and we held out that note nearly as long as we had breath. Before we quite gave out, we heard a grunt and turned around to see the old woman had lifted her head and was staring at us, frowning. I was worried, but then, like a miracle, the old thing grinned a beauteous toothless grin.

She seemed to try to laugh a bit, but then she began to cough hard, as if it hurt her, so I helped her sip some tea and settled her back down again into her robes. Elizabeth went back to tend to her old woman. I soothed mine until she fell asleep. Bright Bird was her name.

CHAPTER 16

Elizabeth and I were standing in front of my tipi rubbing our hands over a fire.

'Mary tells me we are now in the Moon of Frost in the Lodges. It's confusing. The days must not be divided the same way we do it. But it's close enough to call this January. It certainly feels like January.'

'God save us! I wish this cold would break. It makes everything worse. We're still in one place, at least. But who could possibly find us in all this snow?'

'The Cheyenne knew we were here. The more people who know, no matter who they are, the better our chances, don't you think?'

Elizabeth rarely heard me offer up anything encouraging about our situation and she raised her eyebrows. Then, looking at me quizzically, she said,

'I never hear you use any of your new words. You spend so much time with Mary, is she still teaching you the language?'

'I thought it distressed you to hear me saying words in Lakota so I don't practice in front of you. But, yes, Mary is still *trying* to teach me and I am still *trying* to learn.'

'Do you understand any of what you hear?'

'Not much. Sometimes a word or two, sometimes enough to guess the subject of a conversation, though never enough to know what is being said about it. It's like a puzzle with thousands of pieces all scattered, and slowly — very slowly, I'm afraid — these pieces are coming together. Sometimes a short phrase will pop out of the general noise, but I wish I were better at it. I must concentrate harder.'

In fact, I hated to admit how little progress I was making. Mary would give me the name of a thing, or I'd ask her how to say a sentence like 'I am going to fetch water' and I could barely repeat it back to her much less remember it. If I'd had a way to write it down, perhaps I'd have been a better student. But there were so many variations and there was nothing in the root of the language that was familiar, that I could hold on to and build upon. Lizzie, bless her heart, was sympathetic this time.

'It has such strange sounds. I can't imagine what English letters might join to make those sounds.'

'Perhaps that's why it isn't written, just spoken.'

'Old Flower delights in yammering on at me though she knows I don't understand a word of it.'

'Is she still ill?'

'I suspect she has a case of quinsy, she complains of her throat a good deal. I told her to open her mouth so I could see and her entire gullet looked awfully red. Sometimes she seems feverish, but she's a remarkable old thing. She holds on, jokes with everyone who comes to visit, many of whom are also sick. But Old Flower summons the will to yell at me for any reason that amuses her — and I do seem to amuse her. Sometimes she laughs and laughs at me and I never know why, so I laugh right back. She yells at that medicine man for not being helpful enough. He takes it with good humour. I encourage her to drink the infusions he makes.'

'I'm surprised. You're generally so disdainful of his efforts.'

'It does not hurt to make friends with those who might be useful.'

'*Ha!* No, indeed. It does not hurt at all.'

'And he's a kind old man for all his arrogance. I've known a couple of women near where we lived in New York who understood the use of various wild herbs and how to make poultices and such — it's the same art, I suppose. But his chanting and rattle-shaking and all the smoky weeds burning, all that annoys me to no end. And nothing annoys me more than his pompousness. Goodness!'

'Medicine Crow is a sincere holy man, I believe, even if we don't understand his religion. Mary said he has strong medicine. The people certainly respect him. And love him.'

Elizabeth gave me a rather scornful look.

'He's an arrogant old heathen. Sometimes I simply can't abide him and his smug, fat wife.'

I changed the subject.

'I'm worried about Bright Bird. The old thing has become uncommonly sweet towards me.'

'Oh, dear! A sure sign of imminent death!'

We laughed, though I felt we shouldn't.

'I worry she might be fading.'

'But she has not had this malaise of the chest, the cough, that's got hold of so many of them now, has she? I worry about the children.'

'She coughs, but not as badly as some others. But she does not want to get out from under her robes.'

'I can't blame her. Moon of Frost in the Lodges!'

'I help her out to relieve herself a few times a day and she has dwindled to nothing. It feels as if her bones are made of paper and she would blow away if I did not hold on to her. And she will not eat unless I feed her.'

'Ah. I didn't realise it had come to that. But she will eat when you offer?'

'If I bring it to her mouth she will take a little. But I think it's to please me. She will often look at my face with such tenderness as I sit beside her, Lizzie. She talks to me. I can't understand any of it, but once or twice I believe she has called me 'daughter'. I wonder if she once had a daughter.'

'Who would have thought we'd become so fond of our old hags?'

'Yes. It's been a long time since she's hit me.'

We laughed a bit and I fed the fire a bit. We were shivering in spite of layers of clothing, our old dresses underneath the heavy buffalo robes. We had both long since given up our leather shoes — Lizzie's were destroyed, and Jake's boots leaked and weren't warm — and wore winter moccasins now. They came up high on our calves, heavy hide with the fur inside.

'Look at this weather, Sarah. This morning the sun was so bright it made my eyes hurt and now, look at it.'

'It doesn't look good, Lizzie, does it. And the wind's picking up. I hope we're not in for another storm.'

'As we speak of it, look. Snow.'

'Only a few flakes. Perhaps it won't last long.'

But the north wind drove heavy snow before it for six days and nights. Sometime in the middle of the blizzard, I woke in the early morning to find my old woman gone. The pelts she slept in had been pushed aside and were cold. I pulled on my moccasins, wrapped myself in a robe and went outside to look for tracks. The snow came at me full in the face and, looking down, I could barely see my feet. I walked around the tipi and could not see my own tracks when I glanced behind me much less any sign of the old one's.

I stumbled to Elizabeth's lodge, told her what had happened and holding to one another tightly we fought the deep and drifting snow to Mary's lodge where we called her and stood shivering outside until she opened the flap. I shouted to be heard over the wind and the sound of the icy snow striking the tops of the lodge poles and the trees.

'My old woman is gone.'

'Bright Bird?'

'Yes. We must search for her'.

'How long?'

'I don't know, her pelts were cold, so we must not waste time.'

'Her sleeping place was cold?'

'Yes! Please Mary, we must hurry. Maybe your husband would help.'

'We will not find her. '

'*We must try!*'

'Mary is right, Sarah. Look around you. Standing here, we are now well over our ankles in fresh snow. She is gone, I'm afraid.'

'Lizbet is saying truth, Sarah. She goes away to die.'

'Let's not have her dead until we know certainly! Maybe she's lying just beyond the tipi...'

'You said you looked there...'

'I only *looked*! I did not try to feel under the snow for her.'

I remember how the two other women looked at me and then turned their heads away and gazed into the white howling world.

Stores ran low and in many tipis there was nothing to eat. Horses tore at the bark of cottonwood trees. The people shared what they had. Some of the dogs disappeared. Many people were sick with a cough that ripped their lungs and throats. The old ones and the children were especially hard hit. It seemed the snow would never end. Several of the clan died.

Far Cry's people had for a long time adopted the custom of burying their dead, but the deep snow made it difficult to reach the earth and, in any case, it would be frozen hard as stone once they got to it. So they made platforms and put them in the trees. It was too difficult in the blowing snow to make the platforms as high as they might have done. So Medicine Crow consecrated a place at a fair remove from camp. No one wanted to hear their loved one's bones being gnawed by beasts.

With a break in the weather — a couple of days of pale sun — Quick To See, Mary's husband, and four other men, all good hunters, rode off to find meat. When they didn't come back when people expected they should, everyone was worried. In the last few days we'd heard the dull reverberation of avalanches from deep in the mountains. The crust of the snow would melt in a day of sun, then turn to hard ice overnight. More snow would follow and then ice and yet more snow, layer lay upon layer. A dangerous situation, people shook their heads. Mary was very worried. But the people must not starve, so the men had gone hunting.

After about two weeks or so, the hunters were declared lost.

Far Cry took a few men and went out. They had no hope of finding the bodies of the men or the horses but would do their best to bring home food. The women of the lost men lamented according to their custom. Mary Small Wing took hold of her hair and knifed it short. Keening and rocking, the women cut gashes in their faces, chests, arms and legs.

'What in Heaven's name is she thinking? Those could fester and endanger her health and that of her child.'

'It's the custom. It might be better than our way of being so stoic.'

'That wailing is horrible. How long will it go on?'

'I don't know, Lizzie.'

In a couple of days, Far Cry and the others returned with three thin elk and several rabbits. The meat did not last long, but soup was made from the bones and in some tipis, people hung a few strips of gristle from the poles to dry in the smoke from the fires.

CHAPTER 17

More and more people were dying. Hardly a day or night went by without hearing the keening wails of grief. One morning before dawn, Elizabeth came into my tipi in great distress.

'Sarah! Old Flower's dying! Please come!'

Blue Star Flower — whom Lizzie called Old Flower — had been sick for weeks and had been breathing roughly for several days. Elizabeth told me that during the night she had slipped into a strange state, moaning, her eyes darting around as if she were frightened, reacting to things that weren't there. Medicine Crow had come and several women gathered around to sing and wait.

Medicine Crow made a tea and tried to trickle the fluid into her mouth. The old woman rejected it but, in his presence, she was calmer. He threw herbs on the fire and waved the smoke over her, singing softly all the while. Her breathing grew louder and more laborious, the flesh beneath her collarbones sucking inward with each effort. Until it stopped.

Elizabeth wept.

'I cared for her. I'm surprised how much.'

The bitter weather continued week after week with only occasional respite that was not much respite at all. On these days, the sun would rise late, and the gauzy, muted light seemed to barely persevere until night came up over the hills and killed it. But that was a rare thing among day after dark grey day and long starless nights.

I recall feeling more oppressed by the weak sunlight, when it managed to show, than by the relentless greyness. That wan yellow thing hanging in the sky seemed an imposter, bearing false promise. I hated it. A blizzard was, by comparison, the perfect expression of that winter's truth. As was the howling, roaring wind with the branches cracking and snapping, taking others down as they fell. As was the distant rumbling of avalanche. As was the malignant cold. Sunshine was a lie.

Wolves came closer to the camp. Sometimes at night, I could hear them moving through the frozen scrub outside the tipi. I remember a sort of manic glee in wondering how much worse it could possibly get. I kept thinking of a line from Macbeth: 'Let it come down'.

It did.

After Old Flower had been put to rest on a scaffold, Elizabeth moved a few robes and a couple of old horn bowls into my tipi. Mary Small Wing, weak from grieving, kept us company when we went back for the old woman's heavy sleeping skins, more warm robes and everything else that was of use. Mary took some small, soft pelts to give to another woman who'd lost her husband in the doomed hunt and was taking care of two small children. She took the old one's clothing to give away. The bit of dried meat that was left, we insisted Mary take. We were worried about her. Lizzie said she didn't like the way she looked but couldn't be specific about it. Mary never complained.

We were asleep in the middle of the night some time later when we heard the first piercing cry and the sound pulled us both sitting upright. The wail was followed by more and then there was a chorus of lamentation that had become too familiar.

'Who now?'

We lifted the flap and saw firelight and people moving quickly in and out of Mary's lodge, that she shared now with a woman who was cousin to Quick To See. She had moved in with Mary after the avalanche.

Terrified for our friend, we threw on robes, pulled on our moccasins and stumbled through the snow. Just outside the flap were bloody cloths lying where they'd been thrown. Inside, a clutch of women was tight around Mary lying on robes moaning. They pushed us back vigorously when we tried to come closer. Medicine Crow and the women were singing. Between them, I caught glimpses of Mary, a naked haunch, an arm moving, a leg extended and pulled back. Then, suddenly, the women's keening got louder. We stood where we'd been pushed, just at the open flap, among the bloody cloths.

After a bit, the singing got softer, was mixed with weeping, and the women sat back and let us through. Mary was lying in a pool of dark blood but nothing more was coming from her. We watched as a woman retrieved from between her legs a bloody thing not much larger than my hand, someone cut the cord with a knife. We stumbled out. The cold was a relief. We stood holding one another, crying. We had loved the girl. I was angry.

'Why didn't they come for us?'

I turned back to the group around Mary's tipi and yelled.

'*Why didn't you tell us?*'

'Come. There's nothing we can do. Nothing we could have done.'

We built a small fire inside the tipi. We held one another and wept. I was shaking, furious, and couldn't stop weeping.

'They knew we loved her. They should have come for us. Why didn't they?'

'Sarah, you know why.'

'No, I do not...'

'We are not one of them.'

We made tea and sipped that and ate a bit of the coarse meal mush we'd prepared the day before.

I felt betrayed. Those women with whom we'd laughed while doing chores, who seemed to enjoy our company, who had seen how we were with Mary and she with us, had not let us know she was in trouble and had shunned us as she died. Elizabeth was right. We were not 'one of them'. We were enemy women. *Wasichus.*

I looked over to say something about it and was surprised to see that, replacing the rational face she'd shown while laying out the truth for me, Elizabeth's features reflected a gathering fear.

'Lizzie, what are you thinking?'

'We are *truly* alone now, aren't we.'

'Yes, I suppose, in a way, we are.'

'Are we at the end, Sarah? Is winter itself going to kill us?'

'Don't talk this way, dear friend.'

'You're right. I shouldn't. We must not lose hope, Sarah. Promise me you'll continue to hope. Yes?'

I said, 'Of course,' but it wasn't true. I did not indulge in hopeful thoughts, not of the kind Elizabeth meant. I simply went about the days and nights. That seemed more than enough to occupy my mind and body.

'I need to sleep in your robes with you tonight. I can't be alone.'

We pulled the robes up high and lay like spoons. I put my arm over her. We slept.

When we woke, the sky was a hard, high blue and the snow's crust returned the sun's blaze with a fury that made the people reel back into the dark of their tipis. Later, they said of that month it was so bad even the horses went snowblind.

We heard Death songs several more times in the next weeks and each time would hide in the tipi. I got sick with a bad throat, a chest cough and fever and Elizabeth nursed me generously. Then she got it and it hung on for what seemed a long time. I worried about her.

We were both getting very thin. Everyone was getting thin. But occasionally someone would whisper at the flap and have a bit of meat or pemmican for us. The giver would hand it over without a word and immediately turn and go. We'd call our thanks to the person's back. I suspected it was Far Cry looking after us, sending people to make sure we didn't die. Lizzie would have said he was protecting his investment. I often tried to make eye contact when I saw him. But every time I came near to catching his eye, his gaze always seemed to have just slipped to the side and away.

Gradually the days got longer, as they always will, and the sun was out more often and with greater force. The snow began to melt, and mud replaced it. No one cared. To lift one's face and feel warmth — even, sometimes, heat — made up for the mess. The men hunted and we all began to regain our strength.

We moved camp a couple of times and then settled on a spot by a wide stream where the sun had cleared the snow off a gentle slope revealing new grass. Flowers, too. Some pushing their heads up through the packed and dirty snow lying among the still naked shrubs and trees in the woods. Lizzie and I spoke briefly of how Mary Small Wing would have loved the change. The loss of her still hurt horribly.

After we'd been there a few days, a group of a dozen or so people joined us. Apparently friends and relations. They all seemed to know one another. These were mostly women, children and old people, but I did see a few more young men and thought it was a good thing to have more hunters on hand, more fighters.

The big stream was full and fast from snow melt, coming up over its banks in places, covering the new grass so you couldn't tell if the water was shallow or deep. It roiled dangerously. The children had to be kept away. Even a little stream that ran behind the tipi Lizzie and I shared was wild. Though wet and still cold, sometimes at night, very cold, the worst was over and we survivors were greatly relieved.

Song birds were returning and the game had begun to move. So had the predators.

CHAPTER 18

'Ho, me lads! Lookie 'ere! A *comely* pair ta greet us. Ladies!'

The stranger grabbed his hat by the brim and swept it off in a theatrical salute, loosing a few strings of pale hair to wave above his scalp. He was one of three men who'd ridden into the village on mules, with a fourth animal in tow laden with packs of different shapes and sizes.

'How in hell did ye pretty things come to be wi the likes a' these... Wait now! Hoo! I recollect some tattle o two white cunnies, captives held to ransom, and, bless me pucker! I b'lieve I've stumbled upon ye. Are ye these uns? Or wot?'

'Yes! That would be us!'

Elizabeth's too quick, too loud, too eager, and to my mind too stupidly revealing answer came before I could signal her not to speak. She continued to address him in a half-whisper, as if anyone in the camp knew what she was saying.

'We need help! How close are we to an American fort? Can you get to one? Tell them we're here? They must send help as soon as possible!'

The miscreant noticed the look I gave her.

'Don't look so peevish at yer comrade, me fine lady. Nor at me. "Help", says she? Well, me darlin', I'm thinkin' I could be that very thing to ya. In fact, seems to me that I could be yer fuckin' salvation!'

The man returned his hat to his head. His face was pasty and pocked. In spite of this damage, he looked fairly young. The others' features were mostly obscured by full dark beards and dark hat-brims pulled low. All three wore buffalo robes open to long-johns the same colour as their skin. Over these they wore trousers — the leader's pair held up by suspenders — tucked into ruined boots.

The camp had been warned. It was late afternoon, chores had been done for the day, and we were outside our tipi stirring a soup over the fire when the alarm sounded. *Wasichus!* The little girls who now often kept us company, clustering around Elizabeth who played with them, had run back to their mothers. Elizabeth and I looked at one another. Whites? Out here? Her excitement rose fast. Too fast, I thought, before we could learn what sort of people these were.

Far Cry and several of his men were out hunting or raiding or both, so the Old Man Chiefs and others who'd stayed in camp had taken positions in front of their lodges, old flintlocks or carbines held loosely. Far Cry and his men had taken the good guns. Those young men in camp, a few of whom were barely out of boyhood, paced around, carrying their bows, quivers over their shoulders, knives at their sides. The women remained by their cook fires, their children behind them. They continued to stir. Waiting to see what would happen.

The people were not pleased to see this bunch, as if they'd had previous experience of them and it hadn't been good. Neither was I. I certainly did not believe that this leering piece of work would be our 'salvation'. It spoke again:

'Ah! Whelmed to silence by my 'tudinous charms. Gone squaw yet? From the draggled state o yer habiliments, I guess you bin caught in this complexion long enough to want some o that muddy cock. Tasty, eh?'

He laughed loudly and turned to his companions who also laughed, more loudly. He turned back to the two of us.

'I do b'lieve these fancy cunts are affronted by my risibilities, boys. Oh my, oh my. But I'm a fergivin' sort an we got bizniz ta conduct. Now, we'll try agin', polite like. Where's yer head man, m' lovelies? Where's the Chief?'

We kept our eyes on the soup. He leaned in Elizabeth's direction.

'Didja not hear me, darlin'? Who's king o' this ere dung heap? All ye gotta do is point.'

And again she spoke to him. I wanted to slap my hand over her mouth.

'How did you know about us? How did you find this camp?'

'Simple, honest question, simple, honest answer. We're simple honest tradesmen, girlicue, wandrin the countryside, keepin' eyes and ears open. We seen the smoke from yer cookfires. An now...'

As he scanned the camp, I leaned my face against the side of Lizzie's and whispered hoarsely.

'Don't speak to him again!'

The trader made a humming noise.

'Old men and boys. Appears to me yer Daddy's gone a huntin', leavin' pore little children an' the decrepit to mind the stores, an' wi' such valu'ble contraband as yer lovely selves...'

'That's enough. I suggest you take your leave now, while the light holds. There's nothing for you here.'

'*Ye'er* here, yella hair, now aintcha. Who took a cleaver to ya? That'll teach ya ta be so high and mighty. Ye need me, ye battered cunt. Think on't. If I've a mind to, I *might* jes tell yer story when I git to Laramie. '

Elizabeth couldn't contain herself.

'*Fort Laramie?*'

'If I don't feel like headin' ta Paree first, Laramie it is.'

'How far is it? In what direction?'

'This creek, the big un, jines another leads to the Platte North Fork and I intend to follow that beast all ta the easterd. We was on our way when we seen yer smoke. Purty in yer own way, ye are, like a slick brown fish.'

'*How far is the fort!*'

'Far enough t' be far. And in mud-time and with the bitin' insects and the tetchy natives, it's a vexation ever stinkin' bit o the way. But never ye mind. Them at the fort'll be mighty pleased to hear my news an don't you know I'll make 'em pay real purty fer it. Soon enough, ye'll see us ridin' back ahead o the motherfuckin' American Army cavalry. Now! That's only if yer *sweet* to me, real sweet, which ye oughta be, considerin that I've become the pinch o' yer game. To say it plain, ladies, I could change yer life right the fuck around. *Or not.* Dependin' on the delicacies o me moods.'

I spoke to keep Elizabeth from doing so.

'The command at Laramie would be *very* pleased to know of our presence here and I'm quite sure they'll pay you handsomely for the information, and again upon finding us unharmed. The sooner, the better. So you might as well leave, as these people have nothing to trade.'

'Ah, darlin. There's always somethin to trade. Mebbe they'd even trade *the two o'you* fer some good Remingtons. *Ha!* That made ya look lively! We'll be gone afore ye know it, afore yore chief comes, don't doubt it. And don't trouble yersels none, I talk enough o' this lingo to make me own way. Boyos!'

The three dismounted and walked their animals into the centre of camp.

'This is an evil man. I don't like this.'

'He could be the Devil himself, Sarah, and still be the one who achieves our deliverance. That is all that's important.'

'Did you not notice how the people looked at him when they came in? He's bad and they know it. Let's get inside. I wish I had a gun.'

We sat listening for sounds out of the ordinary but could not hear much over the rushing stream. After a time, we walked out and around the tipi together to relieve ourselves. I carried our big knife. It was coming on dusk and across the camp, in the light of a fire, we could see the traders sitting with a bunch of the young men. I couldn't hear, but it appeared they were laughing. I wondered if a trade had already been transacted. The people desperately needed guns, and the winter's cold had meant there were some rich pelts. I wished Far Cry and his men would come soon, but in truth, it could be days.

We went back inside and lay down on our sleeping robes. Neither of us could eat. We sank into a sort of stupor that we were jolted out of by maniacal laughter and the fire snapping and cracking. I moved aside the flap to look. Night had come and the fire — who knows what they'd thrown on it — burned with a high flame and a lot of smoke. The women and children had disappeared. The old men who had guns now held them at the ready. The others had their bows. But it appeared that four or five of the older boys were drinking with the traders.

'This is not good. I'm going to sneak around through the woods to Medicine Crow's and ask for a gun. I know he's got a revolver in addition to his rifle.'

'No, Sarah! I don't want to be alone here and you shouldn't go out there alone. Let's just wait and see. Mostly likely there'll just be noise and then they'll go.'

'Those bastards know this is our lodge, Lizzie. We need to be armed.'

'Wait. Please...'

Suddenly, ecstatic shouts erupted. I looked out to see someone trying to make his horse go through the fire. The animal bolted and the youth fell in the flames but rolled free. He staggered up pumping triumphant fists to howls of acclamation from his friends. The traders had taken off their buffalo coats and their pale colour made them easy to spot.

'Hide under the skins. Here. Take the knife. I'm going for that gun.'

She didn't argue this time. I slipped around back of our tipi and made my way to Medicine Crow's on the other side of the camp.

On the other side of the fire, I saw Medicine Crow standing before the tipi of one of the other old men, holding his rifle. I saw the trader who'd spoken to us — his pale hair and the height of him made him stand out — yowling a song, showing his ass, dancing around not far from our tipi, where Elizabeth lay hiding.

The flap of Medicine Crow's lodge was loose and I darted inside. No one was there. I turned things over, no revolver. I did find a good hatchet, grabbed it, held the flap open a bit, looking for a chance to slip out. Someone had started beating a drum hard and fast and the madness suddenly accelerated. One of the dark traders fired a revolver into the air. I looked across to our tipi and through the smoke and dust saw the tall trader in front of it, looking around. Then he took his knife — the fire's light blazed on it briefly — and ripped off the flap.

Gripping the hatchet, I charged through the melee fast as I could move. More shots were fired. There was shouting. I dodged a sudden surge of older boys throwing themselves at someone behind me. When I reached our tipi, the man was half inside the opening, half out, his bare white buttocks thrusting, his feet scrabbling, with Lizzie under him, pinned and screaming.

I lunged forward, the hatchet in both hands, raised it over my head and brought it down with all my strength between his shoulder blades. I wrenched it out and struck again and then again. The third time, I struck so hard I was afraid it might have gone through to Lizzie, but I couldn't get it out. I grabbed both feet and pulled the twitching, bleeding thing off Elizabeth, dragged it out of the tipi, through the dirt to the other side of our cook fire. I put my foot on its shoulder, pulled out the hatchet and crashed it down on the skull, once, twice, I don't know how many times, then stepped to the side and hacked at the neck. The vertebrae broke easily but I had to push my foot against its back to stretch the skin, muscle and sinew, hacking and sawing the blade into the dirt to cut it all the way through. It was surprisingly difficult to sever the head.

The carcasses of the other two traders had been dragged near the diminishing fire, where some of the women, dispassionately as the town butcher, hacked limbs from torsos. I pulled the trader's body to where the others were and went back for the head, flinging it by the hair onto the pile. Then I ran back in to Lizzie, wiping my hands on my skirts.

Elizabeth, gasping and shaking violently, was trying to clean between her legs with the hem of her petticoats.

'Let me, let me,' I said. 'Lie back. It's over out there. Lie back.'

I moistened a small, soft skin, helped her lift her knees, and gently wiped her. She'd been torn, there was a bit of blood. When I'd done as well I could, I arranged her skirts over her legs and pulled the furs around her. The knife looked as if it had been thrown across the tipi.

'Lizzie! Why didn't you use the knife?'

'*Too fast!* I heard him coming and was standing there holding it, but suddenly, he was right in front of me. I must have dropped it when he threw me down, he put his own knife to my throat. He would have killed me if you hadn't come when you did. *Thank God you came! Thank God! Thank God!*'

She was sobbing and choking.

'Breathe, Lizzie! Breathe! No, don't get up. Stay still. Good. Now breathe. Slowly. That's better.'

We sat for a minute. I stroked her head. The fighting was over. People were moving about, calling to one another, talking. Lizzie's breathing had mostly calmed.

'I'll make you some tea.'

'*No!* Don't you dare leave me!'

'I'll be right out there, Lizzie. The flap's torn open, you'll be able to see me, and I'll only be a moment.'

I poured water into a small pot, took a bowl and some herbs Medicine Crow had given us when we were both sick during the winter, and stepped outside. There were embers left of the cook fire. I hung the pot over it and urged up a good-enough flame. There were drag marks and blood from the tipi to where I'd finished him off, where there was a lot of blood. I got up and, with my foot, mixed up the blood with the dirt. A few young men who'd gotten drunk and hurt were sitting or lying down by their parents' lodges, their wounds being tended to. But there was no wailing.

Women were scooping up the traders' body parts, bundling them in blankets. People were gathering in twos and threes, now, talking more calmly. Occasionally, I'd catch someone's eye and, instead of looking away as usual, they'd return my look. And the quality of the look they gave me was wholly different from anything I'd yet experienced with these people.

I remember all this as if it happened yesterday. I remember sitting before the fire looking at my bloody hands. I stretched them in front of me and looked at them. I was vibrating, but not with fear like Elizabeth. My whole body hummed with something rare to me, something fierce. I liked it.

I said out loud: 'I am no longer who I was.'

Yet, the Sarah who had wielded the axe did not feel like a stranger, and hacking at that man's flesh had not felt foreign. It had felt *right*. Perhaps I'd acted on something long hidden, some legacy suddenly loosed by circumstance. But I could imagine no other possible response to what had happened and I liked very much that I had done it. I was proud. I stretched out my hands again, my hands that had done this thing, and noticed my gold wedding ring. I took it off and threw it into the brush.

I brought the tea inside.

'Drink this, Lizzie. Then I'll do a better job of cleaning you up.'

She sat up and, still shaking, took the bowl.

'No need, Sarah. I can see to myself.'

She stared at the blood on my hands, under my fingernails, on my arms, splashed and spattered over my clothing, on my face and in my hair. Hoping to distract her, I said,

'Well, our people still have their good pelts and now also have new guns. Remingtons! New cook pots...'

'*Our people?*'

'Drink more tea, dear heart.'

She pushed the bowl back at me and I took it before her body collapsed into itself on the skins. Her words came out in choked sobs.

'I can't take it any more, Sarah. I wish he'd killed me. It would be over. I want it over.'

'No, no, no, sweet one. This was *horrible*, but you're *alive*. And you'll feel better...'

'I won't. I might as well be dead. There's no hope for us.'

'We are better off without it, Lizzie. Here, let me help get you under these robes, you need...'

'What do you mean, *"better off without it"?*'

I had said out loud something I'd not yet fully articulated to myself, but I knew to be true. I had to make it clear to Lizzie. Before I could begin, noises outside made Elizabeth gasp. I went to the flap.

'It's the women. Carrying what's left of those bastards to the big stream.'

'The stream. Sarah, he said that it leads to...'

'*Stop! Shut your mouth now!* Don't say it! Don't even think it! Trying something like that again would be stupid, futile. Certain death.'

She was shocked by my tone, but she nodded.

'I know. I know. It's just... '

She was quiet a moment, gathering her thoughts.

'"Better off without hope", you said. I have only been able to survive all this because I've held on to hope. And now it's gone. I don't know how...'

'Hope is a lie, Lizzie. It's good to be rid of it. '

She looked at me incredulously. I wanted to be clear. I wanted to change her mind.

'From the beginning, I tried to share your belief that help would come, but I couldn't. I pretended. More and more each day, I have felt myself settling into this life. I know you won't like this, but it feels *ordinary* to me. Hard, yes, but when has life *not* been hard? We had men die screaming from horrible wounds, bleeding out on our veranda, and if not for my father's money and connections, it could have been worse. It's impossible to constantly be frightened, Lizzie, and it's also impossible to constantly hope for deliverance that *most likely* will not come. No, hear me out. I know you believe in it, but I do not, and I can't pretend any more. I will never again try to escape. I will *not* die that way.'

'How do you propose we live?'

'We'll simply *live.*' I told her we'd wake up in the morning and eat breakfast. Many things would happen and, one day, it might be the thing she wants so badly. But I couldn't think about it, it seemed best, I told her, to accept life as it came, and I told her again that I was done with hope. Hope was a false friend.

'In fact, hate might be a truer ally,' I said. 'It wasn't hope that saved your life this night.'

Elizabeth was quiet for a bit. Then she looked me hard in the eye.

'I owe you my life, I do, but I am not you. I *must* believe that I will get back to my family. Hope is a kind of *faith*, Sarah, and without faith in God, faith in His goodness, despair would kill me. *I* will not die *that* way. As I say these things, I realise that I'm not yet ready to die. I'm grateful to God for that. And I will always be grateful to you for doing what you did. But I will never stop praying for help out of this situation.'

She turned her head away from me. The camp was quiet now, except for the roar of the stream.

'Lizzie, you would not try it alone, would you? The stream? Or some other way?'

She promised she would not. Relieved, I told her to undress, that I'd take her things to the little creek out back and rinse them as well as I could. I grabbed a blanket. Her eyes widened.

'You know how close it is. I'll be back very quickly. Besides, there's no longer any danger.'

A generous piece of moon lit the woods, and a crust of ice lay around the stalks at the water's edge. I took off one moccasin and dipped my foot in. Too cold. I kept my feet in my heavy moccasins, walked in, rinsed our things, rubbing and wringing them in the fast running water and threw them onto the grassy banks. I used my shift to scrub hard the skin of my hands and arms, face and neck. I dipped my head in the water and rubbed my scalp with my fingernails again and again, then swung my head back and stood looking up at the stars, bright points of ice in a black sky. I got out and wrapped myself tight in the blanket, shivering so hard my teeth clattered.

I spread our dresses and underclothing on bushes. If the sky stayed clear, the next day would be sunny. We could wash our clothing again in the morning — I knew we'd want to — and it would dry. I'd wash myself again, too, rub my skin with sage and sweetgrass and get Elizabeth to do the same.

As I was settling into my sleeping robes, she turned to me.

'Sarah. This is *very* important. William must *never* know what that man did to me. When you meet him, *as you will*, promise me that you will *never* tell him about this thing.'

'Of course not. I promise.'

She was breathing more evenly now, which was good. I remembered something that might please her.

'Lizzie? Are you still awake?'

'Yes.'

'I forgot to tell you. When they first rode into camp, while that fool was yammering at us, I saw there were bolts of calico in their packs. We'll mend our dresses, or better yet, make new ones. There was more than enough.'

'The women will divide it up. They won't give us any.'

'Yes, they will.'

'You think so?'

'I have no doubt.'

CHAPTER 19

It was the Moon of Making Fat, or June, as close as we could figure it. Even in the higher places, the snow that had lingered for what felt like a long time, looking like torn sheets among the trees, was gone. There were wild roses, sunflowers, blue aster, red flowers that I think were phlox, and a great many flowers whose names I didn't know. We women and girls gathered strawberries, raspberries, gooseberries, currants. Children's hands and faces got stained with eating them and their mothers had to keep them from overdoing it.

Days dawned bright and noon was hot. In the afternoon we could see clouds being whipped up at the horizon and piled on top of one another so they rose higher and higher. The mass, grey-bottomed and heavy, would begin to roll towards us until it covered the blue and the day was suddenly dark. The wind shivered the leaves before it whipped the branches. Then, lightening and thunder, and a sudden rain pounded the lodges. The people rushed in and closed the flaps.

Lizzie and I would sit and mend our clothing with pieces of the dead trader's calico. I made myself a new skirt, and I suggested she do the same, but she shot me a look. She said she would wear the clothing she'd been wearing when William had kissed her goodbye that day, until she saw him again. 'And that *will* be soon.' So on rainy afternoons we mended — Lizzie sewed her patches on the inside — until the urge to nap overcame us.

After a while, the birds came out again and began to warble in Lakota. We'd step outside and stand around smelling the good smells, noting how the late afternoon sun made everything glitter. Then we women went about building fires and preparing the evening meal.

One morning, we heard the other women up and about much earlier than usual. We dressed quickly, went out and saw that everyone was busy with activity that Lizzie and I now recognised as preparations for moving camp. This unsettled us.

I had become rather friendly with Medicine Crow's wife, Laughing Woman, who could speak a few words of English. A very few. She had about as much English as I had Lakota and neither of us had enough of either for a real conversation. But we'd greet one another, smiling extravagantly, enjoying that simple ritual. Occasionally, I was able to ask a question in a way she could understand and, occasionally, I was able to grasp at least some small part of her answer and pass it on to Lizzie.

Laughing Woman confirmed that the entire village was moving.

'Did she tell you where they are taking us?'

'I think it's a place they always go in the summers. I *think* that's what she said. It must be a good place, everyone seems happy.'

'Maybe it will be closer to one of the trails.'

I turned away, giving my attention to finishing up the packing of our few things. One of Far Cry's men had brought us a travois.

The people made this packing up a kind of celebration. There was much joking and laughter, the children ran around yelping with excitement. All morning, parfleches of dried meat and pouches of pemmican were prepared and packed. Travoises were loaded with lodge poles and hides, cooking equipment and other necessaries, with robes and blankets piled on top. Special travois were cushioned with skins for the old and those too sick to ride.

'We don't have much to pack, do we.'

'No, Lizzie, we certainly do not. If my mother saw this, she'd be aghast. She'd wonder how on earth these women live without a good chifforobe or two.'

'And a decent table and chairs!'

'Couches! Oh, for a cozy couch with feather cushions!'

'But then, can you imagine packing all that so many times as we've moved?'

'No, I cannot! This is better'.

'For now, Sarah dear, for now.'

By late morning, all seemed ready. They had not tied our hands or bound us in any other way for the short moves during the winter. They must have figured that even *we* were not stupid enough to try to make an escape in killing cold and snow. And they had not tied us at the tail end of winter, when all the streams and rivers were flooding and wild. But now the weather was mild and the country before us looked inviting. I wondered if it would be different, if they'd tie us. I hoped not, I yearned for a good gallop. I hoped we'd get good horses.

We'd wrapped our things in large squares of calico or tied them up in skins. We'd dismantled the tipi. Just as we finished that work, one of the men came up with two horses. He attached the travois to the girth wrappings of the larger horse and helped us load it with the tipi poles and hides. To the other horse, he secured leather saddle bags in which we'd packed some food. Then he left.

'They're not going to tie us.'

Lizzie raised her eyebrows.

'Well, I suppose we couldn't get too far dragging this thing and, of course, they know we wouldn't separate.'

'Besides, Lizzie, look at these horses. They're so old and spavined I'm amazed they can walk.'

Medicine Crow went about chanting, wafting smoke from tobacco and herbs on the horses, the travoises, the people, including the children, making them sneeze. Lizzie commented,

'He's like a minister blessing his congregation.'

'He is exactly that.'

'I wonder how far it is. Were you ever able to find out?'

'No, I couldn't understand most of what Laughing Woman was saying. But I'm guessing it's a journey of some distance. She pointed north and thrust her finger in that direction three or four times. She seemed very excited and pleased.'

'Be it what it will, I am glad to be leaving this place.'

'So am I, Lizzie.'

When everyone was ready, our company did indeed turn towards the north and we set off. By afternoon, we made our way down one of those gullies that are invisible until you're upon them. This one was fairly wide with a broad stream running through it and along its banks was a village about the same size as ours had been. Apparently, they'd been waiting for us. In the evening, there was plenty of food and, of course, drumming and singing. No effort was made to unpack, so this was clearly to be a short stay. The weather was fine, we slept outside.

At dawn the next morning, after a quick meal, everyone helped to break things down and pack up. They were to join us. Most of the work had already been done. Before setting off, however, there was the dressing up. The people *dressed* for this move, and dressed the horses, too. It was theatrical and celebratory. We quickly picked whatever flowers we could grab and put them in our hair. We couldn't think of what else to do.

After following the stream in the gully, we came to yet another small encampment. These people were ready to join us right away, the sun was getting very warm. Moving in and out of woods for most of the morning, we emerged onto high prairie, an expanse of grasslands horizon to horizon with distant hills in all directions. From progressing in a long file, usually only two or at the most three abreast, once coming up onto this open land the people spread out, as if we all, collectively and at the same time, took a deep breath, spread wide our shoulders, expanded our chests, and then let that breath out slowly in a long sigh of pleasure. We were not in a hurry. We were at home in the space in which we moved.

For this scene on the prairie, I want you to imagine yourself — you who are reading these pages — standing a good piece ahead of us, watching us approach. Your first impression would most certainly be the marvellous breadth of our company across the grasslands in front of you. And now imagine this line is several horses deep. There were at least a hundred of us. Then you might be struck by the colours: between the blue of the sky and the new green of that short grass prairie, our party was an extravagance of colours.

The Old Man chiefs rode right in the centre of the first line wearing their war bonnets with the fancy beaded bands and long rows of white eagle feathers with the black tips floating out on either side. They sat their horses proudly. Most of the horses were brilliantly caparisoned, their manes adorned with feathers, glass beads and silver trinkets that glittered in the sun and made a wonderful sound. The riders sat on brightly coloured blankets. Imagine reds, greens, blues, yellows, with dramatic black accents. The horses danced as if they knew how handsome they looked. The dogs chased one another and barked for the joy of being dogs on a warm spring morning when everyone was moving and the mood was high.

Beneath the barking and the jingling of equipment and ornaments, was the regular bass thump of hooves and an occasional whinny when a rider kicked his pony to a gallop to get closer to a friend, to flirt with a girl, to start a game or a race. There was also the hum of people talking, accented by someone shouting, someone laughing out loud, and above it all were the gleeful voices of the children.

Imagine this troupe riding towards you across the newly green grass under the blue sky. I hope you can see how magnificent we were.

On both sides of the Old Man Chiefs rode their seconds, their counsellors. The younger chiefs, Far Cry among them, were mixed among the counsellors or just behind, sometimes moving up to speak with one of the older men, then dropping back and sweeping around to run their horses with the other young men, racing, whooping, trying to knock one another off. I had never seen Far Cry so happy, had never seen him laugh so freely. He was beautiful to look at.

We women followed the men, moving more slowly, keeping an eye on the younger ones. Some of the women were pulling travois behind their horses with an old or sick person on it wrapped in blankets. Girls who were themselves barely past childhood had the care of many of the younger children and practiced at grown-up mothering. A few had bound their charges onto miniature travois strapped to very patient dogs. Some were carrying babies on their backs, snug in boards. Groups of boys and girls played running games, sometimes the boys in pursuit, sometimes the girls. Sometimes they galloped as if they were pretending to be horses.

The slightly older boys and girls raced their ponies, moving among the lines. The bigger boys would gallop back to taunt the younger boys herding the horses in the rear. These boys didn't seem to mind. After all, it was a fine thing to be in charge of such a great herd of horses. They must have felt the glamour of it. Or maybe not. Maybe they were just putting on a good show and would rather have been free to careen about with the others.

The *akicita*, the clan's guardsmen, watched our flanks, riding ahead and behind, sometimes following a ridge-top for a better view, constantly on the move, constantly vigilant.

The women gossiped and told jokes. After a particularly animated exchange, one girl fell off her horse from laughing so hard, which made everyone laugh harder. The mirth was contagious. Lizzie and I laughed even though we'd understood nearly nothing of what had been said. And then we laughed about that.

'Sarah, do you have *any* idea what they're saying?'

'Guessing by the gestures and one or two words, I think she said something about someone's penis. I *think* her husband's.'

'What? Really?'

'I *think* so.'

'Oh, my goodness. Talking about their husband's... parts!'

I rolled my eyes.

'Jake Byrd was quite proud of his. Waved it around every chance he got.'

Elizabeth laughed so robustly it surprised me.

'Well,' she said, 'My William is a tall man with long, strong legs and long, strong arms and fine big feet, and...'

Lizzie then indicated with her hands something like a good-sized trout. This did not escape the notice of the other women and we all laughed.

It was good to laugh with them. To laugh, to feel the warmth of the sun on us and smell the clear, fragrant air. And for a time, there'd been no terrible danger and that, of course, made everything easier. I looked at Lizzie's face, her head thrown back, laughing her hearty laugh that I'd heard too infrequently. My friend. The first real friend of my life. I loved her dearly.

The women began to sing songs. We tried to join in on what *sort of* sounded like repetitions of something *sort of* like a refrain, but we stumbled over the sounds and gave up.

'Sarah! Let's sing something we know, you and I.'

'Yes! What?'

'How about... *A Mighty Fortress Is Our God.*'

'Oh! Dear me, I'm afraid I don't know it well enough. I don't imagine you could sing Dixie with me?'

'*Ha!* Maybe, but let's not! How about *God Rest Ye Merry Gentlemen?* We both know it.'

'A Christmas song?'

'What difference does it make? It's a good song.'

'You start. Set a good key, Lizzie.'

Elizabeth began to sing. I hadn't heard her sing full out before, she had good rich mezzo. I joined her and we both sang lustily. Between us, we knew several verses that we embellished with increasingly extravagant arpeggios up to the last chorus that we sang in harmony.

Oh – oh tidings of co-om-fort and joy, comfort and joy,
Oh – oh ti-i-dings… Of? Co-om-fort… And… JOY!

What a wonderful major chord we made! And Elizabeth took off from it, executing a cadenza that brought a great whooping from the women and several others of the company.

The weather was exceedingly pleasant. People would pause to swim in a stream when we passed a pretty one, careful not to get too far behind. We would stop to dig for wild turnips or gather berries. Cicadas buzzed and the small wild bees — with a mean sting! — hummed. The usual rules seemed to have been relaxed and a pair of young lovers might disappear for a while.

After food was eaten in the evening, the women took care of the cleaning up and the gathering in of children while the men talked and laughed softly. Sometimes they drummed and sang. Lizzie and I let our fire burn down slowly. The air traveled a long way over the sweet-smelling grass. Stars dusted the whole canopy of sky and the night creatures called to one another.

CHAPTER 20

One morning shortly after we'd gotten up, we were sitting in front of the fire when the earth beneath us began to tremble. The camp suddenly became quiet. Then we heard a low rumbling, like distant thunder but continuous, and suddenly with hoots and shouts, nearly all the men — except the old ones — grabbed their guns and bows and arrows and were met by boys leading the hunting horses. The older boys, near enough to manhood, joined them. Some who'd run to take part were called back sternly. They stood around looking wronged.

As the men rode off, some of the women gestured to us to follow them up a hill. Beyond it, a cloud of dust rose looking like smoke from a prairie fire.

'Must be buffalo, Lizzie!'

'Or the Rapture!'

We settled ourselves with the other women on a promontory that dropped off revealing a wide valley below to watch the action. Some had brought *wasna* that was passed around.

The animals were enormous. I'd seen a few from a distance, standing and grazing, but never a whole herd this close running full out. It was a river of brown backs, with horns and hooves flashing, and darting in and out at the edges of it, were our friends on their horses. We'd hear shots and an animal would fall, then another and another. The men rode without holding on so they had both hands to aim and shoot. Lizzie and I looked at one another in amazement. We knew these men! The hunt was brave and reckless and thrilling. Lizzie turned to me at one point and shouted how Charles and Joey, her boys, would love to see this.

In the herd's wake, we women went down with knives and skin bags to cut up the carcasses and carry the meat back to camp. Lizzie and I helped others who were clearly expert at the job. There'd be good eating that night and for a while afterward and no one had been killed or hurt badly. One horse had stepped in a hole, broken a leg, fallen and been trampled, but the rider had rolled free and was snatched up by another hunter whose horse barely slowed and the two continued hunting. The men seemed pleased. Some of the boys had had a good chance to prove themselves and were cockily jubilant. It seemed to have been a good hunt.

But later, the men talked among themselves, shaking their heads. Using our now familiar mix of English and Lakota and gestures, I asked Laughing Woman why the men were so serious and she told me the herd was too small.

Carrion birds had already descended on the carcasses. Coyotes would follow and then wolves.

'I'm surprised they left so much, Sarah, it seems wasteful.'

'They took everything they needed, I'm sure. The rest will get eaten by the wild creatures.'

Of course we had no way of predicting what was to come in just a few years, with white hunters from the east killing off thousands upon thousands of buffalo from the safety of train cars, having paid a lot of money to do it, and leaving whole carcasses on the ground to rot. Or the hunters, when the government raised the price of buffalo robes, who came in droves and skinned the animals on the spot. These people, too, left the meat to rot and sold the bones for fertiliser. Decimating the herds, decimating the tribes, that having been the point.

Roasted and boiled meat was eaten fresh twice a day and some made into sausages. Strips of meat were put out to dry in the hot sun. The women made new water bladders, separated sinew to make thread, staked the hides to flesh and brain-cure them. Lizzie and I knew how to do these things and worked along with the other women. Several of the cows we'd shot had good hair and would make fine coats for the winter. Medicine Crow picked out a good-sized skull and worked on it, cleaning the flesh from every tiny crevice, singing spirit songs. Babies got new rattles made of hooves.

Late into the night, the men told stories of the hunt and then, from what I could guess, re-told them with new emphasis and embroidery. From the acting out, we surmised that the trampled horse and the two young hunters was a favourite. All evening, the boys who had been denied the hunt simmered. I could imagine them saying, *Next time, next time.*

Our odyssey continued. One morning, we saw far ahead of us a small band of riders approaching, no more than three or four although the images shifted so it was hard to count. It was even impossible to tell how they were dressed, whom they might be. Lizzie and I looked at one another and at the others. We seemed to be the only ones concerned.

'If they were enemy, we'd know it by now.'

'It's hard to see, Sarah, the heat shimmers so.'

'Lizzie! It's a mirage!'

Our ghost riders turned out to be the bones of a long abandoned Conestoga wagon lying on its side with a few bleached flags of torn canvas fluttering from the bows. It looked like the remains of a huge pre-historic bird.

There were eight stout hickory bows and Lizzie told me that the long tongue suggested six mules or oxen. The big coach had been emptied out. The wheels had been taken away, as had barrels, tools, cooking pots and implements. But just to one side of it, standing in the grass, singular as an icon, was a desk-sized fortepiano. We dismounted to get a better look. When I tried to open the lid, I had to wrench away the dried piece to expose the keys.

'They look like old teeth, don't they? All here, though. Six octaves.'

I spread my fingers to make an A-minor chord and gently pressed the keys. A dull tinkling of sour notes. The lid was gone so I could see that the strings were corroded and the hammers looked as if they'd been half eaten. I tried again and one of the front legs buckled and then the other, as if it were a four-legged animal kneeling. Then it settled, crackling dryly to the ground.

'Poor old thing! I would like to have played it. You could have sung, Lizzie.'

'What in God's name is it doing way out here? Could we be so near one of the trails?'

'Maybe they struck out on their own, wanting to make a home out here somewhere.'

'I can't imagine it. This is too far out in Indian country, Sarah.'

'Beautiful, though, with the meadows, those hills, and we never seem to be far from water.'

'I wonder what happened to the people.'

We walked around the wagon, but there were no arrows stuck in the wood or bullet holes indicating an attack. We looked for signs in the grass right around the wagon but there was nothing. Not a shred of clothing, not a shoe, not a bone. I returned to the ruined piano. It looked sad, lying there. Lizzie was impatient.

'We should go. We don't want to fall too far behind.'

'I miss music. Not playing it so much, I wasn't very good, and neither could I sing that well. But I miss *hearing* it.'

'I miss singing with other people. Our church had a fine choir. William plays the guitar and the fiddle and we had friends who also played. We'd get together about once in a week and sing all the old songs.'

'That must have been lovely. I should try to learn their songs.'

'Whose? The *Indians'* songs?'

'Yes. Those.'

'Please don't! Can you honestly say you like it?'

'I don't hate it.'

'But do you *like* it?'

She was laughing at me.

'I'm trying to understand it. I listen carefully, trying to find, I don't know, patterns... '

'*Patterns?* The drumming is the same monotonous thumping over and over. It gives me headache. And it's not sung — it's shouted, and...'

'Not all of it! You've heard the women singing to their children...'

'That's the same thing only done softly. Why can't you allow yourself to say the music is *ugly!'*

'I'll admit that some of it is... difficult. But we're still not used to it, Lizzie, if we were to...'

She stopped me with a look that made me laugh.

I'd often thought about their music. While Elizabeth slept, if there was singing, I might sometimes quietly rise and slip outside the tipi to listen. If the 'prettiness' of a piece of music is a frill, like the lace on a petticoat, there were no such frills in their music. There was nothing between the singer's heart and the song. It was a cry direct to the universe, direct to their gods and their spirit world. Strange as it was to my ears, it stirred me in a way the music I'd grown up with rarely did. The beauty of certain pieces performed by an artist had moved me, of course. But this moved me differently. I knew better than to say any of this to Elizabeth.

'Come along, Sarah. We must catch up.'

She began to walk toward where our horses had drifted.

'Oh. Here's an old chest with drawers. I wonder if there's anything in them.'

She walked over to the remains of the thing and bent over something in the grass that had caught her eye. With some effort she lifted an oval piece of warped wood a bit taller than her forearm and a little less wide. It once must have been a graceful frame. I couldn't see the other side.

'Sarah, it's a mirror. Mostly blackened but there are no cracks… *And, oh my Lord in heaven!* I'm so sun burnt! I always wore a bonnet in the garden. And, my hair! So much grey in in it, and *dirt!* What a mess I am! William won't recognise me! I look awful!'

'You certainly do not! The colour in your cheeks is wonderful, you look beautiful. Besides, your William will be overjoyed just by the sight of you.'

'Thank you, dearest. But it's a shock to see myself looking like a thing that's been raised by wild animals.'

'My turn.'

I reached for the mirror, but Lizzie's face changed and she stepped back from me.

'Sarah, I'm not sure…'

'What?'

'Your eye… I don't think you should…'

'Nonsense. It's been long enough.'

I had long ago stopped wrapping a sash over it. It was too difficult to keep the damn things tied on and it seemed to make no difference regarding how my eye felt. I could see nothing at all out of it, it was dead to me. When Mary had offered her small mirror, what seemed a long time ago, I hadn't been ready to look. Now I wanted to know. I knew it was bad enough. I knew this from Lizzie's comments early on, and from what that bastard I'd killed had said about it, but I hadn't dwelled on it. Now that I had the chance, I wanted to see it. I *needed* to see it.

'Lizzie, I need to see my face. It's time.'

'Let me hold it for you, then.'

As a child, I didn't think a bit about how I looked. Ruth or one of the other Negro women would have to force me into the bath, scrub me and then rake my hair to get me presentable for dinner with my parents.

Round about age eleven or twelve, after I'd said my good-nights and Ruth had closed my door, sometimes I'd get out of bed, light a candle and stand before the tall oval mirror in my room. I'd take off my shift and look at my naked body. I'd run my hands from my neck

110

to my chest. I had no breasts yet, but my nipples were beginning to bud. My belly was getting rounder.

I felt around to the small hard cheeks of my buttocks. I'd stare at and touch my sex. My mother had never taught me any words, I'm not sure what I called my genitals, if anything at all. And she had certainly never told me of the astonishing sensations that came from touching the soft skin of the outside and the softer places just inside. Finding the tiny knob that swelled under my finger tips, that seemed to be the centre of a particular sort of pleasure that spread throughout my body, seemed miraculous.

Neither had my mother ever told me I would bleed from there one day. When it happened, I thought it was because of touching myself, a punishment. I ran to Ruth who explained that it was natural, that I was now capable of having babies. It was as if my mother had to remain innocent of that part of me, of who I was becoming.

In time, I became aware of how the small world of my parents' social milieu had begun to notice me, especially the men. I liked the attention. When I pleased them, I got more attention. I began to make note of *how* to please these men. Being pretty was a good start. Acting grateful for their compliments, smiling as they looked me over, these were also effective.

I became a vain young woman. Getting ready for a party or changing for dinner, I'd stand in front of my mirror as Ruth dressed me in layer after layer of linens and silks and embroidered cottons. I'd turn to one side and then the other, testing the effect of a fresh frock, stockings and pretty shoes. A cameo brooch, a golden locket on a golden chain so fine you could barely see the links, a gold ring with a small ruby between two pearls. I knew my blonde hair was lovely, as was my clear skin. When no one was looking, I'd enhance the natural high colour of my cheeks and lips with a bit of rouge stolen from my mother. But my most formidable weapons were my two sapphire-blue eyes, framed by naturally curling light brown lashes.

I knew that I was pretty, and when done up, *very* pretty. I learned to use it well. My conversational gifts, thanks to my mother's tutelage, were good enough, but it was the beauty of my face and body that created my place in their world. It was important currency.

Because that girl in my mirror could not tell me who I was other than a pretty thing, I became what others wanted me to be.

I had not forgotten what had happened when the Indians came. I remembered the blow. I felt the scar every time I ran my hands over my face to wash it, could feel the lumpy and partially opened lid when I'd splash water on my eye to cleanse it of dust. Now I had to see it.

Elizabeth turned the mirror to face me. I took it from her. I looked. My knees gave way and I sat down on the ground.

'Oh, Sarah. You've seen now, let me have it back. Let's...'

'No. I have to do this.'

The blow had obviously shattered the brow bone over my left eye and the cheekbone under it. Those bones had settled unevenly, so what there was of an eyebrow on that side was not on the same plane as the one on the other. My forehead on that side had sunk a bit and so had the cheek. From a point about in the middle of my forehead over that eye, down to a point almost level with my mouth — that corner of which was pulled down as if by a string below my jaw — was a thick, jagged seam still dark in its centre.

The ruined eye was hard to focus on, as if my other eye did not want to linger there. The puckered lid was stuck closed on the inside and was slightly open, though immobile, from the middle to the outer edge, revealing a glimpse of the opaque yellowish-white thing that was my eyeball.

Half my face was composed of my familiar features in their proper places. The other half was stove in with the scar running down it, dominated by that awful eye.

Elizabeth again tried to take the mirror out of my hands.

'Not yet.'

I stared at the face staring back at me. I forced my good eye to examine every bit of it as I turned my head slowly in one direction and then another and tilted it up and down, trying to see it from every angle.

'Sarah dear, please. Give me the mirror...'

'*I'm not done yet!*'

I had memorised the damage and now I was looking more deeply. I wanted to see who was in there. I wondered if the killer would show herself. I'd become doubly lethal: like the Gorgon, my looks could kill, and if that didn't do the trick, I could hack someone to death. I sort of chuckled at that. Elizabeth must have thought I was losing my senses.

'Sarah! You must stop...'

She tried to pull the mirror away but I held on to it.

'No, Lizzie. I need to understand. I *must* understand.'

I needed to learn this new face, this face that was how the world now saw me. And who was this 'me'? Who had I become? When one wants to see past a person's façade, one looks deep into their eyes. One of mine was a hideous ruin and the other was full of questions. The young, pretty face in my mirror back home had been unable to tell me who I was, and the scarred woman looking back at me now might as well have shrugged. An aspect of myself I'd believed was important had been obliterated. What, if anything, had been gained?

I slowly lowered the mirror to the ground watching that face, *my face*, the face I would have for the rest of my life, slide away as the glass filled up with sky. Elizabeth took my arm.

'Come. We must catch up with the others.'

We mounted and rode as fast as the travois allowed, but we needn't have pushed ourselves or the horses. That great company of people and animals moved slowly and it didn't take us long to regain our usual place among them.

Finally we came to a place where two good-sized, shallow streams, one coming from the northwest, one from the northeast, converged into a much wider stream. The water moved fast around rocks and flashed in the sun, running away to the south. Along the streams were trees for shade and between them was a broad shelf of grass. Up where the streams were farther apart, as they came from different directions, the meadow spread wider and wider, and rose higher. Away to the north were jagged hills thrust up from the plain.

Between the streams, birds called from the trees.

Summer camp.

CHAPTER 21

Lizzie and I had found a spot for bathing in the eastern-most of the two streams, above and at a bit of a remove from the camp. The others tended to bathe downstream, closer to the largest group of tipis. This particular morning, we had gathered our things and started up to our spot, when some of the women with children came running to fetch Elizabeth. She'd become very fond of a bunch of the little girls and they with her. Laughing, they began pulling her along by her skirts. She went with them and waved me to continue on. I went alone to our place.

I was humming, as I tend to do, and mindless, as I tend to be on a hot summer afternoon — or anytime, actually; one of my many flaws — and I walked farther up the path than usual. Here, the bank down to the water was steep. I kept tripping over roots as I made my way, grabbing tree trunks with my one free hand. A stone toppled towards the water, I followed it with my gaze, and there he was. Far Cry had to have been there all along, standing where overhanging branches shaded that part of the stream, watching my clumsy progress. He was naked.

It so startled me, that I stumbled and slid about halfway down the bank on my bottom. I stopped myself by grabbing hold of a slender tree trunk and ended up lying pretty much on my back, skirts pushed up high on my legs. I sprang up, spun around, bumped against the tree, bounced off it, sat down again hard and began to slide. I grabbed at a bush to keep from going the rest of the way down, my moccasined feet fighting for traction. He was laughing and so was I, in spite of my acute embarrassment.

'It's impolite to laugh so hard!'

Stupid. Not only was it unlikely he understood what I said, but I had shouted it to the trees off to the side so as not to look directly at him. I expected him to leave right away, or make some effort to cover himself, but he did neither of these things.

I was glad he didn't. I wanted to look at him. I wanted to look at him because he'd stopped laughing and I could feel him looking at me and I knew he wanted me to look at him. So I did.

He was gazing steadily at me and smiling as he squeezed water from his hair. His wrists were small but his hands were large, strong, long-fingered. His arms were lean and well muscled. I noticed the shape of his rather short but powerful legs, with the water splashing around his knees. I wanted to meet his gaze with mine and began to lift my head to do so, then, suddenly, I remembered my face.

I snapped my chin to my chest and looked at my feet. I turned my head away and used the bush to pull myself up. I turned my back to him as he climbed, splashing, unhurried, out of the water. I heard him pull a blanket from a bush. I heard his easy progress up the bank towards camp.

I threw down my blankets and bundles of sweetgrass, my clean clothes, and stumbled down the bank and into the stream still dressed in my dirty clothes. I'd exposed myself enough. I hated my face. What the hell was I thinking? That I was still a beautiful woman who could command the gaze of a beautiful man? Never again. And certainly not this man. I lay on my back in the water, then turned over and pushed my face into the onrushing stream, holding to rocks to stay under.

When I ran out of breath, I rolled over again and lay on the surface, looking up. I began to breathe more reasonably. A strange joy began to rise, surprising me. I looked at green leaves cutting into blue sky and it was as if I'd never seen such a thing before. I desired him and he desired me. And, in truth, it had begun a good while back. This time, I'd been the one who'd looked away. Not him. The hopelessness washed away downstream. He *desired* me. Even with my ruined face.

In the following days, when I accidentally — or deliberately, recklessly — looked in his direction, I often found that Far Cry was also looking at me. But I was cowardly about it and would turn away fast.

I used to imagine there was a silk cord connecting us that only I could see, a red silk cord. I imagined that neither of us could move without the other feeling it. *Lovers cannot see the pretty follies that themselves commit.* Oh, I could see mine plainly and didn't care one bit.

At night, with Elizabeth asleep on the other side of our tipi, I'd lie there and conjure an image of him lying alone on his robes in his tipi across the camp. I knew exactly where it was, with his war horse tethered outside. He would be awake as I was awake, the two of us wanting one another. I'd tug on the cord. I longed to tell Lizzie about it, but I knew what she'd say. Red silk cord! I admonished myself as Lizzie might: at the least, this was a silly schoolgirl sort of thing. But I knew she'd see this as nothing more than base hunger for skin against skin. There was truth here. I wanted nothing more than what had fuelled my marriage to Jake. My disastrous marriage. Sometimes, I thought I should cut that imaginary cord with an imaginary knife. I never did.

Before marrying Jake, I had never so much as had an infatuation. I rarely saw any boys my age until my mother began to invite them to soirees designed to find me a husband. My introduction to adult sex was unpleasant. During The War, our house was very briefly a refuge for wounded soldiers. There were bleeding men on the veranda with some on the floor in the great hall, too. One of these, an officer recovering on a couch in our small parlour, liked to reach under my skirts when I'd bring him water or change the dressing on his neck. Mother would send me to do it if her nursing skill was needed elsewhere. Thinking about it, I'm surprised she didn't guess what this bastard was like. He was, after all, a friend of my father's.

I'm not sure why I let him, other than that I'd been taught to obey adults. Especially adult men. Once, he grabbed my hand and pushed it into his trousers, making me stroke him. The air around us became suddenly thick, I couldn't breathe. But this didn't last long. I heard someone outside the door and sharply pulled my hand back. Smiling, in case someone was watching, he whispered that I'd better not say anything or he'd hurt me. Besides, he was an officer and I was just a silly girl, no one would believe me. Not long after that, he left. I never told anyone.

Because of this and all the stories I'd read, I had a sense of what desire could do to men. But I was unprepared for what it could do to me. It deranged me. I confused sexual hunger with the desire for love. I gave the name of love to my *need* for love that would justify my desire to fuck Jake. This was complicated by the fact that I did most certainly enjoy the feeling of pleasure between my legs and had done so for years, long before I'd any notion of sexual congress.

My parents had wanted 'a good marriage' for me. But their ideas of what that might be were very different. It wasn't difficult — thinking about it alone in the dugout after Jake left me — to figure out what my father had had in mind: a merger of Southern royalty. He and Jake's father were old friends. They were the two largest landowners in the region, and between the two of them, probably owned most of the Negroes in Virginia. They owned most of the politicians, too. The useful ones.

My mother simply didn't want it to be Jake. She'd been married to my father at eighteen and had become addicted to laudanum shortly after my birth when she was barely twenty. Perhaps she was dulling several kinds of pain. She didn't like Jake and didn't like his father or any of his family. But I could not believe she was any more impressed by the other available young men than I was. I suspect that, in her eyes, their winning quality must have been that they weren't Jake.

These alternative suitors were introduced at dinners, dances, musical evenings, that sort of thing. Everyone watched. They bored the hell out of me. My father, knowing how things would go, enjoyed the show, retiring early to his study to drink with whatever cronies of his were there.

Jake was by far the best looking of the bunch, not so tall but strong and fast, an athlete. He'd done poorly at West Point, but was an officer. He was dark haired. I can't remember the colour of his eyes, perhaps because he was heavy-lidded and liked to make the most of this cloaking. He knew why he was there. I knew why he was there. We wanted one another immediately. I do recall he had a beautiful mouth.

After dancing and flirting and laughing through a couple of gatherings at my parents' home, pleasing my father, making my mother nervous, we finally, early in one such event, did what *we* wanted to do. Carrying our punch out to the veranda, we oh so casually walked down the stairs, keeping a proper space between us. Just outside the circle of light from the house, we went into the shadows of the great old trees.

He pushed his tongue deep into my mouth and I met it with mine. I'd never done that before, but to my surprise, it came naturally. I liked it. He grabbed my breast. I liked that, too. He took my hand and slammed it against his erection, then reached up under the layers of silks and linens, under my chemise, and rubbed me until I thought my knees would buckle. This was nothing like the wounded man on the couch. I remember saying to myself: I *like* this. I'm not supposed to like this. My mother would be furious, but I like this very much.

From that night forward, Jake was ubiquitous. He seemed to have moved into the house. Sometimes I'd feel sick in anticipation of seeing him. I didn't like *him*, his arrogance was almost as well developed as my father's and he didn't care about any of the things I found important — music, art, literature, aesthetics — yet I hungered for him.

My mother became desperate in her efforts to turn me in another direction. The War barely over, she still managed to bring to the house a handful of boys — good boys, even a few nice looking boys, sons of friends — for lunch or tea or music. Each came credentialed: a *fine* young man; a young officer with a very good record; Lee gave him a commendation. The nice young man would treat me like a perfect lady. At some point, he'd lean tentatively in the direction of my mouth but I'd turn my head so he'd deposit his nice dry kiss on the side of my face. Then I'd go find Jake.

'Done with that pup?'

'And Mother had such high hopes.'

We'd take our walk. He'd lift me a bit and press my back against a tree trunk. He'd rub his cock between my legs. We'd *almost* fuck, but I'd stop him. I was afraid, yet I was addicted.

'You *like* it, girl, don't you fool yourself. Say you like it.'

'Why? Are you in need of reassurance?'

'Say, "I wanna fuck you, Jake"'.

'I will not.'

'Say it! Say, "Fuck me, Jake"'.

'Fuck *you*, Jake.'

'Ha, *ha!* That's my girl.'

We'd go on 'picnics'. After a couple of these, I did away with my reluctance. I was tired of my virginity. Barely intact anyway, it felt like a weight on me. I paid off the 'chaperone' — one of mother's house Negroes, a girl younger than me — in sweets and told her to wait at a certain spot. Jake would drive the buggy to a hunter's cabin, where there was a cot over which he'd spread a couple of horse blankets.

We faced one another and undressed quickly; we did not waste time. He did things he liked to do, theatrical things like grabbing a fistful of my hair and yanking my head back when he went for my breasts with his mouth. He liked to do these things, so I pretended to like them. I was a good actor, and learned how to increase his desire so that what *I* liked would happen more quickly. I liked it when his manipulations and theatrics fell apart and he lost control. It was his only moment of vulnerability. He would pull out of me fast to come on my belly or thigh. I liked to watch this.

'Good lord, girl, I've made you into a wanton. Or maybe it was in your nature all along. I think it must have been... *Harpie!* Now you're *striking* me!'

I did not experience or require or expect a cataclysm of my own that matched his. I took my pleasure later, in the bath, or lying half asleep in my bed, or covertly and rather dangerously, while reading on a chaise longue on the veranda, in the languorous heat of the afternoon.

We were a handsome couple, everyone said so. He was always perfectly groomed, expensively dressed, and well equipped with aphorisms. I admired his way with older men, especially officers, as if they were all equals, discussing history, battles and strategies. He had that way of standing, correct for his class, to show off his power and how relaxed he was with it.

Finally, there were no more friends' sons or second cousins or nephews or friends of friends. Everyone could see the future. Our fathers were pleased. My mother was disgusted. She could barely bring her-self to begin preparations for The Great Nuptial Celebration.

One night, after climbing into my bed with complaints about how my father smelled, we lay side by side on our backs and she took my hand and squeezed it. In her low, soft, laudanum-slowed voice, she told me she had a wonderful plan. We needn't rush into this marriage, Jake was going nowhere. She'd send me to Paris where I would stay with friends from her youth. I could study piano there and maybe art for which she believed I might have some real talent. My French was already fairly good and she said that I would soon become fluent and wouldn't that be lovely? Most important, in Paris I would become a lady among a different kind of society than what passed as such here. What do you think?'

I didn't say anything. She turned her face to me.

'Don't marry that Jake Byrd.'

'Why not?'

'He is not the kind of man one marries, Sarah. He's for... diver-sion. I'm not an idiot about these things, you know. That man is not for marriage and children.'

'Why did you marry Daddy?'

She sighed, turned her back to me, lay there for a bit and then got up and walked out of my room, closing the door behind her.

The wedding was lavish. Afterward, we moved into a small, elegant house on his father's land. The ardour of his courtship seemed to diminish rather quickly. But when he conceived the plan to go west, and sought the assignment to Fort Laramie, all done without telling me a thing, his excitement over the move briefly re-kindled his inter-est in me. I'd missed his attentions. After all, he was my husband and I, of course, loved my husband. I ached for the intensity of our sex.

We could have afforded stage coaches and hotels, but for some reason Jake wanted the grittier experience of a wagon train. My father suggested we take one of 'the boys' who'd stayed, when so many had left. I had to remind him that we no longer *owned* any 'boys'. 'Nonsense,' he said.

During a good part of the trip, I was sick at the stomach and cramping. Finally, I couldn't sit a horse, so I rode in the wagon among our things. All day I'd sip tea with brandy in it. At night, I'd sleep while Jake went from campfire to campfire drinking and playing cards with men he'd found companionable. In the afternoon of one day of impressive pain and convulsive cramping, I started bleeding profusely and, looking at the clotted stuff on my underskirts, saw that I'd just lost a baby. It was about the size of a plum, but it was unmistakable.

I was surprised, but felt no sadness. I'd had no idea there was a child inside me; I hadn't once thought of having children with Jake or of preventing such a thing. I rolled my soiled underskirts in a ball, the plum-baby in the middle of it, and that night, while Jake made his rounds, I added sticks to our fire and burned it. No one noticed. I wondered if maybe that's how every woman handled bloody skirts. It seemed impractical, one would run out of things to wear while traveling in the wilderness. But I didn't know. I'd never had to deal with my own monthly stains.

Soon I began to feel well enough to ride again and often Jake and I would travel side by side. There were some good days, when we enjoyed one another's company. We saw Indians, but only once along a ridge parallel the trail. We saw wolves, various kinds of deer, buffalo and other wildlife. But these excitements soon gave way to boredom and fatigue.

After a short time at Laramie, there was the incident, and the contretemps with the fort commander whom he considered 'a priggish idiot', and Jake moved us into the dugout, leaving me alone there days at a time, until he left me for good. My husband, my love.

And now here was this beautiful man, this Lakota. Jake had been a cruel, corrupt, possibly evil man. I had no idea who Far Cry was. He'd ordered us captured, held us prisoner, and kept us alive only because of our value as hostages. Yet, I knew he *wanted* me. He could have taken me by force, but hadn't. I fantasised all sorts of passionate, *romantic* encounters, and this made me grin like an idiot. Elizabeth noticed. Once I felt her staring at me.

'What are you thinking about?'

'Nothing in particular, Lizzie. Why?'

'You've been staring into the trees for the longest time with a very strange smile on your face.'

'It's nothing but simple-mindedness, dear heart, that's all it is.'

CHAPTER 22

It was late in the afternoon, one day of that summer, in the camp between the streams, that we first walked out together. I was alone in the lodge. I was probably humming some bit of a tune and failed, at first, to hear the sound. Then I heard it but didn't know what it was. I listened more closely and realised that a man was right outside, clearing his throat. The only man I spoke with was Medicine Crow and that was mostly our rather extravagant greetings when we passed one another.

I came to my side of the partially closed flap and said, 'Yes?' as if I were at home in Virginia and someone had knocked on the door of my rooms. I looked down and saw a moccasined foot and part of a leg in fringed buckskin. I'm not sure how I knew, but I knew. I was paralysed, but could not now pretend I hadn't heard Far Cry quietly trying to get my attention. I opened the flap and stepped out.

I stood to the side looking at him. He looked straight ahead and was silent for a moment. We were exactly the same height. He turned to me and we were eye to eye. It was nearly unbearable to be that close. His face was expressionless; he spoke a single sentence in Lakota. I recognised the word for 'sister'.

Mary had told me about courtship among the Lakota. I'd seen it myself. A young couple had married earlier that summer. The girl was quite pretty and for some weeks, several young men had lined up outside her family's lodge. Later, they brought gifts and she — or perhaps her parents, but she was clearly impressed with the boy and seemed happy — chose the one who'd brought two rather fine ponies.

Mary had explained that the lining up outside the girl's tipi is part of a ritual with specific behaviours and language. The young man holds his blanket open towards the girl and says, 'Sister, will you walk with me.' If she chooses to do so, he enfolds her in his blanket and they go off together. I'd asked Mary what they did when they went off and she laughed. 'They talk love!'

He had used the word 'sister' and had briefly held out an edge of the blanket that was draped over his shoulders in symbolic invitation. I nodded. He did not enfold me in his blanket and we walked off a bit apart from one another. The people went about their business, pretending not to notice. I did not know where Elizabeth was and vacillated between hoping she didn't see us, and defiantly telling myself that I did not care if she did. He took a path between the two streams that made straight for the broad meadow. We walked a long way, facing the sun that was getting lower in the sky. The path had given out and we were in grass to our knees. He stopped and we turned towards one another. He took my head in his two hands and, his eyes open, he brought my face to his and touched his lips to mine.

The kiss began as tentatively as any kiss between two people who are not sure of one another. But, for me, and I have chosen to believe it was the same for him, the kiss carried all the force of longing long held down, longing that had matured into yearning, yearning that had blown up into powerful desire. He threw his blanket on the ground and we we lay on it. The grass encircled us.

We reached the edges of the camp at late dusk and separated without a word or glance. Elizabeth was standing by the fire staring at something bubbling in the pot. The air had a bit of chill, so I went inside the tipi to get a blanket to put over my shoulders. I took a deep breath before joining her. She was ready for me.

'What are you doing with that man?'

'With Far Cry?'

A stupid question, a stalling question, and she let me know with a look just how stupid it was. I answered honestly.

'I believe I am falling in love with him.'

'Don't be ridiculous!'

I had no response. Elizabeth continued, her voice low.

'Have you gone mad?'

'I may, indeed, have found a way *not* to.'

Elizabeth straightened up and folded her arms hard against her body. Her mouth formed a tight, straight line and she took a moment to compose herself before speaking. She told me that she'd been watching 'this thing,' as she called it, growing in me, that I'd been 'mooning about' and was so obvious in my infatuation that it would be laughable if it were not suggestive of something sick in my soul. Then she said,

'You are losing yourself. One part of you at a time is going over to them. We spoke of this. First you want to learn the language, saying it's for our own good, and now this, this absurd...'

'Lizzie, please. You are as involved with these people as I am. More so. You're always playing with the children, every day one or two of the women...'

'That's different.'

'How is it different?'

'I am making the best of a horrible situation. I am not trying to replace one life with another. But you... I have felt you drifting away. And now you are drifting towards him. Can you deny it? No you cannot. *Do not forget who you are!*'

'*And who am I?* Can you tell me, Elizabeth? All anyone has ever been able to tell me is who I *ought* to be. I will not hear this any longer. Do *not* speak to me in this manner!'

'I will tell you who we are whenever I feel you're forgetting it. *We are captives of these people and they are our enemies.* For your own sake, Sarah...'

'*Enough!* You asked me what I was doing with the man and I told you. I am in love. *This* is who I am.'

'That man is our enemy, Sarah — no, don't interrupt me! — *our enemy!* When the army comes for us, *and it will*, he will be shot. If he does not leave you to ride off into the hills and escape, he will be shot.'

We stood on either side of the fire, staring into it. I could still taste him. I was in love. I'd never been in love and I was not going to let it go. Elizabeth would accept this. Or she would not.

CHAPTER 23

Far Cry came to the tipi several times when she was not there and we walked together. As soon as we were out of sight of anyone from the camp we fell on one another. At our first encounter, I had lost myself in my hunger for him and I worried that I might behave in ways that would offend him, that I might be too different from what he'd expect from an Indian woman. But his hunger matched mine. Our desire for one another grew stronger each time we made love.

Jake had called me a wanton. Lizzie saw me as a reckless bawd. And a traitor as well. We had barely spoken for a while, she kept her back turned to me when we lay down at night. I missed her good will. I missed *her*.

I decided to surprise her with a gift. Our clothing was badly stained and falling apart. I had the one outfit of calico that I'd made, but I'd not done a very good job with the fit, and besides, that fabric had not been of high quality and had begun to show wear. Lizzie had used the calico only to patch the clothes in which she was captured, the result was beyond eccentric.

For weeks I laboured in secret on two soft dresses made of doeskins Far Cry had given me. Laughing Woman let me examine one of her dresses as I could not imagine how to shape the yoke. Then I made the two garments by myself. I worked on them when Lizzie wasn't around, quickly folding them carefully and hiding them among my blankets and sleeping robes when I heard her approaching. One day they were finally ready.

I waited until she had gone to the creek with her women friends and their children, then quickly pulled them out. I peeled off my old clothes, my under skirt, my linen shift and what was left of my pantalettes that were so badly torn I could hardly keep them on my body, and so badly stained I couldn't bear to look at them. I rubbed my skin all over with sweetgrass and pulled on one of the doeskin dresses. It hung down loosely not quite to my ankles, with simple fringing at the hem and at the sleeves that came to my elbows. They perhaps were not as well constructed or finished as those the other women wore, but I was proud of my work. It was lovely to be bare underneath it and it made me wonder why we had to wear so many layers under our clothing.

I would have liked some beading, but I'd had nothing to trade for beads or other sorts of ornament, did not want to ask and have them feel they had to give me something. And besides, I was in too much of a hurry. It didn't matter, as the dresses had a simple elegance about them that I found beautiful. I still think they are beautiful. And they were soft. I'd worked hard to make them very soft. I hoped Lizzie would like her gift, or at least accept it in the spirit in which I would present it to her, as a peace offering.

I also changed my hair. I pulled out the two sticks with which I tried to keep it knotted behind my head, and let it loose. Far Cry always took it down when we were out walking together and I'd gather it up again before re-entering the village. I made a part and separated it into two sections, combing it with my fingers. I used a bit of grease to smooth it and made two braids. My thin and fine hair made thin braids. So be it. I tied them with thin strips of cord.

I folded the dress for Lizzie and made a package of it, tied with braided grass with a blue flower in the knot. I placed it on her sleeping blankets. I stepped outside. I had not considered how shy I'd feel about appearing in Indian dress for the first time. It reminded me of walking down the stairs of my parents' house for a fancy party, dressed for the first time in a gown that displayed my shoulders, that presented the woman I was just becoming.

I built a fire. The women in the camp made no show that they noticed, but of course they noticed and of course they would not show it. I became increasingly nervous waiting for Lizzie and kept adding to the fire. Suddenly I was seized with an urge to get rid of my old stuff immediately. I ran into the tipi and grabbed up that pile of stinking rags and came back out. I was tearing everything to pieces — the fabric gave little resistance — and feeding them to the fire when Elizabeth surprised me.

'What on earth are you doing?'

'Ah! There you are! I'm burning this old stuff. It's rotting and falling apart, I leave bits of it behind everywhere I walk. It's become ridiculous. But, Lizzie! Lizzie dear, I have a surprise for you...'

'You've braided your hair.'

'That's not the surprise. I should have done this long ago. My hair is too thin to stay in a knot. You have such beautiful, thick hair...'

But Elizabeth was looking at the fire. She'd looked at my hair, and now she was looking at what I was burning. She made a sound something between pain and fury and dropped to her knees. She snatched a piece of my dress from the flames and was reaching for another when I grabbed her arms and pulled her up.

'Stop! What are you doing!'

'You're burning your clothes! What does this mean?'

'This means nothing, Lizzie. It's only a dress, and it's done, this dress, and these underthings. It's all stained with blood, piss, shit, who knows what else. I can't get the smell out. It's all falling apart, I can't patch it anymore. It's all done and I'm done with all of it.'

I took the scraps from her and threw them back in the flames, poking them with a stick. Elizabeth's eyes were hard and her voice harder. It was hoarse, as if she could barely get the words out of her throat.

'You are gone to me! Good as dead to me!'

She started sobbing and sucking at a place on her hand.

'Ah, you idiot, you've burned yourself. Let me see.'

I reached for her, but she violently thrust my hand aside. She started to walk away but I caught her, having to hold on hard to keep her there. I was sick of her dramatics.

'This is about him, isn't it. Not the damn clothing.'

She stared at my doeskin dress as if she'd only just then noticed it.

'Yes, Lizzie. A new *clean* dress. I made one for you, too. I think they're beautiful.'

She tore herself loose and began to half run, half stumble away from me. I watched her go. Her dress was patched with pieces of old blankets and scraps of calico, some from the dead trader's stuff, some that other women had given her in exchange for the hair pins she'd hoarded and buttons she'd taken from her clothes. The sleeves were in shreds, they flapped around her arms, the lace like old spider's webs. Strips of petticoat trailed in the dirt behind her. Her hair was piled on her head in an attempt at her usual fashion but held too loosely with the few pins she had left and a couple of porcupine quills so locks fell all around her face. She was holding her burnt hand to her mouth and her eyes and nose were streaming. A couple of the women looked up as she passed and then quickly away. She looked like a mad woman.

She came back at suppertime with firewood but I had done that already and was standing at the fire, stirring a soup. Elizabeth had washed her face and neatened her hair. She stood looking into the fire for a bit before speaking.

'I told you what happened when I was captured, didn't I?'

'Yes, you did.'

'Everything?'

'You told me how they killed your friends and made you watch. But these are not the same ones, Lizzie...'

'*This is your mistake!* Your romantic idea! They are of the same race, they have the same gods and the same grievances as those others, and if it came to them or us, what do you really think would happen? Never mind answering. I *know* what would happen and so do you. If he had to choose between you and his people, your lover would kill you. Of course he would! No matter what you wear on your body or how many Lakota words you can manage to toss around, you will *never* be one of them. They will *never* fully accept you. Tell me you understand this!'

'No! This is not true. I believe it's possible...'

She didn't wait for my to finish, but stifled a scream and spun completely around before she faced me again. Every head in the circle of tipis looked up and then quickly down. She spoke in a lower voice and so hard I barely recognised it as hers.

'You are so smart, and so stupid, and you're bound and determined to cause me pain. But never mind. Fornicate with this savage, I'll say nothing more about it.'

She walked away but only a few steps. Stopped. I could see her shoulders move and I knew her well enough, now, to know she was both crying and talking to herself. In a bit she turned around and came back, standing closer than before. This time, her voice was softer, and I could see her struggle with her emotions.

'This is horrible, Sarah, I can't stand it. You will do what you want to do, of course you will, and I suppose I have no right to say anything about it. But I feel betrayed. Betrayed! And this hurts me deeply. Do you understand this?'

'I do Lizzie, and I'm so sorry, but I...'

'I know you can't help yourself, Sarah, I know you... Do this one thing for me. *Please,* do this one thing.'

'What can I do?'

'Tell me you will pray for our release every single day we remain in these circumstances.'

'Lizzie...'

'*Say it!* I need to hear you say those words.'

'It would not make sense, I don't believe as you do, I...'

'Say it! Or we are no longer friends. *Say it!*'

So, I did. I told her I would pray every day for our release. The words were the libretto of a ritual reinstating our bond: 'Say you will pray.' 'I will pray.' We both needed the bond, she needed the ritual. Perhaps I did too.

She never wore the dress. I found it on my sleeping blankets when I came in that night. We were strange with one another for while, and then we were no longer strange and could laugh and embrace once again.

It was still high summer, we had plenty of good weather ahead of us.

CHAPTER 24

Far Cry and I found ways to communicate that did not require words. This was fortunate, as I was not learning to speak or understand the language at all well. Friends and lovers with the luxury of a shared language can use words carelessly. Friends and lovers lacking such a thing, must work harder. We used all our senses to understand and be understood. When speaking with one another, we did not break eye contact. We watched for the subtlest cues: a dilation or contraction of the pupil, the twitch preceding a crinkle of amusement, a slight head-tilt that might mean, 'I don't understand, try again'. A tightening that might signal displeasure. A change of tone along with a smile that says, 'Ah, yes, I know what you're telling me and I agree'. We made the most of these things. And we created a rich vocabulary of gestures.

Once, he showed me small marks on his thigh where I had bitten him when Lizzie and I had tried to escape across the river from the big gathering of clans. Who was that woman? An animal doing what any animal does when its life is threatened. Perhaps the kisses I was giving him now, maybe all this 'talking love', was just another way to stay alive a while longer.

Sometimes, while walking together, he would talk to me in Lakota. Every now and then I would recognise a word and every now and then he would use an English word, or even an entire phrase. Soon, I hoped, more words and phrases of both our languages would gather together and we'd be able to converse. I so badly wanted to see his world as he saw it. And it was his world he was offering me in this talking: waving his hand over the grass tops, pointing out birds flushed by our progress over the meadow, picking up a wild herb, crushing it, passing it under my nose and, I imagined, saying its name, speaking of its qualities. After a bit, he would spread his blanket, bending the grass beneath it, and we'd lie down together and hold one another and kiss and stroke and entwine our bodies because that was how we were most eloquent.

It was stolen time, which is always especially sweet. But when that thought would come to me, 'This is stolen time', that word, 'stolen', would strike me in the gut. Our people were at war, as Elizabeth had so often reminded me. She and I had been 'stolen'. And yet, each time Far Cry and I walked out together, I felt more at home with the feel and look of him, with the smell and taste of him, with the sound of his voice, than I had ever imagined I could feel with a man. I did not feel stolen. I felt chosen.

One night, Elizabeth and I woke suddenly to a shout, then more shouts. We'd been asleep for a good while, it was dark. We heard horses galloping, strangers' voices whooping, dogs barking. We stood up and were about to go outside to see, but suddenly there was shooting and we hit the ground. There was more shouting, some from voices we knew, and more shooting, horses galloping back and forth, and then almost as suddenly as it started, it stopped. We stepped outside. It was not the first time we'd experienced this.

Far Cry and his men had ridden off after the raiders. The old men were standing in front of their lodges brandishing their rifles. Even the boys were pacing back and forth, tense, bows at the ready. But that brief, loud dust-up had apparently been it. No one had been killed or injured. Now we had to wait to see who came back and who didn't. Some of the women had begun to build fires. We did the same. The eastern sky was paling.

'It's *horrible* when they do this! Crow again, do you think?'

I told Lizzie I thought it was probably a Crow raid. I thought I had heard the Lakota word for Crow when it began.

'Why must they do this? How different can they be that they have to kill one another regularly!'

It wasn't only Crow, the Lakota also fought Pawnee, Snake, maybe others. I strained to recall what Mary had told me. It was part of life and had been going on as long as anyone could remember.

The men came back before the end of the day. I learned from straining to understand Far Cry and Medicine Crow, by watching their gestures and the reaction to what they were saying, that a small group of Crow had tried to make off with the horses and they'd gone after them. There'd been a bit of a skirmish. One of our young men — not much more than a boy — was being congratulated for, I gathered, counting coup. He'd gotten close enough to strike one of the raiders with his coup stick and then make off with his horse.

The boy pranced around the circle on his horse, holding the new one by its reins and shaking his coup stick in the air. There was dancing and singing that night. Not long after, there was a rather somber ritual that I believe had to do with giving him a new name, followed by a festive celebration.

Not long after, Far Cry and some of his men rode off with no more ceremony beyond Medicine Crow's usual benediction of blowing smoke over their heads and chanting, but the men were carrying their newest rifles, some also had handguns, they all had bows and arrows and war clubs. From the lack of ceremony, I hoped it was just a hunt. Although fresh game had available close by all summer and there was meat drying on all the racks. And you don't need a war club to hunt. Also, he'd worn his red shirt. I hated not knowing. Hated that I couldn't ask him and get an answer. Hated that I could not talk out my fears to Elizabeth, my friend.

After the men rode off, she and I went to gather firewood — an unending task — with some of the other women and their children. Elizabeth started playing hiding and chasing games with the little girls. One of the very little boys wanted to play too. Barely past toddler-hood, he kept trying to hide under her skirts. She picked him up, hugged him hard and put lots of loud kisses on his cheeks. He screwed up his face, turning his head back and forth to escape the kisses, and the little girls and their mothers laughed.

I sometimes tried to join in the games, but if I'd ever known how to play in that way, I'd forgotten. No matter how sweetly I spoke to them, they seemed frightened of me. It saddened me a bit. I was the one who felt a truer sympathy for these people, or so I believed, yet it was Lizzie who was loved by the women, young and old, as well as the children. Even the men smiled at her pleasantly.

The young women were polite to me, but almost as shy as the children. The older women were skeptical, watchful, except for a few such as Medicine Crow's wife, Laughing Woman. I considered her a friend. The men glanced in my direction as I passed and sometimes nodded, as if I were… I still don't know how the men saw me. But as it was clearly understood that I was Far Cry's woman, there was a kind of deference. And, of course, I'd killed someone who'd made big trouble in the camp. And perhaps because I'd killed a bad actor of my own race, they had placed me in a special category. But none of these distinctions earned me the warm feelings they extended to Elizabeth. Elizabeth who called them 'heathen' and 'enemy'.

I envied Lizzie. I loved Lizzie. Her contradictions infuriated me.

The men were gone for several days and I was sick with fear for Far Cry. Then, early one morning, they rode back with about ten new horses. Lizzie and I were outside, drinking coffee while a porridge warmed, blankets draped over our shoulders as there was a slight chill in the air. Everyone ran up to welcome home the men and to admire the horses.

Out of that flurry, and in full view of the camp, Far Cry came towards us leading a filly, an appaloosa, all white with black spots. He handed me the rope attached to a soft bridle with no bit and stepped aside. I stroked her all over. She was well formed. She was easy with my hands on her and had a lively eye, an almost human-looking eye. She shook her head in a playful way. A *fine* young horse. I was moved in my entire being but was careful not to show it. It would not have been proper. He smiled, pleased, and walked away.

This was a strong gift he'd given me, in front of all the people. In front of Elizabeth. It was the kind of gift a man gives a woman he loves. Elizabeth, standing off to one side, had folded her arms in that way I'd come to dread, even sometimes to hate.

'What does this mean?'

'It's just a gift, Lizzie. She's beautiful, isn't she?'

There was dancing that night and I could not take my eyes from my lover's face as he sat smoking and laughing with the men. He returned my gaze often, something he rarely did when others were watching. While I was looking at him, Elizabeth was looking at me. I didn't care.

CHAPTER 25

I should not have looked back. The look on her face as I rode away with him still haunts me. As I was mounting my horse, my beautiful girl, having prepared a pack, I told her I'd be back soon. As Far Cry and I rode out of the camp, I called out to her,

'Lizzie! I promise!'

But she had already turned and gone into what had been our tipi. I watched to see if she'd come out again. She did not. I faced forward.

We cross the stream to the west of the village and turn south, south-west. We are moving through wide rolling meadow of short grass and flowers, high hills behind us, high hills before us and on either side. I can't see a path but he seems to know exactly where he's going.

'When do we come back?'

I hold up my hand and count off days on my fingers, then raise my open hands and lift my eyebrows: it's a question. He smiles, then offers up the country all around us with a sweep of his arm. He laughs a little. He's right. It's a stupid question to be asking now. We continue but I have a knot in my belly. I do not belong here. Where then do I belong?

What a time to fall in love, with the whole human race tearing at one another. Were we ever not at war? Will we ever not be at war? He sees the shadow of my thoughts, pulls close and strokes my face.

Dusk. We've stopped on the banks of a stream among clustered trees and shrubs. The green of mid-summer has faded somewhat, but the cottonwoods have not yet begun to turn yellow. Late July, early August? I don't know and I'm sick of trying to figure it out. I'm no longer sure why it matters or *if* it matters. We water the horses. He clears a place for a fire. I put water in the small pot I somehow thought to bring and make a soup from dried meat and a couple of turnips. It's delicious. We spread a buffalo hide on the ground and lie down with blankets over us.

On our sides, face to face, he strokes my cheeks, my lips, my neck, my breasts, my belly. I wrap my leg over his hips, open myself to him, he enters me. As hungry as I'd been, lying with him in the meadow outside the village, this is different. I should feel free to love him beautifully, but I feel dull, ashamed, nervous. He stops moving and I think, he knows, he knows I don't really know how to love. I'm on the edge of despair when, still inside me, he kisses my dead eye, my nose, my chin. I feel the heart of his kisses and thank whatever gods are with us. We make love. We sleep.

I wake to the smell of coffee.

'Coffee!' he announces in English, nodding his head in a self-satisfied way.

'You are a good man!'

'Yes! Good.'

I pretend we are like any other couple at breakfast. He looks at me and smiles. But we are not 'any other couple'. I wish we could talk. I am certain he understands more English than he would have anyone believe.

'I think you know much English,' I tell him, and I use everything I've got in addition to my words to help him understand. 'I hope so. I am too stupid to learn Lakota.'

He shakes his head, still smiling, and I have no idea how to interpret the response. As we pack up, I ask, using gestures as usual,

'Where are we going?'

'Soon,' he says.

Good enough.

Two eagles circle, high against the sky. Do they see us? Two small figures on horseback moving slowly over this curve of earth.

Elk, deer, buffalo, foxes, wolves, quail, sparrows, snakes, mice, all those creatures and the two of us on our horses.

Green and gold grass, red phlox, purple aster, many more flowers whose names I don't know in any language. Gooseberries, currants, cherries. Hawthorne, cottonwoods, aspen. Plum and red elderberry. The wild blue sky.

I follow him along a deer path through trees, a lively stream just to our right. We come to a small clearing, sunny in the middle, and dismount. I notice a shallow pit encircled with rocks. Fires have been built here.

He goes in the brush and pulls out what appear to be tipi poles. From his pack, he unrolls hides. He knows this place, he comes often, I think. Maybe others use it, too. I help assemble a small tipi. We put the buffalo hide down over the grass floor, place the blankets upon it. While he finishes pounding in the pegs, I gather firewood.

We build a fire. I turn to get the pot, but he stops me. He takes my hand and walks me back to the fire and turns me gently by the shoulders to face him. He lifts off my dress. He also undresses. I think he wants to make love, but he takes me by the hand and walks with me into the stream.

He washes the dust of travel off me in the chilly fast water and I wash him. We go back to the fire. He dries me with a soft skin but won't let me put on my dress. He gestures for me to wait. He goes into the tipi.

The sky directly above is yellow tinged with blue, some green as well, Fragonard's colours, my mother would say, the light is nacreous. I'm shivering, though the air is warm.

He emerges dressed in a breechclout of white cloth with red embroidery and is wearing beaded necklaces I've not seen before. He hands me something white and loosely folded. He hands it to me in a ceremonial way.

It is a dress of soft white doeskin decorated with wapiti teeth and silver and crystal beads in varying hues of blue, green, yellow, red, black. He slips the dress over my head. Then he takes off the necklaces and puts them on me, adjusting their drape over my breasts.

I do nothing. He does it all. He places a blanket on the ground and we sit. He combs my hair with a porcupine comb. Takes a small pouch attached to one of the sashes around his waist, dips two fingers into it and rubs a powder into the part on the crown of my head. He gently blends it onto the apples of my cheeks. I see the stain on his fingers. Vermilion. I remember Mary telling me that brides are adorned in this way. 'It is for the beloved,' she'd said.

He takes a pipe from a beaded pouch, fills it, lights it, takes a long draw, exhales and waves the smoke over his head and mine. I reach for the pipe. I have no idea if this is a right thing or a wrong thing, but I want to do what he has just done. He gives it to me. I mimic his actions. He chants softly.

We make love outside. We take a long time and then lie still together. I *feel* like 'the beloved', I feel like a bride. The moon is almost directly overhead before we think of food. We chew pemmican and drink tea.

I can see through his skin into the centre of his bones, the bones of his face, the hard, protruding cheekbones, the jaw, the chin that juts a bit, the straight brow bone and the strong nose. I can see into the marrow. I see his love for me. I feel mine for him so hard it makes me shake. I shake because the darkness that surrounds us seems impenetrable.

We are not always gentle. Sometimes we slam into one another. I take into my mouth every part of him I can and I always want more. We close our teeth on one another. It is not enough, so we pull harder, thrust harder, reach deeper. Sounds come out of my throat that I have never made before.

We are sometimes silly. We feed one another, pushing the food into one another's mouths with our hands, laughing like children. We race the horses. Wrestle in the grass. I roll him over and pin his shoulders to the ground, pull aside his clothes and lower myself on top of him. We keep our eyes open. We fall asleep entwined. We wake entwined.

'Where are we, my love?'

I ask in the way to which I've become accustomed, using gestures and without expectation. He points to the hills in front of us and to my astonishment, answers in English:

'You say, Big Horn. We say, Shining Mountains.'

He turns, points to the east and says,

'Powder River.'

Then gesturing beyond that, indicating some distance beyond, he says,

'Paha Sapa. Black Hills. *Home*.' And he pounds his fist over his heart.

'Please, *please* speak more English to me! You know many words. Why do you not use your English with me?'

He shakes his head and looks away. This makes me remember what Elizabeth had said about the danger of speaking your enemy's language. I don't want to think of Elizabeth. I don't want to be his enemy.

I wake in the deep dark. Listening. At first, I think the sound is the wind sighing in the trees, and then I know it's not and my skin prickles. The sigh becomes a moan and then another moan rises up from under the first, meets it and breaks off, then another rises, and the pack sings its ancient song.

I want to get up and go to them. Let them sing me into oblivion. I am already dead to that other world. We should not go back. We should just keep going. We should turn hard to the west and keep riding west and north. Go deep into the wild high mountains. Head for Canada. We'll live simply and come to a natural end.

Elizabeth comes into my mind again as if she's doing it through some magic of will. Even *thinking* of disappearing is betrayal. How can I leave her? And 'natural end'? This man and his people will not have a 'natural end', my people will see to that, and neither will I if I stay with him. That is how it is in these hideous times. I know this and I hate it.

He reaches for me and I grab his face with both hands.

'I will stay with you! Do you understand? *I will stay with you.*'

We are heading back to the camp. He is wearing his embroidered breechclout, a fringed buckskin shirt and leggings. I am wearing my white doeskin dress, my wedding dress, with the necklaces he gave me. There's vermillion in the part of my hair and on my cheeks. I will take my things from the tipi I've been sharing with her and move them into the tipi where I will live with my husband. *My husband.*

Saying these words does not ease my fear of facing Elizabeth.

CHAPTER 26

Ah, Lizzie. I had so badly misjudged my friend, as I'd done too many times and will do again and again. She was there to meet me, the whole camp having been alerted, of course, and she held out her arms to me. The first words she said were, 'How beautiful you look!' She gave me a gift, a horn bowl she'd found that had been discarded and that she'd polished so it shone and the light parts were nearly translucent. She helped me move my things from what had been our tipi into the one Far Cry's friends had already prepared for us.

She said she'd been horribly afraid I would not come back and her fear had made her furious with me. She'd again felt betrayed. But she told me she had prayed about it. She'd prayed I'd come back, and I had. She'd prayed for help forgiving me, and she hoped I'd forgive her. She'd prayed for my happiness and, Look! I seemed *very* happy. She *wanted* me to be happy. I believed her. This was Lizzie.

But who was I? If Far Cry had said, 'Let's go now', I'd have turned instantly and gone away with him into the wilderness. I'd have abandoned her. I hoped that she would be returned to her family, that she would be the one to leave me. I wanted to stay. I intended to stay.

We changed camp a few more times during that summer, never going far, just far enough to provide fresh pasture for the horses. The grass seemed to grow back quickly, and ours was not a huge string of animals. Some people had left, so there were fewer tipis, fewer horses, fewer mouths to feed. The work of the camp was what it always was and we did it along with the other women. Elizabeth had begun seating the children in a circle and teaching them Christian songs, children's hymns, that they'd repeat phonetically. The children enjoyed it and it made Lizzie happy. They had no idea what they were singing, neither did their mothers. No one seemed to mind. I wondered if Lizzie believed the words would penetrate, that translation would happen magically in their souls and the children would one day wake up loving Jesus.

Far Cry was often gone, hunting or raiding. On the morning of an expedition of some sort, I'd get his horse ready and hold the bridle while he mounted. His horse knew me now and was not too proud to nuzzle me. I thought I should stand at a sort of attention as some of the women did, but I stroked the horse and talked to him while I waited for Far Cry to emerge ready to leave.

He'd put his arms around me in a hug, and I would try to guess how long he'd be gone by how tightly he held me. I was never right. Once mounted, before riding off, he'd sit still and look at me for a moment. I'd stand and look back at him. Eye to eye, another ritual between us. I wondered how the rest of the camp felt about me being

Far Cry's 'wife'. Perhaps they gave it little thought. After all, one day there would be an exchange of hostages, and I would be gone.

I hated his absences. Sometimes, he would ride off by himself, I never knew why or how long he'd be gone. The other women — wives, mothers, grandmothers, sisters, aunties — were absolutely stoical, showing nothing of what they felt. The men went away from time to time, it was part of life. One hoped they came back whole. Sometimes they were clearly pleased to have the men gone.

The other half of our ritual was to greet him when he returned. There was plenty of warning, of course. The *akicita* would send someone to announce it, one of the boys would intercept the man and race to the camp shouting the news. The degree of excitement upon their return was proportionate to how long they'd been gone and why. If it had been a good while, there was a great bustling of activity as the women began to prepare food. The old people and children, and anyone who had not gone with the party, would gather outside the tipis. In addition to tending to the cooking pot, I'd tend to myself. If I had time, I'd quickly wash. I'd smooth my hair and change my clothes. By the time he came riding back with his men, I'd be stupid with desire. But I knew how to behave.

If they'd been hunting, there would be meat. If it had been a raid, the men came back painted and, if they'd been lucky, showing off stolen horses. Injuries were rare. I came to understand that the point for both sides was not to eliminate an enemy. If they did that, they'd eliminate an opportunity to show off the superiority of their horsemanship and the virtues of their horses, the quality of their weapons and their skill with them, their strategic abilities, their bravery, the magic of their songs. Boys would have no opportunity to prove they'd become men. It was who they were. A good strong enemy was a fine thing. Everyone played by the rules. The whites, on the other hand, did not respect such matters. Another reason to hate them.

When the men came back from a successful raid, after the feasting, there would be singing and dancing and acting out what had happened, showing off around the fire. Far Cry never took part in the dancing and storytelling, instead, he sat smoking with the older men. I would sit with Lizzie. If the women began a circle dance, one or two would come and grab our hands, make us join. I know it was Lizzie they wanted, but they'd include me. We both liked it. I'd catch a glimpse of her laughing face in the firelight and think, Ah! She'll come around! After a bit, she and I would leave the dancing and retire to our separate tipis. After a bit, Far Cry would join me.

Our lovemaking never again reached the levels of passion we'd found on our 'wedding' trip. I wondered about that, but did not feel deprived. Jake had shown off his prowess with a kind of theatrical ecstasy. This man would look at me lovingly as he undressed, then crawl under the robes without hurry. Our kisses were generous. He'd find his way, or I would guide him home. That wild passion had astonished me, but in so very many ways, this simple loving was better. Sometimes, we'd just fall asleep together without making love. And that, too, was lovely.

When he was away, Lizzie and I would eat together, sitting in front of one of our lodges. These were pleasant evenings. I remember Lizzie telling me it reminded her of summer evenings back home in New York.

'This is like sitting on our porch at home with my mother and a couple of friends, shelling peas and gossiping.

'Yes. This *is* nice. We had evenings like this, too.'

But I had never in my life sat on the veranda of my parents' home doing anything such as shelling peas. I had no idea who shelled the peas we ate. Ruth, who did most of the cooking? No, probably one or two of the black girls did it on the porch off the kitchen. Elizabeth had had a more 'normal' life than mine, filled with these sorts of homey activities. But now our situations were more similar. We were both women with husbands. Women-with-husbands. This was a culture unto itself and I allowed myself to imagine I was a part of it.

Elizabeth stretched, arching her back.

'I do miss having a chair to sit on, though.'

She told me there were two rocking chairs on the porch in front of the house William had built. They'd brought them from New York. After putting the boys to bed, and when the weather was gentle, she and William would sit there of an evening and William would play his guitar or his fiddle. I decided not to tell her about pulling my chair out of the dugout to drink whiskey, hoping to hear wolves, wondering if I should just go on and shoot myself. Good god! What might she have said about that!

Many of the old men had chair backs of woven willow that were a bit off the ground. We figured that in order to get such a thing one had to be old. And a man. We laughed about that. It was good to laugh with her.

We never tired of watching the children. We'd been around long enough to see them grow and change. It amused the hell out of me to watch them play war games. One side would put kerchiefs around their necks like soldiers. They lost every battle. They insisted on changing sides, after a bit, but no one wanted to be a *wasichu*.

The way the men ambled towards one tipi or another and gathered in the evenings reminded me of my father and his friends. Except for the whiskey. And that these men, our Lakota men, were good people. They would sit and smoke, talking very seriously. Or I would think it was serious until they'd all break out in sudden laughter. A few of the older boys hung around them, listening, trying to appear mature beyond their years. Learning.

The dogs lay quiet in front of the lodges. The warriors' horses — always tethered right outside, as was my own beautiful girl — would nod their heads. Gold bands of late sun slanted across the camp. Bits of dust and ash from the cook fires drifted into the light, blazed for an instant and disappeared in the constant stream of stuff drifting and rising and falling.

I remember thinking: *This* is what it is to be human. To sit in front of a fire among others, talking gently, keeping company as the sun goes down. Everything else is incidental, and the differences in these incidental customs can't possibly be worth the organised murder of war and the adding up of atrocities.

It was a naïve view, born of fatigue and the desire for love in a quiet time, for a kind of innocence I'd never known.

CHAPTER 27

Overnight, it seemed, the foliage lost its lustre. Leaves on some of the trees were brown at the edges and had a bitten look about them. Willows were suddenly yellow and the cottonwoods were getting there. The days were shorter and the nights were sometimes quite chilly. Several times, I'd seen Elizabeth standing in front of her tipi, looking at the sky. The joy that had been there in the height of summer, especially when she was with the children and their young mothers, was diminished. Greatly.

One late afternoon, when the men were gone and we were having supper together, she looked at me and her eyes were wet.

'I won't survive another winter, Sarah. My heart will break.'

I reached out and took her hand but could think of nothing to say. I had become certain we'd never be found. It had been too long. I thought it likely we'd been given up for dead. I had a personal theory, more a wish than a theory, that Far Cry must have made some other arrangement regarding the young men in jail, that this explained the lack of sign that negotiations were in progress regarding our exchange. It was a stupid wish.

Often over the summer, visitors had come to wherever we were encamped. Friends and relations of Far Cry's band never seemed to have difficulty finding us and they were always warmly welcomed. People would stay a few days and nights and there was usually feasting. People would go from tipi to tipi, but I never had to play hostess. I was never introduced in any formal way. My feelings about that were mixed. I wondered how Far Cry explained me to them. But maybe an Indian man was not asked about his woman, especially if there was something unusual about the arrangement. I had no idea.

The presence of strangers made me nervous, as if one day someone would come and Lizzie and I would be told that a deal had been struck, it was time to go. Nevertheless, I made certain I was well groomed, and that the tipi was tidy. Then I mostly stayed inside.

Late in the summer, however, a particular group of men came to the camp on two different occasions, intent on conducting serious business with Far Cry. They stood outside our tipi to speak with him and when I saw a particular muscle in his jaw contract, I gathered up my sleeping robes and joined Elizabeth. After their second visit, Far Cry rode off without speaking with me. I went back to our lodge and waited, sleepless. It was several hours before he returned. He got under the robes but turned his back to me.

In the morning, I asked him who those men were. I almost didn't expect an answer, but he surprised me with an English epithet I'd heard Jake use for the Indians in a ragged encampment around the fort, often drunk, wanting something from the soldiers they clearly couldn't get and yet they stayed.

'Loaf abouts.'

Then he spat a Lakota phrase and walked away. I'd seen the 'loaf abouts' at Laramie, and the men who had come to visit did not strike me as being like those rather derelict people. They'd angered Far Cry and yet he'd felt he had to receive them twice. I wondered why he called them 'loaf abouts'. I wondered if these men had some relationship with with one of the Army's forts that Far Cry didn't like.

Then came a visit from a group of five that included two older men wearing bonnets with eagle feathers. These were very clearly not 'loaf abouts'. These men had gravitas and obvious prestige. Far Cry greeted them with respect. He invited the men into his lodge. One of them greeted me in English, nodding his head and saying, 'Good evening'. I answered politely, served soup and retreated to Elizabeth's tipi. It shook me to be acknowledged by someone other than a member of our tight group. The talking went late into the night.

It was grey dawn when I heard them ride away. Elizabeth and I came outside and started a fire. Women who generally smiled a good morning to us — to Lizzie, at least — seemed unusually attentive to their own fires. She looked at me.

'This had to do with us. What do you think?'

'I don't know.'

But I strongly suspected she was right. I walked over towards Far Cry who was standing outside our lodge holding his horse's reins. He looked at me with no expression then got on his horse and rode off. He was gone four days. Nearly every night he was gone I dreamed of death. I could never remember upon waking whose death, but I was so consumed with anxiety I felt nauseous. One morning over coffee, Elizabeth pressed me.

'It is clear that something is going on that concerns our future and I find it hard to believe that you don't know *anything*.'

'Lizzie, I don't speak Lakota. Many things could be going on among all the different groups of people Far Cry's involved with. It doesn't always have to be about us.'

She was quiet for moment and then said, uncannily, some of what I'd mulled over myself.

'Sarah, think about this. Perhaps among those "friends and relations" who've visited over the summer there are those who are telling him to give us up. Perhaps the jailed Indian boys are in danger of being hung, or shot, and they want him to *do* something finally. Or perhaps these boys have already been killed. Perhaps there's a reward for our return, or a threat if we are not. With all these "friends and relations" coming and going all summer, don't you think it possible that *someone* has said something to someone else about the two white women in his camp? And that the word has spread, as it tends to do? And that Far Cry knows much that he's not making any effort to tell you?'

'I don't know, Lizzie, and I don't understand the point of this constant speculating. We'll know when we need to know. Let's eat our food and get on with the day.'

The sympathy I'd felt for her when she first told me her fears was becoming replaced by irritation. What she wanted, what I wanted, what we feared and why, who we were as people — none of this had ever really been compatible. Now the differences were starker. What she *hoped might* happen, I *feared would* happen. The fissure between us was widening.

When Far Cry returned he walked into the lodge purposefully and immediately set about gathering up and packing our things. When I stopped him to ask, he held me very tightly for a long moment, then released me.

'We go,' he said. I nodded. We packed.

I watched people watching us dismantle the lodge, the men standing in front of their own tipis or gathering in small groups. No one seemed to know what he was about and this made me particularly nervous. Before loading our things onto a travois, he went to speak to them, going from lodge to lodge, finally gathering the men together at Medicine Crow's tipi and going inside.

Elizabeth was horrified.

'What is this! *You're leaving?*'

But I knew nothing. When the men finally emerged and dispersed, people began to break camp. I helped Lizzie pack. People hitched their travoises, mounted up, and when they began to walk the horses out a bit, it became clear that the village had separated into two groups.

Fewer than twenty people were going with Far Cry: his closest men with their families, and a few young warriors without wives, people who, it occurred to me, could move fast if necessary. The older ones and most of the women and children, most of Elizabeth's favourite families, were with the other group. Elizabeth looked at me as if I were responsible.

'This is unbearable! Unbearable not to know what is happening!'

'I'm sorry, Lizzie. I don't know. I wish to hell I did.'

Medicine Crow and Laughing Woman, the only people who knew a bit of English and who seemed to genuinely like me, were among that other group. It hurt my heart. I embraced Laughing Woman and we both had tears in our eyes. Medicine Crow took from around his neck a small beaded pouch on a leather thong, a spirit pouch, he called it, and put it around my neck.

'Strong for you,' he said, 'will help you stay strong.'

And the two of them turned to mount up.

Elizabeth and I got on our horses. Elizabeth, tears streaming down her face, was waving and calling out farewells, as the others, many of the young women also tearful, rode away from us. Wanting to go closer to say farewell to some children she loved, Lizzie began to trot in their direction. Suddenly, three of Far Cry's men surrounded us. One blocked her way, and then the three flanked us and herded us back towards the group following Far Cry. Elizabeth shouted at me.

'Do you see, Sarah? *We're captives! Nothing more!*'

Her pain moved me, but my sense of things felt solid. I had been a captive, but I'd become something else. I would miss my friends, but I was glad we were moving.

We traveled due west when the season's logic would have been to go south. I did not know what Far Cry was doing, but I liked the way it felt and knew I had to be careful not to let Lizzie see this. It had become easy to keep my feelings hid behind my face. The journey felt endless, and I liked that as well. It involved fording a wide, rough river. A few travoises were lost, but the people all got across safely. We camped on the other side and in the morning, I wondered in what direction he'd take us and was pleased when we continued west. We entered into an ever-wilder terrain of jagged peaks, deep ravines with pines growing out of the rocks. The difficulty of this passage required strict attentiveness to one's horse. I'd named her Pretty Thing.

Far Cry was more than usually cold in front of the others, but more than usually ardent at night. Following his example, I feigned indifference to him as we rode. I enjoyed hiding my strong pleasure in the distance we were placing between ourselves and everything that was part of that other life. When Elizabeth caught my eye, I smiled and pretended not to see her despair.

There was nothing in the world to think about but this movement from *what had been* to *what would be.* The farther we moved away from the former, the happier I was within the small of circle of *what is now*: that place in time and space under the robes with my love.

When we finally came to rest in the place it appeared we'd stay for a while, I found to my surprise that I wanted to keep traveling. I felt restive and short-tempered. But then I began to take in the shattering grandeur of where we were. The mountains appeared to have forced themselves up from the earth's crust with great violence, it was a place both majestic and deadly and it felt utterly remote which pleased me to my core.

The travoises were unloaded and people began putting up tipis along the broad banks of a stream. Far Cry and I put up ours then

I looked for Lizzie and went to help her. One of the other women joined us. When that was done, Lizzie and I stood in front of it, looking out at the stream and the mountains in silence. At some point, we looked up to see a chevron of geese flying south.

CHAPTER 28

Have I told you how beautiful he was? Have I written of this? My lover, my husband. I asked him once, during that trip, about his religion. He pointed to the sky and said, '*Wakan tanka*.' I assumed this was his people's name for their chief god. Then he used a gesture to include everything around us — sky, water, dirt, grass, me, even the coffee we sipped — and he said, 'All is *wakan*'. I took that to mean that everything was holy. This made beautiful and perfect sense. It reminded me of how I had felt as a child alone in the woods.

I will tell you about his face. His cheekbones and nose were the perfect mould of strength (think of the profiles on ancient Roman coins), yet his mouth was sensuous. His lips were beautifully shaped. Apollo would have been envious of those lips. I wanted them on every part of me, every chance I got.

His eyes were long and different from one another. His right eye was the same size as his left, but it was never opened as widely, as if the lid lay more heavily on it. This eye was thoughtful, it took things in as they came, rested softly on things that pleased him. This eye expressed his tenderness and, perhaps because I knew the story of his murdered wife and baby, his profound sadness. I also saw in this gentle eye, his capacity to love.

His left eye was opened wider than the other, and was hard. This eye scanned the terrain like that of a hawk or an eagle, looking for trouble, ready to go at it. It could be cruel. Whites used such clichéd descriptions as proof of the primitive nature of his people, of how 'savage' they were. And he could be savage when he had to be. So could I. I admired the qualities reflected in this eye. He had to be vigilant. My people wanted him dead.

It was a face full of complexities. It could, when he chose, be impenetrable. But when he chose to show his love and his humour — his humour was always a delightful surprise! — his face moved me like no human face ever had. I remember hoping his child would look like him.

CHAPTER 29

I had not known the early signs. And when they became too much to ignore, I still managed to push them out of my mind most of the time. While traveling with the Indians in the first months of our captivity, neither Elizabeth nor I had bled with any regularity. In fact, we'd barely bled at all. She had been relieved when she first bled as she hadn't been entirely sure whether or not she'd been raped by the Indian who beat her and nearly scalped her. But the bleeding was either less than we remembered or more, and would come unexpectedly or not at all.

The hunger and sickness of the winter further interfered with our bodies' functioning. When we did begin to bleed somewhat normally, we were discomfited by the lack of the right sort of cloths. The women used what I think was milkweed fluff wrapped in something, we watched them gather it, but that was a seasonal thing. Mary had already died, and we were too shy to ask anyone else. We bled onto our clothing, washing them as needed.

I learned later that some Indians insisted that women sleep in their own small tipis while they were bleeding. It was considered bad medicine for the men to come into contact with them — the hunt would go bad, or a raid would end in deaths and injuries — but Far Cry and his people didn't hold with that.

I must have become pregnant the first time Far Cry and I made love. Whenever it had happened, it had happened. I couldn't remember when I'd last bled. My breasts that had always been small, were swollen and sore, and there was a roundness where I'd been shallow between my hipbones. I was afraid to tell Elizabeth and afraid to tell Far Cry.

Elizabeth was still considerably chilled towards me since the separation from her friends and the incident with Far Cry's men. While traveling, I hadn't cared, being too involved with myself and my love. Now that we'd returned to the kind of domestic routine in which we'd formerly shared every little thing, and *now*, in particular, I needed her. I pursued her forgiveness, appealing to her in every way I could think of short of simply asking for it. And, finally, as I trusted she would, because of her generous nature, she softened. I still could not bring myself to tell her.

But one morning, sipping tea outside her tipi — Far Cry was gone again and I did not know where or why — when I got up to stretch my back that ached constantly, I let drop the blanket I'd draped over my shoulders and I saw her notice the movement of my breasts under my loose doeskin.

'*Sarah!*'

I burst into tears. She stood up and gathered me in her arms as I cried.

'Oh, no', she said over and over. 'Oh, no, oh no.' And then she said, 'This is *horrible!*'

I pulled away from her sharply. I was frightened in many ways, but I hated hearing her say that my pregnancy was 'horrible'. I asked her to *please* not say that again. She sat down and regarded me seriously. She motioned for me to sit down.

'Sarah. I'm sorry, I should not have been so sharp. But... Oh, Sarah. With you bearing his child, he will not want to give you up. What will that mean for *us?* Forgive me, but how can I not ask this?'

I told her I had no idea. I didn't know what to think. I could not stop crying and she took pity on me.

'Come. Drink your tea. We won't talk about that now. We must first think of your health. *And* the health of your child. It is, after all, a gift from God.'

Though I noticed she'd not said this with great enthusiasm, for once, I was grateful for her religiosity. As her feelings for Mary Small Wing had grown upon learning of her pregnancy, her feelings for me seemed to soften and deepen. Her nature was compassionate. She said that no matter what happened she would help me stay healthy. She did. She watched to see that I ate well and ate enough. She insisted I sleep with her whenever Far Cry was away. She insisted I nap in the afternoons. She tried to take over many of my tasks, but I wouldn't let her. She mothered me. She kept her fears to herself.

I was sick with it, which she assured me was normal. But often while vomiting behind the tipi I would retch so hard that I thought the little thing might be ejected. There were times I hoped it would be. Lying awake at night, I'd talk to it, tell it to leave me, that I would not know how to care for it, that I wasn't fit to be its mother. Sometimes, in fear and anger, I told it I wanted it to die. That because of it, I might lose both my lover and my only friend.

I told it the world was a cruel, unforgiving place, that as a half-breed, it would be treated badly. I begged it to leave me. I made myself work hard when Elizabeth told me to rest. Sometimes, I put my finger down my throat after I ate to deny both of us nourishment. While having a bowel movement, I'd squeeze hard enough to invert my guts, hoping the contractions would abort it.

But it was strong. It held on. It grew.

One night, lying in the robes, before Far Cry had come back from visiting with a few of his men, I thought I felt it move. Then I thought it must have been my imagination, or a minor upset in my belly. But whether I'd felt the baby move or not, in that moment, I strongly sensed its life. The baby was speaking to me, telling me that it *would* live, in spite of me. And, suddenly, in that moment, *I wanted it to live*. I wanted to have this child. I whispered into the robes that the two of us would live together or die together. I could no longer separate myself from it, our fates were conjoined.

From that point on, I spoke to it nearly constantly, in whispers and silently. I told it I belonged to it as it belonged to me and confessed my anguish at ever having felt otherwise. I begged it to forgive me. I told it I would protect it from harm. I could feel it coiled in there, hearing me, understanding me, knowing me, loving me. I told it how much I loved it. And, oh, I did love it. There were times I was beside myself with joy. Lizzie saw and was happy for me. Or she appeared to be, for my sake.

Far Cry returned late one night from one of his sudden solitary departures, having been gone for about ten days. An unusually long time during which I was not only sick with the pregnancy, but sick with fear for him. Usually, if he came back late at night, he slept alone in our lodge and greeted me in the morning. This night, he stood outside Elizabeth's tipi and softly said my name, a thing he never did. I got up and came into our lodge. I built a small fire inside, as the night was cold, then we undressed and lay together under the heavy sleeping robes. I'd missed him horribly. He began to stroke me and then stopped abruptly, yanked off the robes. By the dim light of the fire, he looked hard at my body, felt my belly, weighed my breast in his hand, looked into my eyes. He knew.

It was the only time I ever saw him weep. We held one another and wept together.

My heart is still not healed from everything that followed and there is much that followed. I hate to hear people say that suffering, when it comes, is 'God's will'. I've seen too many innocents suffer at the hands of people who say this in sanctimonious tones, brandishing their god's name like a battle flag. I have utter contempt for that god and his cruelty, and for that god's believers who do cruelty in his name.

Neither do I like to hear, 'Time heals all wounds'. It doesn't. Rather, you get intimate with sorrow. It becomes part of who you are. Not like a thorn that might get wrapped around by tough skin keeping it *in* the body but not *of* it, sorrow penetrates, spreads to every part of you, mixes with older pain, mixes with joy. One eye is dead, I see clearly with the other. It's all one.

But this philosophising comes in the luxury of reflection. During the time of which I'm now writing, the fear of the losses and the pain I knew was coming, was nearly unbearable. It clouded my reason.

CHAPTER 30

It was mid-morning and I was still lying in my sleeping robes. I heard riders. Very few, it sounded like, and approaching slowly. I listened to the dogs, to people's voices. These were not 'close friends or relations', but they were not unwelcome. I'd stay where I was. Visitors made me uncomfortable. Besides, I had awakened tired to the marrow, as I did often, and somewhat nauseous.

Elizabeth burst in. We had, through an unspoken sense of what was proper, never entered one another's lodges without asking permission. Before she was even entirely through the opening, she spoke breathlessly:

'A white man is here! A priest, I think, and there's a woman with him, an Indian woman. We must speak with him. Hurry! Come!'

Sudden terror. I was not certain my bowels would hold.

'I can't, Lizzie. I'm sick.'

'Did you not hear me properly? *A white man!* Come! We must catch him before he goes, ask for his help.'

She grabbed my arm and pulled at it, trying to get me to sit up. I shook her off.

'Lizzie, stop! I'm feeling too poorly this morning. You go ahead.'

'What? *No!* Pull yourself together, Sarah. This could be... Who knows what this could be. You *must* come! Will you come?'

As she was speaking, my head cleared and I realised that I *had* to come.

'Yes, yes, of course. But give me a moment to make myself presentable.'

'Let me help...'

'No. Please, Lizzy, just wait outside. And *wait* for me. Don't go without me. I will be only a moment.'

'Hurry!'

A white man. She'd said a priest. Traveling with an Indian woman. Why would a priest come all the way out here? But this was beside the point. He was a *wasichu*, so he was the enemy. I could not let

Elizabeth speak with him alone, she would give us away. I needed to direct the conversation and I had no idea how. My legs shook as I dressed myself and neatened my hair.

'*Sarah!*'

I walked outside feeling as if I had no blood in my veins. Elizabeth's excitement was nearly intolerable. She tilted her head towards my face, her eyes wide, and whispered,

'This man has been sent by God!'

'That's what you said about the trader who then raped you.'

She stared, looked surprised as if I'd slapped her, then shook it off, put her arm around my waist and pulled me forward, walking fast. A toddler intercepted us, leaping at Elizabeth who, without slowing down, swooped her up and carried her on her hip to meet the priest.

A white man and an Indian woman, neither of them young, were removing packs from their horses. The man wore a threadbare cassock that had once been black. A simple wooden cross and several beaded necklaces hung down and over the top of his round belly.

His round head was bare and bald except for a fringe of white tufts. The woman's dark hair was grey-streaked. They were both small and round with round, smiling faces. They looked like people who spent a lot of time in the sun. They looked like happy people. I could see they had great sweetness about them, but I would not let myself be seduced. Lizzie obviously hoped they'd be the agents of our rescue. I was not in need of 'rescue', didn't want any part of it.

They'd spread a blanket on the ground and were setting out cakes of soaps, jars of honey, rolled lengths of ribbons — a very popular item, the young women sighed to see them — strings of beads, folded pieces of printed cotton in various sizes, and other small items to trade. Several of the women had already gathered to look, and the priest was speaking with them softly in Lakota.

When he saw us, his mouth opened in a wide O as if he might begin to sing. He walked to meet us beaming with delight, arms open. Elizabeth greeted him in a voice ringing with joy, as if he were a long lost relative..

'*Hello! Hello!*'

'Ah! Quelle surprise de voir commes vous! Mes chers jeune femmes! Qui êtes-vous?'

With his first words, I felt as if a door had cracked open and from another room, I'd heard the sounds of a solution. The language he spoke offered a way, if I could think of it. And, if having thought of it, I could rise to it. If I could rise to it, I could direct this situation. I must rise to it. Elizabeth turned to me.

'That is French, is it not? And you know French!'

'Some, yes. Do you?'

'No, not a word. What did he say?'

'He said it was a surprise to see people like us and asked who we are.'

'Well, speak to him! Tell him!'

I gathered myself and began tentatively:

'Bonjour, monsieur! Je peux imaginer comment vous seriez surpris. Parlez-vous Anglais?'

'Non, je suis désole. Mais vous parlez Français très bien!'

'Un petit peu. Pêre? Frêre? Monsieur?'

The man said I must call him Jean. 'Tout simplement, Jean!' He said he was an 'ancien prêtre', a *former* priest. Then he began telling his story as if delighted for the chance to tell it to someone who might understand. He'd fallen in love with this woman — here he turned to her and they smiled at one another — and, though he'd loved the priesthood no less for loving her and perhaps more, as she was God's gift to him, he was told he could not keep a wife yet continue to be a priest.

He shrugged, smiling. He loved his story. He'd made his choice and married his beloved and been expelled from his order. But that was a long time ago. Now, if anyone desires his priestly help — to be confessed, to be married, to pray at a death, to baptise a child — he is pleased to do these things in God's name. He is still a servant of God and so is his wife, though she also believes in the old gods of her people. It is all the same, he said. 'C'est le même, le même.' They were traveling south from Canada and lived by the kindness of others and the few things they were fortunate enough to trade. He was very happy to make our acquaintance.

Elizabeth was impatient.

'What is he saying?'

'He was a priest once but he fell in love with this woman, and...'

'Ah. Do you think you could ask him how far we are from an American fort? We must tell him that we're...'

'Elizabeth. I know what to tell him.'

'Of course you do. Forgive me. Please, continue.'

I was trying to think of what to say to him when he asked how such as we had come to be with these Indians. He had told his story and now he wanted to hear ours. I was afraid he might have heard, as those other traders had, of two white women with a small band of Lakota, but he did not say anything suggesting this. He asked,

'Êtes-vous Americaines? D'où êtes-vous?'

I told him that, yes, we were Americans and that we were from the east. Then I choked. I could not think of what to say or how to say whatever I might think of. I forced myself to continue, saying it was very difficult to explain our situation. Then I was lost. The silence was sickening. To fill it, I feigned a coughing spell.

'Sarah, are you well?'

I nodded, smiling, coughing, gasping, clearing my throat, smiling some more, sputtering like an idiot.

'Can you not speak? Are you ill?'

'No, I'm all right.'

'Good. Then continue, continue. You must tell him who we are. Tell him *now*. We are desperate, sir. Gather your wits, Sarah. Explain that we...

'Elizabeth! Do not press me.'

'I know, I know, but... please. *Tell him everything.*'

As Lizzie and I were speaking, Jean had been watching us, examining us, sensing the tension between us, or so I imagined. I saw that he was aware of Elizabeth's urgency. Perhaps he'd caught the word 'desperate'.

He smiled at the baby as she played with Lizzie's hair. He smiled when she kissed the child, put her down and shooed her towards the women speaking with his wife. He noticed my doeskin dress with its fringes, and Elizabeth's calico dress, like that worn by many of the

Indian women. I saw him notice our skin, coloured by the sun, and our arms, strong from the work we did.

I began to see him from an oblique angle and a bit of a distance. He said he'd made a choice to go against the rules. He'd broken a holy promise, left his own kind for the sake of love. His words about his god and his wife's gods being the same had stuck in my head: 'C'est le même, le même.' And, suddenly, I knew how to begin. The rest would follow. *Something* would have to follow.

I apologised for my poor French and repeated that, yes, we were Americans, as he had guessed, but that we had been away from our people for a long time. By now, they certainly believed we were dead. But, I said, there existed a far more serious problem. A desperate problem.

He was immediately attentive, said he'd suspected something was wrong. He understood my friend had asked about an American fort and he was sorry to tell us that we were a very long distance from the immigrant road and its forts. But he said that he and his wife might come nearer to them as their journey south and east progressed. Was there anything he could do for us?

Elizabeth broke in.

'Sarah, I can't stand not knowing what you're saying. You must tell him to go to the nearest fort as soon as he can. He must tell them...'

I abruptly lifted my hand to stop her. Her response had hit too close to the mark. I was taken aback. Jean had understood a bit of her English. She said she did not *speak* French, but had she understood some of what he'd said? Might she know more than she admitted to?

'Lizzie, are you following *any* of what is being said?'

'*No!* I don't know French. I told you.'

'Not even a little?'

'Why are you asking me this! You should be...'

'Calm yourself. The others must not see this conversation is at all fraught. I will tell him everything he needs to know. But please, *please* do not interrupt me again. I can't concentrate. It's difficult enough to find the right words, especially as I'm feeling ill. I want to be certain he understands everything perfectly.'

'Of course. Forgive my impatience, dear. Go on, please, go on.'

I told him that I had been moved by his story about having fallen in love and making a difficult choice. I said I understood him perfectly, that we — gesturing to Elizabeth and I — had also made a hard choice. That it had been, in some ways, the same choice he had made, 'Le même. Le même.'

I began inventing a tale and, as I told it, was amazed at how it fell into place. The words rushed one after the other, often ahead of my ability to put them in French, making me stutter. I told him that as young girls on the way west, our families had been attacked, parents killed and we had been taken captive by the Indians. But that had been long ago. We had been with the Indians a long time. As he could see, my friend now has a dear child by her Indian husband. I also have a husband I love — I gestured vaguely towards the camp — and a child coming. I told him that we were happy with these people. Because part of this was true, the part that was not, *felt* true enough.

'Nous sommes heureux.'

We are happy. It felt good to say it, so I said it again.

'Nous sommes très heureux avec ces gens.'

A slick of sweat came on my upper lip. He'd asked what he could do for us. There was only one answer. I had to make very clear that he must tell no one, *absolutely no one*, that he had seen us. I implored him.

'Je vous en prie, mon cher Jean, *absolument personne.*'

Then I added: 'Ou nous sommes mort.' Or we are dead.

I'd gone too far. My jaw shook in a spasm that, for a second, I couldn't control. He made a movement with his head, pulling it back a bit in surprise. I had no idea how to follow this statement. I did not know with what words I could explain it. But my justification for the lie was all around me in the surprising warmth of this day in the Moon of Leaves Turning Brown. These good people. My lover. The baby. This was my life. I would hold on to it any way I could.

I had to say the right thing and I had to say it right then. The two of them were waiting, I could hear them breathing. I opened my mouth and, somehow, again, words came out.

I've tried to remember exactly what I said, but I cannot. Something about being named as traitors in a time of war. We gave information to the Indians that helped them win a big battle not that long ago in which all the American soldiers at one of the forts had been killed. We had seen terrible things done in reprisal and in evil malice, *méchanceté*, to people we had come to love. Our loyalties were with the Indians. I told him again that we were in danger for our lives. If found, we'd be hung for treason.

I was afraid he would question me for details, but I had used up all the words I knew, had exhausted everything I had. I was done. My legs were shaking. To break yet another horrible silence, I told him again that no one must know where we are. *No one.* '*Personne, personne.*'

'Très grave,' he said. I nodded.

He looked at us for what felt a very long time. Then he reached out and took our hands in his, leaned into us and said with sincere emotion,

'N'ayez pas peut. Confiance en Dieu. Tout ira bien, mes enfants, tout ira bien.'

Elizabeth turned to me.

'*Please!* Sarah!'

'He said we must not be afraid, to trust in God, that all will be well.'

We could not rejoice openly, of course, we whispered our gratitudes, our very different gratitudes, which he accepted simply. Then he gestured for us to follow him over to the blanket and gave us each a bar of lavender soap. 'Savon a la lavande!' he said, kissing his fingers as if it were something good to eat. The little girl came running up and pulled at Lizzie's skirts. She picked her up and smacked her cheek with many kisses, making her squeal with delight. They walked back towards the centre of the village to find the child's mother.

Alone with Jean, I thanked him again. I looked directly into his eyes, wanting to make certain he had understood all I'd tried to tell him.

'Vous me comprenez?'

'Oui. Je vous comprends, ma chère enfant. Tout ira bien.'

I went back to my tipi and lay down. I held the fragrant soap to my nose. I had crossed a line. I had betrayed my friend. But what else was there to do? That spring, I'd killed to save Elizabeth. Today I'd lied to save myself and my unborn child. In order to survive, it can sometimes be necessary to do evil. But this was not evil, I told myself. This was for the best. For her as well, once she surrendered to it. Her family had surely gone on with their lives. We must go on with ours.

Elizabeth came into the tipi, again without announcing herself, but it was alright this time.

'Now, tell me *everything* you said and everything he said.'

'Yes, of course. Would you like some tea?'

As I prepared the tea, I told her that I had responded to his story, told him ours, that he had said he would help, that all would be well. Elizabeth, of course, wanted more, but I was empty.

'I told him everything, my dear. Please don't make me repeat it word for word, I'm exhausted. You must trust me.'

'And what did he say?'

'He said he understood the gravity of our situation and that he would help in any way he could. He told us not to be afraid. That all will be well.'

'You're certain he understood you?'

'Yes. Quite certain.'

'Oh, let it happen! Let this be God's will.'

'Yes. Let it be. Do you feel better now?'

'Oh, my dear friend!'

She sighed. Then she looked at me appraisingly.

'You do look peaked. I have a soup bubbling, come eat, then sleep this afternoon. This could be it, Sarah! A wait, of course, I am prepared for that, but this could be the end of... of all this. I will see my little boys! My husband!'

The love in her voice gave me pause.

'Lizzie, I don't think we should place all our hopes on what this man might be able to do. He said we're far from the trail...'

'I know all that. I'm not an idiot. But I must trust in God and then, of course, I will accept whatever is His will. But I have a good feeling about this man, and *I will hope!* You know this about me.'

I did. I had my own hopes for the future.

Jean and his wife did not stay long. As they were packing up their things with the help of some of the women, he saw us sitting outside Elizabeth's tipi and walked over.

He told us — I translated for Lizzie as he spoke — that they had been working their way slowly south from Canada for many weeks. His wife believed she was nearing her death. She'd been separated from her sister as a child, both having been captured by different tribes, and she'd come of age with the Ojibwe. She did not remember who her original people were and did not know where her sister might be found, but she had a strong sense she must go into the country of the Southern Cheyenne. She could feel in her heart that her sister was also searching, and that they would find one another. She wanted to see her sister's face before she died. They had no children, no other relatives, so they'd begun this pilgrimage together. Jean said it might be God's will they would both die on this journey.

Then he shrugged. 'Mais peut-être pas!' But perhaps not.

He was a good man. Lizzie believed he would save us. I felt he already had. *Tout ira bien.*

Our people waved as they rode away.

CHAPTER 31

It had become common, now, to see frost on the ground in the early morning before the sun was well up. The nights were cold and the top branches of the trees along the riverbanks were mostly bare. One morning the men sat outside their lodges, cleaning their guns. New arrows were being made and bows restrung. Preparing for the autumn hunt.

The men gathered early one fine morning a few days later. I readied Far Cry's hunting horse. I'd put on my white dress with the wapiti teeth, my wedding dress. I always wanted him to be proud when we appeared together in public. He was wearing his red shirt. (I never did learn the full story behind the shirt. It has remained one of the mysteries about him. It doesn't matter.) He placed his hands on my shoulders and pulled me to him. We held one another tightly, then he mounted and rode off with the other men. We women trilled until they were away from the camp, and then we turned back to daily life.

These were good days. I might look up and the sky would be an absolute, ultramarine blue. When I looked into it deeply, it would pulse like a living thing. But that night, a wind might blow, and keep blowing the next day and maybe the next and the next. The sky might then hang low, dense and slate-coloured, with the gold and crimson leaves in contrast against it.

Sometimes in the early morning a mist white as milkweed fluff would move down the river into the camp, keeping low over the ground, stealing among the tipis. Then the sun would pierce through and drive it off. At sunset, the whole western sky would be on fire.

There was goldenrod in the meadows, and something that made a purplish haze. The wild plums along the stream were almost ripe. I took this beauty into myself hungrily, savouring every little thing. These images were so imbued with love, they became Love, and on this foundation, I built my dreams. A sort of religion, I guess, and I was every bit as fervent with mine as Lizzie was with hers. I made sentences that, strung together, were a prayer.

I will have Far Cry's baby. We will be a family. I will help Lizzie learn to love these good people. We will move yet deeper into Indian country, yet farther away from whites and their forts and their roads. We will move out of range of their guns, always bigger and more lethal than ours. We will move away from their greed and their lies. We will remove ourselves from the horrors of this endless war that we cannot win on their terms. Lizzie and I will forget what we need to forget. The days will follow one upon the other and we will live our lives.

The falling leaves skittered across the ground and into the tipis, delighting the babies. I remember stopping from time to time, looking around me and thinking, this must be what people mean when they say *happiness*. How surprising this is! To be *happy*.

And then it was over.

It happened on a day of brilliant sun.

The Five Important Men, as I'd begun to call them, those men who had been serious with Far Cry and polite to me, had come a few more times. With the last visit, when they left in late afternoon, Far Cry had gone with them, without ceremony or explanation. I was, as always, in a state of horrible apprehension until he returned a few days later.

Lizzy had asked me about those men once, in her perpetual fear for our status, and I'd been unpleasant. She had not asked again. But I had come to believe — in fact, I was certain — that these men were negotiating with Far Cry about us, his captives. I prayed hard to every god I could think of that they would find a way to return Lizzy to her family. And I prayed they would leave me here, with mine.

The afternoon before the day it happened, Far Cry and I made love. He built a small fire inside and threw in some sweet smelling herbs, then surprised me with a playful seduction. We were with one another as we'd been in the beginning: the loving looks, the gentle kisses, the strong kisses. Naked on our sleeping robes, he stroked my round belly and whispered to the baby in Lakota. 'What did you say?' He shook his head. We lay together from early afternoon until nearly dusk, when he got up. He dressed quickly, then, and began gathering his things.

He said he was going to meet old friends and relations, some Cheyenne, who were encamped not too far away at a place known to all the Indians. He pointed north and east, and from his description, I was fairly sure I knew the place he meant. We'd been there together a couple of times, and he'd told me that many people used it for sun dances. He then said — and he was careful to make himself under-stood, as if to make clear the importance of these plans — that tomor-row morning, Lizzy and I must ride out together to meet him, with some of our good friends, people who knew the way. We must arrive before the sun was at its highest. He would be waiting with others whom I would be happy to see. He mounted his horse, leaned down and stroked my face, then rode off with a few of his men. He was not wearing his red shirt, but I had watched him pack it in his roll.

I wondered if these Cheyenne might be some of Mary Small Wing's people. I could not understand why he had to go out ahead of me, why we could not have gone together. Our afternoon had been so sweetly intimate. But as with so many other questions, I did not ask and I would not let myself dwell on it.

Later that evening, over supper, I told Elizabeth about the plans for the following day. Anything that departed from the ordinary tended to unnerve her, so I invented a bit. I told her that this gathering *was* with Mary Small Wing's people and would bring together families that hadn't seen one another for a long time. There was to be a celebration. I was relieved when she received the idea warmly.

As I told her my version of the plans, elaborating on the beauty of the place and other details that I can't remember now, I began to believe in them. It *might* have been true, all of it was possible. I began to look forward to the next day. In addition to whatever else it would bring, I told Lizzie I was eager for Pretty Thing to have a good gallop.

I had never thought of a better name, but called her that from the day Far Cry gave her to me, my fast little spotted horse, my Pretty Thing. I loved her as much as I'd loved any horse I'd ever had, as much as Pegasus, maybe even more. I'd loved one or two dogs this well, and had befriended a couple of the camp dogs from puppy-hood, they were good dogs. But Pretty Thing was an important companion in the way only certain animals can be: intuitive, patient, unequivocally loving.

'Sarah, did Far Cry say how long we might stay?'

'He did not. But I think we should prepare to stay several days. It will be nice, I think, don't you?'

'Yes. It sounds wonderful.'

We said goodnight and went to our tipis. I don't recall whether or not I slept. Perhaps I did. I was always tired those days.

The morning it happened, I am changing into my wedding dress when I hear Lizzie's voice outside. I step out into the dazzling air, the sun on its way to the meridian, to see Lizzie smiling down at me from her horse. With her are six men, Far Cry's companions. They're carrying bows and guns, they nod in greeting. Good company, but where are the women? I'd thought the party would be larger. Perhaps some had left earlier and I hadn't heard them, or perhaps they'd join us later. I hadn't noticed who'd remained in camp.

Lizzie and I are riding side by side at a walk, the men in no particular order behind us. We've left the shade of woods and are squinting in the sun, now directly overhead. The land is higher here and rolls. We're climbing a long grassy hill rich in wildflowers, more trees are off to the left. In the distance ahead, the hills rise higher, with snow still on the peaks.

'How beautiful it is today!'

'It is! Lizzie! When we get to the top of this rise, let's run the ponies. We might see them on the other side, we should be almost there.'

'Yes! But you'll have to hold *her* back a bit!'

We laugh. Boys would ask to borrow Pretty Thing hoping to win races, she did so love to run, but I never let them.

As we make our way up the hill, three of the men move up to Lizzie's left, so we're in a row with the other three just behind. I'm more or less in the clear on the right. Some are watching the ridge, but I see that others keep looking off to the left towards the woods. I'm wondering about this when I hear it, only faintly at first because the wind is brisk and coming from behind.

'Lizzie, do you hear that?'

'What? I don't hear anything...'

'Listen! Music. I think it's music.'

'Oh, yes. Now I hear *something*. What is it?'

I pull Pretty Thing to a stop. We all stop. We are less than a hundred yards from the crest of the hill. We stand there listening, trying to figure out what it is we are hearing, because the sounds are wrong, they don't belong on this hillside, in this day of sun and birdsong. Then the wind shifts, and now I hear it clearly and so does Lizzie and we both know what it is. I see that the men have lifted their rifles. Lizzie raises her head to the heavens.

'*They've come! My God! They've come!*'

Brass instruments, pumping out a melody, piercing descant of pipes, percussion of trotting hooves, and up over the rise, the big horses, the blue uniforms, banners with gold fringe flapping, sun flaring off brass, the garish striped flag, whipping in the wind.

I yank Pretty Thing's head up sharply so she rears and pivots. We make a run back down the hill, heading for the cover of the woods down there. I hear Lizzie screaming, '*SARAH! NO! NO! NO! NO!*'

Horses are behind me now, heavy horses, cavalry horses, but in the corner of my eye, there's Far Cry, I see his red shirt, there's a band of warriors with him riding in fast from where our men had been looking, they'd been looking for Far Cry and here he comes riding hard! Then again she shouts my name, but her voice gets lost because we're in the woods now, dodging, jumping, turning this way, that way, and my head is low, pressed hard against Pretty Thing's neck, I feel the heat of her muscle, smell her skin, she's breathing hard, her hooves are pounding and I'm shouting, *Faster, faster, faster, faster!*

I hear shots but it's back there on the hill, they're fighting one another and we are getting away — *we are getting away, we will get away!* — and then I hear a crashing from behind us, they are in the trees too now, the cavalry, I hear them close behind us in the trees, getting closer.

Of what followed, I remember these two things:

The whiz of one bullet as it passed very close to the side of my face.

The crash of another as it shattered the hard bone of my pony's head and we went down.

And that is all I remember of our 'rescue'.

PART TWO

WINTER AT FORT LARAMIE

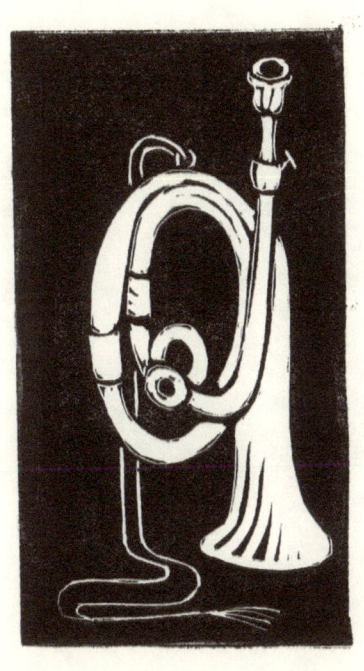

Her body. I remember when they pulled her body out of my body. I remember astonishing pain. I remember that the doctor didn't want me to hold her. Elizabeth was there and the woman I later learned was named Mary. I remember begging them to please not take her from me, I remember the pathetic sound of my voice and that it seemed to be coming from somewhere else in the room. They placed her in the nook between my breast and my left arm and I covered her body with my right hand. I could cover her entire body with my hand. She was still warm. I fell asleep. When I woke she was cold and I let the woman take her.

I remember periods of dark and light and dark again. I remember that sometimes I lay in the dimness of a single low lantern flame, wanting the deeper dark of unconsciousness to come back. I remember the taste of laudanum. The woman named Mary mixed it with water, and the sound of the spoon against the glass as she stirred the tincture filled me with gratitude.

The light increased bit by bit and became the natural light of very early morning. It was coming from a window off to my right. I was lying on a wide bed with a low wood frame in a big room. The wall across from the bed, many feet away, was dominated by a large armoire of dark wood slightly to the left of centre. In the middle of the wall to the right was a window. Pale curtains covered dirty glass panes. A round table of dark wood with graceful legs, large enough for two people to sit at and enjoy a meal together, stood in the middle of the room, quite near the foot of the bed.

The table seemed out of place, as if it had been pulled there for convenience, probably from the corner between the armoire and the window, where a single small chair of the same style as the table stood alone. On the table was a large pitcher in a bowl, several small glass bottles, and a stack of what appeared to be folded white cloths.

To my left, rather nearby, was a dresser with drawers. A piece of white linen lay on top of it, the worked hem hanging a bit off the side. A tray, it appeared to be pewter, in the centre of the table held another pitcher, smaller than the other, a small glass flagon with an emerald green stopper, and two drinking glasses. A large, framed mirror hung above it, reflecting the light from the window across the room. Further down was the door. It was closed. On this side of the dresser, a chair had been placed against the wall. A woman was slumped on it, her head fallen on her bosom, she was snoring lightly. I was fully conscious by this time.

The woman woke when I stirred. 'Ah! Mrs. Byrd. You're with us, I see. And your eyes are looking pretty good and clear.' I asked where my baby was. She looked at me with a sorrowful expression and shook her head. I told her I knew the baby was dead, remembered she'd taken her and that I needed to see her. She said she'd bring her to me shortly. I told her I needed a dose of laudanum. 'Are you feeling pain?' I told her I wasn't at that moment, but did not want to. She smiled and put a few drops in a glass of water. I told her to put more in the glass. She looked at me again, but did as I asked.

'My name is Mary. Do you remember all that's happened to you, dear?'

I told her I knew where I'd come from but did not know where I was now nor how I'd gotten here. I knew I'd been injured, had given birth too soon and that the baby was dead. I repeated that I wanted to see her body. Mary said again that she'd bring her to me. She told me that my friend Elizabeth and her husband were coming soon. They intended to bring me to their farm today, so that I could recover there. She said they'd prepared a place where I could bury the baby. They would gladly wait a day, if necessary, that someone was taking care of their boys.

'Do you not remember talking about all these arrangements, Mrs. Byrd?' she asked. I told her that I did not, and to please call me Sarah. I did not care about the formality and, more to the point, I had not felt like 'Mrs. Byrd' for a long time. I told Mary I was certain I could go with them that day. I asked when they were due to arrive and she told me it should be around lunch time, they'd planned to start before dawn. The sudden press of time made my heart race.

I told her I had to have the baby right away so that I could cleanse her body before she was dressed for burial. I said those things as if I knew what I was talking about, but I'd never done it. As a child, I'd watched it done a couple of times by our Negroes. I was fascinated by the ritual until Mother found out and forbade me to ever go to their cabins again. During The War, I'm not sure what happened with the men who died on the porch. Maybe our Negroes took care of them as well.

But I wanted to take care of my baby, mine and Far Cry's.

Mary — she told me everyone called her Irish Mary for obvious reasons; her accent was pronounced — looked at me again with an appraising expression I would come to know well: as if she understood I might not be telling the whole truth, and I should know that she understood this, that she'd go along with me — up to a point and I'd owe her something. She nodded her 'yes'. Then she poured water from the pitcher into the bowl on the table. From something at the foot of the bed, she took a small blanket, folded it several times, and placed it by the bowl. She took some cottonwool from a pocket of her apron and placed it on the blanket. She said she'd be right back and left the room, leaving the door slightly ajar.

I got up from the bed, walked the few steps to the table and stood leaning against it. I was weak but not as bad as I feared I might be when I first woke. I walked to the window, looked out at what must have been the parade ground with a flag staff prominent. Fort Laramie. Of course. I heard Mary at the door, she used her back to open it and her foot to close it again. Cradled in both hands was a small thing wrapped in white. I met her at the table and held out my hands. I was shocked at how light my daughter was. I placed her on the blanket and slowly unwrapped her.

I reeled and Mary's arm immediately shot around my waist. While the baby had been inside me, I'd perceived her vitality, her personhood. In my ignorance, I'd imagined she would be like a doll, a miniature of the baby she'd have been in another four months or so. But she was not.

Her nearly transparent skin, a darkish yellow membrane, barely concealed organs and vessels whose various darker colours showed through. Her eyelids were entirely closed and her mouth, also closed, seemed oddly wide, with thin lips. Her head was too large for her body. I'd imagined there would be hair, dark as her father's, but there was only a fine down of no particular colour.

Her ears were not in the right place. This disturbed me greatly at first. But they were *almost* in the right place, and as I looked more closely, I could see they were perfect. The tiny whorls of skin and cartilage were perfectly shaped. I could see where eyebrows would have grown. At the end of the thin, rather long limbs were hands and feet that that had the smallest nails, finer than the finest flake of shell, finer than anything I could think of. I reached out and took one of her feet in my fingers and stroked it. Then I held one of her hands. Because of the position of the fingers, I could imagine we were holding one another. They were exquisite, her feet, her hands.

I began to see my baby as *my baby*. I was her mother, and she had a father. Both of us had given something of ourselves to her blood and these strains had mixed with her own... what? Essence? Lizzie would have said 'soul', so that's the word I chose. I imagined that something of her soul was still there, inside that unfinished skin, and just outside it, too. I could *feel* her. I assumed this was an illusion born of pain and desire, of the moment's lightheadedness, but I didn't care. I welcomed it.

There was stuff stuck to her skin in spots. I wanted it gone. I took the cottonwool, dipped it in the water, squeezed out the excess and moved to clean her. Mary quickly put her hand on mine.

'Soft. Soft. You'll take her flesh off, dear. She wasn't yet ready for this world. Go lightly.'

So I stroked her ever so gently until she was mostly clean. I put away the cottonwool and folded the cloth she was lying on over her, pressing gently, to take up the dampness. I stroked the tiny dome of her head. I touched her eyelids with two fingers of each hand. I traced her lips with my thumb.

I brought my face close and spoke to her silently. I told her I loved her, would always love her. My throat tightened and my eyes stung, I felt a sob gathering in my chest. The spirit pouch I'd worn since Medicine Crow gave it to me fell from the neck of my gown and onto her body. There was a sort of jolt and something came to mind, an idea that pulled me from the edge of despair.

'Sarah dear. You'd better lie yourself down. You're looking peaked and there's much to do yet.' I shook my head. She said she'd prefer I lay down now rather than fall causing her to have to lift me and strain her back.

She helped me onto the bed. Without ceremony, she lifted my gown and examined dressings she took from a sort of pouch between my legs. She told me a Norwegian woman she'd known had knitted the thing and she'd copied it. Quite useful, she said. She dropped the bloody cloths on the floor, wiped me as if I were myself an infant, put fresh cloths into the pouch, pulled down my gown and covered me again. I began to sit up, but she told me to stay put for a bit. She brought me a glass of water, helped me sip some, then sat down on the chair in which she'd been sleeping.

She said I'd bled but nothing like earlier and nothing to worry about. Besides, it was to be expected considering it had taken many hours for the baby to work her way out of my body with Doc's help. I asked if she had been dead when she came out and Mary said she'd been alive but that 'the poor mite' had died almost immediately after. She said they'd been worried about me as I'd lost a good deal of blood, and also there was a good sized knot on my head that Elizabeth surmised must have happened when I fell from my horse. Mary told me the doc had said I must surely have been concussed as there were no other injuries to explain why I was two days and nights mostly out of my senses. And there was that subtle look again. I felt she believed I'd chosen to remain senseless. She might have been right.

As she was talking, she reached down and took things from a wooden box on the floor by the dresser. Just last night, she said, she'd found an old linen pillow cover with pretty embroidery and was making a gown for my baby to be buried in, a simple thing to slip over her head with a ribbon at the neck and the embroidery at the bottom. As she took scissors, needle and thread from the box, she told me she'd also found a soft woollen shawl in which to wrap her. These had belonged to Doc's wife who'd 'passed'. They were on a shelf in the armoire, where there were also several dresses and a few pairs of shoes.

She told me I'd been set up in Doc's own house that he'd shared with his wife until she died of the pneumonia at the end of last winter, poor soul. And poor Doc. How he'd loved her!

'What is his name? The doctor.'

'Dr. Martin Thomas. But everyone calls him Doc. And he's a good doctor, he is. Oh, it broke his heart when he couldn't save her. His own wife. He hasn't been the same man since.'

'Have I taken his bed?'

'He set himself up to sleep downstairs. The post infirmary is downstairs until they build another one and next to it is a small bedroom. He told me he sleeps better there. When his wife was here, they slept in this room. So, everything in it makes him think of her.'

It was strange to be lying there having a conversation with a woman I didn't know, about a woman I had never met, the dead wife of a man I remembered only as a hallucination, while looking at my daughter lying still and naked on the table, very real and very dead. I should have covered her. I tightened my grip on my spirit pouch, grateful they hadn't removed it when they changed my clothing. I felt certain it was Elizabeth who'd made that decision.

Mary's voice went on telling me things, but I'd stopped listening. My mind had slipped from my body, up and over the bed to the table where my baby lay. I hovered, looking down on her. I willed myself to move closer until we were face to face, almost merging.

'You should not be dead. Or we should both be dead. I will kill your killer. I swear to you, my baby, whom I love so horribly much. I had no idea, no idea. This is like no other love. I swear to you, I will kill him.'

I swore it on her heart, that tiny organ. How big could it be? The size of a robin's heart? I swore it on the soul of my mother. On my own soul, though I didn't think it worth much. I swore on my love for her father. On my love for Elizabeth. On every truly good thing I could think of.

I came to consciousness, lying in bed sobbing with Mary standing over me, stroking my hair. My daughter was dead and, except for luck, I should also have been killed. So much shooting. And Far Cry, leaving the night before with no explanation. Nothing unusual in that. But he gives specific directions on where and when to meet. So we go, Lizzie and I. And we meet the cavalry. Then he comes wearing his red shirt, riding in fast with warriors. We could *all* have been killed. I told myself there'd been a plan and it had gone horribly wrong. Not his fault. I'd learn the details of what had happened, who was responsible, and I would avenge our daughter's murder. This was a good reason to stay alive.

'Good, darlin'. Good. Breathe deeply, now. Yes. Good girl. Ah. That's better. Calmly, calmly. I am wondering if you truly are well enough to do this today.'

'It was a dream,' I told her, as I breathed deeply and willed the breathing to quiet my mind and body. I had to be strong to do everything that needed to be done. 'I'm alright, it was only a bad dream.'

'You're a tough thing, aren't you, tougher than you look. That's good. I will show you something that I hope will make you smile. Look. What do you think?'

She proudly held up the gown for my approval. I said it was lovely and thanked her. I began to sit up but she told me to stay comfortable, that she would put it on her. Then she put her sewing things, shears, needles and thread, back in the box by the dresser.

'No! Please. Let me. I must be the one to do it. I'm quite strong enough to stand again.'

'Very well. And so you shall. I'll be just here...'

'Mary, I want to be alone with her. I want to say goodbye. Alone.'

I can't recall what else I said, I might even have said that I wanted to pray over her. I knew exactly what I wanted to do, it had come to me when my spirit pouch fell on her. Mary nodded and said she'd be down in the kitchen, she had cooking to do. I could simply call her name out loud if I needed her, otherwise, she'd come back up when my friends arrived. She warned me she would bring a cup of broth when she came and I was to drink it all. She shook her finger at me.

She reached down under the bed near the foot of it and took a rather small basket that she placed on the bed. A folded shawl was in it, I imagined it was the one she'd mentioned from the doctor's dead wife. She scooped up the bloody cloths and put them in the bowl with the soiled cottonwool, but I saw that on the floor by her chair she'd left clean white scraps from the pillow case. She went out the door and pulled it shut after her.

I had wanted to take her heart, but holding the shears over her body, the blades seemed too large. I decided to take one of her hands. It would fit easily in my spirit pouch that was not quite the length of my middle finger and a bit wider than that finger and my index finger together. Laughing Woman had stitched it from soft doeskin and decorated it with beadwork and Medicine Crow had put herbs in it he'd said would keep me strong. I did not know what they were, but they smelled pleasant and I hoped they would help cure that little bit of flesh. The gown had no sleeves, so no one would see what I'd done.

Holding her arm and hand, I assumed the deep colour was from pooled blood that would leak, so I went back to Mary's sewing basket and cut a length of sturdy thread. I also grabbed some of the scraps of white linen from the floor. I was proud of how quick I was in my movements, how agile. I tied some of the thread tightly around her arm just above the wrist, and made another binding right at the wrist. I'd cut between the two. I was careful not to pull the thread so tightly that I'd sever the fragile limb. It was no thicker than one of my fingers and it did not feel as if there was hard bone in there.

I cut off her hand. There was only slight leakage that I staunched easily. I bound her hand with its beautiful fingers in a piece of linen, then secured it with the rest of the thread, pulling it around and around again and again tightly, making it as small as I could. Then I took the pretty beaded pouch from my neck and worked my baby's hand into it, among the dried herbs. I pulled the thong to close it, tied it tightly, and put it back around my neck.

I heard Mary's steps on the stairs and quickly placed the gown over my baby's head, pulling it down its full length and tying the ribbon at her neck. I stuffed the shears under the mattress. There was no time to do the other thing I'd thought to do, what Mary Small Wing and the other women had done when their men died in the avalanche, what the women had done when Mary Small Wing died, what others had done during that horrible winter of all the deaths, what the women did when a loved one died. I could not howl my grief in that house, though I had thought to chop my hair and slash at my arms and chest with the scissor blade. But there was no time, and somehow, I did not have the right heart for it. Mary knocked on the door and I told her to come in.

She put her hand on my shoulder, grasped it firmly, held it there briefly, then let go. It made me uncomfortable. I didn't know her well enough yet to interpret all her looks and gestures. I was everywhere an alien. She handed me a cup of hot broth and I drank it as I'd been ordered to. Then she unfolded the shawl — a soft cream coloured thing — and draped it over the basket. 'Ah', she said, 'she looks pretty, she does.' She stood by as I lifted the baby from the table and placed her in the centre of the shawl, arranging the folds of the gown so Mary would see how I appreciated her work. I leaned down and kissed the tiny body over her heart. The pouch moved a bit as I did so. My daughter.

I should feel more, I thought, cataclysms of grief. I should be like Hecuba beating my fists on the floor. I was not without emotions — profound sadness, and the stirrings of rage — but their stronger expression seemed distant. I was an empty battlefield. I folded the shawl over her body. I did not want Elizabeth to see her unfinished face. I wanted her to imagine, as I had, that she was beautiful.

'They've arrived, dear,' Mary said, 'let's get you ready.'

CHAPTER 2

Elizabeth and William had waited downstairs while Mary helped me dress. I'd picked out one of the doctor's wife's dresses, a simple, dark blue serge that seemed appropriate. It was a bit short and too wide. Mary quickly threaded a needle and took in the bodice seams and was annoyed at not being able to find her shears to trim the excess fabric. I reached under the mattress and handed them to her. She raised one eyebrow then went on with her work as I washed myself. Mary helped me with my hair. She handed me a pair of buttoned shoes with a small heel. They were too small — my feet were long, it had been an embarrassment to my mother, she complained about it humorously with her friends — but I agreed to wear them instead of my stained moccasins.

Mary pulled from her pocket a dark blue velvet eyepatch and tied it around my head with a black grosgrain ribbon, making a bow in the back. She had me look in the mirror — I'd avoided the damn thing — and I liked the look of it. I told her so and, obviously pleased, she said she'd already made me another and would make a few more. Before she left to bring Lizzie and William upstairs, I told her I was afraid of feeling pain and not having anything to subdue it. Did she have a small bottle or flask in which I could put a dose or two? She did not give me one of her looks — I'd readied myself — but rummaged a bit in the dresser, found a metal flask, poured water into it and several drops of laudanum. I thanked her. She smiled at me and left the room. I packed it in the carpet bag she'd taken from the armoire.

I heard my friends come up the stairs. They entered the room quietly, respectfully. William stood by while Lizzie and I held one another. She pulled back and looked at me, said it was good to see me up and about, that I looked quite well, considering. She indicated the eye-patch, smiled and said it was a very nice idea. We laughed a bit. Her eyes were wet.

Lizzie's William was almost exactly as I'd imagined him from her descriptions. A sweet faced man with regular, well-made features. His skin was tan and rosy at the same time, he had wavy dark brown hair, a nicely groomed beard, and blue eyes that crinkled at the edges. He was quite tall and stooped a bit, as if he wanted his eyes to be more on a level with those around him. Or, as Lizzie later joked, because he had always to avoid conking his head on low lintels.

He was carrying a small coffin. I nodded toward the basket on the bed and he placed the coffin beside it carefully, as if not to disturb my dead baby. It was beautiful. Oak, he said. He'd smoothed and oiled it so the surface was satiny and on the lid, he had carved a small circle in which was a tiny bird, a leaf and a flower. Beautiful delicate work. I remember saying it seemed a shame to put such a lovely thing in the ground. It was an odd moment. My daughter was a lovely thing.

The lid had been loosely nailed to the box and William removed it. Inside, Lizzie had placed a soft blanket, clearly knitted for a baby. I tried to object but she wouldn't have it. She made a sort of nest and I lifted my baby wrapped in the shawl and placed her in it. Lizzie folded the edges of the blanket over her. William placed the box on the floor and with a small hammer that Mary had brought up for the purpose, nailed the lid shut. The hammer strikes were jarring. We had all been speaking so softly.

I suddenly thought of my mother and that she did not yet know that I was alive. It upset me greatly. I told them they had to wait while I wrote to my mother. I could do it quickly but I had to do so right away so it could go out with that day's post. I barked at Mary to bring me writing things. But Lizzie said it was best to leave right away as they hoped to get to their home before dark and we were starting a bit late. I'd write my letter, have supper with the family, and sleep in their house that night, the bed had been readied for me. The burial would be first thing in the morning tomorrow and then I could stay as long as I wished.

My heart hurt so with guilt and longing for my mother, that I was unable to move. Mary reminded me that I'd been mostly unconscious until before sunrise that very morning and that, since waking, I'd been tending to my own child. I was far from recovered even now.

Lizzie told me she had pen and paper at home, I could write to my mother tonight and that William would bring it to the fort first thing in the morning. I agreed this would be the best thing to do.

I'd forgotten how flat the country is around Fort Laramie. Grass as far as you can see. Deceptive, though. Quite suddenly you'd descend into a draw, at the bottom of which might be a spring or a creek with shrubs or even trees, the tops of which hadn't been visible until you were right upon them. Lizzie and William remarked on how warm it was for the time of the year.

September. Back in Virginia, the days would still be hot, but the nights would just have begun to get cool. As a girl, I would suddenly notice that the lushness of summer had faded. This had made me melancholy in a delicious sort of way. Looking around me in this place, I felt only a sick sadness. It was this month a year ago that I'd been taken captive by the Indians. And days ago, the Army had yanked me back, without asking me if I wanted to go. In the high country where we'd been living before the cavalry came, it was golden autumn, with cobalt skies and air like the fresh, fast water in the streams. Here, it was mostly flat. Hot in the sun.

It was only the three of us. Mary said she would have my room all freshened up for me upon my return. Lizzie told me the fort commander, Colonel something-or-other (this was not the same officer with whom Jake had had the infamous disagreement), had told William to convey his condolences. Lizzie thought he should have presented himself and spoken with me in person, as he'd made such a proud to do about his part in our return. It made no difference to me.

By the time we were in the buckboard I was tired to the bone and not sure I could remain sitting up for the entire trip. I wanted it over. I wanted a shot from my flask, but did not want to take it in front of my friends. Though they would not have known what it was, even if they'd noticed, which they probably would not have done.

Mary had packed a lunch that we ate in the shade of cottonwood trees down in a draw on the banks of a creek. I nibbled a bit and then lay down. Soon, we were bumping along again, out in the sun.

My eyes searched the horizon, wondering if we'd see Indians and which ones they'd be, when it suddenly struck me that perhaps I'd done a wrong thing in separating my child's hand from her body. Indians did that sort of thing to their enemies.

Hacking up one's enemies rendered them helpless in the afterlife, but I suspect this belief had evolved to support a natural desire for vengeance. An ancient inclination. I'd felt it myself when I removed the head of the man I'd killed before he could kill Elizabeth. Triumphant, vengeful hatred. I was glad I was capable of it.

But I had cut off my baby's hand. I'd mutilated her body. What did *that* mean? What sort of afterlife did I believe in? Nothing. But looking out towards the horizon, feeling the air against my face, smelling the grass and the earth warmed by the sun, hearing the voices of birds and the hum of the universe of living things, all of which was holy to Mary Small Wing and Far Cry and Medicine Crow and Laughing Woman, all the Lakota I'd lived with and loved, I wondered if I'd dishonoured my child by dishonouring their religion. Perhaps it was immaterial that I did not believe in it myself. Should I have nevertheless respected it?

I took hold of the pouch and felt the barely discernible shape of my daughter's hand. I relieved myself of that particular question. I was glad I had that much of her to hold. Her soul was her own and it had flown free of her body. She'd lack for nothing.

I remember being surprised at how poor my friends' house was. The unpainted clapboards were already beat up a bit by the weather. But Lizzie pointed out the second story, and the large glass windows. She was proud of them, they'd carried them from New York and William had built the house around the windows. Behind them I saw white curtains. There was a good-sized porch in front with the rocking chairs Lizzie had spoken of. Along the side of the house facing us as we approached, were tall sunflowers and other plants below them. Lamps had been lit inside and the glow was welcoming.

Her two boys were standing on the porch and right behind them was a short, wiry man. As we approached, he took off his hat and the boys came down the steps to greet their parents. I was introduced to

Charles and Joey. They smiled at me shyly. They did not look at the coffin. Then I was introduced to Bron, a neighbour, who nodded his greeting.

As he helped me down, William said he and Bron often helped one another with jobs that needed two strong backs and four strong arms and two good pairs of hands. Bron had spent the day repairing a shed to return a favour. He said that the boys had helped, had proved themselves fine workers. Putting his hat back on, Bron said he had to get back to his wife who surely had supper waiting, and walked up towards the nearby barn. His house was just out of sight on the other side of a hill behind the barn.

Inside, the house was sparsely furnished, but sweetly, with little touches of domesticity, most of which must have been carried from their former home. But there were also small tables holding jars filled with flowers, a corner cupboard and other pieces that I suspected had to be William's fine carpentry. There were pillows here and there that I was sure Lizzie had decorated with her needlework. It was cool in that room, and quiet. Peaceful.

She laid out a nice supper but I had little appetite. I drank a glass of milk and ate some bread she'd baked, spread with butter. The boys spoke lovingly of their cows. I was profoundly tired and worried I might be bleeding from the jolting ride.

Before leaving for Laramie, Lizzie had set up beds for the boys in the hay loft in the barn. They were excited and happy about it. I was to sleep in the big bed in Lizzie and William's room, while they took the beds in the boys' room. But I would not have them give up their bed, so Lizzie turned down the covers on one of the boys' beds and brought in another pillow.

'Here is a nice one of goose feathers, brought from New York, and a nightdress. I think the bed will be long enough, William made them so there would be room for the boys to grow.'

'It will be just fine for me, Lizzie. But if your boys grow to be as tall as their father he'll soon have to make new beds!'

I sat on the bed and motioned for her to sit beside me. I complimented her on the loveliness of her home, how tasty her bread was, how fresh and sweet the butter, the creamy milk. I rushed through these niceties to get to what I really wanted to talk about and felt she could sense it. So I came right out and asked her to please tell me what had happened the morning the cavalry came.

I said I remembered riding out with her and the six Lakota. We'd run the horses a bit, or had we only spoken of it, I couldn't remember for certain. Then suddenly there was music and the mounted soldiers coming over the rise. I remembered turning my horse and running away. I remembered seeing Far Cry and some warriors ride in. I remembered racing through woods, being shot at, then nothing more. I wanted to know everything she knew.

'Must it be now?' She urged me to rest, as she could see how done in I was. She reminded me that tomorrow, the burial, would be hard, that there was time later for this story. But I said that as William and I would return to Laramie immediately after the burial, there would not be time tomorrow to talk at length and I could not rest until I knew more.

'I had hoped you'd change your mind and stay a few days', she said. I stammered that I did not want to inconvenience her, and before she could argue with me, I asked her again to tell me what she recalled. I told her that I badly needed to know. I was hurt and my baby had been killed and I couldn't rest until I understood how these things had happened.

She placed the pillow behind my back and said she'd get water for me to have in the room. While she was gone, I quickly checked the cloths between my legs and was relieved to see I'd bled very little. The room was small and clean, with toys that must have been made by both William and Lizzie. She came back with a pitcher and a bowl, a towel over her arm, and two tin cups. She poured us each some water and then sat down next to me.

She began by telling me what William had told her.

William and the boys were coming back from Fort Laramie with supplies. He and the boys would say hello to their friend Robert and the children, and then Elizabeth would join them and they'd all four go home. He and the boys were talking about home and what they'd have for supper when he saw smoke on the other side of a small rise and felt an immediate horror. Robert's house was there.

He made the boys stay in the wagon while he went into the house. Though the bodies had been burned and animals had been at them, they were not thoroughly destroyed. He could tell that Elizabeth was not among the dead inside the house, and in a quick look around, there was no sign of her body outside. He circled the house several times, widening his search, but she wasn't there. He hurried home with his terrified children, assuring them over and over, 'Your mother wasn't there, she got away and we'll find her. We will find her.'

The next day he left the boys with Bron's wife and the two men went to Fort Laramie, where William made a report. Then they then rode back out to take a thorough look. Elizabeth said that Bron was widely known as one of the best trackers in the territory. He told William how many Indians there'd been, in what direction they'd come from, in what direction they'd ridden off, and that there were two riders on one of the horses. There'd be no reason to carry off a dead body. They'd left the others where they lay. William was certain his wife had been taken alive.

William and Bron immediately returned to Laramie and told the Colonel what they had seen. They arrived just ahead of an ice storm. As it happened, two soldiers, young enlisted men, had come in shortly before to tell of a burned dugout and a missing woman. There were a lot of tracks. They'd gone out before dawn that day to deliver supplies, something they'd done several times before, and figured whatever had happened, had happened the day before. The Colonel told them this woman's husband, a Lieutenant Byrd, had ridden off with a whore some months previously, leaving his wife. Byrd had left money to deliver supplies to the dugout, saying she'd sooner or later come in to the fort. She hadn't and the money had run out. What was the Colonel to do. She couldn't be left to starve.

He'd told his men to convince her to come to the fort but she'd always refused, saying she expected her husband back any day. This particular time, he'd told them to order the woman to pack a bag, saddle her horse and to return with them to the fort — at gun point, if necessary — that he was sick of shouldering responsibility for her. Well, now the Indians had taken her. He thought he still had an address for the wife among Byrd's records and said he'd write to the family. William said to give him the address when he found it, that he'd keep the family informed of how the search was going.

They believed the massacre at Robert's home and the capture of Byrd's wife must have happened on or near the same day. The Colonel sent out a party of soldiers. William went home to his boys whom he'd hated to leave, as they were still terribly upset and frightened for their mother and themselves and for their father when he was not at home. Bron rode off to join the search party. But by that time, sleet and icy rain had been falling hard for a good while and the trail was cold. Even Bron couldn't pick it up.

It was long weeks after this — 'terrible weeks, William told me, when Charlie tried not to ask and Joey cried himself to sleep every night' — when a couple of soldiers came riding up to the farm with a message from the Colonel.

He'd said there'd been sightings of two white women with a group of Indians at a big pow-wow up near the Tongue River, but he told William not to get his hopes up until there was some way to verify the report and identify the women. William asked what the Colonel was doing in that regard and he was told there were problems with marauding Indians all up and down the Bozeman, the savages were angry about late annuities or whatnot, that he had his hands full but would do the best he could. So William sent letters to everyone whose names he could think of in Washington including the President and wrote to newspapers, too, trying to put pressure on the Army to move on the situation.

Months passed. Winter came. Lizzie asked me, 'Remember how bad that winter was?' I remembered. William had told her he'd tried not to think of how hard it must have been for her, but that he had never stopped believing she was still alive. He told her he'd felt her presence and prayed for strength.

'His thoughts were one unending prayer to God for my safe return, as were mine. Do you see, Sarah, how powerful a thing that is?'

With spring, William went more frequently to the fort. On a trip in for supplies, the Colonel told him he'd been about to send someone to tell him some good news. Word was out that some rogue Sioux had two white women they wanted to exchange for a pair of their young hooligans held at Fort Reno, he thought it was Reno, not that far up the Bozeman trail.

From the descriptions, William knew that one of the women was Elizabeth. The other was taller and light haired and the Colonel told him it had to be Byrd's wife. He said he'd met me when we first arrived at the fort before we went to live in the dugout.

Summer came and nothing more was heard. No one knew which band of which clan of which circle of Sioux held the women. No one had any idea where they were. Except General Custer. William was very pleased. Something would be done now...

'*Custer?* George Armstong Custer?'

'Yes. He's the one who arranged the exchange of hostages.'

My knowledge of him went back long before our move west. Jake was only a few years behind Custer at West Point. They'd both been dedicated carousers. *Custer*. So. If not for him, my daughter wouldn't be dead. I'd promised I'd avenge her. Well, I'd kill him. I'd kill Custer.

Apparently, based on information from his Crow spies, Custer had decided it was Far Cry who held the women. He was told that Far Cry had broken from a larger group and was said to be travel-ing farther and farther away from where, according to the last treaty, the Sioux had been told they had to remain. He'd refused to collect the annuities due his band and refused to attend meetings about the hostages.

So Custer ordered his men ride into a particular village before dawn and kidnap a highly respected Lakota medicine man, an old man, and from what William had been told, a relative of Far Cry. Custer put him in jail at Reno with the two Lakota boys. They'd killed several in the camp, possibly including the old man's wife, when shooting broke out as they dragged him from his tipi. Elizabeth did not know if the man taken hostage had been Medicine Crow and if Laughing Woman had been killed. It made us both sick to consider it.

She asked if I knew whether or not he and Far Cry were related. I did not. We'd both observed a deep regard between them, yet when the clan had broken up towards the end of summer, they'd gone in different directions. I had thought then that Medicine Crow, his wife and the others with them had chosen to go to the reservation, but maybe not. I asked if she knew whether or not Medicine Crow and the boys had been returned after the cavalry had taken us. She had not heard of any such thing, and she didn't recall having seen any Indian boys among the soldiers who'd come for them, but it was all too chaotic, she couldn't be sure of anything.

Apparently, Custer had met with a few important chiefs from some Sioux and Cheyenne clans — again, his spies told him upon whom to call — and told them that they must inform Far Cry that if the two women were not returned within a month, all three Indians in jail would be shot and white soldiers would begin killing *all* Indians — women, children, old ones — in every camp they could find, in ever widening circles from Fort Reno, until the captive women were returned. These had to be those Indians we'd called the 'five important men' who'd come to the camp several times. Now we knew why they'd come and why Far Cry was always so disturbed by those talks with them.

And that was all Elizabeth could tell me.

'Sarah, I've told you everything that's been told to me. I don't know any more. I don't *want* to know more, and I can't talk about it any more. I'm *home* now. I was afraid you'd been killed that morning. I saw you fall in the shooting but then soldiers grabbed my reins and galloped me back down the other side of the hill. You can imagine my relief when I learned you'd not been shot and would live through your injuries. But, please, Sarah. That part of my life — of *our* lives — is *over*, for which I thank God with every breath.'

It was not over for me, but I reached out and touched my friend's cheek on which there were tears. She took a sip of water and we sat still a moment. Then she said she hoped that after spending some time in her home, among her family, I would come to understand why she could not give in to that other life. I told her I already understood. It was true. The difference in her was remarkable. She held her body differently and her face had softened with relief and joy.

She took my hands in hers and asked if, in spite of what I'd lost, was I not also relieved. I could go home to Virginia now, I could see my mother, of whom I'd so often spoken. Lizzie said she would miss me terribly, but that I could now go back to 'my real home', to 'my own family'. Did that not make me happy?

I told her that I did, of course, look forward to seeing my mother, that I missed her terribly. But I did not tell her that the idea of the trip back to Virginia filled me with dread. I did not want to see my father.

And, 'my real home', 'my own family'?

I'd truly loved a man for the first time in my life and had become pregnant with his child. I'd made pictures in my mind of this new family — the man, me, the baby — part of a larger family of people who were, after all, not so different from the soldiers among whom I'd come of age. Men of a warrior class and their wives and children. And yet they were *very* different in ways that I'd not only accepted but had come to admire.

And it was not only the man. I'd fallen in love with the country through which we'd traveled, with the drama of its seasons and topography, a place whose foreignness had excited me on first encounter and that still held me enchanted. I'd fallen in love with a life that, while strange and hard and sometimes horrifying, also offered a kind of everyday happiness I'd not known was possible.

She'd asked if I were not relieved, 'in spite of what I'd lost'. But I had lost everything. I did not know who I was now, if indeed, I'd ever known. While sitting with my dear friend on one of her sons' beds, in a room in the house built by her beloved husband, smiling into her happy face and returning the pressure of her hands, it took an extreme effort to behave like a rational person. I did not know how long I could keep it up. My entire demeanour was a lie. All I wanted in that moment was a strong draught of my drug, and I wanted to be alone so that I could begin to plan how I'd kill Custer.

I told Lizzie I needed to lie down. We held one another for a long moment. Then she got up saying she'd be setting out a bit of food a little later and asked if she should call for me. I told her no, thank you, I only wanted rest.

At the door she turned and, with her great warm smile, said, 'Oh! I must tell you! The boys like your eyepatch very much. Joey says it makes you look like a pirate in one of his picture books. Isn't that dear? *All* my boys are in love with you! Sleep well, Sarah. God bless you, my dear, dear friend. I will call you for breakfast.'

The bed was narrow and the mattress hard. My limbs twitched. My various wounds seemed to have conspired to inflict pain all at once and even parts of my body that had not been injured hurt. My skin hurt. I took the flask from my carpet bag, shook it, and took a large swallow. Then another. Finally, I slept.

The smell of coffee woke me. I went to the window and saw it was just coming on dawn. We'd planned the burial for right after breakfast. How much better it would have been, I thought, to have walked alone with my baby far out onto the prairie and left her to the animals and carrion birds. They could have had me too.

CHAPTER 3

The sun had not yet dried the dew. We walked up a bit of a rise beyond the barn. I insisted that I would carry the coffin while William carried a small polished wooden cross up to where there was a single young cottonwood tree standing alone. A seed must have been carried there and dropped, taken root, sprouted, somehow survived and was now a tree. Slender still, it had a lot of growing yet to do, but its leaves made some small shade. Off to one side and down a gentle slope, there was a small, flat meadow rich in flowers, and a bit farther down, a good sized stream with thick growth along its banks. William saw me notice and nodded. It was a good place.

Not too close to the stem of the tree — William explained he wanted to leave room for its roots to spread — but still in the dappled shadow of its leaves, was the hole he'd dug, the dirt piled on the side. A small hole. I wondered if it was big enough. But when I looked at the coffin in my arms, I saw that it was plenty big enough.

Just to the side of the newly dug hole were two small wooden crosses like the one William carried, sticking up out of the ground no higher than my knee. They were nicely finished, with tiny flowers carved at the heart of each. One was for 'Annie Brown' and one for 'Janie Brown'. The date on each was March 14, 1865. One date. Born and died the same day. I looked at Elizabeth.

'I lost them at about six months into my pregnancy. Twins. I didn't know I was carrying two babies. I was hoping for a girl and would have had two. We'd have been a big family! I let the boys name them. One day, we'll have nice stones made.'

I said I was terribly sorry, and she smiled.

'You haven't mentioned a name for your baby, Sarah. Have you thought about it? If you want him to, William will carve a name into her cross and a date, too. He said he'd do it today, if you'd like.'

I thanked them but said there was no need. I wondered why Lizzie had never told me about the twin babies she'd lost. When I asked a good while later, she said she'd started many times to tell me, especially once she'd learned I was pregnant, but she'd not wanted me to carry around such sad thoughts. William reached out his arms and said, 'Well, why don't you let me have her then.' I handed him the coffin.

The boys came forward but Lizzie told them gently 'not yet'. I hadn't noticed they were both carrying bouquets of wildflowers. She looked at all of us to see if we were ready and asked me if there was anything I'd like to say. I shook my head no. She asked me if I wished for her to read two brief verses from the Bible. I wished she would not, but couldn't possibly say so. I nodded yes. The verses were brief, as promised, a good thing as I was feeling lightheaded.

'Suffer the little children to come unto Jesus', said one, 'for such is the kingdom of God'. Another said it was 'not the will of God that even one of these little ones should perish'. What kind of god is this, I wondered. Did this god's kingdom include our Indian friends and relations? Mary Small Wing and her unborn baby? This god, Lizzie's god, had let *my* little one perish and hers too. If it was not his will, was it *against* his will? Not much of a god. Many little ones perished every day as a result of our evil towards one another. Or as a result of bad weather. Of falling ill. Of falling down. Bitten by snakes, drowned in creeks, struck by lightning. They died of bad luck. I began to itch as if insects were crawling on me. I'd had enough.

Lizzie said she'd end by reading Psalm 23. This I could stand. I let it wash over me like music. When it was done, she asked if there was a hymn I wanted us all to sing. I was sweating profusely. My head hurt, my back hurt, my womb hurt, my genitals hurt, the dress chafed my skin, my feet did not like the shoes and the damn eye-patch kept slipping. I wanted my drug. I did not want a hymn and shook my head, looking into her eyes so she could see I meant it.

Lizzie nodded, and I silently blessed her. She looked to William who knelt, looped a rope around the box and gently lowered it into the hole until it came to rest. With the soft thunk of it hitting the dirt, I had a sudden, compelling desire.

'*Wait!* Please. Wait.'

I suddenly did not want my daughter packed into the earth without a name. I wanted her to have my only friend's name.

'I *do* have a name. It's Elizabeth. Her name is Elizabeth.'

Lizzie was visibly moved.

'I'm honoured, dear friend. She should have a second name as well, her family name. Shall it be yours? Byrd?'

I'd always liked the name, Byrd, except that it belonged to Jake and his hideous father. But I suddenly thought it would be different if it were spelled B, I, R, D, instead. That would evoke our sweet, dead friend Mary Small Wing. I explained this and asked what they thought of Elizabeth Mary Bird, spelled B, I, R, D. Lizzie explained the difference to the boys who nodded seriously. William said he would carve the name into the cross that day and the date as well.

He pulled up the rope and Lizzie gestured to the boys to toss in their flowers which they did with great solemnity. Then they each placed a sunflower on the other two graves. When that was done, she said, 'God bless you, Elizabeth Mary Bird, and keep you among His angels, as He keeps our Annie and Janie. May they greet you with joy, dear little one. We will join you by and by.' William filled the hole with the dirt he'd taken out of it. He picked up the small cross and we started back down the hill.

When we passed the barn, Charles and Joey wanted to show me the loft where they'd spent the night. Lizzie shook her head, but I told them I'd like to see, so we went into the barn. They were proud of themselves, pointing to the hay mow and the rope ladder they used to get up there and pulled up after them. They'd heard an owl, or at least that's what they thought it was, and something else in the distance that scared them a bit, but all they had to do was look out towards the house where their mother had kept a lamp burning in her window all night. She rolled her eyes and we laughed gently.

As we approached the house, I told Elizabeth that I really wanted to go back to the fort right then, that I did not want to impose on her any longer. She frowned a bit. She told me she would pack up a lunch for us, and if we started off right away, it was possible William would be home by dark. But she had some worries about this plan. The days were getting shorter and the weather could suddenly turn, there was no way of knowing. She said, 'Please consider this idea, instead.'

I could write to my mother now as I'd wanted to do before leaving Laramie yesterday, then eat a bit of supper and spend the afternoon in bed. She said with some emphasis that she felt I sorely needed to put up my feet and rest. Later, we'd enjoy a good dinner. I would stay that night, at least, but she hoped I'd stay longer, she wanted us to have more time together. But she would, of course, agree to whatever I wanted to do. She asked me to please think about it. She took the boys into the house and I remained on the porch.

I did not want to stay. The hospitality of these people went beyond simple generosity, but I needed, urgently, to get back to my room at Laramie. I had to take off the doctor's wife's clothes. I had to take off her damn shoes that were too small. I had to smell my body's smells, feel the ridges of my scars. I needed to stand naked in that room, cleanse myself head to foot, fix a strong dose of my drug — Mary had made the traveling concoction of 'my elixir', as I'd come to call it, too damned light — and confront my reflection in the mirror. I had to talk to that woman who'd stare back at me. I had to figure out who she was. I had to get her ready to kill Custer.

I was not a person deserving of the love being offered, as I was proving by getting ready to refuse it. William changed my mind.

He came up quietly beside me on the porch. We smiled at one another. He stood a bit, looking out at the bright, already hot morning, then he said that if I really wanted to go back to Laramie right then, he'd surely take me. But wouldn't it be good to eat a nice lazy supper, then sit out on the porch and have a bit of whiskey? Hell, we didn't have to wait until after supper for our whiskey, we could have a taste right then in the bright light of morning, it had already been quite a day. That way poor Lizzie could finally take a deep breath. We could leave the next morning early.

I stayed. William and the boys went off to do chores. Lizzie gave me writing paper and pen and ink and set me down at her kitchen table so I could write to my mother. I wondered when William would bring that whiskey, but he'd gotten busy away from the house. The letter was harder than I'd imagined it would be. I could not remember when I'd written last and what I'd told her. I was certain I'd never told her of Jake's discharge and defection and I wasn't going to do it now.

After destroying several pieces of good paper, I decided the simplest truth was best. I wrote that she had not heard from me in so long because, as she had probably learned by now, I had been captured by the Indians the previous September and had only been returned very recently. I explained that I'd been part of an exchange of hostages brokered by Lt. Col. George Armstrong Custer, whose reputation I was certain she must be aware of.

I wrote, 'A woman who has become my dear friend was also taken and she is most relieved and grateful to be returned to her husband and two young sons. She and her family are a source of great comfort and company.' I did not mention my own husband. I wrote that I could imagine how difficult it must have been for her 'not to know of my circumstances and condition all these long months.' Now, I wrote, she need not worry any longer.

Then, after much mental stammering, as I'd never expressed myself to her in this way, I wrote that through it all, she had been always in my mind and heart. I was recovering well from 'the ordeal', comfortable enough at Fort Laramie under the care of a fine physician stationed there. Perhaps she would wire me money for the journey home and I could begin to make arrangements. I wrote that I longed to see her. 'Your loving daughter, Sarah'.

I put it in the envelope Lizzie had given me and took it up to the boys' room. I took off the eye patch and lay down on the bed I'd slept in the night before. The bed was made up and ready for me. I was surprised to wake up, my hands crossed on my chest still holding the letter, to Lizzie softly knocking at the open door.

She said I'd slept through supper and all afternoon, but dinner was ready — could I smell the good smells? — and they'd be most pleased if I'd join the family. I wondered how I was able to sleep so soundly without a dose. I said I'd be most happy to join them. Before I made it to a sitting position, she said in a soft voice to be certain to wear my 'nice eyepatch.'

Lizzie had cut up a chicken and baked it with onions, small potatoes and carrots from a garden started by William and the boys. There was more of her fine bread, and water or fresh milk to drink. I don't remember what we talked about, but it all seemed to flow easily and I was part of it. This was due to their graciousness alone. Afterward, the boys and I helped Lizzie clear the table and clean up, or we tried to, but she shooed us out onto the porch where William was tuning his guitar. I was quite ready for my whiskey. He must have guessed. He told me to sit in one of the rocking chairs. He smiled and winked as he passed me on his way inside the house.

Lizzie came back onto the porch with him. He handed me a generous portion in a ceramic cup. She said she never was much of a drinker, though she liked the smell of it on William's breath. They looked at one another and laughed in a way that showed another side to their love. Lizzie sat in the other rocker and William sat on the edge of the porch, his feet on the steps. The boys were still running around between the house and the barn. They were being soldiers and Indians. I turned to Lizzie and we both smiled. Our Indian boys had played the same game. But among them, no one ever wanted to be a *wasichu*.

William played and sang songs like *Lorena, Listen to the Mockingbird*, and *Aura Lea*. Lizzie sang harmony with him — they sang well together — and I was happy to listen. In a bit, Lizzie brought out slices of a pie made from dried apples William had picked up at the fort, he'd planted some fruit trees but they weren't doing so well. 'Yet!', said his wife. We enjoyed our dessert and then it was time for the boys to get to bed. They'd wanted the loft again, but Lizzie had made up pallets for them in the big bedroom. They both said, 'Good night, Mrs. Byrd,' and then Lizzie took them inside. I heard her tell them to wash while she tidied up, then to call her when they were ready for her to hear their prayers.

Fireflies began to appear. The whiskey was good going down and I said yes to another. We sipped in companionable quiet.

Upstairs, I had lit a lamp and was about to undress when Lizzie knocked on the door and softly called my name. I told her to please come in. She held a packet of envelopes of different sizes and colours tied up with twine.

'The Colonel at Laramie gave us these when we came to get you. He said it took a while to find them. I sometimes doubt the competence of those people. They're all from Virginia, dear friend.'

As she put them in my hands, Lizzie said she'd planned to give them to me earlier in the day, but I was sleeping so soundly she hadn't wanted to wake me. I thanked her and we embraced. She said 'God bless you'. Then she said, 'You know I love you dearly, don't you?' I said I did and that I loved her too. I did love her, more than I understood at the time.

I walked to the window holding the letters. The whiskey warmed my belly, and the taste of Lizzie's pie sweetened my mouth. I caressed the spirit pouch. *Elizabeth Mary Bird.* My daughter with Far Cry. Born and died September... I did not know the date, I would have to ask. I had named her and buried her early that morning. Now it was deep dusk and stars were beginning to show. I put the letters on a small table by the bed, next to the one I'd written to my mother. I decided I would read them once I was back in my room at Laramie. I swallowed the last of elixir in my flask. I slept. Early the next morning, William took me back to the fort.

CHAPTER 4

The tincture had to be strong enough but not too strong. I could always fix another if I needed it.

Mary had brought me supper, but I'd had no appetite. I rearranged the stack of letters so the oldest would be the first I'd read. These were from my mother. There were many and I saw that the handwriting on the envelopes was inconsistent, sometimes the letters were beautifully formed, sometimes her hand must have shaken badly enough for the nib to scratch the paper. Several letters from my father followed. The last were from a Richmond law firm. One of the names on the firm's envelope was that of a man who'd spent time with us on numerous occasions. He and my father would sequester themselves in his office to discuss business until dinner to which he was invited, and then back to the office for brandy and cigars. But never for long. This man seemed to prefer dessert and tea with my Mother. He made her laugh, as I recall.

I read the letters one after the other. Then I mixed a stronger dose, drank it down at once, and read them again. It took a long time, some sentences I read over and over, the pain in my chest was sometimes almost unbearable. I replaced them in their envelopes, put them in order, retied them with the same twine, then put them out of sight in the top drawer of the dresser. All except those from the lawyer, as they required immediate attention.

I had another strong dose of my elixir, my drug, my dope. I got into bed and let it take me away.

I still have the letters. Not long ago, I opened them for the first time in many years and spread them out on my table, read them again. I was surprised by what sounded a bit like love for me in my father's letters. He'd never shown it, and I felt it was a pose, a manipulation. And my poor Mama. What would it have cost me to have been kinder to my mother when she was still alive?

I am trying, now that I'm older than I thought I'd live to be, to forgive the child I was for her cruelty. She was a child, after all, and no one had told her anything. All she knew was that love was a prize you had to win by obeying certain rules. If you were a woman, you had to sacrifice yourself.

I will write down fragments of a few of these.

My darling Sarah,
Sweetest child,
Dearest daughter,
Lovely girl,
Dear you, who can't imagine
Oh, my beloved daughter!
Fascinated by your stories, always, but
A dugout? Surely not! I can hardly write the word without cringing
cozy, perhaps, but a SNAKE falling onto your table! My word!
glad to hear you are riding daily in such striking country
Don't you miss your lovely home? Your dear mother? I am joking with you
those base types at the fort. Don't forget your
sending you canned cherries!
Are you truly not afraid?
more Negroes left today, I don't know how
you never write of your husband, one hears
too long, my sweet, too long
Perhaps you are not well?
Ruth said they all want to be paid now, I know it's just, it's right, but
One of the girls stole a brooch, can't trust
Where are you? I can't bear
horror, must be, otherwise
Someone needs to tell me the damn truth!
Ruth is the only
May God forgive me, forgive us all
I'm tired, my darling girl
I want you home with me, to see your face, touch
You will never know the depth of my love until you are a mother.
No more of this pap.

Your silly mother
Yours, Jane Grey Blair: Mama!
Your doting mother
I hold you in my heart, my sweet daughter
With all my love
Your own, your
I am forever your loving Mother

My dear daughter Sarah,
My own Sarah,
Sarah, child,
Sarah, beloved daughter,
I am sorry to have to write such sad news
she had not been well, as you might know, a nervous condition
hardships of The War and then such fears for you
heart failed, her doctor said
never did trust that son-of-a-bitch
I suspect some other cause
If you are still alive, as I will continue to believe
very encouraged by word of sightings!
too bad your mother couldn't
Mr. William Brown, husband of your friend, writes that negotiations
You must stay alive
Return to your home, child!
I have made arrangements that you must
as soon as you are able, please
Your father
Your Father
Your Daddy
Your grieving Father
Your old father

Mrs. Sarah Blair Randolph Byrd.
Mrs. Sarah Byrd.
Dear Sarah.
If you are able

I am so sorry to have to inform you that your father, Thomas
  Huntington Randolph
during an altercation at the home of Mr. Jackson Byrd, Sr.
Believing you to be alive still, reports of sightings, then word of
His instructions, made several weeks before the incident
The deed reverts to you
entire estate, more extensive than perhaps you understood, but
  debts and the expenses of
Currently Freedwoman Ruth Randolph and her eldest son, Ezekiel,
  kept by Mr. Byrd as sharecroppers, but
Contact me at the above address within one year of the date of this
  letter
will be offered in sale to Jackson Lee Byrd, Sr., the proceeds to pay
Send the following documents, if this is
I remember you fondly and will look forward to serving your father's
  intentions and your mother's wishes
With sincerest hopes for your safety and wellbeing,
I continue to trust, as did your father and your dear mother,
John W. Sands, Esq.

CHAPTER 5

I had been too exhausted and overwhelmed to cry. Not even for my
mother. I tried to think of her, bits of memory came and went, but
I couldn't hold on to much at all and wondered if the injuries to my
head had robbed me of some of my childhood. And I couldn't sleep.

After reveille, when the sun got high enough, I mixed myself a
quick dose, had a bite of the buttered bread and a sip of the tea that
Mary insisted I have, then went out and made myself do what had
to be done. I was close upon the lawyer Sands' deadline. I wired him
that I was alive though injured, and that when I was fully recovered,
I'd come to Richmond to settle things. I'd soon wire him with spe-
cifics. But in the meantime, I needed money. He should free some
from the estate and wire it at once. The fort commander would

attest that I was the person I claimed to be, should he require this, as I had no documents in my possession, no proof to send him.

I returned to Doc's house and went upstairs for another dose. Because it was still early in the day, I made it a light dose, then lay down on the bed and waited for it to take possession of me.

I must tell you about the feeling when the dose perfectly fits the need, in case you're not familiar with it. When one's affair with a drug is still new — as when a love is new and one is hungry for the lover's touch, still innocent of the sickness of obsession — the first feeling of it in your body is a relief so surprising it makes you inhale deeply and then exhale slowly. Makes you smile. You smile knowing that in another moment, you will feel even better. You feel the drug slow your breathing, slow your heart, ease your clenched stomach. When the body releases itself of postures of shame or fury or fear or guilt and gives in to pleasure and only pleasure, the mind follows like an eager pup. When you have achieved this state of ease in your body, and you're still capable of clear thought — or what you imagine is clear thought — you feel above the fray. You are strong. And smarter than anyone you know.

Having reached that state, I lay with it a bit. Then, because it was good but I wanted it better, I took more. I did not return to my bed. I wanted the sun on my face, wanted to feel the air that was cool and pleasant that day. I got up, straightened my clothing, came down the stairs and sat outside in a chair on the porch facing the parade ground.

I settled myself and stroked my skirts smooth over my lap, a movement that felt delicious both to the skin of my palms and to the flesh of my belly and thighs under the fabric. The breeze on my face was as good as I'd hoped it would be. Floating on it, from somewhere off to my right, I heard what I believed to be a flute. It was not a martial tune, but a folk song of some sort. The player practiced the same mournful phrase over and over. It came and went with the wind, with the low hum of voices and other sounds, punctuated by an occasional horse's whinny and the constant flapping of the flag on its pole.

People passed in small clutches or singly, at different speeds, in different directions, some went diagonally across the space, slicing a long line or cutting corners, some stuck to the well-worn pathways. All their bodies seemed to leave visible eddies and wakes in the air. When one body stopped to speak with another, the air around them slowed a bit, but was stirred again as others passed. The breeze, too, ruffled these currents, swirled and lifted them along with dust and bits of debris, up and up. The sky was too bright to look at directly.

A pair of officers in crisp uniforms, chests out, swaggered past, talking seriously to one another while looking straight ahead. An enlisted man ran by, heedless. *Watch yourself, soldier! Yes, sir! Sorry, sir!*

Men in buckskin passed. Traders? Guides? There were a few broken men, tattered and dirty. A very drunk one of these stopped in front of me, stared, weaving, tried to ask a question but was unable to speak. I was glad when he lurched by and was gone. I saw several obviously drunken soldiers. So early in the day. How did they get away with it? Jake had told me of the rawness of the rank and file there. The bastard had been right.

A few families looked as if they were taking the air on the street in some nice town, smiling as if they were not walking among drunks and killers. They came and went, shading their eyes from the glare. They kept tight hold on their children, some of whom clung shyly to skirts, some tugged like untrained dogs on leashes, some broke free and were running like mad things making their mothers call shrilly.

Voices rose and fell. English in varied accents, different Indian tongues, Swedish, Bohemian — when I didn't know, I made something up — then, suddenly, French! The sound of it gave a jolt of pleasure, though I couldn't hear well enough to understand. I tried to identify the speaker and saw a man I decided had to be French by his looks, walking with an Indian woman and a child.

Young white women whose soldier-boy husbands must have been out on manoeuvres were showing off their dresses. Whispering under their bonnets, so close together they had difficulty walking properly. Tittering, simpering. Officers' wives were no less foolish in their promenading, despite a more conspicuous confidence in the cut of their clothing.

A few whores sashayed by. I liked them for their colourful

dress — what hats! — their make-up, their brazen manner.

An Indian man, young, sharp-featured, stained khaki trousers under a blue uniform jacket, wide-brimmed Army issue hat sporting motley ornaments, swaggered past and shot me a look. Crow, I decided, paid guide for the Army. As he passed I saw something off about his gait, he was not quite sure of his boundaries, not quite certain where to place his foot with the next step. Was the whole world drunk?

Other Indians with faded blankets pulled around their shoulders, men and women, some with children, walked slightly folded in on themselves as if warding off a blow. I remembered Far Cry's derision of 'loaf abouts' at the forts, looking for handouts. These people didn't look as if they deserved anyone's censure.

The bugle by which the fort ran, and to which I'd become so accustomed that I hardly heard it, suddenly sounded. The blare echoed off every hard surface around me and hit the bones of my skull. I pressed my hands hard over my ears, shut my eyes tight, put my head down to my knees, fighting nausea.

I straightened up slowly, and opened my eyes to a shocking brightness. There was a *throng* passing by — where had they all come from so suddenly? — changing direction to look at me, slowing as they passed, putting their hands to their mouths and hissing to one another. They'd heard all about me and here I was, plain as day.

I'd taken off my eye patch upstairs and had forgotten to put it back on. I was naked, exposed for who I was, right there at their holy white parade ground, the stars and stripes whipping on its pole. They spat in my direction.

Wouldja lookit that!
No Christian woman
With that savage
Pregnant by him
Heard she lost it
Good! One less breed
Whore!
Squaw!

Traitor!

CHAPTER 6

I could not rise from the chair. The high had left me and I was sick. I needed more elixir. I told myself to sit still and breathe until I could stand, then to hold on to the chair and breathe until I could walk. Then to get myself upstairs and into my room and close and lock my door. A small dose, then sleep. I was working hard at this breathing when a man with a boy separated themselves from the crowd and came towards me. *Good god. Now they're coming after me.* Both were smiling, though, and took off their hats as they climbed the stairs.

The man announced himself as Garrett Augustus Robinson and held out his hand. I stared at it. He said I need not introduce myself, he managed the sutler's store. He'd packed up the supplies delivered to me in the dugout — adding some extras when he could — and lately he'd been keeping Irish Mary supplied with beef bones to make stock for my recovery. I leaned away from him, pressing against the chair back. It was hard to focus on his face and voice, but his manner was calming, and after a bit I was able to hear what he was saying.

He introduced his boy who had the wonderful name of Singer John Robinson. With unforced good manners the boy said, 'How d'you do, Mrs. Byrd, ma'am.' Behind them, the parade ground was as it always was, people going about their business, the flag gently waving.

Robinson's hair was so dark it was almost black and so was the boy's, but the boy's shoulder-length hair was thicker and, while his father's waved a bit, the boy's was straight. Both were rather dark complected, but the father's skin had been tanned by the weather, and the boy had the colouring and bones of an Indian. A beautiful boy. Robinson watched me figure it out and then said,

'His mother was Lakota. We named him Song Maker, but I just call him Budd. Always have. He is my best buddy and has been for all his eight years, no doubt about that.'

They smiled at one another. Then Robinson told his son to go into the house and fetch some water for Mrs. Byrd. 'Looks like you could use some.' I nodded. I concentrated on breathing, on not vomiting, on holding myself upright in the chair. The boy came back with a cup of cool water. Robinson told me to drink it and I obeyed, taking a tentative sip. Then he told the boy to please head on over to the store, he'd be there in a minute or two.

'Do you mind if I set a bit, Mrs. Byrd?'

Incapable of speech, I nodded again. He sat on the step. I learned he was from Tennessee where he'd been a blacksmith and before that, a farmer. He'd had a wife from that state who, after losing a couple of babies within a year of being born, had come out west with him around 1851, right before a big treaty with the Sioux was signed there at the fort. He'd been trading skins and other goods, they'd staked out a homestead, but she lost a couple more babies out here, then lost heart, went back home and died.

He'd met Budd's mother on a visit to her people to trade. She'd died of cholera when his son was a baby. He shook his head. So many ways to die. He sold his homestead for not much money round about 1863, and the Army hired him to run the store. The job came with quarters for him and the boy. He felt lucky just to wake up in the morning, more or less sound in body and mind, his boy in good spirits.

He asked if I'd learned to speak Lakota and I shook my head. I sipped the water, it was not helping.

'Well, you and Mrs. Brown had each other to talk to. If you'd been alone, you'd a learned it. Budd's mother talked not even the littlest bit of English. That's how I learned it. Learn one pretty good and others come easier. So, along with a few different Lakota tongues — there's differences, you know — I got some Cheyenne, Arapaho, Crow, Ree, others. I can make myself understood in most of the languages of these plains.'

I was feeling sicker. I was afraid I'd faint or vomit or die before I asked him at least a few of my questions.

'Do you still have contact with many Lakota? Any of the smaller bands, perhaps, those broken off and moving on their own?'

He said he knew a few, it was common for groups to separate from larger clans and then come back together, say, for the summer. But some people that had been friends with him just a little while back, weren't friends any longer. He was a *wasichu* and things had gotten worse.

'It's been nothing but bad since the '51 Treaty. And, now...' He shook his head. 'Now there's talk of a new one. They've sent out the word, want all the chiefs to come in and touch the pen in a couple of months. But people are angry.' He looked out over the river. 'It's like fire weather out there. This whole prairie...'

I interrupted him.

'I have to ask you, Mr. Robinson. You seem to know a good deal about me, so you must know, everyone seems to, that I had an Indian husband.'

'Yes, Ma'am, I do. The Lakota, Far Cry.'

'You knew his name! There was a fight when I was rescued, and he was involved. Is he alive? Do you know?'

'I've heard only a little... Complicated story...'

'But what do you know of him now? Is he alive?'

'I'm afraid I don't know that for sure, Ma'am. That was a terrible shame, what happened to you that morning, shouldn't have gone that way.'

'Can you tell me exactly what did happen, Mr. Robinson? I have yet to understand exactly what happened that morning.'

'Well, I doubt anyone could tell you *exactly* what happened.'

He looked off, shaking his head. His stalling infuriated me.

'That's ridiculous. Someone must know.'

I was sick. Sweat was running down between my breasts in front and my shoulder blades in back. My face dripped, and I'd begun to shiver.

'You're looking a bit poorly, there, Mrs. Byrd, are you sure now's the time? Listen, I'm here whenever you want to talk...'

'We're talking *now*, Mr. Robinson. Tell me what you've heard.'

'Yes, well... You do not look well, ma'am, drink some more of that water.'

'What do you know? Tell me, now! Please.'

'Far Cry had been hard to find. So, a while back, Custer had his men surprise a village and they took an old man who...'

'I know about this. *Tell me about that morning.*'

'Well, it's pretty near impossible...'

'*What the hell happened!*'

'Some say Custer didn't have no intention at all of making a trade. The plan was that once he'd got you two women under his control, the rest of that troop was to take out the village. But something went bad. No one expected Far Cry to attack the column, Custer's scouts had got something wrong. Seven soldiers are dead and no one knows how many Indians. Far Cry was shot but his men got him away. There was a magazine writer along, and he's dead. Someone said Custer did it. But, here's the thing, Mrs. Byrd. There's another story says that he wasn't even there. No one talks about it. It's like it never happened.'

'But it happened! I've got a dead baby in the ground and a husband lost or dead. *I deserve to know the truth!*'

'The truth? This is the Army, Ma'am. There's a *war* happening here, and we're way the hell out where nothing makes sense. My best advice to you is to go back home and try to forget you ever came to Indian country. You're young. Start over...'

I leaned over my lap and began to retch.

'Oh, no. Here, now, let me help you upstairs. Slowly, now. It's okay. I'll get Mary to come along quick and we'll get you comfortable.'

CHAPTER 7

Maybe it started in my mind or maybe the dose had been too strong or maybe I'd have gotten sick in any case, but I sank into a deep affliction. Doc and Mary and Lizzie were in and out. I couldn't get out of bed. I did my best to stay high. I'd say I had severe pains in my body and needed a stronger mix of my elixir and Doc obliged me, or I thought he did. I slept or watched the light change on the wall until night.

I remember seeing the first snow of the season. I went to the window, opened it and leaned out. The snow was falling steadily at an angle. I liked the deep quiet. It was like having a taste of death while still alive. Just a soupçon, just enough, I said to myself. But, in fact, I wanted it to snow forever. I mourned hard. I mourned my mother's death and that I hadn't been there to tell her I loved her.

One day, not long, I think, after that first day of snow, Mary came up to tell me Lizzie and William's friend Bron was downstairs having come to get supplies. She gave me a note from Elizabeth in which she suggested I come back with Bron and spend some time with the family. They'd keep me warm and well fed. She missed me and wanted to take care of me. *Your loving friend, Lizzie.* I told Mary to say I was still too sick to travel.

I closed my door, waited a minute to make sure Mary didn't have some new reason to knock. I mixed myself a very strong dose, stronger than usual. I couldn't remember when I'd had the last one and didn't care. I got back into bed. A couple of deep breaths and I felt that some beneficent deity was pulling a black velvet comforter up over my body. Oh, it was good. I could almost believe in god and angels.

Then, suddenly, Doc was at the side of the bed shaking me, haranguing me in a stream of sentences with no breaks between them. He looked into my eyes, felt my pulse, listened to my chest. He said I owned a body stronger than I deserved. If I wanted to kill it, I'd have to be less cowardly about my methods. A bullet to the temple, maybe. But I should go home, damn it. And I had to get off the goddamn drug now, before it got too hard.

'I'm not addicted.'

He laughed out loud.

'You're on your way, but quit now. The worst is behind you. Go home, girl.'

I told him I suspected the worst was ahead of me. There was nothing and no one to 'go home' to. My mother was dead. My life was worthless. He said if I really felt that sorry for myself, he'd fix up a syringe for me right that moment. Hell, he'd even inject it so I wouldn't fuck it up. But he told me I was a fool to think that way.

'How old are you anyway?'

'Twenty? Maybe not yet… No. Twenty.'

'Jesus Christ,' he said. 'I thought you were older. The scar makes it hard to tell. Well… You'll stay here till you're off the laudanum. Then you need to go home.'

I told him I couldn't yet get off it entirely, too much pain. I began to cry. I was terrified of quitting.

'It's alright, it's alright. We'll go slow. I know there's some pain still from what happened to you, but I suspect you've got a weakness for this stuff.'

I told him it was possible. My mother had used laudanum, she'd started after giving birth to me. I got in control of my voice and told him I understood what he was telling me, understood the danger I was in, but I needed more time. I had things to figure out and it helped. I wasn't ready.

He looked at me for a bit, then took a small bottle of laudanum from his pocket. He poured water in my glass and fixed a light dose that he gave me to drink.

'It's got to be your decision. Be an addict or don't be. But you need to get the hell away from here. *Go home.*'

I gave him back the glass which he put on the table. He put the bottle beside it.

'I don't want to be an addict.'

'Good. Then, Mary and I will help you get off this. You will get regular small doses for a while, getting smaller and smaller. If you decide you don't want to quit, you'll have get the hell away from here right then. I don't want to find your corpse in the bed where my wife died. Understand?'

I nodded. He turned to go, and I was suddenly afraid to be alone.

'Doc. Come lie down next to me. Just for a bit.'

'Oh, dear girl. I am not…'

'I just want someone to lie by my side a little while. Stay outside the covers.'

He put his bag on the table and lay down next to me. He lay on top of the blankets and took my hand in his. I told him I didn't want to die, but I didn't know how to live.

'I can't give you any answers,' he said, 'but I'll tell you a story about addiction. I was top of my class at Jefferson Medical College in Philadelphia. Then The War broke out. When it was over, I could have built a nice practice in Philadelphia, lived a normal life. I'd married a girl from a good family, well educated, wonderful girl. My Jane.'

'My mother's name.'

'Been a long time since I've said her name out loud. God! How I loved her. But when you're doing medicine in the middle of a war, you're called on in a way that's not like anything else. I was addicted to the madness of it. And then it was over. How the hell do I replace that? "Normal" life? What the hell is that? Then I learned they needed doctors out here. I talked her into coming with me.

'Jane had all these ideas about The Noble Savage. Neither of us had ever even *seen* an Indian, but she'd attended lectures, done a lot of reading. She believed that he could be "civilised" and that we should be part of that effort. She was a fervent assimilationist. Know what that's about? Ask Elizabeth. I'd bet money that if she doesn't know already, she will soon. So we came out here and she died, goddamn it. Pneumonia. I couldn't save her.'

He was quiet for a bit.

'Are you asleep yet?'

I told him I wasn't, but that I liked his choice of bedtime stories. He laughed. Said it was a good thing that I could make a joke. But he hadn't yet gotten to the part about addiction.

'After she died? Heroin and cocaine. *Fine* mix. I fucking loved it and I sorely tested my limits, but I wasn't ready to die. I assessed the situation and decided I didn't have *time* to die. With more immigrants coming out here all the time, I was too busy. I'm still busy. I stay busy. Staying so busy at your work that you don't have time to think is another addiction, but it's a useful one. I treat Indians, too. Some whites get richly pissed by that. *Don't that make you a traitor, doc?*

'But the way I see it, we're not all that different. On these plains, the whites and the Indians share a cult of death. We're both warriors. We both say we're protecting our families. We both believe that we, and only we, know the Holiest of All Paths. And the truth, as I see it, is that what we both want most in this life is to wipe the other off the face of the earth. Feeling justified. With a band playing, cheered on by our women. I don't believe in God, but Fate makes a kind of sense. It's their fate to lose this one, and ours to win, though we sure as hell don't deserve it. I am sorely tired of it all. But I keep going.'

'Why?'

'I've got the habit of staying alive. I'm addicted to what comes next. To wondering just how bad it can get before it gets better. If it ever does.'

I did not believe he was right about what the Indians wanted, not the ones I knew. And I *would* not believe it was their fate to lose.

'Sarah, find something clean and good to get addicted to. Or at least something that makes you feel useful. But, I warn you, you're not going to find it out here, not in these times.'

When I woke very late, possibly close to dawn, Doc had gone. Though the room was quite dark and I couldn't see the bottle, I knew exactly where it was. I knew where the pitcher of water was and where my glass was, with a spoon to the right of it. I could see the outline of the table-top not far from the end of the bed. Everything I needed was within easy reach. I imagined how it would feel to close my hand around the smooth edges of that small, rectangular bottle. It was a pretty little thing and would feel cool to my hand. I knew the weight of it. I knew the weight of the pitcher and what it would sound like to pour water into a glass, then drip in the drug. I could imagine the small clink of the spoon as I stirred. I knew how it would taste. I knew how it would feel.

I thought of my mother. By choosing not to fix a dose, by choosing to stop this march towards addiction, I was placing myself in judgment of her, I was placing myself above her. I hadn't loved her well enough while she lived, and now that she was dead, I was betraying her by choosing not to become her.

I begged her forgiveness as I emptied the bottle of laudanum into the chamber pot under the bed where it mixed with my piss. I was done. For a time.

CHAPTER 8

Doc's face came all alight when he remembered the trunk. Mary, Doc and I had finished dinner at my table — in Doc's old room that had become my home — and were having a bit of brandy when he thought of the trunk.

I'd declined Lizzie's invitation to Thanksgiving dinner, but Christmas was coming. I'd been invited to spend the holiday and had said, Yes. But I had no gifts. There was no time to order anything from any city large enough to have suitable gifts. I ought to have anticipated this, ought to have been a better friend. I said something about it to Mary and Doc.

Mary said not to worry, she'd been busy knitting. Much of the wool she'd gotten from unraveling things left behind — 'God bless deserters and their women!' — and washing the wool. She'd make mittens and I could say they were from me. She also said she'd doing a lot of baking for the men and their families and planned to put aside some cookies and pies for the Browns whom she'd come to like very much.

She squinted at me.

'I might even let you into my kitchen to help me bake, but you will follow my orders precisely and in all matters, or out you will go.'

I agreed, but was still glum about it being too late to order something special from the east. Especially for Lizzie. Her dresses and her one cloak had gotten threadbare.

Then Doc remembered the trunk. He pushed back his chair so suddenly it nearly fell over.

'I'd just about forgotten about all this. It's time, goddamnit.'

He went to a corner of the room, removed a lamp and a faded linen cloth from the lid of a large old trunk, and dragged the trunk right up close to the table.

'My Jane's things. After I buried her — right out there, actually — I packed them up. I don't know why I left those few dresses hanging in there. Maybe I had a sense they'd be useful to someone. But, in here... *Fuck me!* I locked it, of course, and have no idea where the damn key is. Damn it to hell!'

'Just hold on there!' Mary ran out of the room, downstairs, and ran right back up with a hammer. She hit it hard and the lock broke.

'I'm going to leave you ladies to plumb the depths of that thing. Use it all. She'd be happy.' And he left.

Doc's Jane had had good taste. There were four or five dresses of good wool, one of pale blue velvet with lace trimmings. There were fine linen or silk petticoats and shifts, prettily embroidered. I was most excited by a boiled woollen cloak of midnight blue lined in black satin, with a hood lined in silver fox fur. 'Lizzie will be so beautiful in this!' There was a pale green silk quilt with what felt like goose down in it. Somehow, no damp seemed to have gotten to the trunk's contents. There were several sachets of lavender among the layers.

I held one of the dresses up to me.

'I believe they can be made to fit her beautifully. Mary, what do you think?'

'For you they'll need tucking and lengthening, but...'

'Nothing for me, these must all be for Lizzie.'

'Take one, you idiot, you have no decent clothes, I'll make it fit. But I suspect they're nearly perfect for our girl. I'll give you a paper of pins, so when she puts them on, if there's a tuck needed here or there, you can mark it and bring it back to me.'

I pulled a small, unpainted pine box with a lid from a corner of the trunk and in it, wrapped in cottonwool, were six glass Christmas ornaments in different shapes, different colours. Mary had never seen anything like them. I had.

'My mother's friend in France sent her some like this. We had them on our Christmas tree back in Virginia.'

I knew William would be making toys for Charles and Joey, I'd help Mary bake, and with these things, Christmas was solved.

Mary, as I'd suspected, would not be able to come to Lizzie and William's home for Christmas. There were officers and enlisted men on the fort, most of whom were lonely for their families, and she would stay and create a feast for them. William or Bron would come to fetch me early Christmas Eve morning.

The day before, once Mary had completed her own work, she called me down to the kitchen in Doc's house. She used it consistently now, as the kitchen she had been using before was too accessible to the rank and file.

'Those fellows would come in and out without so much as a by-your-leave, and dip their nasty fingers in the sauce!'

The place smelled like a glutton's heaven. I'd been getting healthier and hungrier by the day.

I had told Mary I wanted to make some pies — peach, apple, pear, cherry? — and maybe a cake of some sort. She'd raised her eyebrows, said she'd see what she could gather together and we'd do the best we could and be happy with it.

Lined up on a counter were several cans of peaches, and she showed me burlap bags filled with dried plums and cherries. She had flower, sugar, many different spices, 'and that fresh butter you so love.'

'Then there's this.' She pulled forward a wooden box, opened the lid and lifted out a large plate on which sat a domed thing, wrapped in what appeared to be several layers of deeply stained linen.

'A Christmas cake! Doc found it months ago, left behind in an officer's rooms after he'd been killed. Poor man's wife must have sent it to him. Smell!'

The aroma was dark and rich, a bit mysterious. It looked like something long buried. I was worried how a year-old-cake would be, but Mary said that covered with linen and regularly soaked in liquor — which she'd done since she found it — they can last a very long time. She'd been waiting for the right occasion and this was it.

I turned out to be a poor pie baker and a messy cookie maker, but I was a fine drinking companion to Mary that night. She told me about coming to America, what New York looked like when she and her parents and two older siblings got off the boat. She was the only one to survive the first couple of years. They'd lived with a lot of others from Ireland in a part of the City called Five Points, and in 1849 cholera struck, killing so many it was a struggle to bury them all. Her entire family was taken. She was twelve years old. When I asked what she did then, and how she made her way here, she refused to speak of it.

She filled our cups with more whiskey.

'In that small pot over there is some chokeberry wine I want us to taste. It's getting warmed up with a bit o' this and that to spice it up. You'll have to tell me what you think.'

We had to stop what we were doing to laugh out loud many times that day. When we finally got to it, the spiced chokeberry wine was syrup, we tasted it and found it superb, but we were very drunk and perhaps not very critical. She poured it over the linen-wrapped Christmas Cake. I said I would cut a piece a bring to back to her. She thought that was a fine idea.

CHAPTER 9

It was slow going through the snow already on the ground, and a light snow was still falling. But Bron's horses got us to the house just as dusk was settling in on Christmas Eve. Since I'd last seen it, the house had been painted white with dark green shutters. Each window downstairs showed yellow in the blue air, and smoke was coming out of the chimney. Bron called out, the door opened and there they were, Lizzie, William, Charles and Joey, silhouetted against the glow of their home.

A flurry of activity followed, parcels going hand to hand then carried inside. This was done in a hurry so Bron could get back to his house.

The gifts were placed carefully under the tree, festooned with homemade ornaments. Dolls of straw and wood, ribbons, bits of lace, dried flowers, cookies shaped like stars, tin cups that held tiny candles. The boys told me they'd gone out with their father early that morning to cut it, and the family had spent the day decorating it. I agreed that it was, indeed, the most beautiful tree ever.

Elizabeth took my coat and carpet bag and carried them upstairs.

William handed me hot coffee with whiskey in it. 'It's pretty cold out there. I figured you'd need this.' The pies and the Christmas cake were carried into the kitchen and I was ushered to a cozy chair in front of the fireplace where a fine blaze was crackling over a bed of coals.

Candles had been placed all around the room, and all the lamps were lit. When I'd last visited, this same room, that then been unfinished and spare, had been a cool relief from the heat outside. Now it was the very heart of comforting warmth. I did my best to ease into the pleasure of it.

Lizzie popped to attention and said she must go finish dinner preparations, we'd be eating quite soon.

'I'll help you...'

'Absolutely not! You're our guest! My boys — all three of them! — have been looking forward to your visit. Sit right there by the fire. Please!'

I convinced her to first open one of the gifts I'd brought, as it was for the whole family. I handed the parcel to Charles who was sitting on the floor against his father's legs, and, leaning in to look him in the eye, told him to open it with care as what it contained was extremely fragile. He accepted this responsibility with gravity. Joey scooted closer, and Lizzie came up to where I was sitting and put her hand on my shoulder, I placed my hand on hers.

Charles untied the ribbon then unfolded the paper carefully, revealing the pine box. When he pulled the first of the glass ornaments from its cottonwool nest, he gasped. We all did. As if he could not trust his hands, he looked to his father. William gently took it from him and held it up so the fire and all the room's glowing lights reflected on the shiny sphere. This one was a bright apple-red ball streaked with sparkling gold. William handed it to Lizzie. I'd tied silk loops so they could be hung on a tree and Lizzie did so right then. One by one, all six were lifted, admired, and after some discussion over where was best, hung on the tree. When all were in place, we sat for a minute and looked at them. Red, gold, green, blue, purple, silver. Each reflected the light differently, and the effect dazzled us. Then Lizzie said she absolutely *had* to get dinner on the table or it would be ruined and she swooshed out of the room.

She placed a venison roast before us, surrounded by potatoes and turnips and carrots and onions, and on the side, a compote of canned fruits mixed with dried berries. There was a basket of breads and rolls with fresh butter and honey. The boys had milk to drink, and we grown people had some hard cider William had gotten at the fort. Bron had given them the meat. He kept them well supplied. I asked if he and his wife might not be joining us, and a look passed between Lizzie and William.

Bron and his wife had stayed at home, Lizzie said. She was ill and didn't like to leave her house. Later she told me there were serious troubles in their home. Bron's wife was from Warsaw, born and raised in that city, but he'd met her in New York where they'd arrived a short time before. She was quite young, pretty, seemed lively, from a large, poor family who'd come to America hoping to better their circumstances. He'd wanted a wife, was smitten by her, and gave her family some money. But starting with the trip west, there were difficulties.

He'd told William he thought the very vastness of the plains, the emptiness, intimidated her over much, that all the way over and even once here, she'd clung to his side 'like a scared pup'. But he'd been certain she'd get used to it. He said that when she wasn't frightened, she was 'an affectionate little thing'. He was in love. But it wasn't enough. Lizzie told me that, while we were enjoying Christmas dinner, she was probably lying in bed. She rarely left it, now, though she never spoke of pain or physical illness. Often Bron could not get her to eat.

The boys fell asleep while William was reading from Matthew about the first Christmas. I nearly did as well. My belly was full with the roast and I was lulled by the fire's warmth and William's soothing voice. Lizzie roused the boys and took them upstairs to bed. William poured us each a bit of whiskey and we sat watching the fire. Soon, I, too, was ready for sleep. I passed Lizzie coming down as I was going up to the boys' room. She'd prepared it for me as last time. We hugged on the stairs. 'God bless you, dear friend', she said. I thanked her for having me there. I felt full of good food, of whiskey, and most especially, of the good will of my friends. I remember thinking, 'This is better than laudanum!' I had to laugh at myself.

I woke before dawn hearing the boys. 'Please, Mama!' 'But it *is* morning! *Christmas* morning!' 'We've been *so good!*' In a bit, we were all downstairs.

Things seemed to happen all at once. A fresh, crackling fire was built on top of coals still live from the night before, griddle cakes and coffee were had, candy and coins and tops and other small toys pulled from the stockings, parcels were distributed with excitement — 'but we will not be greedy!' — paper and ribbon were pushed aside as each of the gifts was opened and exclaimed over.

For his wife, William had gotten an opal pendant from a trader who happened to be at Laramie and was desperate to make a sale. William had put it on a black silk ribbon and tied it around Lizzie's neck. She brushed tears from her cheeks. The green silk feather quilt from me also made her weep. But the cloak from Doc's Jane was the grand prize. Lizzie stood to put it on — it fit her perfectly — she pulled up the hood and swirled the skirt. Seeing their pretty mother in that deep blue wool, the silver fox fur hood pulled up, seemed to shock the boys. William, too. All three stared, wonder-struck.

Lizzie had knit me a sweater in soft purple yarn that I put on immediately. William had carved for me an exquisite small casket polished to a soft sheen, a flower and leaves twined round one another on the lid.

Then the boys were layered up in their new scarves, mittens, socks, sweaters, hats — 'Seems they should save these for...' 'For what, Lizzie girl? Take a gander at these fine looking fellows!' They put on their boots and coats and went outside. It was a bright day. We three sat amid the ruins — William had to insist that she sit, all would get straightened up in time — and drank more coffee. I was glad I'd thought to bring a good-sized bag of it, and sugar, too. Lizzie cut some of the Christmas cake. William and I liked it very much, she wasn't so sure. 'The boys won't care for it. Too rich.' 'And that's just fine', said William. 'More for us.' I had a feeling I'd be taking plenty back for Mary.

Later, it was just Lizzie and me before the fire, quiet, content. She turned to me and said, 'This is quite a different sort of Christmas from the one we knew last year, isn't it? My heavens!'

'Well, of course, Lizzie. Your lovely home. Plenty of food to eat. And we're *warm!*'

'Yes! Thank the Lord! That cold was endless. One storm after another, each worse than the one before.'

'Impossible ever to get warm and stay warm.'

'And so many people dying. With that horrible wailing each time. Makes me shudder just to think of it!'

'It had its purpose, though. It *has* its purpose.'

'It sounded like animals screaming.'

'It was a very difficult time. But, Lizzie, our spontaneous little Christmas was rather sweet, in its way. Mary was happy and starting to get big with her baby. She was the one who told us it was Christmastime. Remember? The avalanche had not yet happened, our old women were ailing but still alive. It *was* very cold, but not nearly as bad as what was to come.'

'You're right. It did, indeed, get much worse. But it was around that time, Christmas, that everyone seemed to get that horrible cough. People died of it and with each one, oh, that wailing. And the cutting of hair, the slashing of arms and legs, and faces! Horrible!'

'But that night, Lizzie, the two of us managed, in spite of everything, to share a bit of Christmas, even if only for a few moments. Remember? It was lovely.'

'Yes, it was. We were able to forget for that brief bit. I remember your stories about Christmas in your home. The women in their beautiful dresses.'

'It was certainly fancy,' I said. I'd left out of the story my mother's terrible anxiety for perfection in the decorating, her pacing back and forth, yelling at Ruth, 'Not there, you fool!' And how, if they failed to follow her orders exactly, she'd sometimes strike out at the servants who were moving the furniture, hanging the tapestries, draping the sashes. Then, at dinner, all was transformed. The house was a vision, the food was delicious. Everyone was spectacularly beautiful, and in a short time, spectacularly drunk.

'Then, when I became so sad with missing my family, you put

your arms around me and began singing. What a lovely thing to do, Sarah. I still think of that with gratitude.'

'And you joined in. We sang softly so as not to wake my old one — what was her name? Awful that I've forgotten it... *Ah!* Bright Bird! — but we managed to sing an entire verse. In harmony. And you sang a pretty descant at the end. Remember?'

I could see by her expression that she did not.

'Don't you remember? We tried so hard to sing softly, whisper-ing almost, but we got a bit carried away at the end. Then, when I heard her cough, I thought, Oh, no! We've awaked her, and she's so sick...'

Lizzie's expression was now quite quizzical.

'Lizzie! You *must* remember this! We held out that last note, grin-ning like children, tears streaming down our cheeks, and then the poor old thing started coughing...'

'Sarah, I'm afraid you're mistaken. She didn't exactly cough...'

'She did! She suddenly began coughing hard. It startled us, but when we turned around, we saw she was *smiling.*'

Lizzie shook her head.

'Sarah, dear, I don't recall it quite that way. Not at all, actually. We never sang a full verse. Only a few lines. You began to sing and just as I joined in — and we were *so* quiet — she heard. And, sweet friend, she didn't *cough*, she *hissed* at us. She'd half lifted herself up and was trying to say something, but all that came out was hissing and sputtering, she was gesturing with one of those hands like claws. We were both very much taken aback. Dearest, she was not smiling. She looked at us with purest hatred.'

Her choice of words, 'purest hatred', shocked me. I told her this was impossible.

'There would not have been *hatred,* there *couldn't* have been hatred at that time. No, Lizzie. You're mistaken.'

'Perhaps not hatred, but certainly anger. She was sick and very angry to have her sleep disturbed by these two silly white women. Right away, you broke from me to bring her some water. I whispered my goodbye and went back to my tipi, to my own sick old woman.'

I could not speak. Lizzie's interpretation felt like a betrayal. In my calmest voice, I said,

'How interesting that we recall this same event so very differently. I don't know what to make of this. I've always had a good memory and this one is so deeply etched that I can *see* it.'

'Goodness. I'm certain of my recollection, as well. But let's not pursue this any further right now, Sarah dear, I need to begin preparations for dinner. Besides, I don't believe it's really so important, this little difference. Not really important at all.'

I started up to join her in the kitchen, but she told me to stay where I was and rest. Her family had sent some issues of Harper's that were on a shelf under a small table, and I might find them entertaining. She'd call if she needed me. She asked if I wanted more coffee, or tea, or a bite of something to eat. I told her I did not and thanked her. The exchange felt awkward and superficial.

I took an issue of Harper's, opened it and stared at the page. She'd said it was not important. It was *very* important. I was *not* wrong. Lizzie had altered the scene's details to fit with her hatred of the life we'd lived with the Indians. I took a deep breath. I did not want to be angry with my friend on Christmas Day in her home.

Then I felt a stab of doubt: Could she be right? Could *I* have been the one to invent? Had I felt the need to make a romance of the experience in order to survive it? No. I would not have done that. I would not have felt any such need. And that particular memory was quite clear. I may have lost parts of my childhood, I may not recall precisely when things happened, what month, what year, I might forget names, but how my world looks, feels, smells, tastes, what people say and how they say it, these things stay with me, and are very precise.

I sat back and closed my eyes. I was to spend this night as well in their house, and wished I were not. Once again, I felt I didn't belong with these people. I had little in common with Elizabeth's vision of the world, reinforced with Bible reading. Her ignorance about things beyond her cozy domestic sphere annoyed me. William followed events, but I wondered if he discussed anything with Lizzie other than homestead matters.

The last I'd spoken with Garrett about the Indians, he'd said that most had refused Sherman's latest order to move onto the reservations, and both sides were hair-trigger itchy. Efforts to bring in the big chiefs to sign a new treaty had been put off until the spring. All of this was important. Elizabeth lived in the midst of it, but never seemed interested unless it was to voice her fears of Indian depredations.

I wanted to be back at the fort. News of Far Cry, or news that might tell me something of his circumstances and that of his people, could come at any time. This was not my life, this tidy, pretty home, prayers at dinner, prayers at bedtime. I wished I'd put elixir in my flask and stuffed it in my carpet bag. I'd not tasted the stuff since I'd seen Doc, but I wanted it right then.

Later that day, there was more good food, and while the boys played with their new toys, William and I enjoyed our whiskey. After dinner, he took out his guitar and everyone sang Christmas songs. Lizzie asked if I knew any special songs of the season that were sung in Virginia. I told them I'd sing a carol my mother had taught me. It was not from Virginia, it was French, one of my favourites as a girl.

I sang it first in French, to show off, no doubt, but also to reinforce for Lizzy in case she ever questioned it, my ease with the language. But then, feeling guilty, I sang it in English, softly, like the lullaby it is: *Here 'mid the ass and oxen mild, sleeps, sleeps, sleeps my little Child...* A pretty song, I kept it to one verse and everyone seemed to enjoy it. Then even before the boys went up, I said my goodnights and climbed the stairs.

I slept fitfully and, finally, in the middle of the night, got up and wrapped a shawl over my nightdress. I wanted whiskey. I'd seen where William kept it, I knew where the cups were, I'd help myself. I had brought two bottles from the fort, so did not feel I was taking anything I shouldn't. I was in the kitchen looking out the window at the moon on the snow, about to sip from the cup...

'Mind if I join you?'

I hadn't heard William come down. I told him it would be a pleasure, that I'd been unable to sleep, muttering something about the excitement. He poured himself a cup, lifted it, I lifted mine, and we toasted one another happy Christmas.

'And let's hope the new year brings better times for all of us,' he said.

I was not optimistic, but that seemed a good thing good to toast nevertheless. We stood sipping our drinks, looking at the scene outside, the perfect, white quiet of it.

'Are you well?'

I told him I was well enough. That I had to make arrangements soon to travel back to Virginia, to settle things regarding the plantation.

He suggested I wait until spring as the weather could blow up bad of a sudden out here, making travel treacherous. And the Indian situation was not good and was likely to get worse. I said I'd heard the same thing and would take all this into consideration. Then he said,

'You know, our Lizzie is hoping that one day you'll decide to stay close by. She said I wasn't to tell you, but I think you should know she wants me to build you a cabin down in that bit of meadow near the stream. She wants me to get started on it soon as I can.'

'Ah. Bless her dear heart. And yours. But, William, please don't build me a cabin. I have no idea what my life will be, where I'll need to live, anything.'

'Yep. That's about what I told her. You're like a sister to her, you know. You've become like family to all of us. She told me about how you saved her life once, when a drunken trader tried to kill her. You'll always have a place here, Sarah. But I told her to give you time to figure things out. There's been so much...' I finished the sentence for him.

'Life.'

I drank the last of my whiskey and thanked William for his family's many kindnesses. I lay awake all night and was dressed and ready when I heard Lizzie go down to start breakfast. I waited a bit before I joined her. I stood at the foot of the stairs and watched her from the back as she went about preparing the morning meal. She was humming softly.

CHAPTER 10

March. After a stormy, frigid winter, the snow was finally beginning to melt. I'd seen little of Lizzie and her family, but I felt at home in my room at the fort. William and Bron came for supplies every now and then, and I'd have a whiskey with them. Bron's wife had died. Sometime in January, he'd gone hunting and been delayed in getting home. A sudden vicious storm had blown up and he'd had to spend two nights in a shelter he'd made from deadfall, digging himself out when the snow let up enough to see where he was going. The house was empty. Both front and back doors had just about been ripped from their hinges by the wind, and snow had blown into the house. It was still snowing, there were no tracks. He searched for days but it wasn't until a sudden thaw a couple of weeks later that he found what was left of her. She'd been partially eaten. Bron hoped she'd died of the cold first. He wasn't doing very well. William told me it was hard for him to stay, but he couldn't think of anywhere else to go.

But William, Bron, Garrett and I, Mary too when she wasn't busy, and Doc when he was around, kept good company until William and Bron had to head back home. An old friend of Garrett's had come by, and stayed in a tipi down in the Indian camp. Garrett said this man used to make a good living as a trapper until men stopped wearing beaver skin hats, preferring silk. Frank Bell, though no one ever used his first name, was English going back several generations on his father's side, but French on his mother's side. He said he spoke French, Spanish, German, maybe others. He also claimed to know the languages of most of the plains tribes.

He was dark and angular, rather tall. I told him once that he looked a bit Indian. His reply was, 'Maybe, some. You know the French.' Years back, he'd lived a while with the Brulé Sioux, and after that, he'd spent a good amount of time with the Cheyenne. He'd had a Cheyenne wife. His time with the Brulé had also, apparently, involved a woman.

He was a trader, but I was never clear about what he traded. Guns, definitely, unapologetically. He said that though it would never be a fair fight because of the numbers, the Indians should at least have small arms on a par with those of the whites. Mary told me he sometimes sold opium to wealthy European hunters who thought it was exotic, something to talk about back home.

Sometimes, he said, he took work as a guide and interpreter. But he hated interpreting between whites and Indians because each side heard only what they wanted to hear. And if they didn't, they accused *him* of lying. It was a dangerous profession, so he'd pretty much priced himself out of it. I think he was older than Garrett, but I've never been good at judging such things. After a few drinks, he told a good story and was sympathetic to the Indian, so I liked him.

I ended up knowing Bell for a long time and he never spoke of it, but Garrett told me that his Cheyenne wife and young daughter had been murdered not far from their village down in Kansas territory. The girl was only about five years old when she and her mother and a few other women were digging turnips and were all shot to death by a couple of drunken soldiers. Nothing was done. When questioned, they said they'd killed some savages who threatened them. They'd been hired by the US government to kill Indians, right?

I had noticed that Bell could get restive, touchy. After a bit, he'd simply disappear, to rejoin us after a bit, easier in manner. It took a couple of repetitions for me to catch on. Then, once, when he excused himself, I caught Mary's eye and she nodded in affirmation. He was using opium, preferred to inject it and kept the implements in a beaded pouch he wore at his waist. I could hardly hold it against him.

On an afternoon in late March, Mary came out with some biscuits and jerked beef left over from the noon meal to enjoy with our whiskey. All spring, the talk had been about a new treaty. The signing wasn't going to happen until April, but Indians were already starting to arrive, adding to the already sizeable village just outside the fort. Garrett said business at the store was brisking up, more soldiers had come, and more traders prowled among the growing number of tipis. The new grass was barely up and the Indians' horses were chomping it right back down.

The men would tilt back their chairs and tell stories. They

lampooned the officer class currently stationed at Laramie, a fairly squalid bunch, but the enlisted men were worse. They'd discuss the prevailing attitude towards the Indian among the country's leaders: that he was a ferocious, sub-human being. They talked about the impeachment of Andrew Johnson, and who'd succeed him come November. They talked about guns, horses, different places they'd been, work they'd done, just about everything. Except women. I guess that with Mary and I sitting there, they knew they were outclassed.

But with the treaty signing coming near, the talk was mostly about Indians. These white men talked about Indians as if, having lived close to them, and having married into the culture, they had uniquely valuable insights. They did. I'd thought the same of myself, though no one ever asked me about it. They both knew of my history with Far Cry's band, yet those men never asked me for my opinion. Be that as it would, if any of us had any slight edge on understanding the Indian, it did the Indian no good whatsoever.

Yet here we were, yammering on about Indians: four *wasichus*, the most dangerous predator on the prairie, sitting in chairs on the porch of a comfortable two-story wood frame, white painted house, on a US Army fort in that tinderbox frontier, drinking pretty good whiskey out of glass tumblers. Protected by uniforms and Howitzers, we watched the Indians arrive for this event that had been made by whites for the good of whites, and sold to the Indians through exaggerations and lies. 'Just another mean-assed deal,' Bell called it.

We'd see them riding in from a distance, and when they got close, the men in the front line would gallop their horses. They'd be dressed in full battle array, the chiefs with their eagle feather bonnets flying behind them, the horses caparisoned gayly. They'd be followed by their families, several dragging travois with the makings of tipis and everything they'd need to set up camp. The women among those already there greeted the newcomers with the tremolo. We'd drink to them.

Shaking their heads, Garrett and Bell said they were pretty sure how things would go, and their pessimism annoyed me. Mary never offered an opinion, she was skeptical of the motives of men in general.

All those whites prosecuting the war against the Indians, politicians, bureaucrats, military brass down to the rank and file soldiers in the field, shared one important piece of certainty: They would win. Doc had said pretty much the same thing. Many of the chiefs knew it, too. They wanted to make the shift of power go as well as it possibly could for their people. So they'd come to touch the pen.

Both Garrett and Bell had strong doubts about the personnel in the Peace Commission that had been traveling all over Indian country for months, talking up the treaty, making promises, trying to round up signers. They described as officious, patronising, dangerous, pompous, alcoholic, incompetent and cruel those men who would preside over the signing in a few weeks.

'Harney? And General Philip "The-Only-Good-Indian-is-a-Dead Indian" Sherman? Shit.'

They told me that very few of the Indians who would make their marks on the thing would understand what they were signing.

'But interpreters will be present, will they not?' I asked. Bell and Garrett said there would, indeed, be interpreters for *most* of the languages represented. They went back forth on the nature of interpreters, Bell having an inside perspective.

'Mr. Bell. Think they'll find any who aren't drunks?'

'No sir. But maybe they'll find a few honest drunks.'

'Not likely.'

'Not likely. But what the hell difference does it make? As if anything Washington promises, written down on paper and signed or not, has any meaning out here.'

Because when the document with the Indians' marks on it would finally get delivered to the halls of power in Washington for ratification, all sorts of 'adjustments' would be made, of which the Indians would have no knowledge. That is until they broke the new rules, or demanded something they were no longer entitled to, and then they'd be punished. The entire exercise, as my friends described it, was pretty much a charade.

CHAPTER 11

On the twenty-ninth day of April in the year 1868, Garrett, Bell, and I walked down to the Indian encampment, swollen to at least three times its usual size. We walked through to the big, canvas tent where the signing was taking place. We stood near the entrance and watched people walking in and out.

In the deep shade of the tent, the Commissioners, in their brass-buttoned blue uniforms, sat on chairs at tables, piles of papers in front of them, several ink pots and pens here and there. Light filtered though thick dust that moved with the coming and going. The Indians, chiefs of their people, their blankets folded around them, sat on the ground. I saw they were on a level with the tall leather boots of the whites, having to look up past the boots in order to watch the Commissioners' eyes while the reading and interpreting droned on and on. I wondered how they felt about that. Why were there no chairs for the chiefs?

Garrett pointed out Harney, with his white bushy beard and red face. I said he looked like Santa Claus.

'*Santa Claus?*' Bell made a rough sound in his throat. 'That's "Squaw Killer Harney".'

I asked him how he got that name and he spat, 'Blue Water. He killed about a hundred Sioux there because some hungry Brulé boy killed a Mormon's half-dead cow the year before and somewhere else. Did you never hear about this?'

I hadn't. So, while standing there, glaring at Harney, he told me a brief version of the story. A stupid young officer named Grattan had fired a howitzer in the camp of a chief named Conquering Bear, killing several. The Indians — Brulé, Oglala and some Mniconjous — had been friendly, had taken pains to be known as 'friendlies', but when Grattan fired on them, they became justifiably enraged. Conquering Bear's men fought back killing Grattan and his whole bunch.

Bell continued, 'The next summer, Harney came upon a camp of Brulé on Blue Creek, over there off the North Platte. These people had had *nothing whatever* to do with the Mormon and his cow. I doubt Harney even knew they were Brulé, but an Indian is an Indian. If one Indian kills a white, you kill the first ten Indians you come to, or as many as the occasion allows. Harney killed about a hundred, mostly women and children. "Squaw Killer Harney". People aren't too happy to see him.'

I asked him when that had happened and he told me summer of 1854.

'A long time ago,' I said.

'Nothing out here is *long ago*,' Bell told me. 'It is all *now*.'

The tipi village seemed to grow by the hour. People had brought their horses. It was quite a herd. Quite a crowd of people, as well. Not only *all* the relations of all the chiefs who were to be the treaty's signatories, but many warriors, seconds in command, had also come and they had also brought their families.

I was tired of standing at the opening to the tent, so I walked into the heart of the village. Groups of men sat and talked in serious tones. Women had gotten cook fires going and were preparing food, but they would stop stirring from time to time to listen to what the men were saying.

If the adults were wary, they had not passed it on to the children who ran around playing among the tipis. Boys chased one another with sticks for rifles, followed by happy dogs. From somewhere, I heard soft humming. I followed the sound and, around the corner of a large tipi, came upon a little girl singing to her doll that was strapped to her back in a cradleboard.

I immediately thought of Elizabeth and imagined how, if she were there, she'd find some little one to scoop into her arms. If, indeed, she would be inclined to do so under these circumstances. And if, indeed, under these circumstances, the children's mothers would allow it. I'd not seen Lizzie in a while and I suddenly missed her sharply. But the emotion took me in a strange way: *I missed being with her among Indians.*

I missed being among Indians. Missed it hard. I felt as if I'd been shot in the gut, the pain was such that I couldn't move from where I was standing. The village swirled around me with its smells and sounds and colours, and I was no more than a snag in a stream. The rhythms of the language were music I had *lived* within. I'd built dreams within that music.

And I missed Far Cry ferociously. From the first days that we four had sat on the porch watching the Indians arrive, I had not stopped watching for him. I strained my eyes, hoping to see that red shirt. I looked for him now among the men sitting and talking and moving around the village and in and out of the tent. I was suddenly afraid he might not recognise me in my white person's clothes. I'd gone out with a hat on my head — Mary was a great believer in hats — so I pulled it off and carried it. Then I yanked my eye patch down around my neck.

If Far Cry was there, or anyone who'd traveled with us when Elizabeth and I were part of his group, I wanted to be easy to recognise. There I stood in my skirt, my underskirts, my shift, my blouse buttoned up to my neck, my vest, my fitted, buttoned up jacket, my hat in my hand and my eye patch around my neck, offering up my ruined face, stupid with hope. I turned my head in all directions. I barely stopped myself from calling his name. My love for him was alive as ever, clawing and tearing at me from the inside.

I thought of our dead daughter and pulled the pouch containing her bones so it lay on top of my clothing. *Where is your father? Where are his people? Are they all dead? Everything is changing. Is there nothing to be done?*

Garrett and Bell found me and said we should get to the tent, things were approaching the climax. Bell looked away, but Garrett asked if I was alright. I had not realised I'd been weeping. I wiped my cheeks with my hands, replaced my eyepatch, put my hat back on my head.

'Too much dust.'

CHAPTER 12

I told Bell and Garrett that when Elizabeth and I had been taken two years back, in '66, Far Cry had brought us to a huge gathering of Indians — I told them there had to have been a thousand — on the banks of a river. I wasn't sure where. I explained that a young Cheyenne woman, our dear friend Mary Small Wing had said the chiefs were being pressured to sign a new treaty, so a great many clans had come together to decide what to do. I asked if they knew anything about this pow-wow, and if the treaty they had been debating was the one being signed this day.

Bell and Garrett said that, yes, I was right. They were most likely arguing the points of this very treaty. Bell elaborated.

'Gold had been discovered in western Montana, a much larger strike than ever before, and people were crazy to have a piece of it. But to get to it, whites had to go through territory sacred to the Lakota. And the Lakota were not exactly welcoming.'

He explained that the Bozeman had split off from the Oregon Trail and now headed north and west. It was a shortcut to the gold — more and more whites were using it, there was no way to stop them — but on its way to the mines, the Bozeman ran right through the middle of the Powder River valley, traditional Lakota hunting grounds ever since they'd taken it from the Crow, or as long as anyone could remember. The Big Horns, or what the Indians call the Shining Mountains, formed a boundary to the west, and the sacred Black Hills, Paha Sapa, were part of the eastern edge.

I told them I knew the Powder River country. This was where Far Cry and I had traveled when we'd ridden off together. I knew they'd never give it up. They would certainly not give it up easily.

Bell told a story about a meeting with Red Cloud at Fort Laramie earlier in '66, months before the big pow-wow farther north to which Elizabeth and I had been taken. The Commissioners had promised the chief and his Oglalas that if they agreed to stop killing whites coming through on the trail, the white soldier chiefs would *never* build forts along it, and *no new settlements* would *ever* be allowed. The Powder River valley would belong to the Sioux *in perpetuity*. They knew that if Red Cloud signed, the other important chiefs would probably follow.

Red Cloud and some others agreed to talk. The promise of no new forts ever, no new settlements, and no whites in the Powder River valley ever again was a strong draw. They were going back and forth via interpreters in a tent down in the Indian village, when suddenly, there was a great commotion outside. Men shouting and oxen bawling and the creaking of heavy-laden wagons brought everything to a stop.

A sweaty Colonel Henry B. Carrington strode into the tent. The Commissioners tried to usher him out fast, Bell said, worried that the Indians would quickly learn why he was there. Which they did. The oblivious Carrington announced that he and his men were goddamn hungry and tired and pissed off that they hadn't been received properly by the fort command. They were on their way north with supplies to start building the first of at least three forts to go up along the Bozeman.

Three new forts where it was promised there'd never again be any, and the paper stating this was there on the table, and the Commissioners had been urging the Indians to put their marks on it. A furore erupted.

'Red Cloud pulls himself up, flings his blanket over his shoulder, glares at the Commissioners and tells them, "the White War Chief offers paltry gifts in exchange for a part of the Indians' *home*, and then, while the Indian is thinking about it, and has come here *where he was told to come* to talk about it, he learns that the White Chief has already stolen it, breaking his word yet again."'

Bell was shaking his head in admiration as he told the story.

'Red Cloud then told them, loud and clear, that he'd *not* leave the home of his ancestors and that he would *never* stop fighting to keep it. Then he and his men stormed out. Fine thing to see.'

Hostilities continued. Raids against whites accelerated and became more bold. Indians in the southern plains started coming north to join in what was being called Red Cloud's War.

'The Fetterman fiasco followed short upon that, did it not, Mr. Bell?'

'Yes, it did, Mr. Garrett. The Battle of One Hundred Slain. In December of that year, I think, or maybe early in '67, I'm not sure.'

'I know about that,' I told them. It excited me to be able to add to these conversations. They so rarely took me seriously, these men friends of mine. 'Criers came into the camp with the news.

They said it had been a prophesy. It was talked of for a long time, that fight.'

They said that every soldier on on every Army fort in the west talked about it a great deal, as did every politician in Washington. Ulysses S. Grant was General in Chief of the Army at the time. Sherman screamed in his face that it was long past time for aggressive action against the Indian, even if it meant killing them *all*, men, women, and children. Grant told Sherman it was more critical that he give his attention to protecting 'overland lines of travel', saying that completion of the Union Pacific Railroad would be 'as great a victory as any in the war'.

Diplomacy was urged. So Sherman and Harney once again sent out messengers asking to meet once more with Red Cloud, promising all sorts of gifts if he would just come in to talk. They returned with the answer that Red Cloud was 'too busy' to talk. Apparently, upon hearing this, Harney turned to Sherman, red in the face, demanding to know how many men it would take to eradicate the entire Sioux nation, '*Right now!*'

On that windy April day in 1868, my two friends and I stood outside the tent looking at the company gathered to sign the new treaty. The men noted that it seemed to be mostly Brulés and other friendlies.

'There's Spotted Tail, and Iron Shell... Recognise anyone else, Garrett?'

'Not really. Oh, wait, I see the priest. De Smet. Friends with Sitting Bull, but I don't see the chief himself. Thought he'd be here. And no Red Cloud, either, which is no surprise.'

'No. I didn't expect him.'

The government warned the chiefs in no uncertain terms that it could back out of any agreement if the Indians failed to adhere absolutely to all the treaty's terms. Bell and Garrett found this disingenuous at the least. Absolute adherence would require doing things that were not only contrary to Indian custom, but were damned near impossible for *anyone* trying to survive in that vast country with its harsh and unpredictable weather.

However, the Commissioners promised that if the Indians *did* adhere to the rules, no whites who had not obtained Indian permission would be allowed to pass through the reservation that would be put aside for them. Bell and Garrett rolled their eyes. The Commissioners finally came to the last Article of the treaty: all the existing military posts in the Powder River basin would be abandoned and the road closed. The Black Hills would again belong only to the Sioux.

I had not expected this. I watched as the Indians listened to the translation, but their faces, of course, revealed nothing. I looked at my two friends, they too were stone-faced. *Was this not very good news?* The Indians talked quietly among themselves for a bit, then one of them lit the pipe, offered it to the four directions, and smoked. They passed it among themselves. Then they stood one by one, walked to the table and made their marks on the paper. Their Indian names were written phonetically alongside these marks, and also the names by which they were known to the whites. If they were known. Most were not. It took a long time and we didn't stay for the entirety of it.

I felt as if I'd witnessed a great thing. *All the Army posts abandoned! The Bozeman closed! The Lakota would keep Paha Sapa! No whites allowed on Indian land!* But Garrett and Bell shook their heads. When some reason arises to take back the Powder River Valley and Paha Sapa along with it, they said, the government will take it. Mostly, this treaty was designed to protect the railroad.

'*The railroad?*'

'That's how those fools got here,' Bell told me. 'The railroad from the eastern cities to Cheyenne, stage coach to Laramie. It's being built west to east, too. The spans are supposed to meet pretty soon, but the Indians keep killing the workers, which slows things down. Fact is, no one cares one whit about the Bozeman anymore, those forts are useless. Closing them officially is something to mollify the tribes, distract them from attacking railroad workers. I told you what Grant said. This has all to do with the railroad. With expanding westward. With money.'

We headed back to the fort. Bell and Garrett hadn't had any expectations of the exercise, but I was distressed — deflated, angry, sad. Already, a good number of the Indians had left, the ground was bare dirt where they'd been, others were dismantling tipis and packing travois. I tried to discern their mood by looking at them closely, but no one made eye contact with me. I needed a drink and said so. The others cheered that idea, and we all agreed we wanted some of Irish Mary's fine cooking, too. It had been a long day.

About three weeks later, on May nineteenth, the order came from Washington that Fort C. F. Smith, Fort Philip Kearny, and Fort Reno would be closed and the Bozeman abandoned. The local commands were to begin the process immediately. On May twenty-fifth, Sitting Bull and his men, along with some Mniconjou, some Yanktonais and Arapaho, chiefs who hadn't been there in April, came in to touch the pen. Neither Harney nor Sherman were there. Only about five whites — the only brass being two Captains and a brevet Major — witnessed this signing.

Red Cloud, possibly the most important of the Sioux chiefs at that time, did not come. He derided Sitting Bull for selling out for crackers and molasses. But there had been a drought and the buffalo herds were severely diminished. Sitting Bull had been to Washington. He'd seen the rivers of whites rushing to and fro in the streets. He knew about the railroad. He was a realist.

CHAPTER 13

The night before I was to leave for Virginia, Mary made a special dinner in my honour that we five companions enjoyed at the table in my room. I helped her bring up bowls of beef stew and a couple of loaves of fresh bread. Peach cobbler for dessert. Afterward, we all brought our dishes down to the kitchen and then went out on the porch for whiskey. There were cigars that night, too. And, though I didn't smoke with any regularity, I'd have Garrett or Bell roll a cigarette for me every now and then when we were all drinking, I did, that evening, enjoy that aromatic smoke.

We were all comfortably full of dinner — Mary, Garrett, Doc, Bell, and me — and getting comfortably drunk. It was just turning June. The grass was green, there was still snow in the high places, so the streams were full and fast. Migrating birds were coming home. The moon was coming on full and that kept us out longer than usual. Doc was the first to say his goodnights.

Then Garrett said he needed to see about his boy. He said he didn't know when or if he'd see me again, he was thinking of going back east himself. He was worried about life for his boy with things turning so bad for the Indian out here. He tipped his hat and left. He'd been a good friend, and he was right, I never did see him again. Mary went to the kitchen, leaving the nearly empty bottle — we'd finished one, already — on the small table by my rocking chair for Bell and me to finish.

After a bit, Bell and I looked at one another. I felt a stirring I hadn't felt in a long time. He spoke.

'I'd like to go up to your room and get into bed with you. No strings. Just another kind of companionship.'

I don't recall thinking too long about it.

'Well, come on then,' I said, or something like that, and I took the bottle and headed toward the stairs with him right behind me. As I passed the kitchen, Mary was near the door. I caught her eye and she grinned. Well, good, I thought. We have Mary's benediction.

I closed the door to my room, he put his hat on a chair. I lit the lamp and took out two glasses, poured us each a shot. We put it down fast, looking at one another, and then, simultaneously, slammed the glasses down on the table. *Thunk!* We laughed out loud. The kiss happened fast, and was a good one.

We were more drunk than we realised — there were too many damn buttons on all our clothing! But finally the skirts and pants and shirts and vests and braces and stockings were in a pile we kicked to the side as we got into bed.

He fucked with the manner of a person who is good at a thing, knows it, and is relaxed about it. Like a good dance partner, he could both lead and follow. I thought of the two other men I'd been with. One was a bad man, one a very good man. This man, the third lover of my life — and he was to become something like that, for a while — was complicated. But he pleased me and so did this kind of fucking, without romance, without expectations.

When we were done, I told him that I liked to sleep alone. He was good about it.

But I did not sleep. My head was too full of images of the afternoon: the numbers of Indians who'd come to sign the treaty, still believing; the little girl playing with her doll as if all were well; the chiefs sitting in the dust of the stifling tent; the Commissioners' tall black boots and their condescending tones as they stated the provisions of that so-called treaty; my naïveté in thinking there might have been even the slightest intention among Washington's power elite to treat the Indians honourably.

As the light in the window paled so the room looked as it had when I first saw it, still bleeding from the loss of our daughter, I thought of Far Cry. I wept for myself, and I wept for him. '*What can I do?*' I asked whatever gods might hear me. I got no answer.

PART THREE
RUTH

CHAPTER 1

The whistle shrieked so piercingly I was amazed birds didn't fall out of the sky. Clouds of steam billowed. I settled myself by the window and looked around. An effort had been made towards comfort, and there were even, here and there, details promising future opulence. I knew there were trains in the east, some of which were apparently quite fancy, but I'd never been on one.

I had everything I needed in two bags, my old carpet bag — rather, Doc's dead wife's old carpet bag — and a soft, dark green leather bag Mary gave me, left behind by some officer's widow, for which she'd made a new lining. She'd packed some food for me, but in the rush of leaving, I'd forgotten it. People were running along the platform, hurrying to board right up until the last minute. Fortunately, the car in which I was sitting was sparsely occupied. I'd been advised to spend money so that I might have more room.

I was adjusting my clothing for comfort as the whistle sounded again, and there followed a cacophony of clanking and creaking, with a lurching forward, stopping, lurching and more lurching. I felt the engine's metal turning the wheels and felt the metal wheels grabbing the metal rails and pushing off and pushing off and pushing, pushing, pushing, until the sounds and vibrating of the lurching and pushing were all of a piece, and a rhythm asserted itself. So, here I was: sitting still in a great metal thing hurtling itself east at a shocking speed.

The window was streaked with dust so whatever colours might have been visible outside were muted. Everything was pale brown and ochre or muddy-green with suddenly something darker or lighter appearing — a clump of trees or a house or barn, or a flash of sun reflected in a window — coming, passing, gone. Mary had gathered up a few magazines and some newspapers for me. I tried to read, but couldn't concentrate.

Preparations for the trip had been a helpful distraction. Mary insisted on dressing me down to my skin. 'You're a lady, you can not travel east on a train with mended underthings, they must be new-made. Now hold still, or blessed Mother of God, I'll stick pins in your bum!'

I refused any sort of bustle as I could not imagine sitting all that time with that volume of fabric at my backside and the stiffening required to give it shape. Neither would I wear any sort of corset. Mary fashioned two skirts of reasonable proportions, a jacket with a peplum sort of arrangement at the back that was comfortable enough, and a few blouses. She'd also found a decent pair of shoes another widow had left behind that actually fit. And, of course, under it all, around my neck, I wore my beaded pouch. My daughter.

There had also been the distraction of telegrams going back and forth and money coming and going, tickets to purchase, connections to be made, and all the complications of changing trains, overnight stays, finding my way to where I would need to go to catch the next train and the one after that. I'd never done anything like this before. It made me want my damned elixir. I'd forsworn it and done alright, but felt sorely tested. I'd taken Bell aside and asked him to fix a strong tincture for me, enough to fill my flask, in case of need. I had no intention of using it, but felt better knowing I had it. I'd wrapped the flask in clothing and buried it in my carpetbag.

Now, finally, I was on my way. And now, finally, I had time to imagine the ride up to the house in which I'd been born. My parents were dead. Who'd be there? The letter from Sands said Ruth. Was that still true? Was the house still standing? Maybe not. The bolus of fear I'd been nursing swelled and crammed my belly.

I should have left it all to the lawyers and sold the damn thing to Jake's father. I'd have taken the money and... what? No. I had to do this. Too much was unsettled and I wanted a last look at the place. I wanted to see Ruth again and her boy. Who knows? I might want to stay. Besides, here I was. I reached under my jacket and loosened the fastenings of my skirt.

I looked out the window, ignoring the flash of things appearing and passing, all the way to the horizon. Odd how things up close flew past with dizzying speed, and things far off seemed to move more slowly. But, of course, none of these things were moving at all, it was me, and all these others on the train, all headed east while the rest of the country was heading west. The noise and rocking lulled me into a light sleep.

I was jolted awake by a sudden strong *thunk!* and a shudder that seemed to come from my side of the train a couple of cars ahead. This was followed by jolting and jerking and screeching of metal against metal. As the train slowed, everyone in the car came to look out the windows on my side. I pressed my face against the glass as we slowly rolled up to and passed a black and white horse, writhing on the ground at the side of the track, bleeding, its mouth open. Even with the noise of the train braking I could hear its screams. Not far from it, an Indian lay face down, his legs oddly bent. People were saying, *What the hell? Crazy Indian! What was he trying to do?*

Suddenly, a horror rose in me.

I thrust people out of the way, yelling, 'Let me through! Let me through!', pushed open the door onto a sort of vestibule between the cars, still rolling slightly. I jumped down onto the ground, got up from my hands and knees and was running towards the man's body when a man in a dark blue uniform grabbed me, yelling at me to get back on the car. Others had followed me out, and this trainman was trying now to herd us all back on the train but no one wanted to go. Everyone wanted to get closer. The horse was dead, now, and the man appeared to be also.

The man was the right height, and the proportions of the body were as I'd remembered Far Cry's. One hand, open on the ground near his chest, had the same fine bones, the wrist was the same. The hair was the right colour and texture. But this man had fastened in it a small, dead hawk — his medicine, I assumed — and that was not a thing Far Cry would do. The Indian was in full battle dress, with a beaded quiver of arrows still slung on his back. He was lying on his bow. The other arm was stretched out and, still clutched in the fist, was his coup stick.

Though fairly certain now that the man wasn't Far Cry — no red

241

shirt, for one thing, and if he'd planned such a thing as this, he'd have worn it — I had to see his face. I pulled down my eyepatch — a completely illogical thing I will still do sometimes if I need to see more clearly — and forced a couple of men aside to get closer, fighting off the hands trying to pull me back. 'I have to see his face!' The trainman looked at me as if I were mad, took me by the shoulders and firmly turned me away.

I turned back and tried to lunge towards the body but the trainman kept hard hold of me. Others had moved up and, between them, I saw someone use the toe of his boot to turn the Indian over. It wasn't him. I think I said it out loud. Still gripping my shoulder and standing between me and the bodies, the official told the passengers to get back on the train.

'All right, now, there's nothing more to see here. Get back on board, please. We have a schedule to keep.'

'What about him?' I asked.

'There's nothing to be done, ma'am.'

'Are you just going to leave him there?'

'There's nothing else we can do for him now, is there. Please get back on board, ma'am.'

The several men who'd left the car with me began to climb back on board. I caught a few snatching a look at me and snapping their heads away quickly. People at the windows were still looking at the dead Indian and his horse, and also at the woman with the scar who was weeping, wiping her face with her hands. For the first time, I noticed several men outside different cars with rifles ready, searching the horizon.

Finally, the man in the uniform said, softly, 'Please, ma'am', and offered his hand. On the vestibule before the door of the car, he asked quietly if there was anything I needed. His sincerity surprised me. I said there wasn't unless he could provide me with a shot of whiskey. He nodded and said he'd have some brought to me. I settled back into my seat, replaced my eye-patch, collected myself.

A Negro brought the whiskey in a glass wrapped in a napkin. He made no eye-contact as he handed it to me. I thanked him and asked what I owed for it, but he shook his head. The conductor, as I learned later was the proper term for the uniformed white man's position, then came in and, moving the Negro out of his way, announced: 'In approximately one hour, there'll be some light supper served in a car newly fashioned for the purpose. I'll be back to show you to your tables.'

As the train began to pull away, I took the whiskey in about two gulps. The Indian was still gripping his coup stick. He'd intended to count coup on the train. Good god! I imagined his wild gallop, forcing his horse's head at the engine. He'd come from somewhere up the track, riding towards the oncoming train. I hoped he'd be considered a hero by his people, whoever they were, he could have been from any of the plains tribes.

He'd counted coup on the train. I felt like standing up and explaining the meaning of this gesture to my fellow passengers to whom he was just a crazy Indian. They'd settled back into their newspapers or their conversations or their naps. Alone, he'd challenged the iron beast cutting up his country. He'd struck an honourable blow against this huge iron beast and died.

I remembered the thrill of encountering a herd of buffalo, once when we were moving camp. We women watched from a hilltop as the men rode, weaving in and out among those massive animals. What if from that hilltop, we'd suddenly heard the shriek and clatter, had seen this enormous smoke-belching dragon scream across the grasses, fast, heartless, inelegant, cruel, unnatural. We'd have been horrified. More so, if we'd been able to foresee what all it meant.

But the train was here. The country needed it, everyone said so, for the success of farms and young towns, for the livelihoods of people such as Elizabeth and William. It would not be stopped, yet it cut up Indian country irrevocably. The Indian who'd sacrificed himself had understood this. And for a brief moment, I'd thought it might be Far Cry. He'd not have made a gesture so obviously suicidal, too many depended on him. Besides, he was most likely dead. Wounds sustained in that debacle with Custer might have done it, or some other fight. Along with ongoing skirmishes with whites, there'd been no cessation of warring among the tribes. Traditions were maintained.

I tilted my head back, swallowed the last drops of whiskey and put the glass down beside me on the upholstered bench. I took off my eye-patch and wiped my entire face with the napkin, over and over. I wondered if my love thought of me as I thought of him. I doubted it. It had been a long winter, and now it was late spring. Far Cry and his people had become part of me, had penetrated my being. When I was with them, I'd thought they'd felt the same for me. I no longer believed this was true. Why should they? But my love for Far Cry was still alive in me. Goddamnit.

Where are you? Why did you never try to see me? I reached into my bag, felt for and found my flask. I had not imagined I would need it so soon.

CHAPTER 2

I saw Ruth's son before he saw me. A mulatto boy standing straight and tall on the platform of the Richmond train station. He'd been a spindly little kid when I'd gone west with Jake, but I knew him now by his resemblance to his mother. Their faces were quite similar. But his hair was wavy, not nappy like Ruth's, and seemed to have a reddish shine.

Though it had not been so very long, I doubted he'd recognise me, changed as I knew myself to be in so many ways. But he came up immediately to take my bags.

'Welcome home, Missrus Byrd.'

'Thank you, Ezekiel, but, good heavens! Please call me Sarah.'

'Very well, Missrus Sarah.'

'Ezekiel! Just Sarah! Please!'

'Well, then you call me just Zeke, please. Like you used to.'

He was grinning. The visit was off to a good start.

Richmond was a ruin, frantic in its efforts to re-make itself. Signs of construction were everywhere. Once we were out of the town, I dozed off and slept on and off most of the way, waking when I felt the buggy turn off the main road. The driveway up to the house was rough. Stones and roots, small branches, pine cones, detritus from storms past needed to be cleared. The ragged shrubs that reached out from all sides needed trimming.

Yet, the sun through the pine boughs brought a gentle, dappled light and the earth breathed up familiar scents of sun-warmed pine straw, cool mulch. White dogwood bloomed here and there in the woods. Then, around a bend, suddenly, there was the house with its tall windows and pretty columns. Proof of my parents' vanity and wealth, scene of our love for one another, imperfect as it was. The place that had formed my young self. It looked smaller than I recalled it, forlorn, neglected.

Ruth was waiting on the veranda. She too had changed, a bit thinner, yet she held herself proudly as she always had, her spine straight, head high on her long neck. Her hair was not slicked back into a tight knot as she used to wear it, but gathered loosely in a way that allowed its texture to be seen. There was a little grey in it. I had forgotten how beautiful she was. The bones of her face were elegantly modelled and her eyes were large. When I looked into them, I was not sure what emotion they reflected, if any at all, but I was suddenly awash in it. I rushed up to embrace her.

Thwack! She struck my face with the flat of her hand. Not hard enough to knock me down or hurt me, but hard enough to bring me sharply to attention.

'Didn't expect you to come rushin' up on me like that. C'mon inside. There's tea.'

I followed her into the foyer and through the door on the right, into the room we'd called the small parlour. Sheets of white muslin were draped over most of the furniture.

'Nobody usin' this place, as you can see.'

But in one corner, she'd pulled two chairs with embroidered seat cushions up to a small, round table near the window. She'd set out my mother's favourite tea service on a pale yellow linen tablecloth, and had a fire going in the fireplace. A welcome thing, as it was a bit chilly in the house. She'd opened the shutters to the tall window to let in the light. My mother had enjoyed taking tea here, as she could look out over her favourite flower garden. It got the morning sun.

'Set yourself down now.'

I sat. I picked up the exquisite cup, English bone china, pale robin's egg blue with a single pink rose inside the cup. Her colours. 'Fragonard's palette', she used to tell me. The rim of the saucer was gold. Ruth had put out the silver tea spoons. I traced the roses on the handle and stroked my mother's monogram with my index finger. Three perfect yellow rose buds stood in a crystal vase.

'It's exactly as mother would have done it.'

'Yes, it is. Just like it. Put your cup down now, so I can pour. I heard you all comin' and got the water started. It's been hard to get good tea, but this will do. And these little lemon cakes come out nice. You always did like 'em.'

Then she pulled out the other chair, sat down, and poured herself a cup of tea. I hadn't noticed two places had been set.

'Lot's of things different 'round here now.'

'Yes. Of course, they are. It's good, Ruth, it's better.'

She gave me a look.

'We got a lot to talk about. Not much of it gonna be easy. Fact is, most of it gonna be hard.'

'I can imagine.'

She lifted her chin and delivered another hard look.

'No. You can't.'

I bristled. Not that long ago, she'd been my servant and would not have dared to talk back to me. Even to me. Clearly things were different, I'd have to learn in what ways. I'd have to listen.

'Please, Ruth, before anything else, know that it is *very* good to see you. I am eager to learn everything you have to tell me.'

The quick movement of an eyebrow, a small change in the position of her lips, a slight tilt to her head as she looked me in the eye. She lifted her cup to her lips.

I admired the tea and the cakes, and looking out the window, could see that my mother's roses were beginning to bloom. They looked healthy.

'Josiah, you remember him? He was the only one your Mama'd trust with her roses. They don't grow all that easy hereabouts. Oh, how she loved her roses! Josiah goes 'round now to different houses with gardens and makes money workin' his magic. For them that has any money. Lot's who did once, don't now.'

'I gather we have some money still. Mr. Sands, my father's attorney, has written to me.'

'I've got know that Mr. Sands, and he knows me. Your father fixed things so there was money to run the place 'til you was to take over. *If* you lived. Your husband, that Jake — Mr. Jackson, I mean — he still alive?'

I told her he was not. I had no proof of this, but had decided that he was dead. In any case, he was dead to me.

'Good.'

Without waiting to see how I might react, she continued:

'Your dead husband's father, that other Mr. Jackson Byrd, controls what's done with the tobacco and wheat, got sharecroppers to work it, but to my mind, they ain't done too good. Zeke is in charge of the dairy cows, horses, oxen, chickens, turkeys, dogs, hogs, all o' them. A lot a work, so we hired a man to help him. White man, Slovak, I think. Good with animals and him and Zeke get along. I take care of the vegetable garden. Good care. It's a big one and feeds us all. Get enough, most of the time, to sell to different houses. Sell milk and butter, too. I keep account o' what goes out, what comes in. Zeke and me do it together. I'll show you the books whenever you ready to see 'em. Me and Zeke are 'sharecroppin', as that Mr. Byrd calls it, but that ain't gonna last much longer. I reckon you'll be talkin' to Mr. Sands.'

'Yes. I'll have to contact him soon. I never liked my husband's father, to tell you the truth, and I'm not at all pleased that he's involved with this house's business. I suppose my father made that arrangement, to the benefit of them both.'

'They was like brothers, them two. Seemed like they was in a game to see who was the worst of 'em. I'm sorry to speak like that about your father, since he's dead. But I ain't interested in talkin' nothing but truth now.'

'I would not want anything else, Ruth.'

I looked around at the little parlour. Everything other than the table and chairs where we sat was draped in white, giving the place a dreamlike appearance. In chilly weather, my mother would sit to read in a small armchair with a hassock, close to the fireplace, her tea on this table. There was a china cabinet with glass doors above and drawers below, and there was a wooden trunk she'd used when she traveled to France — all were draped in white. The only colour, other than the furniture we were using, came from a couple of paintings on the walls.

I looked over my shoulder to the big parlour and straight through open French doors to the dining room where Mother had given her dinner parties. The long table under the three dusty chandeliers was draped in white, as were the sideboards and another, taller, china cabinet. I'd not understood back then that when Mama had referred to her 'grand hall', she'd been joking. In the dusky light of the shuttered room I could see that it wasn't grand at all.

On this side of the French doors — I don't think I ever saw them closed, Mama liked the open space — the parlour's three divans were covered, as were the chairs and hassocks and small tables. I could see the shape of the piano forté also under muslin.

There were the curving stairs to the second floor and, just off the foot of them, was the door to Father's rooms. He had an office and a small sitting room with a privy. We had indoor privies before anyone else around, of which my mother was very proud. Across the foyer, I could see the entrance to the kitchen and through the open kitchen door, there was a glimpse of green, bright in the afternoon sun.

There had been several women and girls always at work keeping the house as Mama had wanted it kept. Ruth did the cooking, assisted by a girl she named Sue-Shef — the name prevailed with every girl who filled the position, they had no choice in the matter — and other girls who worked in the kitchen. Then there were those who did the washing and ironing, dusting, mopping, tidying. All under Ruth's supervision.

'Who helps you in the house now?'

'Help? Child! Ain't no way they'd be money for help. Besides, ain't enough to do that I need help doin'. Had a Scottish woman come in for a couple days to help with some cleanin'. Was a fire did a bit o' hurt to the back outside walls — you'll want to take a look at that — and all the linens in the house smelled like smoke. Carpets, too. She helped with that, and with washin' down the walls and windows, and then I let her go.'

All the while we talked, she was examining my face.

'What happened to you? That's some kind of scar you got down your face.'

I told her in brief of the capture and how I was injured. She knew that I'd been taken by Indians. 'It was a torture of fear to your Mama.' She said she wanted to look at the eye, so I pulled down my eye patch. She leaned closer, and turning my face towards the light from the window, examined it.

'You might want to get that eyeball took out some time, might could cause you trouble.'

'It hasn't yet, fortunately.'

'Hm. You was a pretty girl. Ain't no more.'

'It has taken some getting used to. But I've accepted it. This scar is part of who I am now.'

'*Part o' who you are.* Good for you, girl, good for you. How it needs to be.'

She looked at me a moment, then said,

'Now, I'll show you mine.'

Ruth stood up from the table, unbuttoned her blouse and put it down on the chair. She turned her back to me, pulled her shift down off her shoulders, pulled her arms out of it and pushed it to the waist of her skirt, exposing her back. Swipes of different lengths, some longer than my hand, some shorter, crossed back and forth over her skin. They looked like the branches of a dead tree. In places where they crossed one another, the healing skin had formed thick ridges.

'Feel 'em.'

I hesitated.

'Go on. Feel 'em.'

I began to touch them gingerly.

'You *scared* to really feel 'em? Follow my hand.'

Ruth held up her right hand with her fist closed. She moved her arm in arcs, as if she were striking someone's back.

'Now! Follow me and feel 'em!'

In concert with her movements, I stroked the scars gently with my fingertips, going over the rough places as if they might still be painful to her.

'You ain't *feelin'* 'em! *Feel 'em!* You got to feel 'em to understand what this is!'

She whipped the air in front of her with more violence, and I answered the motion with my fingers, pressing and sweeping them across her back, following the lines the whipper had made. Finally, slowly, she brought her arm down to her side. I followed a thin branch of scarring over the right side of her back to where it ended just under her last rib. I had used the same finger to fondle the petals on my mother's teaspoon. She stood still while I wiped my face.

'I am so sorry, Ruth. How horrible! Who did this to you?'

She shook her head. Stood for moment, then pulled up her shift. She put her blouse back on and sat down again.

'So, you don't know. Well, I guess there wasn't no one who'd tell you. Never mind. I got...'

'*Wait!* Did that happen while you were here?'

'It did.'

'Who...'

'That's for another time. A long story. I got marks on my legs, too, and that ain't nothin' but the usual story. I was always and forever "a uppity nigger bitch". I was a uppity pickaninny! I was born with this in me, my Mama had it too. For this alone, they punish you. But I am proud to tell you they didn't *never* punish it outta me. So, now you see. These marks are part o' who *I* am.'

She sat back, looking at me.

'How come your hands be shakin' so bad?'

She took hold of my hands, looked from them to my eyes, looking hard into them for a solid beat. I lowered mine. She leaned into my face and sniffed. My face was wet, but from tears. She dropped my hands.

'You your mother's daughter, ain't you.'

'Oh! No. Not the way you mean. I might have been, might have become that way, but... No.'

I told her I'd fixed myself a flask-full for the journey because I'd been frightened of what coming here would feel like. But that something horrible had happened shortly after we'd begun and I'd finished it on the train.

'Nothin' left in one of them bags you got?'

'Yes. I had the last drops pulling into the Richmond station.'

'Laudanum.'

'Yes. How did you know?'

'You feelin' sick now?'

'No. I'd not been using it for a while before this trip, and then stopped. But I was... afraid. I didn't bring much. I'm not feeling sick, but I am very tired. And, your back... Good god, Ruth. That it happened here... I hadn't known.'

'Lots you didn't know. You still scared? Wishing you had more of that drug?'

'No. I don't want it. There'll be times I will want it, I'm sure of that. But I can't have it in my life anymore, and I'm sure of that, too. I'm done.'

'Good. 'Cause I ain't gonna nurse you like I did your Mama. Now, enough on all that. I saw how you enjoyed them cakes, girl! You hungry?'

She changed course so fast, I had to take a breath to catch up, but it was a relief to answer a simple question.

'Yes! Those cakes were even better than I remembered. I guess I am a bit hungry.'

'Well, we gonna put some meat on them skinny little white bones!'

She led the way into the kitchen.

'This is where we gonna eat from now on. Here or in my cabin that's fixed up real nice. I took some things from the house to do it, which, if the wrong people were to find it out, could get me hung. That's how it is these days. I got some nice soup ready on the stove and fresh bread and butter. You'll have a glass of milk, too.'

She showed me where to sit at the clean white-painted wooden table, and started ladling soup into two bowls.

'Now. I come in here to fix breakfast for Zeke and me round 'bout six in the morning. You can eat with us, if you want, but if you don't, you fix your own breakfast. Same with dinner in the middle of the day, and with supper.

Let me tell it to you plain: I ain't your *slave* no more. I *work* for you — for now — but I got plenty to do without *servin'* you. Zeke too. It *all* changed. You got that?'

I told her I understood, but she looked at me skeptically.

'Do you have any idea how your daddy got so rich? Ain't such a big place here.'

She made a sweep with her arm that included the house and the yard outside, and the barns and stables and fenced paddocks and slaves' cabins and everything in and around and beyond, all the way out to the fields and woods that belonged to my family.

'Not really, Ruth.'

I had no idea how my father made his money. I knew he'd inherited the plantation from his father, being his only son, and I'd assumed the rest was from crops. And from moving money around so it made money, I'd overheard him talk about this with his cronies. I assumed this Mr. Sands advised him along those lines.

'Well, maybe you don't want to know. Maybe you should just sell the place to Byrd, take your money and get out.'

'I want to know everything.'

'Gonna take some time.'

'I'll be here for a while, Ruth. I have to see Sands, figure out what to do about all this.'

'Well, before anything else, we gotta get some of my good chicken soup into you. Nobody does it good as me.'

CHAPTER 3

After dinner, Zeke carried my bags up the stairs to my room and Ruth told him to heat water for my bath. She had opened the long shutters, so the late sun flowed through the glass and lay on the floor.

She'd taken away the sheets covering the furniture, had dusted and polished so my old room looked as I remembered it. My silver-handled brushes and combs were set out on my dressing table. The linens on my bed were fresh and fragrant and a nightdress was laid out on top of the cover. Zeke filled my bath, then left me to it.

The last bath I'd taken there had been before my wedding. Ruth had soaped me, rinsed me, dried me, powdered and perfumed me. She and at least one young girl, maybe two, had dressed me and arranged my hair. They'd helped me put my feet in the pretty shoes my mother had ordered from New York. They'd draped the pearls around my neck, those Mama had worn as a young girl. They'd hung the sapphires — also from Mama — in my ears.

Then Mama had rouged my cheeks and lips ever so subtly, and dabbed perfume on my wrists and behind my earlobes as if she were anointing me with something sacred. It was sacred. Her childhood friend now living in Paris had sent it to her, she'd had it forever. I missed my mother.

Sometimes, when I was still living there and my father was away at night, I would hear my door being quietly opened and a white form would drift towards my bed. Our four pale feet would find one another under the covers and rub together like cats. But if her breath smelled of her tincture — she liked her drug with brandy — I'd abruptly roll over.

'Why'd you turn away, sweet girl?'

'The smell of your mouth makes me hate you, Mama.'

'One of these days you'll understand how much I love you. I hope it's not too late.'

I finally understood, and it was too late.

This night, lying in bed, I could not stop thinking about Ruth's back. I could still feel the ridges of hard skin on my fingertips. I raised my arm and moved it through the air over me as she had done, as if I were the whipper. I could imagine the scene with so much clarity it made me choke. And this had happened at our home, while she was part of our family. And yet she could fix me dinner, laugh with me.

How many others of our servants — that's how my mother referred to our household slaves — how many others of our *slaves* had we had striped like that? Where was it done? Was it done often?

Of course, I'd known there were the occasional whippings. My father would order his overseer to whip a field slave from time to time, but only when there was good reason. I'd never witnessed it, so it had to have been fairly rare. Just as, every now and then, in one of her sudden rages, my mother might cuff a girl or boy working in the house, calling them 'stubborn' or 'lazy' — as sometimes they must have been — but no one was ever badly hurt.

My father made a point of saying that it was simply good business to treat 'your people' well. You got more and better work out of them.

Yet someone — most likely someone to whom my father had paid wages — had taken a whip to *Ruth*. What would warrant such a thing? She called herself proud, 'an uppity nigger'. She'd said, 'For this alone, they punish you.' She'd had to have done something more than just be 'uppity' to be so horribly injured.

Writing these last sentences, I am struck by how wilful ignorance, such as mine in my youth, lack of curiosity about the truth, such as mine, makes room for evil. I am deeply ashamed still. I'm also horrified to realise that I'd thought, even briefly, that Ruth's scars must have been, at least in part, her own fault. '*She'd had to have done something*' to deserve them. Good god.

My father was a mean son-of-a-bitch, I knew that to be true. Jake had said so, with admiration. So was Jake. The men who smoked cigars and drank brandy in my father's office celebrated their talent for violence. At dinner, as long as no one got too drunk, all was courtly. A scrim of gentility obscured the corruption, the blood-letting.

Yet, I believed that many of our 'servants' loved us. My mother had said so. Certainly, Ruth and the girls in the house had loved us, they'd showed their affection in all sorts of ways. Ruth's husband Jewell had loved me when I was a girl, and I'd loved him. I was loved and so was my mother. My father was most likely feared, he was, after all, *Master*. But he was respected and perhaps that's a kind of love.

I remembered being terribly angry when my father sold Jewell. He'd taught me to track, to shoot a bow and arrow; he'd given me skills that conferred a kind of confidence nothing else and no one else had done. Slaves came and went, they were bought, sold, rented, borrowed, like one might do with a good tool. But this was *Jewell*. My father had gotten rid of my beloved teacher. Worse, he'd done so without telling me why.

As the language of this memory came to mind, I realised that it did not reflect, and I do not recall that I gave, a single moment's thought for Ruth or Zeke. I had not considered that my father had gotten rid of Ruth's husband, Ezekiel's father, and what that must have been like for them.

I was waiting for Ruth in the kitchen when she came in from her cabin a bit before six in the morning. I'd found coffee, made some, and there was more in the pot.

'Damn, girl! I didn't expect you to be up so early today! You don't look like you slept too good.'

'I didn't sleep at all. There's too much I don't understand.'

I didn't know where to start, but Ruth simply looked at me, waiting for me to go on.

'For one thing, I cannot understand how you could have continued to love us, with all that was done to you.'

'What makes you think I *loved* any o' you all?'

I kept myself from backing up a step or two.

'Well, then, I apologise for that assumption. Still, I don't understand...'

She interrupted me. Said she couldn't do this kind of talking without a good breakfast in her. Zeke would be there in a minute. Again, I had to acknowledge the strangeness of having a black servant interrupt me.

Ruth had me follow her around the kitchen to learn where everything was. She took me down into the cellar where root vegetables were kept and even milk and cheese stayed cool enough for a while. I helped her make breakfast — hot cakes with preserves — and the three of us ate together as the sun came up full. Rather, they ate. I couldn't manage more than a few bites. I cleaned up while Ruth went out with her son to 'get things started'. I made more coffee. I left the plate of hotcakes on the table with the preserves and butter. Sat down, sipped the coffee, and waited for Ruth.

I will not try to reconstruct the entirety of our conversation, it went on over a good while. My account will not be complete and not at all in order. The talk was circular. We'd break off — I'd be completely done in by what had been said, sometimes we'd both be done in — and then resume.

My part was simple compared to hers. I told her details of life with the Indians, of my love for Far Cry, of the horrible violence of our 'rescue', that I hadn't wanted leave him, hadn't wanted to leave that life I'd come to respect and love. I spoke of my despair at the loss of our baby. She reached out and took my hand. I showed her my spirit pouch and told her what it held. She raised her eyebrows and sat back a bit, made a humming sound.

I described my deep affection for Elizabeth, how this loving friendship somehow endured in spite of our many differences, and how I'd come to love her family, that I was still amazed at how they'd embraced me.

I told her a bit about watching the treaty signing, the lies, and how whites' clear hatred of the Indians infuriated me. She raised her eyebrows at this as well.

Then Ruth told me her story.

She went back and forth between the more correct English my mother surely encouraged, and a more relaxed, plantation speech. I can only hint at this. I trust she'll forgive me. She told it to me over meals cooked and eaten in the kitchen of the house I grew up in, the house in which she'd been our slave.

CHAPTER 4

'First, my Mama. She gave me my name, said it was from the Bible, said to hold on to it. Sing-song sort of way with her talk — I was little, but I remember that. People said how proud she held herself, "like a queen". Maybe she been one before. She was a dark black woman, said some other black people took her from her mama, sold her by the ships. She hadn't never seen the ocean. I don't know about my daddy, maybe he was white and that's how I got this colour. Delta Negroes call it "caf-ay oh-lay", French for coffee with lots of milk in it. I asked Mama if I had a daddy and she told me, "All children have a daddy in the Great God up in Heaven." She had a strong laugh. I could hear it all the way across the yard of that big Georgia mansion where she birthed me.

'Talkin' about coffee makes me want some more. And this here is *real* coffee. Good, ain't it? Trade eggs and fresh milk for it. And you eat one o' them hot cakes, hear? You need some strength in your body. You lookin' puny.

'I remember Mama and me is in a cart with a coupla others goin' someplace. I think it's fun, but I can see Mama's mad. She shake her fists, jingles the chains on her wrists, kick her feet, jingle them ankle chains. Strange kind of music.

'Then — I can still see this so clear — she's standin' up naked on a kind of raised floor in a big room full o' men, sun shinin' on her from tall windows. She smiles down at me so I clamber up and take a hold o' her hand. A man pulls me down, does it rough. "Ain't your chile no more." Mama rears back her head and lets out a *howl*. I howls, too. *Mamaaaaa!* and I'm reachin' for her, but that man got me good.

'Men pullin' at her, but she gives 'em the eye and they let her be for one second. She looks at me, tells me things without sayin' one word. Then she stand tall, turn her head and they take her away. Never did see her again.'

Ruth told me she was also bought that day, she was maybe five years old, and given as a birthday gift to a little girl a couple of years older. The little white girl got a puppy to play with and a slave to clean up after them both. When Ruth cried for her mother and wouldn't stop, the child's mother beat her, told her that her mother was dead. She'd been a 'damn uppity nigger', did she know what that meant?

257

The woman told Ruth she fed uppity niggers to their dogs and that she'd best watch herself, because she had 'uppityness' in her blood.

This was the first in a series of dangerous women. The cruelty of the plantation master and his paid help was well known, but their wives often matched them, sometimes surpassed them, in brutality.

'The Misruses. Sweet Jesus! Some of 'em? They could be like the Devil's in 'em. Don't know why. Maybe 'cause they ain't got nothin' to do but be hateful. Some of 'em hate their men but can't beat them, so they beat their Negroes. Some get beat by their men, so they beat their Negroes. Some gotta prove they got *dominion* — like in the Bible — over *someone* on this earth, so they beat their Negroes. And they got a *right*! God's with 'em, so they beat their Negroes 'til the skin open and the blood flow. Then it's, "Hey, nigger! Get yo' black ass back to work!"'

But Ruth said it was under one of the worst of the owners and his wife, on one of the richest plantations, that she met the woman who taught her how to stay alive. This woman taught her how to hold on to her pride, keep her humanity, and passed along a set of invaluable skills.

'I was mostly in the kitchen of that house, and I do thank Jesus, 'cause that's where I found my second mama, my dear Maimie. I already had a kind of grace on me from my Mama, but Maimie taught me how to be among white folks. "Do what you 'spose to do and do it good, but don't get saucy. Keep yo' smile sweet, keep yo' eyes low. And don't you *never* let show on your face how bad you hate 'em."

'I stuck close to Maimie. She taught me how to set up the table, how to serve proper. She was from Louisiana, learned cookin' in a big house down that way and taught me how. 'You my Sue-shef!' Not many little black gals could make a roux. Showed me all about different plants and herbs, how to make curing teas and tinctures.

'One day, she sees me staring at the words on a bag of flour, running my finger on the letters. She hisses so no one hears. "*Stop that!*" When we was done cleanin' up after dinner and the white folks was all in they rooms, she walks me to her cabin. Takes her Bible from its hidin' place in the wall. Niggers weren't 'sposed to own a Bible in

258

that house, in lots of houses. Then she takes out a cloth and unwraps some rolled up paper and a piece of pencil. These last two she holds like they's holy things.

'She taught me my letters, Maimie, showed me how letters make sounds, and how to put 'em together to make words. I made letters in the flour I spread to lay down dough, traced words in mud on the kitchen steps. She taught me my numbers, too, and how to cipher. She told me to not *never* let *any* white folks know I could read even a little.'

I asked Ruth why it had to remain a secret, thinking that an owner would find value in a slave who was smart.

'Oh, no, child. A nigger who can read, is a nigger who'll get ideas, and a nigger who got ideas, is a nigger who'll run. You'd think any slave would run first chance they get, but lots don't. And it ain't just the general hopelessness of it and what'll happen when they catch you. Some niggers believe God *means* for 'em to be a slave, and if they get to thinkin' there's more to life, then they goin' 'gainst God and deserve to get whipped. Every whippin' is God's will. Imagine that! *Think* on that!

'Well, sweet Jesus. We been freed. Yes, we have, but not much is changed. Not yet. But it will. With Jesus' leadin' the way, we will rise up like the Israelites in the Bible!

'I'm makin' more coffee. And I'm gonna start fixin' some biscuit an' gravy for us for later. Gonna *make* you eat it!

'The Mastuh of this house where I'm with Maimie rents me out to a friend o' his for a fancy party. They need someone servin' dinner who can do it right. I was to stay the night, then get took home next mornin'. By this time, I'm pretty, and I can put a bowl of soup in front of someone like I'm doin' a dance. I know how to smile, but I ain't *never* saucy.

'Dinner is over, folks leave, that Misrus gone up to her rooms, me and the others is cleanin' up. That Mastuh, drunk as a man can get and still walk, come slammin' into the kitchen. Grabs my arm, "C'mon girl, you gonna earn your fee now." None of them others says a word, don't even look up.

'Next day, when Maimie sees my face she knows. She takes me to her cabin, cleans me up and gives me salves to rub where it hurt. I am shakin' with hate. "Hate that bastard all you want", she says, "but don't let it show one little bit. You bein' tested."'

Ruth said it was a hard test. The man who owned her decided that, since she'd been broken in and wouldn't bring as much in a rental arrangement, he'd use her when he felt like it. He used her hard. She got pregnant for the first time when she was not quite twelve. Maimie gave her a concoction to drink that expelled the baby. Then she was sold again.

'When I got sold away from Maimie, I cried like I was losing my own mama all over again. But she said I'd do just fine if I kep' my head on straight. She'd be prayin' for me like she always done.

'By then, I'd figured out I could take just about anything this life might throw at me. Good to come to know this, no matter when in your life you get it. But you gotta be easy on yourself when you fall down. 'Cause you will.

'Oh, my goodness sakes alive! I'm 'bout to burn these biscuits! Got some cheese in 'em and good butter. Ain't nobody but me does 'em like this. Can you smell 'em? Look at 'em! They's just *glamorous!* Ha, *ha!* And I got this nice piece o' ham and I'll make us some gravy. Gettin' on to supper time. You gonna eat, now, girl!

'Before coming here, at another one of them big North Carolina places, I got raped by the overseer. Child, we *all* got raped by the overseer. Know what I'm sayin'? By the Mastuh or any white man work for him, and don't forget his daddy and his sons and his brothers and his cousins and all his friends, too. That's how it was.

'I got pregnant and it come way too soon. Not much baby to come out, but that time, I felt different about it. My heart hurt for it. I wanted my own baby. I told that to one of the women, and she jus' shook her head. Said there was no worse hell than having your child took from you and sold down river to where you know it's bound to die a bad death.

'She said she knew women who killed their babies fresh from their wombs. Let that baby die before it knows it's a slave. I still wanted my own baby.

'Your papa bought me from another North Carolina man. Private sale, paid *fifteen hundred dollars*. I knew it was a lot of money and was kinda proud. I was that stupid.

'When we got here, they put me in a cabin with four other women, all older than me. One of 'em looks me over and says, "New brood mare. Got some time yet, maybe." I didn't know what that meant. Your papa told me I was to take care of his wife, your Mama. She'd had a hard time birthin' you and still wasn't healed. You was three or four, I was maybe fourteen, fifteen. Doctor come by every few days with her medicine. You asked me how I knew you'd been usin' it? Oh, I know all about laudanum.

'Your Mama was like she was made outta glass. You're stronger n' her. She was nice then and you was a sweet little girl, so I thought, well, could be a good house finally.

'But it weren't too long before I learnt what a "brood mare" was on your daddy's farm. I was bought to have pretty babies your papa could make money off of. Not off o' the *work* they'd do when they was grown, but off o' they *bodies* when they was sold, and they could get sold any time.

'Did you hear me?'

I had heard her. I couldn't speak. My father had bought, bred, and sold human beings as if they were race horses or hunting dogs. He'd bred people. My father.

'Did my mother know?'

Ruth cocked her head and looked at me. Of course, she did. She'd known and condoned it. I'd grown up in that house, and I'd skipped along the surface of our life and never bothered to look down through the layers. Maybe I didn't want to look, maybe I'd had a sense there was something rotten under it all, maybe I'd glimpsed the truth and suppressed it. Maybe I was simply shallow. A shallow, selfish, stupid girl.

'Where d'you think the money come from for your pretty little life? Tobacco? Wheat? *Livestock?* That money come from *human* livestock. Oh, your daddy took good care o' his Negros, we slep' under blankets when it was cold, we was never hungry. We was your daddy's most important *investment.*

'When he was lookin' me over before he bought me, he was *measurin'* me. How much leg to how much body. What about the length of my neck and size and shape of my head. Was my teeth hard and placed right? Was my back straight and strong? How wide was my hips, my shoulders. He liked my light colour, run his hand down my flank, said my skin was "specially fine". My old Mastuh told him I'd have healthy, handsome babies, if bred to the right stud.

'Breathe, child. We gonna have some supper now. Oh! Forgot the okra. Well, won't take more n' a minute. And, you know? I'm gonna give you some o' your Mama's rose pink wine to sip, still so many bottles left. Look like you need some.

'Zekiel! Since you jus standin' there, go down and bring us up a bottle of that pink wine, you know the one. And then, you get on outta here. Take you some of that ham biscuit on your way out and stay out now.'

I wasn't hungry, but I was ready for the wine. I'd have preferred whiskey, I wanted to be drunk — I'd barely arrived and so much had come at me already — but I'd take the wine.

We were then interrupted by a neighbour woman who knocked on the back door, saw me at the table and came right in all a'flutter. Said she'd heard I'd been rescued from being tortured by the Indians 'and worse' — this last she delivered in a hoarse whisper — and was back home and she was so very glad to see me. She'd been a friend of my mother's.

'Jane was the loveliest woman! We all admired how beautifully she kept her house and gardens! And how prettily she dressed herself — and you! — in those fashions from New York. Paris, too! And, oh my! What parties she had! I don't think I missed a one! You must remember me, don't you? So much has changed, since… The Tragedy.'

I did not, but pretended I did. She'd stare at my eye, look away, look back, unable to help herself. I'd stopped wearing the eye patch.

She had two satchels full of dresses she wanted to sell — 'These are hardly even worn, and in remembrance of your dear mother, I'll give you a good, fair price!' — but when she began to pull them out, I begged her not to. Said I had no money for dresses. She said no one had any money any more. 'Look at me', she said bitterly, 'I can't even dress myself proper!' I told her she looked just fine, that it was hard times all around.

Ruth had been gathering up some food for her, wrapped it in a clean towel that she tucked into one of the woman's bags. A thousand things went across that woman's face before she nodded, turned and walked out again. Ruth said the woman had been there a few times before. She'd bought a housedress from her once, and always gave her food.

Ezekiel brought the wine, Ruth poured me a generous glass. She wouldn't have any, told me she'll have a bit every now and then in the evenings, but not often. Then she pushed the ham biscuits and okra towards me with an imperious look. I had to admit it smelled good.

CHAPTER 5

After supper, Ruth resumed her story as we cleaned up.

'One of the men your papa bought the same day he bought me was part Cherokee, part black. Dark skin, smooth hair. Most beautiful man I ever did see.'

'Jewell?'

'*Good!* You remember him. Oh, I am *glad*. You asked about love, well, *he loved you*. And, girl, he was so proud of you. "That is one *fast* runnin' chile! And gettin' good with that bow!" Remember that little bow he made for you? Arrows to fit it? You lost it somewheres. I was so mad at you but he said, "No, no, no, Ruthie. She gettin' to be a real girl now. Different things to think on. How it ought to be."

'Didn't you never wonder how he come to have all that time for you, and wasn't *ever* out in the fields? And him so strong? Jewell was your daddy's prime stud. Your daddy wanted him to conserve his "vital energies", is what he called it.

'He made babies with a coupla other women, and them babies got sold. Your daddy said I wasn't to lie with nobody but Jewell, said he had a feelin' about our "blood lines" mixin' good. But somehow it didn't take. I didn't get pregnant. What did take with us, though, after a bit, was love. When he was doing to me what he was bought to do, I never looked in his face and he never looked in mine, but we was decent to one another. That turned into bein' nice to one another. Then *sweet* with one another. We'd talk a bit, laugh a bit, while he was gettin' his clothes back on, but we didn't never kiss.

'Then one night, he gets up to go, candle still lit, we look at one another a good long look. He blows out that candle. When he gets back in the bed he kisses me and I kiss him back. We made love. Two people can do that, you know, they can *make* love. And that night's love-makin', made babies. It was like the love itself brung 'em. Two babies. The woman who midwifed us all said she could feel they was two, said one was a boy and one was a girl. How d'you know that, I asked? Said she knew babies.

'We was in love with each other, and we was in love with them babies even before they was born. And then — seemed like it happened so fast! — there they was! Out in the world! Jus' like she said! One boy and one girl. Prettiest babies you ever did see. Darker-skinned than me, about as dark as Jewell, and *beautiful*. Strong, too.

'Your mama was sometimes in a bad way then. Sick with headaches, pains all over her body, but mostly, I believe she was sick in her heart. Your damn father, like all the rest of 'em, would bed anyone he took a fancy to. Him and that bastard father-in-law of yours, Mastuh Byrd, they'd go out together. Your papa'd come home drunk, your Mama would say somethin' and he'd beat her. I could see it next day — bad marks on her body — but we'd neither of us say a thing.

'She was usin' the drug, and I could understand how she'd need it. I'd help her mix a dose, time to time.

'We all heard about the war that was surely comin', that if the North won... but it hadn't come yet, so we didn't let ourselves think on it. I had my babies and I had my man. We was a *family*. I thanked the good Lord for every bit of grace.

'But your Mama was startin' to change. When she was her sweet self, she was real sweet. But there was another Missrus Jane Randolph inside her. Sometimes women, white women more than us, I think, go through some hard times when they start gettin' a bit older. But this was somethin' else. She was losin' her mind.'

'What do you mean?'

'I'm tellin' you. One afternoon... Sweet Jesus.'

Ruth put her hand over her mouth and looked out towards the cabins.

'Tell me.'

'Fixin' to.'

She got up, brought another glass to the table, poured herself a bit, and took a swallow.

'I'm sittin' outside the cabin watchin' my children play. Late in the afternoon, work is done for a bit, I'm easy in my body and mind. Jewell's been gone couple o' days, rented out to some friend o' your daddy's for carpentry work, comin' back next day. I look up, and here comes your mama walkin' towards the cabin with this pretty white woman. Says she met her and her husband at a Bible meetin', wants to introduce 'em to me and my "darlin' babies".

'Young, only a little bit older than you are now, with dark brown hair, dark brown eyes. She's wearin' all black, black silk with lace and black beads, pretty little hat with a black veil pulled back off her face.

'Your Mama says her "sweet friend" is in mourning, her own little girl-child, not yet a year old, died of fever about six months before. Woman says she don't know why she keeps on livin'. Can't get pregnant — doctor said not to — can't stop dreamin' about her dead baby. She starts to cry. I reach out my hand and she takes it and I tell her I'll pray for her. She squeezes my hand.

'Then she sees my babies. "*Oh!*" she says, and claps her hands. "Jane, you were right! These are the prettiest children! Oh, *oh!* This little girl! My Marie..." And she starts to cry harder, folded over like it hurts.

'Your father comes up just then with the husband who sees how she is and takes her in his arms. Your Mama asks if they wouldn't rather go on up to the veranda to talk where it's more quiet. But the woman says, "No, no! Please! I want to stay here with these angels." She sits down and starts cooin' to 'em, opens her arms, and, friendly babies as they be, they come right up, gigglin'. "Look! They like me! *Both* of them do!" She has them to climb up onto her lap. We're all laughin', it's a sweet thing.

'Your Mama tells me to go get some of that rose-pink wine, and some liquor for the men. I should fix a little something to eat, too. I go do that, get a couple of the girls to help me. In a bit, we're bringin' everything out, the food and drink, dishes and glasses, and a clean white linen cloth to put on my outside table. I even got a little vase with a rose in it. I'm thinkin' how nice it'll look.

'We're almost back to the cabin and I see everybody's standing up. The two men are talkin', noddin', smilin', and your papa's puttin' something in the pocket o' his vest. I see the woman's got my boy in one arm and is holdin' my girl by the hand. Then, I see your Mama coming outta the door of my cabin with one of my baskets and I see it's full o' their toys, things that Jewell and me's made for 'em.

'I drop the tray and I'm runnin' hard, yellin', '*No!*' I'm just about to where I coulda grabbed my girl, I'm reachin' for her, but your papa throws me onto the ground, pins me down. Your Mama and them other two is runnin' towards the house and *they got my babies!* My babies are reachin' back, cryin' out for me, like I cried out after my own Mama when they pulled me off o' her, and I'm screamin', "*No! No!*" I'm fightin' but he hits me hard. *Hard.*

'When I wake, it's dark. I'm on my back on my bed, tied to it, hands and feet. Your papa's on top o' me, slammin' hisself into me. I ain't sorry to tell it plain.

'When he's done, he says the next baby I get better have red hair like him, 'cause light-skinned, light-haired, light-eyed babies fetch a whole lot more money than little black nigger babies, like them he just sold that afternoon.

'All I can do is spit in his face, so I do it, and he hits me again. After he's gone, one of the older women comes in, lights a candle, unties me and sets herself down on the bed, starts wipin' the blood off o' my face. I can't stop moanin', "*Nooooo, nooooo, nooooooo...*"

"'Hush," she says. "What d'you think them babies was for? Did you forget where you is? *What* you is? Them babies was *never* yours. Thank the good Lord you're alive your own self."

'Next mornin', I don't get up. I'm waiting on Jewell, thinkin' he'll kill all o' you all. Finally, ah, my Lord in Heaven, I hear him callin' my name, and I can tell he knows. By the sounds he makes callin' me, I can tell he knows. He runs in, sees how it is, grabs his bow and arrows, runs right out. They kill him.'

I interrupt her.

'*What? No!* He couldn't have... My father told me he was sold! He said Jewell had made a mistake and...'

'Oh, he made a mistake, alright. For a moment in time, he forgot he was a *slave*, thought he was a *man*. Another man ripped his children away and raped his wife. So, he takes hold of his weapon and goes after that man. My dear Lord God.'

I couldn't stay in my chair.

'Don't go nowhere, yet. There's more you gotta hear about this.'

I sat back down.

'I look at his body, put my hands on him, kiss his face, but someone takes me away, takes me back to my bed. I try to die right then, go right down into that other Hell. But all of a sudden, your Mama's at the door, blockin' the light, hair all in her face, screamin' at me, crazy like I ain't never seen her, like some wild thing.

'She's yellin', "*Get up! It's over! It's done! Now, get up! Who the hell do you think you are? Lazy bitch! You're nothing!*"

'Oh, I get up. I fly at her. Grab her throat with both hands and we're down on the ground, each of us tryin' to kill th'other. But I'm stronger, beatin' on her hard's I can. Then your papa and his man come runnin'. Man's got his whip.

'They drag me to the whippin' post, tie me to it, side o' my head slam to it, and they rip down the back o' my dress. Before that man even raises his arm, in the corner of my eye I see your Mama movin' fast, see her skirts swirlin', see her grab that whip away from him and lean back to make it fly.

'She's the one done it, Sarah. Your Mama was the one done it to me.'

I'm sure I cried, but maybe I didn't. Ruth puttered in the kitchen and let me be. I sat at the table, not able to say anything until, after a bit, I told her how, as I had lain in my bed unable to sleep after hearing her story and feeling her scars, I'd lifted my hand — so very like my mother's — closed my fist tight as if on the handle of a bull-whip and started moving it back and forth with increasing violence, as she, Ruth, had moved her arm while she told me of the whipping, *as my mother had moved her arm while she did the whipping*. I told her how with each stroke, holding that imaginary whip, I could *see* the flesh open, I could *see* the gouts of blood.

Ruth nodded.

'That was your Mama, come into your body to help you to *feel* it, so's you'd *know*. But the story ain't over, girl. Go out, walk a bit, but not for long. There's more to tell about your mama, and I am tired.'

CHAPTER 6

I had trouble getting out of my chair. I gulped the rest of my wine, then walked unsteadily to the back door, down the steps, and and stood facing the vegetable gardens. Beyond these and to my left were chicken coops, other outbuildings. Off a bit to my right and down a gentle green slope were the slaves' cabins. The whipping post must have been somewhere right near there, apparently it had been knocked down. What a thing that must have been, to get rid of it. There were trees — it was a beautiful place — and beyond these, the fields of wheat, tobacco, whatever else was growing out there. The afternoon sky was low and heavy. I hoped it would storm.

When I looked back, Ruth was still sitting at the table. I watched as she slowly lifted a glass to sip Mama's pink wine. Good god, Ruth. How hard all all this must have been to recall and tell. Hard enough to live it once. I hoped she'd had enough for the day. I went back into the kitchen and was about to tell her I was done, but she motioned for me to sit. She poured me another glass of wine, and poured a bit more for herself, too.

'Your mama wasn't done with me. Later on that same day, she comes to the cabin and I think, well, now she'll kill me. But she tells the two women with me to get outta her way. She tells them bring clean water, clean cloths, and she wants fresh jars of salves and ointments. Her doctor comes next mornin' with a whole bunch of different salves and ointments.

'She stays with me all day for about a week. Then she says for me to come back *when I'm ready*. To have someone let her know *if I need somethin'*. What am I 'sposed to think about that?

'Soon I'm back in the house. I do my work, but I don't speak if I don't have to. One day, she's in her bed and got them pains, asks me to mix the dose for her, but make it strong, and I think how easy, *how very easy it would be*. But I'm too dead inside.

'Your Mama starts actin' real strange. She be watchin' us while we work, like she's tryin' to figure who we was and how we got there. Girls was scared of her. I'd say, 'Yes'm?' She'd shake her head and walk away.

'One day, she takes a buggy and, by herself, goes to the fields, walkin' the rows in the sun, no hat nor nothin', watchin' 'em pull tobacco. Tells the man to bring water and she serves 'em herself. That night, I'm puttin' out supper for the two of 'em, and your father's poundin' his fist on the table.

"Stupid bitch! Stay in the goddamn house where you belong!"

'She's just... lost. So, I ask the Lord to help me forgive her. She's sick, I says. One mornin', I'm puttin' away her clean clothes, and she says, "Ruth! Stand still!" She sees I'm pregnant and she *knows*. She's sayin' "Oh, Ruth! Oh, Ruth! What can I do? Tell me what to do, I'll do anything." I tell her this baby ain't gonna be sold. I'll keep doin' for her and for you, I'll stay charge o' the house like I always done, but I ain't makin' more babies, not with nobody, and this baby is *my* baby.

'I tell her she needs to tell her husband that's how it's gonna be, or the worst thing she can imagine is gonna happen. Says she'll tell him that very night. I wonder if she can do it, I wonder if it'll make a difference. I have no hope in any of it.

'Four months later, Ezekiel is born and you know the colour o' his hair. When he was a tiny thing, it was *red*. And he got them greenish eyes, light skin. Few weeks later, one fine mornin', I come into her little room with him in my arms. Your Mama strokes his cheek and says how pretty he is.

'Then I bend so I'm right up close to her face, and keepin' my voice low, I say to her, *Look at his face, smell his baby sweetness that's like the Lord's own breath. Remember what I told you? This baby is my baby, I'm his Mama. I will kill him dead if your husband comes near him and then I will kill myself. I will not let him get sold, and I won't make any more babies.*

'Your Mama's face is lit by somethin' fierce inside her. She says it *will not* happen. "*It will not*," she says. She says it again and swears it on her own life. This time, I believe her. He didn't never bother Zeke or me from then on. And Zeke was my last baby.'

'So, Jewell wasn't Zeke's father.'

'No, child.'

'Ezekiel is my brother.'

'Yes, child. Your half-brother.'

We sat in silence for a while. Then Ruth spoke.

'You asked about *love*. Didn't me and them others *love* you Randolphs. Think, child! How you gonna love someone who sees you as somethin' to be bought, bred, sold, used to death and then someone takes your place and it all goes on and on and on. From your grandma, to your mama, to you, to your children and grand-children and their children. They get the shape o' your face, and they get the shape o' your soul. They get your cuts that don't heal. Your scars. Your deep fear. It'll run in the blood of them you'll never see, them who you can't explain *nothin'* to. Ain't nobody explained it to you. Ain't nobody ever been able to tell you how come they hate you so bad. White people.

'Strange thing was, I did come to love your mama. I did. But I'm done talkin' for now. I ain't hungry an' I see you ain't neither. You a little drunk, so I'm gonna leave this bottle here.

'And Sarah. I gotta know real soon what you plan to do about this place. Time gettin' short for me and Zeke. We got our own lives to live.'

She stood up, but there was something I had to know, it came out in a rush.

'Ruth! Where was I? When my mother was whipping you, *where was I?* How could I not have known? I should have known, I could have made her stop. I could have done something!'

She looked me for a moment before answering.

'You was only about ten years old! Even if you was older, if they was bound to kill me, ain't *nothin'* you could have done.'

'She'd have listened to me, I could have...'

I was falling apart, sobbing uncontrollably and Ruth was quietly, somewhat scornfully, laughing at me.

'Girl! You are givin' me headache. Go on to bed. Sweet Jesus.'

She turned to go, stopped, turned and faced me again.

'Sarah, girl. I know you mean it well, but you feelin' guilty for what your parents was, what they done, what you didn't know and couldn't have done nothin' about, don't do me no good. Don't do *you* no good, don't do *nobody* no good. But listen here. The War's over, we been freed, no more slavery, so they say. So they say. But they *still* got their foot on our necks, they still tryin' to kill us. You ain't a child no more. What you gonna do *now?'*

CHAPTER 7

I woke early. After Zeke left for the day's work, Ruth and I lingered over our coffee.

'I wish I'd known my mother better.'

Getting up from the table, Ruth said, 'Come on. Bring your coffee.'

I followed her upstairs and she opened the door to my mother's bedroom. All the furniture was draped same as downstairs. Her big empty bed, her armoire, her dressing table, a chair, a hassock, everything, all draped in white, and the curtains were drawn so the air was stuffy and dim. We went to the door of the small room she'd called

271

her 'writing room'; it had been her inner sanctum. If, as a child, I'd run in uninvited, she'd say, 'This is where I come to be quiet, Sarah. Now, what is it that's so important?' Ruth reached into the pocket of her apron, pulled out a key and opened that door.

Yellow light poured in through the two east-facing windows. Ruth walked over and opened them to let in a breeze, too. The room was alive with a clutter of pretty things.

'I'm gonna leave you alone in here, but first, I gotta show you somethin'.'

With a very small key, Ruth opened one of the drawers in my mother's desk and pulled out a rectangular item wrapped in a linen napkin and handed it to me. It was a copy of a book by someone named Harriet Beecher Stowe, titled 'Uncle Tom's Cabin'.

Ruth said that a couple of months before her death, my mother had started having tea regularly with a few ladies from her church. Then the preacher began to come. They'd meet in this room and Ruth said my mother had told her she was not to tell *anyone* about these gatherings. This would bring grave danger to everyone involved. The War was going on.

When Ruth brought up tea, she could see people holding a book with a picture on the cover of a little coloured girl. She was able to sound out what the title said. They'd stop talking when she entered and wait until she left to resume talking. Finally she felt she had to ask my mother about this book.

'I was nervous to ask, but she said she was glad I did. She told me to read the book and then we'd talk about it, she had questions for me. I was embarrassed to tell her I couldn't read good enough and, bless her heart, she said we'd read it together.'

My mother started inviting Ruth into her room. They read the book together, discussing it, comparing the story with Ruth's experience — and the truth of Ruth's younger life apparently shocked my mother — and then my mother started having her join the discussions in her room.

Ruth told me it was around this time that my mother wrote down the name of the family's lawyer, engaged by my father, John Sands, Esquire, of Richmond — the man who'd written to me — and gave it to her. She'd given her the address of his office and told her that he was an honest man who was not opposed to sliding off to one side of the law in order to serve a good cause. He knew all about the meetings. She told Ruth not to hesitate to contact him should the need arise. She made clear that he was a friend of *hers*, and not of my father's, and told her she'd be wise not to let the Master know she had this information. Ruth said she still had that paper tucked into her Bible.

After my mother's death, Ruth brought the book to her cabin and used it, keeping it hidden from my father, to teach Ezekiel. But he was already way ahead of her. He'd been reading her Bible and everything else he could get hold of, surreptitiously asking for help from the occasional literate workman. She said that, once she saw how hungry he was, she brought down some of my books so he could read them. When she learned I was coming, she brought all the books back to my mother's room and put them away.

'Here's the key to this door, and this little key to her desk drawer. You keep 'em now,' she said. 'When you get hungry, come on down to the kitchen, we'll have somethin' to eat. '

She paused, looking around her.

'You know, towards the end, your mama tried to get me to call her "Jane". Ain't that somethin'? But I couldn't. Just felt unnatural. Old ways… Well. Reckon I'll see you later.'

Ruth closed the door gently as she left. I stood, holding the book, looking around. Small sounds came from outside, otherwise it was perfectly quiet. I took a deep breath and could smell my mother.

Shelves upon shelves of books. I saw my old much used volumes of Shakespeare, and my beloved Greeks — Homer, Nathaniel Hawthorne's collection of the myths with my childlike drawings in the margins, plays by Aeschylus, Sophocles, Euripides. There was Flaubert, too, that she'd used to teach me French.

Against the wall were stacked the paintings that had been hung throughout the house, except for a few that were on the walls in the small parlour when I first arrived. Ruth must have replaced them to make me feel more at home. I saw the landscape painting that had enchanted me as a child. I moved others aside to stand back and look at it.

It was smaller than I recalled. I turned it over and read a note written on the paper backing the frame: 'This is only a study, he says! Imagine! I had to beg him to sign it! I do hope you will like this. I believe he has a future in art. Your loving friend always, Cecilia.' I turned it back around and the artist's name was in rather large capital letters on the lower left side: COROT.

In a small trunk lined in fabric were my dolls, dressed in their beautiful dresses, many of which Mama and I had sewed together. I wondered if she'd hoped that I'd one day have a daughter who'd enjoy these things. Well, I'd had a daughter.

Her desk was of a coppery-coloured wood with beautifully modelled legs. It was rather wide and deep with a set of small drawers and compartments at the back. There was a stack of letters, and on the top were some that were ribbon-wrapped. I recognised by the hand that they'd come from me. I opened one. It was so awkward, so impersonal that I couldn't bear to read it.

There was a lamp, a set of pens in a leather case lined in blue velvet, various ink pots, in one of the drawers was fine writing paper of different sizes, and a small, white leather covered New Testament.

Wrapped in layers of brown paper were several Daguerreotype images, each separated by cotton wool. They'd apparently been taken during a visit to Cecilia in Paris, the Cecilia who'd written the note on the back of the painting.

My mother had spoken of this friend of her girlhood often. Cecilia had shown early talent as a painter, had gone to Paris to study, met a wealthy businessman, married him, had a child, and had never come back. One of the images was of my blonde Mama and her darker-haired friend Cecilia sitting side by side on a settee just large enough for the two of them. Cecilia has one arm draped over my mother's shoulders. They appear to be laughing, and my mother is the one laughing the fullest, head back, mouth wide. I'd never seen her look like that. She is wearing the pearls I wore on my wedding day.

I sat and looked out the window. The sun had moved and the light in the room was not so potent as before. I was exhausted. I noticed that, though it had been many months since my mother had spent time here, there was no dust. The rose in a vase on the table was fresh.

CHAPTER 8

I took 'Uncle Tom's Cabin' to my room. When I finished the book, I could smell food cooking so went down to the kitchen. Ruth was stirring something in the big black skillet. When I came in, she turned to look at me. I held up the book for her to see. She smiled, nodded, then turned her attention back to the stove. I told Ruth I was so dizzy and exhausted by everything I was learning, that I could barely move.

'Well. Jus' *be* dizzy. Then get over it. And get over bein' tired too. There's things you gotta do about all this here. It's time.'

Her tone was impatient. She stirred food. I sat. Then I suddenly remembered that in the letter from my father about my mother's death, he'd written about her heart's fragility, and I assumed he'd meant her physical heart, that it had given out. But he'd made other comments that had made little sense to me, suggesting that her long-time doctor had failed her somehow. He hadn't been clear.

'Ruth, how did my mother die?'

She stopped stirring and turned to face me.

'Laudanum. I found her in her bed, empty bottles on the floor, must have been savin' 'em up. Told me so many times she felt like she didn't deserve to live, and with you most likely killed, she told me didn't *want* to live. I told her to hold on. You'd been seen and you'd be comin' home soon, and you'd be needin' your Mama. But she done it and I wish to God she hadn't. She loved you with her whole heart. I hope she's found rest in the Lord's Heaven.'

I got up from the table with difficulty and turned to go. She asked where I was going. I said I needed to go lie down. She raised her eyebrows at me, disapproving. I got angry. I told her I'd just learned my mother had killed herself and I had a right to go weep for her in the privacy of my own damn bedroom.

She was unmoved.

'Sit back down. I need you to help me chop these onions for our dinner.'

The onions and a large knife were on a board on the table. She gently pushed it in my direction.

'Best to just get on with life. Ain't nobody gets off easy, child. Chop 'em up good and small.'

Life was 'getting on' with me faster than the train that had brought me back to Virginia. In no more than a few days I'd learned that my father's primary cash crop had been human beings; that he was a murderer and a rapist; that Ruth's son, the shy mulatto boy who grew up playing with the other slave children, was my half-brother; that my fragile mother had beaten Ruth half to death a few yards from where I moved through my days and slept through my nights in luxurious stupidity. I'd learned that my mother, the granddaughter, daughter, and wife of slave-owners, had become an abolitionist, that she'd been hosting meetings that would have been ruled seditious by her husband and his friends, and that she'd invited Ruth to participate — a mortal danger to them all, but especially to Ruth. And I'd learned that she'd ended her life by suicide, using the drug I'd so recently depended on to get through the day, and might use again should a strong enough need arise.

I chopped the onions.

I asked Ruth about my father's death. The lawyer, Sands, had written something about an altercation at my father-in-law's house. Apparently, he'd died doing what he loved best.

Ruth said he'd been carousing with Mr. Jake Byrd, Sr., and some other men at Mr. Byrd's home. They'd had some 'fancy women' entertaining them, Negro women — Mr. Byrd's wife was at her parents' home in Charleston — and an argument had erupted. Shots were fired and my father had caught a bullet in the chest, died instantly. One of the women had also been killed, and two or three of the men had been seriously wounded. Ruth said she learned from the woman who'd cleaned the place up, one of Byrd's Negros, a woman with a small child who'd stayed after The War for the pittance Byrd paid her, that it looked like a slaughter house, blood everywhere.

When Mr. Byrd came by the next day with a couple of his boys to deliver the body, he told Ruth that 'things had just got out of hand', and that he — Mr. Byrd — had handled everything, no need to notify any authorities. But before he'd expired, Mr. Randolph had said he wanted to be buried beside his beloved wife, and that when his daughter's body was returned, if it ever was, they should all be in the family plot together. So, here he was.

Byrd gave Ruth a packet of cash in US dollars, 'to buy a stone'. When he leaned down to hand her the money, he'd nearly fallen off his horse, he was so drunk. He told Ruth that if he heard she was telling tales about it, or if she should feel the need to contact that 'asshole nigger-lovin' lawyer, Sands', well, things would get very rough indeed for her and her boy.

Of course, Ruth got word to Mr. Sands right away. He came from Richmond with a policeman and the coroner who issued the death certificate. This was necessary in order to activate several documents pertaining to the disposition of the property and to Ruth and Ezekiel's legal standing, as well. Mr. Sands and his associates then went to see Mr. Byrd and came back to Ruth with another envelope full of cash.

'Mr. Sands told me it was from Mr. Byrd to "help tie them over until the young mistress returns and we make a sale", but we knew it was to keep me quiet. There was some big politicians there that night playin' them games, and Mr. Byrd couldn't afford no scandal.'

Then she said, 'Your daddy's buried out close to where your Mama's laid, but not too close. I'll take you out there whenever you want to go.'

I told her I wanted to go first thing next morning. I asked her why she hadn't taken me out there sooner.

'You knew your folks was dead, but you didn't never ask me about it 'til today. I figured you wasn't ready and I wasn't gonna tell you 'til you was.'

I asked if there'd been a funeral service for my mother.

'This was maybe the one good thing your daddy did for her. He had the preacher from her church to come, the one she had at her secret meetings, and say some words, read from the Bible. Some other white people come, guests to them dinner parties from before

The War. And them abolition women, they come to pay respects. Us Negros who was still here prayed and sang over her. We all put flowers on her grave. He got a stone for her, got it carved nice.'

I asked about my father.

'We just put him in the ground.'

CHAPTER 9

June passed and then came the lush Virginia heat of July, and then the deeper heat and thick air of August.

My mother's roses flourished and their fragrances — there were several varieties — were intoxicating. Ruth and I filled vases with them. I had them in my room, on the kitchen table where we ate, on a table on the veranda where we'd sit and talk of an evening. Ruth kept a fresh rose on the small table in my mother's writing room.

The vegetable garden was producing and I told Ruth I wanted to help her work it. It felt good to be using my muscles again, felt good to sweat. I'd grown soft over the winter, but it didn't take long for me to regain strength. We didn't talk much while we worked. There was the sound of our hoes in the hot dirt, the slice of knives on thick stems, the hum of insects, birdsong.

We mostly ate vegetables. There were eggs, and about once a week we'd cook a chicken. I was surprised how much I enjoyed the cooking, something that had always seemed a chore for which I'd had no aptitude. But loving good food is fine inspiration and Ruth was a fine teacher.

One day I found the pond on the property I'd swum in as child, a path from the far end of the garden led through trees right down to it. I told Ruth I remembered how she'd catch me in it, remind me that Mama didn't want me in there because of snakes, but that she'd let me swim anyway. She said she'd rarely seen one, but that Zeke and the hired man kept the grass short all around the end of it by the path and a good way up both sides. She said it was likely mostly free of snakes.

'Likely mostly free' didn't fill me with confidence but I wanted to swim a bit and tried it. It felt good on a hot day. I was just walking out of the water one afternoon as Ruth was coming towards it, barefoot with a cotton blanket draped around her. I'd swum in my shift and drawers that clung to me now, bunched and sopping. Ruth laughed.

'Girl, ain't but one way to do this, and that's to go in with no more 'n the skin the good Lord give you to get born in. This here is like yo' mama's womb water.'

With that, she dropped the blanket and walked in up to her hips. There it was, the tree on her back. The sight jolted me. Mama did that, good god. Ruth leaned into the water that was the colour of tea and moved forward slowly with only her head above the surface and barely a ripple following her. I took off my wet things and followed her.

The water was silky on my skin. It was warm for about a foot or so down and below that, cool. Ruth said it was fed by a couple of springs and was pretty deep in the middle, with plenty of fish — she reminded me I'd eaten a few sunnies since I'd come and one nice bass — turtles, frogs that we'd hear in rich chorus at night, and, yes, snakes.

I became addicted. I loved it in the morning right after breakfast. At mid-day, when the heat was oppressive, after working in the garden, I practically ran down the path. I even swam once in the rain. Only occasionally did Ruth and I find ourselves heading towards the pond at the same time. We'd chat on the way, but when we took off our clothes, our thoughts turned towards the water. We swam in silence, respecting what I believe we each, in our own ways, found holy.

Every few days, I visited my mother's grave. I always brought flowers and there were always flowers still there when I arrived, still fresh, yet Ruth and I never ran into one another coming or going. I'd sit against the stone and try to talk with her. She and I had not talked much when I was growing up. It was no easier now.

But one day I lay down on the ground over her body and, speaking softly, begged her to forgive me and said that I forgave her. I told her how proud I was to be her daughter, how much I loved her. I told her about my own daughter, Elizabeth Mary Bird, and how sad it was they'd never meet. I said I wanted us to be at peace with one another. I was crying and had nothing more to say, so I lay still.

I felt a shift in the air. Not in the temperature or movement, but a shift in some quality without measurable aspects. The constant hum of summer changed timbre. Light was neither brighter nor dimmer, but it was changed. This moment of grace lingered briefly, then dissolved. I've chosen to believe it was my mother telling me she loved me too. I lay for a good while on that bed of roots and twigs and fallen leaves, looking up through the canopy of branches at a pale circle of sky, amid the buzz of life above her bones.

Letters came from Elizabeth and even one from William. Irish Mary wrote a short note telling me that she had moved to San Francisco, was now running her own 'house' and had six 'comely and smart young women' working for her. She offered me a partnership. I wrote her back declining the offer but saying I hoped to visit her one day, that I missed her company. I never heard back.

Elizabeth's letters were written in a lovely hand. They were mostly filled with stories of Charles and Joey, of course, how they were growing and how smart and curious they were, how well they could read and cipher, what good people they were becoming, how helpful.

But in one letter, she wrote that the 'Indian problem might seem fairly quiet for the moment where we are, but everyone is terribly uneasy'. Apparently many were of the opinion that 'the Big Treaty' had been 'a clear indication that the Army, indeed, the US government in its highest levels, has given up subduing the tribes'. People said the treaty was 'a declaration of defeat that would embolden the Indians to new and more horrible predations'.

Lizzie seemed to need, always, to consider the worst of possible scenarios with the Indians, as if to be better prepared for whatever happened. I answered her letters with chatty ones about Ruth and Zeke, the vegetable garden, the animals, the flowers — I'd save serious matters for when I saw her next.

William wrote that Wyoming had been officially declared a Territory of the United States. I hadn't known it wasn't. He had decided to go entirely into beef cattle, as it was too difficult to make anything grow out there. I immediately thought of fences, and how that would affect the buffalo herds.

He wrote that Elizabeth was suffering from the heat and working too hard. 'When you come home, I hope you will speak sense to her. Come home soon, Sarah. Lizzie insisted I go ahead and build that cabin, so I have and it awaits you. Lizzie has made it into a lovely domicile as only she can do. Come home.'

Often, in the evenings, we'd sit on the front veranda, admiring Mama's roses. Not only those in the carefully cultivated beds, but she'd planted wild roses on both sides of the short walk down to the drive that led to the road to Richmond. One of the dogs had befriended me, a sweet old girl, mostly white speckled with brown. She had a soulful face.

Ruth said Zeke had found her in the woods one day last year when he was out bird-hunting. She was half-starved and came up to him barely able to walk, but unafraid and gentle. He took her home. When the Grayback fell and people had no way of getting US dollars, they'd hold on as long as they could and then leave their farms hastily. Animals were eaten, or left to starve.

Zeke named her Sally, they'd become inseparable. She liked me, as dogs often did, and would circle and plop herself down near where I was sitting. But if Zeke came to join us, as he often did, carrying a book — I'd given him the key to my mother's room where all the books were, and he was never without one — she'd go to wherever he was. Sally was his dog.

Zeke was always shy with me, but every now and then I'd catch him studying my face. One soft evening on the veranda, he looked right at me and said, 'I want to come visit you when you go back. I want to see this West you talk about. I'd like to meet some Indians. I'd be interested in talking to some. I want to understand, if I can.' I told him I thought that I would like that very much. I'd write to him when I was settled and, when he was ready to come, I'd send him the fare. He nodded. I said, 'After all, you're my brother.' He nodded again, then turned and walked away. Ruth and I smiled at one another.

CHAPTER 10

I finally sent a note to the office of John W. Sands, Esq., and he sent a note back, with a request to come to the house to discuss matters. He was probably about forty, a bit shorter than I, stocky, energetic, with a healthy complexion and thinning, light-brown hair. A straightforward talker, with a slight accent I could not identify, he looked at me directly when we spoke.

Ruth had set up my father's office downstairs so he could stay the night. He said he planned to see 'that miscreant Byrd' the following morning. I suggested we all sit in the kitchen to talk, and that Zeke join us. He seemed genuinely pleased to be in Ruth's company and Zeke's as well, and they were glad to see him. He seemed to hate Jake's father as much as we did.

Shortly after I'd arrived, Jake Byrd Sr., having heard that I'd been rescued and was back at the house, had sent a boy with an invitation for a tête-a-tête. I'd sent the boy back with my refusal. Furious, he'd ridden hard up to Sands' office in Richmond, telling him to get me to sell and sell fast, so he could afford to hire more hands and bring in a tobacco crop. It might already be too late, but if the weather held, what there was might be saved. He wanted the entirety of what he could get for it, rather than having it go into the estate to be 'deliberately bungled up by that Negro, Ruth', as my father had arranged. 'After all, who can trust a damn nigger.'

Sands put him off several times, then when they finally met — Byrd had more or less forced himself into his office — he told Byrd he'd conferred with me and I wasn't interested in selling, that I intended to stay on and bring in that crop myself, and perhaps expand the wheat fields as well. He also said I was rather curious about soybeans. I laughed out loud at this. Byrd apparently 'went apoplectic', then raised his offer. Sands said it was as good a price as I would get in those times.

He also told me that my father, seeing how the Southern economy was about to devolve disastrously, had on his advice invested a good deal of money in a variety of enterprises in New York and London, and they were beginning to show good returns. And, incidentally, he'd been a major investor in the Union Pacific Railroad. If I chose to do so, the value of his shares — now mine — would allow me to travel back and forth in a luxurious private car.

'Hell,' he said, 'you could live your life in one, going back and forth from New York City to San Francisco, stopping when and where you wished, and be served all your meals on fine china.'

He also pointed out, pushing forward one of the many documents he'd spread out on the table, that Ruth's management of the part of the plantation for which she'd been responsible had been excellent, costing the enterprise less than had been anticipated and bringing in more revenue than expected, all contributing to Byrd's interest in making a deal. Ruth said, 'Well, that shouldn't be no surprise. I can cipher good as anybody. So can Zeke. And when I do a job, I do it good, to please the Lord and please my own self too. Zeke is just the same.'

What followed involved Sands traveling back and forth to Richmond, and back and forth from my house to Byrd's, with documents to be signed and an advance on the sale of the property handed over to me in US dollars. Byrd had wanted us to be in the same room for much of this, but I had, of course, refused.

I was established as Executor of the Estate, and an account at a prominent Richmond bank was opened in my name. My father had had several accounts there, and Sands told me that, on her request, he'd opened an account in my mother's name, a secret account, that my father was not to know about. The balance was sizeable. I wondered what her plans had been. All existing funds from both accounts would be transferred to mine, as would all revenues and receipts from the income of the property up until the sale was finalised, from the sale of the property, from the principal of my father's various holdings and any and all interest going forward. There might have been more but I can't recall.

A notarised document, signed snarlingly by Byrd, was filed in Sands' offices stating that if Byrd were to delay, if the full balance of the sale was not readily available for deposit on the date agreed upon, Byrd would forfeit the advance and lose the sale. If any misfortune should befall Sands or Mr. Randolph's daughter, Sarah, or any of her current employees and associates, including the freedwoman Ruth Randolph and her son, Ezekiel, all was forfeit and, in addition, he would be placed under arrest for suspicion of instigating, if not committing, the crime.

Sands said he'd leave us to consider all this and went to the veranda to smoke a cigar. We did not need much time and Sands seemed as pleased as we were with our decision.

As soon as Byrd's money was deposited, which he said would only be a few days from then, he'd send word. We should let our few remaining workers know right away there'd be a change in ownership and management, to give them time to make their plans. Ruth said they would do that and would settle those accounts.

Sands suggested strongly that Ruth and Zeke plan to leave the area entirely, he'd give them papers. He said we all should travel light. And, as there were all manner of 'fucking brigands' on the highways, we should let him know exactly when we planned to leave and he would meet us on the road to Richmond with an armed escort. He pressed this as being '*most important*'. He would arrange for an associate to call Byrd down to Charleston to discuss 'a scam, invented entirely for the occasion, but certain to prove irresistible to that nearly bankrupt scoundrel', so he would not be at the house when we departed.

Ruth and Ezekiel had decided they would go to Chincoteague Island where an uncle of hers lived. The island had not joined the Confederacy and there was a community there of free Negros who made their living as watermen, exporting oysters, blue crab, and other delicacies to fine restaurants in Philadelphia and New York City. Asking my help — though he certainly didn't need it — Zeke wrote to this man immediately, telling him when they'd be departing Richmond. We'd leave the house together, they'd see me off at the train station and continue on to Chincoteague.

Ruth got word that her uncle was overjoyed with these plans and would meet them at the Richmond train station with a few friends of his, all well-armed. It was about a four-day ride to the island, and the two of them shouldn't do it alone.

She said I should come. We'd eat the best food I'd ever had, and would swim in the sea. She'd never seen it before. Neither had I and the idea appealed, but I missed Elizabeth. I could feel her heart pulling on mine. I felt Far Cry pulling at me, too. Though I had begun, reluctantly, to accept that I would probably never find him, I needed, at least, to try to learn what had happened to him. And, though it surprised me, I longed to be back in the west. The land itself, the light, the wind in the grass, even the storms that could kill, it all called to me.

Sands said he'd book my ticket once I gave him the date, which I promised to do within the next few days. I declined the offer of a private car, but was glad to follow his suggestion and have him arrange a situation more commodious than I'd had on the trip east. A nice Pullman berth. As he was getting into his buggy to deliver some documents to 'that miserable fucker, Byrd', I asked him why he hated him so much.

'It is in the interest of self-regard, my dear, and a taste for revenge of a classical sort. If there is one thing Byrd hates worse than a nigger, it's a Jew. My people are from Poland. My name is Jan Wiktor Sandowski and it gives me great pleasure to nail that bastard's balls to the floor.'

Within the week, Sands sent an employee with a letter and copies of the pertinent documents, informing me that the balance of the sale had been transferred to my account.

Suddenly, it was time.

As to traveling light, I took his advice. Mostly. I put two silver candlesticks, the linen sheets from my bed, and my mother's pearls in my carpet bag. I carefully removed from its frame the painting by Mr. Corot, rolled it up and packed it along with a few volumes of Euripides in my other bag. Ruth found a large, drawstring reticule for me, in which I stuffed some clothing.

I urged Ruth to take from the house whatever she wanted with which to begin a new life, cookware, linens, china, cutlery, any of the silver... She interrupted me.

'You ain't got a brain in your head, girl! They got Black Codes now, and if they think you a *vagrant*, they gonna ask for papers. Mr. Sands give us papers, but if they look in that wagon — and they'd do that very thing, don't you wonder about that — and find a load o' rich stuff, we'd get lynched on the spot for being "thievin' niggers". We goin' with the clothes on our backs.'

That being the case, I told her that, together, we'd sew pouches in their clothes, into which I'd stuff good US paper money. She began to object, but I told her it was some small part of wages owed that she'd never otherwise see. We did it together one morning.

And one afternoon, while she was down at the pond, I slipped into her cabin and left on her table my mother's beautiful white leather bound New Testament, and for Zeke, Homer's 'The Iliad' and 'The Odyssey'. I'd wrapped them in two yellow linen pillow cases that my mother had embroidered in pink roses.

CHAPTER 1 1

Ruth had poured all the lamp oil into two big buckets. We each took one, and starting upstairs, we threw it on the curtains, on the muslin covering the furniture, on the beds, the rugs, the upholstered chairs and settees, we splashed it on the wallpaper on the way down-stairs, on everything downstairs that would burn, including kindling we'd gathered and piled high in the middle of all the floors in all the rooms. We anointed every part of the house as thoroughly as we could. I worried it might not be enough. Ruth said it would be plenty. The summer had been unusually dry.

Ruth had stashed a bottle of oil on the veranda; she poured it over several torches she'd made, saturating them. She took a tin box full of matches from her pocket, and told me to go on out to where Zeke was holding the horses, down the drive a bit and around a bend.

Zeke had been afraid they'd get spooked and run away with the buggy. I objected but Ruth said he might need help. She touched my face, then turned and ran back into the house. I turned and went down to the bottom of the steps, then stopped. I'd stay there. I had to be near Ruth and I had to see from close up what was about to happen.

I heard her from upstairs, shouting, 'Hallelujah!' and 'Praise the Lord!' I heard her as she ran down, 'Yes, Lord!', and I heard her from the back of Mama's grand hall and from my father's rooms and from the small parlour, 'C'mon! *Light!*', 'Yes, sweet Jesus!', '*C'mon, c'mon, c'mon!*', 'Dear Lord in Heaven!' I thought I saw her run — blurred, ghostlike — across the dark foyer into the kitchen. Then for a horrible moment there was nothing. I nearly ran in after her but suddenly, hair loose, skirts billowing, she flew around the side of the house to where I was standing and pulled me back from the steps.

Holding one another, we faced the front of the house and waited. The moon was just then rising. We didn't have to wait long.

White smoke began to drift from the upstairs windows, but the first sight of flame flickered from Mama's grand hall downstairs. We watched through the tall windows of the little parlour as the red zig-zagged forward, tentative at first, tasting here and there with smacking sounds, feeding on the kindling, feeding on other stuff, on everything it came to. Then smoke started coming out all the open windows downstairs, not much at first and grey-white, but soon there was more, then more, and we could see the red advancing, with gold and orange and sometimes flashes of blue.

Now the fire danced all over downstairs, fat and flaunting itself, we couldn't take our eyes off it. In the midst of the pop and crackle of small explosions and the crash of things falling, and though I couldn't tell for certain what it was, I thought I heard a wild twanging of piano strings and it pulled at my heart. Suddenly, there it was upstairs. It had the whole house, now, and smoke spewed out all the windows, rolling out and up, shadowing the moon, changing colour — dirty white, grey, blackish, and a sick shade of amber.

The flames reached and fell and leapt. At times dancelike, almost lyrical, and then not lyrical at all, but lascivious, roaring with obscene pride, making a horrific noise, it exploded all the windows, the shards flew all around us.

Ruth and I, grasping one another's shoulders, began to dance, jumping up and down.

The fire made openings where there'd been none, ravaging whatever blocked its way, reaching out to join other parts of itself, reaching out as if it saw us and knew us and would devour us too. It broke through the roof here and there, and then those fires came together as if they could no longer bear to be apart, but swirling into one another became one avenging Fury that rose high and higher, and in a triumphant orgy of reprisal, brought the house down.

We howled, Ruth and I. In a rain of sparks, some lighting the pines on either side of us, we stomped the earth. Tears streaming, holding one another, we shouted songs the origin of which neither of us would know to tell.

Zeke came running, fearful, and seeing we were drunk with what we'd done, he pulled us apart, pulled us back from the still hungry flames. He grabbed his mother's hand on one side, mine on the other, and we ran. Once around the bend in the drive, we were free. We were free. We ran to the buggy and clambered in, Ruth and I beating the sparks from one another's hair and clothing and laughing like mad people. The fire roared, Sally barked, my brother Zeke untied the terrified horses from the tree, leapt onto the bench, slapped the reins, and we took off fast towards the road to Richmond.

PART FOUR
ELIZABETH

CHAPTER 1

I ran both my hands over the top of their new kitchen table. It was like satin, yet I could feel in its density what had been a living tree. William told me it was maple. At first he'd thought to paint it white or 'a nice blue', but together he and Lizzie had decided to keep it just the way it was, so he'd worked the wood over and over with finer and finer stuff. It was a soft gold, about three fingers thick. They were pleased I'd noticed it.

'William did well, didn't he? I think it's perfect.'

'Yes, he did indeed, Lizzie, it is perfect.'

She and I faced one another across the width of it, and on this, my first night back, that table felt as wide as the distance between Virginia and Wyoming. But she stretched out her hands towards mine, I reached towards her, and between the coffee cups and empty pie plates we entwined our fingers.

'I feel it's been forever since I've laid eyes on you,' she said. Though I'd only been in Virginia for a few months, I hadn't seen much of her and her family all winter before going east. It had been a long time.

'How was it to see your home? Your letters were wonderful. Was it hard to leave again? Will you go back? I want to hear everything!'

I wasn't ready. I told them I was very tired, to please forgive me. Lizzie jumped up and made apologies about supper, saying she'd kept a nice chicken stew warming and there was good bread, too. I must be hungry. A good supper would make me feel better. I apologised even more abjectly and asked if William wouldn't mind helping me with my bags, as I wanted to put my things in the cabin and settle in for the night. I saw Lizzie's disappointment.

'Let me at least put some bread and good butter, a jar of fresh milk, in a basket for you to take with you. You need some nourishment, dearest. We can heat up this stew tomorrow.'

I said that would be lovely and she set about doing it. William offered me 'a taste of whiskey', which I, of course, welcomed. We sat at the table and sipped while Lizzie made a basket for me. I asked about the boys and Lizzie called them.

'Charles! Joey! You can come down now and greet Mrs. Byrd.'

They appeared in her kitchen instantaneously.

'You were waiting on the stairs, weren't you.'

'Yes, ma'am', they answered in unison, grinning.

They'd gotten taller, it seemed. They were even more handsome than I remembered, with impeccable manners. They both said, 'Good evening, Mrs. Byrd', and shyly reached out to shake my hand and I took their hands warmly in mine. They kissed their parents and went back up to their rooms. Lizzie sat down, placing before me a basketful of 'nourishment'. We talked only small things while finishing the whiskey.

I signalled it was time and we all stood. William went to the front room where my bags were, and I walked over to Lizzie and embraced her. We held one another tightly. I began to apologise for not being ready to talk about Virginia and she interrupted me, saying she was at fault to charge right in with all her questions. 'We have all the time in the world,' she said.

She told me she'd put enough in the basket so I could make breakfast for myself in the morning if I chose to, and that she had put some supplies in the cabin earlier that day, 'coffee, preserves, that sort of thing'. She said I was welcome to breakfast with the family, they'd eat at about seven in the morning, but that I should feel under no obligation. I must take my time making myself comfortable.

'I hope you'll find the cabin suits you,' she said, 'there is more we'd like to do with it, and the furnishings are a bit sparse, but it should be good enough for the time being. If there is *anything* at all that you need, you must tell me. I want you to be happy, here, Sarah. I hope you will feel at home.'

Her emotions were so close to the surface, I feared she'd draw mine up, too. I quickly said I was sure it would be lovely, told her goodnight, hugged her again and met William on the porch. Though there was still some light, a soft, dusky light, he'd lit a lantern and we walked across the bit of meadow and down the small hill to the cabin. I could hear the stream as we got nearer.

CHAPTER 2

It suited me quite well, the cabin. William was excited as a boy for me to see it.

'You'll get a better look tomorrow, of course, when the sun's coming through these windows, but I want to show you around just a bit now.'

He put the lantern on a small rectangular table just to the right of centre front, and lit a lamp that was standing next to a pitcher filled with wild flowers. 'The boys picked them.' He said the door and the window next to it faced west and south, while the back wall, up against which I saw a bed with a small window above it, faced north and east. One of the first things I noticed was a fine-looking cook stove.

'That stove is iron and will heat the whole place good and warm in the winter,' William told me. 'I started a small fire this morning to take off the chill, and there's probably still some coals, so before I leave I'll put in a couple of logs. There's plenty of wood stacked on the side porch. Oh! And that, sitting beside it, is what they call a Hoosier cabinet. Two houses side by side in town were up for quick sale and each of them had one. I got Lizzie the larger one. Did you notice it? I didn't get this one at first, but a week later when I went into town it was still there and the owner was *very* eager to sell it. So, here it is! I can't begin to tell you how pleased our girl was about that. You can put all kinds of things in there. You'll have to tell her you like it, even if it's not something that you...'

'I love it, William. And believe it or not, I've become a pretty fair cook. This is wonderful, and I will be glad to pay you for this, and for that good stove...'

He wouldn't let me finish, but beckoned me to follow him to the back. He carried the lamp as it had gotten pretty dark. He pointed to the right, where there was a narrow door in the long wall, near the corner.

'Lizzie insisted on this, we have one now too.' It was an indoor privy, a wooden commode with a cover, and shelves above it.

'It's a bit rough, just soil, but I've learned how to make good compost from the waste. Think about it! You'll be contributing to the abundance of our garden!'

We both laughed.

'And look at these chairs!' And he went back to the front of the cabin, doing it in a few strides of his long legs, to put his hand on one of the graceful armchairs placed on either side of a small round table holding a lamp. They were against the wall across from the stove and cabinet. 'Velvet-covered. And the cushions are feather. They're from a Boston family who decided to move on, to California, I think. Lizzie thought they'd fit this place fine. They practically gave them to her! She made the rug we're standing on, and that little one back by the bed.'

He went on, still excited to show me everything. He lifted the lamp towards the windows he'd found. These, too, were from people moving on, as Laramie was a town in great flux. Each was hung with fresh, bleached muslin, Lizzie's work no doubt. He described in detail the qualities of the stove. There was a big iron pot of water on it. 'Still warm, and I'll light a fire now, so it'll get hot fast and you can wash up.'

He took a couple of pieces of stove wood and some kindling from a tin bucket and got a small fire started. 'The nights are getting chilly now.' I put the basket of food from Lizzie on the porcelain surface of the cabinet and saw that she had stocked it far more generously than she'd let on.

'We can make any changes you want, Sarah, if there's anything you need...'

I was beyond tired. I told him that I couldn't wait to see it in the daylight, but from what I could see at night, it was beautiful, that he and Lizzie had done a wonderful job and I was grateful. He went in the back and lit a lamp that was on a small table by the bed. Then he said goodnight and reminded me that I was welcome for breakfast at seven but that they wouldn't wait for me. He figured I'd want to spend some time getting acquainted with the place.

'Oh, and here's this.'

He took a small bottle of whiskey from the pocket of his jacket and placed it on the table near the stove with a smile. Now, there's a friend, I thought. When he closed the door behind him, I looked in the cupboard on the top of the cabinet, found a glass, poured myself a couple of fingers, brought it over and sat down on one of the velvet chairs. It was comfortable. I sipped the whiskey and looked around. What generosity. I didn't deserve it and wondered how I could possibly repay it.

After a bit, I blew out the lamp and went into the bedroom. The bed was larger than I'd thought it was at first, and the wooden head and foot board was clearly William's work, simple and graceful. Lizzie had made it up with clean soft sheets and covers, and there were two extra blankets folded at its foot. There was a cotton flannel nightgown laid out across it — I recognised it as the one she'd made for me last Christmas and that I'd left in her house — and a soft shawl I'd not seen before. I was glad for these, as I had not remembered to stuff a nightgown in my bag.

Lizzie had also placed a washcloth, towel and small bar of soap on the bed, on top of the extra blankets. I carried the pot from the stove and placed it near the bed, the water was now hot. I wiped the trip off me as well as I could, pushing the warm soapy cloth into my hair, all along the back of my neck, under my arms, between my legs. I washed my feet good. Then I went over every part of me again before putting on the clean nightgown.

I spread the blankets on the bed, blew out the lamp on the bedside table and got between the smooth sheets. In a minute, the light from the night sky, stars visible in the high window above the bed, filled the room with a soft luminescence.

I fell asleep with my hand holding my daughter's.

CHAPTER 3

The milk had not soured overnight and the coffee was good. I unpacked and put my few things around the cabin. I put my bed linens from home on a shelf in the bedroom. I put my mother's pearls on the little table. I'd need more shelves, I'd need a chest of drawers. The silver candlesticks needed candles, but I put one on each table in my 'parlour'. I would ask William to help me frame the painting.

Then I put the shawl over my shoulders, took a cup of coffee and sat in a rocking chair on my porch, I hadn't seen it last night. After a few moments, I saw Lizzie coming down the hill and watched her closely. She walked jauntily enough, I was glad to note, and wondered if William's writing of how tired she was might have been the exaggeration of a worried, loving spouse.

She suggested we do our laundry together, so I gathered up my traveling clothes that I'd left in a pile on the floor, came out of the door and met her at the bottom of the steps.

'The stream?'

Then I noticed she was not carrying her laundry. She laughed and said she had two large wash tubs up in the barn, plenty of soap, and even an extra scrubbing board. She'd already pumped water, heated it, and filled the tubs. There was coffee keeping hot in a pitcher wrapped in a towel, and some cookies to fuel our efforts.

We sat on stools leaning over the tubs in her barn. A couple of cows munched softly in nearby stalls. She had a large pile of muddy clothing by her side, and I had my small bunch. Watching her suntanned hands and forearms working the fabric in the soapy water reminded me of the last time we'd washed clothes together in Indian country.

'This is certainly better than rubbing our things against rocks in a cold stream.'

'Well, yes! We're very civilised here, now. You and I had enough of that, I think, back then. In *very* cold water most of that time.'

'And without real soap. Look, Lizzie. You have so much more than I do, let me help you.'

'Thank you. It gets tiresome washing for three fellows who seem as drawn to dirt as dirt is drawn to them. It was the same when I was growing up. My mother and I did the wash for my father and two brothers. Farmers! It must have been nice for you not to have had to do this as a young girl.'

'I never thought about it, Lizzie. It just got done.'

'Goodness.'

'That's... how things were.'

'Well, it must have been nice for you and your mother not to have to do it all yourselves.'

'It was.'

'Remember when we were given to those old women as slaves?'

'Yes! Funny old things. Hitting us with sticks!'

'Shrieking with laughter! And the others would join in. Everyone found it terribly funny!'

'But they softened, after a while.'

'We got stronger. And those women didn't take advantage of the fact they owned us. They were not cruel, by nature.'

'No, they were not. Not at all.'

I almost said, 'Not like many others.' I almost said, 'Not like my parents and all their friends and everyone else we knew.' I stopped myself. Lizzie was enjoying her memories.

'How very attached we became to them. I was surprised at my feelings for her. My grandmothers died young, both of them.'

'So did my father's mother and I never met my mother's parents. Strange. But we did come to care for those old things. And they cared for us.'

'I was very frightened at first, at being made a slave. The horrible images that word conjured! But you relieved my mind when you told me how well your family treated yours, and in truth, I never felt in danger of them.'

'Our old women were sweet at heart.'

'Your home must have been an unusual situation, though. I did hear about mistresses and slave women sometimes having close attachments, but mostly we heard of beatings and runaways getting shot, Negros worked to death, and all that. Well, it's why we fought, isn't it. But I have to admit I was relieved to learn that your family was an exception, taking good care of the Negros who worked for you.'

'To be honest, Lizzie, I can't say that "taking good care of the Negroes" is what we did. And you must know that they didn't "work for us" because they chose to. We *owned* them. They were forced to work. They had no choice.'

'Of course. I understand that. But you were not cruel, like some…'

I could not allow this to go any further.

'Lizzie. I have to tell you. I was badly mistaken about my family. I didn't lie to you, but if I say nothing now, it would be the same as lying. I am ashamed to tell you that we were just as bad as *any* of the others. Worse than many. We were among the worst. We raised slaves to sell them.'

'What do you mean, "raised slaves to sell them"?'

I explained the nature of my family's wealth, and what came from it. Parents were routinely separated from children, children were ripped from their parents and sold while still very young, families were destroyed. All of this. She stared at me.

'You never spoke of any of that.'

'I didn't know.'

'I suppose I can imagine how you might not have known…'

'You are being kind. I cannot imagine it. I *cannot*. I've asked myself a million times, now that I know what I know, how I could *not* have known when I lived there. Ruth told me about a great many things that I had not seen because I had clearly *refused* to see them. I'd kept my head turned, my eyes closed. I'd effectively blinded myself to my family's evil. Ruth also told me her own story which was an endless string of horrors, all the more horrible for not being unusual, before she was bought by my father. And *then* my parents made it worse.'

I told Elizabeth about Ruth getting yanked away from her mother as a young child and sold, about her history of beatings and rapes. I told her about Ruth's children being taken from her, and about Jewell's murder and who'd done it. When I came to the story about the scars on Ruth's back, I re-enacted the movements of the whipping. Lizzie put her hand on my arm.

'Stop, please. Stop. I am so, so sorry, Sarah. Your *mother*. How awful it must have been to learn that.'

'Yes, it was. It is. I will always be haunted by it. I have my mother's blood in me. My father's, too.'

'Why on earth did Ruth stay once she was free to leave?'

I explained that she had a son to raise, and she was being paid a pittance to keep the house going.

'Oh. Jewell's child?'

'No. Ezekiel is my half-brother.'

Her eyes opened wide. I told her about all that. And I told her about the complicated love between Ruth and my mother, and how my mother died. I explained that with both my parents gone, it was to support her son that Ruth had agreed to stay on as a sharecropper, which is another kind of slavery, until I returned or the place was sold to my corrupt and hideous former husband's corrupt and hideous father. I'd gotten back just in time. It was awful to imagine what would have happened to Ruth and Zeke if I hadn't.

'Sarah. I don't know what to say.'

'There's nothing to say, it's done and over. Ruth and Ezekiel are both well.'

'Did you sell to your husband's father?'

'I did. And gave Ruth and Zeke money to get started with a new life — we sewed it into their clothes — then we left in the middle of night. And, oh, Lizzie! This is the best part. Just before we rode away, Ruth and I... *We burned that house down!*'

'You did *what?*'

'We burned down that house!'

'Your house? *Your family's home?*'

'It was no longer my home. What my family had done there was evil. I had to destroy it.'

'So you and the slave woman who...?'

'*Ruth!* Her name is Ruth.'

'You and Ruth... You burned it down?'

'*Yes!* To the damn ground, Lizzie! A magnificent blaze!'

She seemed confused. I'd wanted her to exult with me, I'd been eager to share this enormous event with my friend, but she'd pulled back and was quiet, thoughtful.

'Your childhood home...'

Disappointed, I began to object, but she continued.

'No, dearest, I'm sorry. Of course it was no longer a home to you. How could it be? It was good to do that, you and Ruth. Very good.'

She looked at me, then reached out and took my hand.

'Please know, Sarah, that you will never be without a home. William and I have talked about this a great deal. You will always have a home here with us, for as long as you want it. And I hope and pray it's a good long time.'

She opened her arms and pulled me to her. Something shifted in me, an old reluctance lifted. Our differences were no match for what we'd been through and the loving friendship we'd forged, mostly because of her, because of her generous soul. I had to change my life. I *would* change my life. I could begin to do this in the warmth of this friendship. I could begin in this place. I would make myself into a better person. I'd begin on this very day. It was a beautiful day, the air fresh and promising good things.

I wrapped my arms around her more tightly and suddenly became aware of what I hadn't seen last night in her kitchen, or earlier this morning as I'd watched her walk down the hill.

Her shoulders and arms had too little flesh on them. I felt hardly any breast or belly against me, and even through the deprivations of the winter with the Indians, my Lizzie had been a substantial woman. I pulled back and looked at her face. How could I not have seen this? Exhaustion had reduced and drawn down the flesh of her face. She saw that I saw.

'What a morning! You must still be tired from your trip. Come on inside the house,' she said. 'I don't know about you, but I want more coffee.'

CHAPTER 4

The rest of September and into October was warm with more sun than usual. Lizzie and William had a vegetable garden on the south side of their barn, and flowers on the south side of the house. Often I'd wake to find that someone — one of the boys? Lizzie? — had left a bouquet of late blooming flowers on my porch. I helped Lizzie take in the last of the vegetables, those that might not survive a frost, and together we'd put in the ground things that would be covered with mulch to come up in the spring.

'It feels like a religious act to do this, Sarah. We put things in the earth in the faith that they'll emerge in the spring, and in the summer, bear fruit. Makes me think of Easter and the resurrection. I know this kind of talk annoys you, but I feel this planting is a kind of sacrament. Do you understand?'

I understood how uncharitable I'd been in the past regarding her faith. This was truth to her, and I responded to the poetry of it, which is another kind of truth.

'Of course I do. The Greeks also had a story about this. I'll tell it to you if *you* aren't annoyed by a tale told by heathens!'

She laughed at me and said, 'Don't be silly! I want to hear, and if it's one of your Greek stories, I'd wager the boys would like to hear it, too.'

So I told her the story of Demeter and Kore, emphasising that the love of Demeter for her child was so powerful that she stood up to Zeus, brought down winter on the earth, putting his precious humans in mortal danger of cold and starvation in order to get her daughter back from Zeus's brother, Hades, who'd abducted her when she was picking flowers in a field, and taken her to be his bride. After this, Kore was with her mother for a good part of the year and the crops flourished. She went back to Hades as the Dread Persephone, the Queen of the Underworld, for the rest of the year, bringing winter on Earth.

Lizzie hadn't heard the story and asked if I would tell it to the boys. Then she asked if I would tell them more Greek myths. '*All* of them, Sarah! Every one you know!' They'd heard all the Bible stories — 'and they're quite bored with them, though they'd never dare show it!' — and she thought it was important they hear those of the Greeks.

She said she and William, though mostly she'd been the one to do this, had been teaching them to read, write, and cipher since earliest childhood but there was not enough time to do it properly, and she said that neither of them knew much about literature or history. For a while, an officer's wife had conducted some classes at Fort Laramie, but they were inconsistent and it was too far, the boys couldn't stay for an entire session unless they spent the night. She said that I could introduce the boys to far more than she and William could. Would I please consider it.

So I began tutoring Charles and Joey. I was surprised to find how much I enjoyed it. On a trip into Laramie with William, I ordered books. 'Uncle Tom's Cabin', as I felt it important that they know this part of the history of their country, I did not want them to grow up ignorant as I had been. One day they'd meet Zeke and Ruth, and I wanted them to understand something of their lives. I also got copies of the Declaration of Independence and the Constitution. Then, of course, 'The Iliad' and 'The Odyssey' and as a companion to these, a book I'd loved as a child, Nathaniel Hawthorne's 'Wonder Book for Boys and Girls'. There was one of Charles Dickens books, I can't remember which, and 'Moby Dick', though I'd never been able to finish it.

These were the first of many books. I also subscribed to a number of periodicals discussing political and cultural matters, and I arranged for delivery of 'Scientific American', as I knew nothing about science and hoped to learn along with the boys.

They turned out to be good students, serious, wanting to please me and their parents but also wanting to learn for its own sake. After the lessons were done, I read to the boys, and Lizzie would take the opportunity to go upstairs to rest. When she seemed especially tired late in the afternoon, or often, just because I felt like it, I'd cook dinner for the family. Southern cooking. Or my approximation of it. These dinners with the family, all of us around the table enjoying food together were a source of surprising pleasure. Of joy.

One afternoon while chopping onions for a stew, or doing some other simple thing in preparation for a meal, with the murmurings and easy movements of the others going on around me, I suddenly realised that I felt at home. I stopped what I was doing and considered this idea of feeling 'at home'. I'd felt happy for a while with the Indians, but did I feel 'at home'? I didn't speak the language, couldn't fully participate in the life. I had my love and my unborn baby and a dream of family. A dream. But here it was: a real family that had opened its arms, drawn me close. The small, utterly mundane activities of this life seemed remarkable.

True to myself, however, I was quite happy to return to my cabin at the end of the day, maybe after a bit of whiskey with William. I was happy to get into my bed alone, to sleep and wake alone, think my own thoughts in my own time.

With my help giving her more opportunity to rest, Lizzie seemed to be getting stronger. Following Irish Mary's example when treating me, I insisted that when William brought beef for us to eat, there be some bones and enough good meat to make a broth. I enriched it with onions from the garden and a bit of brandy as Ruth had taught me to do. Lizzie drank it willingly. I believed the meat would help her get stronger, and it did seem to be having that effect. Her colour was better.

One brisk sunny afternoon when I released the boys from their school work, Lizzie came downstairs and we sat in her parlour for tea. She'd come to like it better than coffee. She said she felt the latter was too strong, it made her heart feel 'shaky'. She'd told me earlier she had something special to talk about and as soon as we were seated and had had a sip, she began.

'Sarah. I've been waiting to speak with you about this for a good while. I had to think it out thoroughly and talk with my friends — you've met one or two, I think — but watching you teach the boys has made me certain about this.'

She paused to take another sip of tea, and so did I. Her eyes were bright with excitement.

'I think we should start a school. Either in the town of Laramie, or somewhere on our land. I've spoken to William and he'd re-build a town property to suit, or put up a new building here. We'd need you to invest, of course, but we'd get the parents to pay a bit, those who could, so you would get your money back and, though it might take a while, perhaps provide you with a salary as well. You'd teach the children all the things you teach Charles and Joey.'

She paused for my response but I was dumbfounded, I couldn't speak. She laughed.

'Isn't this a wonderful idea?'

'Forgive me, I'm completely taken by surprise. It might be quite wonderful, Lizzie, though I'm sure you could find a much better teacher. And where would the children come from? The town and the nearby farms? Army families?'

'Well, we've been thinking a great deal about that and I think you will approve. In addition to those you mentioned, I would want to have children from the Sioux reservation as well.'

'The Sioux reservation? But, Lizzie, if I remember the map — I saw it, you know, in April, when the chiefs met to sign the treaty — the southernmost part is still far north of here. A long way away.'

'Yes. I know. And because of the distance, we would have to provide housing for the Indian children. And board, too, of course.'

'But those children would not be able to speak English, it would be terribly difficult for them. And what about their families?'

'Teaching them to speak English would be a great part of the reason for the school. When they are separated from their families and among American children only, they will learn quickly. And you are such a gifted teacher, they will *want* to learn!'

'Separate them from their families? Lizzie, you must remember how close Indian children are to their families, to their mothers particularly. It would be terrible to separate them.'

'But, don't you see, Sarah? It would help — no, it would be necessary, actually — in order for them to learn to see the world as it is now.'

'What do you mean, "as it is now"?'

She looked down at her hands holding the pretty tea cup and saucer, then back at me. She had her argument well organised, perhaps rehearsed, her words fell all in a row. Her voice was soft, her tone weighted with rectitude.

'Their old way of life is over. Those who are not already living on the reservation must move there. This is part of that last treaty, as you know even better than I. They cannot continue attacking white people, needless to say. And the raiding of enemy camps, stealing horses, anything else that is part of that violent way of living, must come to an end. Also part of the agreement is that they must send their children to white schools. If they obey the rules of the treaty,

the government will provide for them until they become self-suffi-
cient. And they must, if they are to survive. This is simply the way
things are. The children need white schooling, and we would give it.'

I put my tea down on a table by the chair and sat back.

'More tea? Some bread and butter?'

'No, thank you, Lizzie. Let me just think a minute.'

We'd been with Far Cry's band for a year. They hunted to live. When
game was scarce, they got thin. In that hard winter people starved,
there was sickness, many died, but when the weather changed, they
moved, they hunted, they got healthy again. They *had been* 'self-suf-
ficient'. Yes, they raided the Crow who raided them, back and forth
in a kind of chivalric game, but they stayed away from whites.

True, others didn't, and these groups had to be dealt with one
by one. But I believed that *most* Indians did not want any part of
fighting with whites. Theirs was not an easy life, but it held meaning for them beyond just getting fed. This land had all been theirs
and they'd already had to change a lot. Why should *they* have to
change entirely?

I then tried to imagine a classroom of white children and Indian
children. Fights would break out. It would be an impossible atmosphere in which to teach and, in a very short time, the Indian children would go back to their families. That would be the best of the
possible results. I suspected it would likely be much worse.

'Lizzie, it's been my impression that most of the white people I know
don't care much at all for Indians, to put it mildly. I doubt the parents
of white children would want them to associate with the Indians.'

'Sarah, listen to the deeper part of this plan. My friends who have
studied this matter believe that the best way for us to go forward
together is for the Indian children to become more like us. There
would naturally be a period of adjustment — for everyone — but in
our school, we'd keep them all so busy, they'd not have time to dwell
on difficulties. We'd provide them with proper clothes and shoes.
We'd have Sunday school, and church, and once they learned the
scriptures and accepted Christ, they could be baptised. As Mary
Small Wing was. We'd teach them American songs! We'd have square
dances! Now, wouldn't that be lovely?'

'What about *their* religion? Our dear friend Medicine Crow was a gentle, compassionate, and profoundly moral teacher. Would we want to deprive them of people like him?'

'Sarah, the old religion would only hold them to the old life. I could begin their religious instruction, until we could find an ordained minister to do it. A good Protestant family man.'

'What about the rituals they'd grown up with, the ones that taught them how to be good Indians? The Sundance?'

'*The Sundance?* Sarah, you cannot mean it. That brutal horror!'

'Nailing Jesus to a cross was not a brutal horror? Commemorating the sacrifice every year with a holiday? Isn't that…'

'You're missing the point, dear, and it's really quite simple. The Indians *must* be civilised, or hostilities will continue. The outcome will only be tragic. *For them.* You must agree…'

'You're talking about… Doc told me about this, what did he call it… assimilation.'

'*Yes!* That's *exactly* what I'm talking about! Our school would provide a beginning towards that end, Sarah.'

'You would force them to become just like white people.'

'That might well be the only way to save them.'

This discussion had gone too far. I tried to speak but she interrupted me.

'The Indians *will not* stay on the reservation. While you were gone, the Cheyenne went on one rampage after another down in Kansas, raping women, murdering whole families…'

'Have you heard what our government wants to do to the Indians? Kill them all, men, women, and children. 'Nits make lice', someone said. You've heard what the soldiers have done in peaceful villages…'

'All the more reason to bring the Indians to a state at which they no longer do things that incite such fear and anger. The sooner they become Christian citizens, the sooner we can all…'

'*Christianity?* Sherman would say quite loudly that he is a Christian. So would Custer, so would…'

'The Indians are outnumbered now, Sarah, and every day there are more of us and fewer of them. *That is how it is.* I must believe that this is how it is *meant* to be. It's clearly God's will. They must learn to be another way.'

I had difficulty controlling my voice.

'You were not willing to give up your religion, to "be another way" when it seemed the only way to survive. Why should they?'

'I did not see it as the only way to survive! I *knew* we'd be rescued. I trusted in God! My faith saved both of us!'

I wanted to slap her hard in the face. I took a deep breath.

'Elizabeth, this is still a big country, a very big country. Do you not think there's some way we can let one another live in whatever way our own religions would have us live and do it without molesting one another?'

'We need the land to build this country, Sarah, and we should have it. We deserve it. We can't have the Indians roaming about where they will, unpredictable in their ways. The reservations were put aside for their use, and that's where they must settle.'

'We *deserve* it? Why? Why should *we* have all the land we want, even their holy places...'

She interrupted me, her face livid.

'Because they don't *do* anything with it! They waste it! Besides, it's in the Bible. "Be fruitful, and multiply, and replenish the earth, and subdue it, and have dominion..."'

'*Subdue! Have dominion!* My father, the slaver, would have agreed heartily with you!'

Lizzie stared at me then broke down. She spoke through loud sobbing.

'I want the violence to end! *I want to help!* I'm at least *trying* to do something! *But you!* You, who say you love them so much, what are you doing? *Nothing! You're doing nothing!*'

William had come in, hearing our raised voices, and had heard part of the argument. He went to Lizzie's side and said she should go up and lie down and that I should go home. He said he 'hoped to Hell' we'd had enough of this subject.

I'd never before seen him angry.

Sigrid Heath

CHAPTER 5

So much of what had often infuriated me about Elizabeth when we were with the Indians came back in force. They'd loved her, those Indian women, and their children, too. I'd believed she'd come to love them. She *had* loved them. How could she now think of them as being in need of training to be fully human?

And yet, she was right about me. I did nothing to help. I had no answers. But why should the Indians be forced to give up everything? Because we can make them do it? Because we're capable of annihilating them to get what we want? I remember someone, maybe Bell, telling me the translation of the Lakota word for whites, *wasichus*, is 'the fat takers', the ones who take the best for themselves. Who gives us this right? Lizzie would say God does.

I began to see it as not much different from our relations with Negros as Ruth had revealed it to me. We had *the right* to enslave them, to make them part of our money making machinery, because we could. And as Lizzy had said, and Doc had said, whites could point to verses in the Scripture that proved we were given that right by 'God', whoever or whatever that is. And we were willing to kill great numbers of them to get the rest in line. And short of killing — though Ruth made clear to me that most white people she'd known would be happy to see *all* Negros dead and gone — we'd use torture to keep them docile.

Ruth had said it wasn't over. In the place I was raised, it's against the law for a person with black skin to do things a white person takes for granted. And these laws, with the force of religion — and commerce! — behind them, get tweaked regularly to make sure slavery persists in all ways but name. Just like the whites' so-called treaties with the Indians, broken one after the other to serve our unending, ever increasing greed. It is now criminal to live as an Indian in Indian country.

I knew there was much I didn't know, that I lacked sufficient history to make a reasonable argument. But I suspected it would be

308

difficult to find enough people with unbiased views to come together and agree upon a humane solution, one that would unite the country. I was partly right. It would not be 'difficult'. It would be impossible. The Negro question and the Indian question seemed to me a single question, one of white greed and hatred. I could imagine no solution.

I felt sick. Impotent. Complicit.

William knocked on the door. He'd brought an offering of whiskey and a grave face.

'You must yield to her, Sarah,' he said to me.

I was too stunned to answer. I put the glasses on the table and he poured. *Yield to her?* Yield to ideas that were anathema to me? What did that mean? He answered before I asked.

'Nothing will come of anything the two of you say to one another over tea in our house. That's a fact. If you calm down for a minute, you'll see this is the simple truth. She won't ever get her school. Let her have the fantasy of it.'

I began to argue with him, but he interrupted me.

'She's mortally tired, Sarah. Can't you see that? And though it's been better since you've been helping her, she's sicker than she lets on. Let her have her big ideas, they feed a kind of hope. Truth is, all she really wants is to love her family. And that means you too. She lost a sister, you're... She admires you, how smart you are, all that reading... She loves you, Sarah. Even if she is mightily worried about your immortal soul.'

He said that last with a small smile.

'Are you worried about my immortal soul?'

He poured more whiskey in my glass.

'What do you want me to do, William?'

'Apologise to her. Do it for love of her. The winter's coming, and I'm worried about this one. She's not well at all.'

'Has she seen a doctor? Is Doc still...'

'She won't go. I can't talk about it, Sarah, I promised. And don't you dare tell her I said anything.'

I promised him I would not.

'I'm going to talk to my friend Juan. You've met him, I think, Juan Cisneros, good man, he took Bron's house, just over the hill behind the barn. Juan and me, we help one another out. His daughter is coming up here to live with him. Her mother died some months ago, down in Chihuahua, and she wants to live with her father, become an American girl. I'm going to ask him to let her help Lizzie. I don't want her doing all the housework alone any more. It'll be a chance for the girl to learn English and I'll pay her something, too.'

I told him I'd come by shortly after breakfast in the morning and make peace. His whole body sagged with relief. I walked him to the door. It was dusk already. Every day now was shorter than the day before.

CHAPTER 6

Lizzie and I gathered the last of the wild plums down by the creek and I helped her put up preserves. She invited me to join in the conversation when those women friends of hers would arrive in two buggies to discuss assimilation, but she knew I'd decline. Those women seemed to think they were advancing a Great Cause over pies and coffee. I'd met one or two and they annoyed the hell out of me.

Maria Cisneros arrived shortly after William and I had talked and began coming to Lizzie's house every day except Sunday. Her English was actually quite good and seemed to get better very quickly. She was fourteen or fifteen then, I think, about Lizzie's height, a stocky, strong girl, bright and with a good heart. Pretty, too. She reminded me of Mary Small Wing. Lizzie agreed.

The boys and I grew closer. They wanted to know about life with the Indians, and I told them a bit, being careful not to stray into areas that would upset Lizzie. They wanted to know how my face had been injured and my eye destroyed, so I told them that, too. They noticed my spirit pouch, and I reminded them that they'd helped me bury my baby girl, Mary Elizabeth Byrd, who'd been born too soon and died. I said a lock of her hair was in it.

But my old restlessness was simmering, and from time to time I wanted badly to get away for a bit. With the road to Fort Laramie now a real road making it a faster trip, and the road to the town also having improved, I would be able to do it more often. William told me a soldier had been asking if anyone wanted to buy a horse, he had to sell him fast to settle a cash debt. So I went with him the very next day and came back with a horse. A big fellow with spirit and good manners. The kid had known horses.

I got a rifle, too, a good Remington, and a new Colt revolver. Lizzie was pleased with that, as she was still certain that one night Indians would lay siege to the house. Now we would all be armed and ready to try to fight them off. And now I could go off by myself upon occasion.

I liked this freedom. I saw Bell from time to time at the fort. He was good company. Garrett was no longer sutler. As he'd told me he might before I went to Virginia, he'd moved back east with his son.

There still seemed to be a full complement of soldiers coming and going, some with families, so the new sutler kept the store fairly well stocked. And what was now calling itself the City of Laramie had grown enough that the fort was no longer the only place where one could get food stuffs and other supplies. There was at least one proper bank in the town and a Post Office.

I gave William and Lizzie money to cover what I thought was good rent for the couple of months I'd spent in the cabin already, and for the following year in advance. They tried to object, but I insisted. I also paid for the stove, telling Lizzie it was a good one and I'd have bought the very same model for myself. That's what I said, though the only real cook stoves I'd been introduced to were the very large one Irish Mary used at Laramie, and the one on which Ruth taught me the little I knew about cooking.

I knew money was a concern for them, and I didn't care a bit about it. I had more than enough for my needs. Sands and I corresponded regularly. He kept me informed of various happenings in the state and federal governments (most of which made me furious). He also told me that, unless there was another War Between The States, or a Revolution — he capitalised such things — or unless I suddenly became Greedy for Grandeur of some sort, I should not have to worry much about money for a good long time.

One day in late October, while the weather was still fine, I suggested to Lizzie that we take the buggy to Laramie one day soon to do some Christmas shopping, in case there was a lot of snow as the season advanced. I'd seen a shop that sold fabric and some ready-made clothes for both women and men, children, too. There were buttons, thread, needles, scissors, ready-made lace, ribbons, things I had a feeling Lizzie would like.

I told her it was a rough place, but I was sure that the two of us together would be fine. I'd carry my rifle and keep the revolver in my pocket. She said she'd also carry a gun. William had told us stories about this City of Laramie.

The first mayor was said to have been a good man, but he'd quit just a few months previously. A gang of brothers, one of whom was the town's marshall, ran things from their headquarters in a saloon they owned called the 'Bucket of Blood'. They threatened settlers who refused to sign over deeds to good property, saying they'd shoot them if they didn't. They'd already killed about a dozen people. This was the marshall! But the county sheriff had organised a committee of citizens who were determined to clean things up and the warning seemed to have worked. It had been quiet lately.

We left just after dawn on a day that William, in his avowed wisdom regarding such things, said would be excellent weather all day. Lizzie had packed enough food for a picnic for half a dozen people. We found a nice place to stop, sat in the shade of the buggy as the sun was surprisingly warm, and enjoyed our lunch. I asked her if it felt good to be away from the house for a bit. She said she was enjoying herself, though it was not something she needed to do often. There was really no place she'd rather be than at home with her family.

After leaving the buggy and our horse at the livery, we walked a bit. Laramie was coarse, but I found the rough vitality stimulating. Lizzie was less impressed, but optimistic. 'It's a new place. It will grow,' she said, 'and it will serve all our needs one day.' We planned to meet at the Post Office in about an hour.

When the time came, I watched from just outside the Post Office door as she walked across the street in my direction, laden with parcels. I was glad she'd found things she liked. Her step seemed a bit off balance, but the road was a mess. She stopped for a moment, a serious look on her face. I thought perhaps she'd forgotten something, but when she saw me, she brightened and came quickly across the street, out of breath but smiling. We picked up our mail. Both of us had gotten letters we were anxious to read so we decided to stop for a cup of coffee in a restaurant at the front of a new hotel. It looked clean enough.

I had a letter from Sands, which I put in my bag, but Zeke had written to me. How wonderful it was to see his name on the envelope! I opened it eagerly. Blue ink, a wide nub, on about three sheets of good white paper. He wrote carefully, his words well chosen. I was impressed almost to tears.

Ruth was still on Chincoteague working with the man she'd said was her uncle, but they were not actually related. He exported oysters and other shellfish to Baltimore and New York City, but he was also a good cook and had started serving food on his front porch or in his parlour. Ruth had torn up his vegetable garden the very day he showed it to her, moved everything around, replanted things, planted new things. Once he tasted her cooking, he decided they should go into business together. They moved their establishment to another house he owned and were doing quite well.

But Zeke! He was now in New York. He said Mr. Sands had an associate there, a Mr. Herzog, also a lawyer and an abolitionist, who had told Sands that he had work for 'an intelligent young man willing to spend long hours'. With Sands' recommendation Zeke was now working for this Mr. Herzog and was being treated quite well by everyone. This was all good to know, but the next thing in particular thrilled me. Mrs. Herzog was helping him with English composition. He was reading the books I'd given him, and many more. He said he was up late every night reading. He wanted to go to college! I decided I'd immediately write to Sands and arrange to pay for Zeke's education, wherever he chose to go. I'd send a wire that day, as soon as we finished our coffee and the slices of pie we'd ordered.

I looked up to tell Lizzy this good news and saw that she was wiping tears from her face. I asked her what was the matter. She put down the letter she'd been reading, spreading her hands over the paper several times before speaking in a soft voice.

'My mother has died. It was sudden, probably her heart. The funeral was two weeks ago.'

'Oh, no! Lizzie, I am so very sorry.'

'My brother writes it was a lovely service, in the church we all belonged to. There were a lot of people, she was well loved. But my father is taking it hard. He hadn't been so well himself, and my brothers are worried about him. I should have been there. I should be there now.'

'Why don't you go see them, Lizzie? You can make train connections all the way to Albany. I can help you, I have stock in a couple of the lines, I'll ask my lawyer, he'll help. And once in Albany, someone could meet you and bring you home.'

She was quiet for a moment and then shook her head and said,

'It was my first thought. But I can't.'

'If it's the money, I'll be happy to pay for your ticket, you and William have been so generous with me, I would be honoured...'

'No, Sarah. Thank you. Thank you, but no. I can't.'

'It would give me such pleasure to help you do this, dear Lizzie, the money means nothing to me...'

'It isn't the money, dear friend. It's... more serious. You know that I haven't been well. The trip would utterly exhaust me. The worst of it is that, once there, I'd be a burden to my family. It's hard enough now, after Mother's death and with my father not well. I couldn't do it to them. I will not.'

'Ah. I was beginning to wonder if this might be what's worrying you. Listen! I'll go with you. I'll go the entire way, you'll not have to do a thing. I'll handle all the arrangements, I'll take you by the hand, we'll ride in comfort. You'll arrive in fine shape...'

She interrupted me.

'Sarah, dear heart, that is very kind of you, but you're not *hearing* me. But it's not your fault, really, I'm not... Oh, this is hard. I didn't want to talk to you about this, not yet, at least. But I see that I must.'

And then Elizabeth told me that she was dying. I told her she must see a doctor, and when she told me she would not, my reaction, I'm ashamed to admit, was anger. When I pressed her about this, she said that William had also pressed her so persistently she'd had to speak sharply to make him stop. She knew her body, and she had prayed and prayed for her God to make things clear. He had, she said. She had no doubt that her time had come and she was not going to fight what was so clearly 'God's will' for her. This, of course, infuriated me. I didn't believe her. Thought she was dramatising for some reason.

Then she turned to look out the window. In the strong light I could see what I'd refused to see before that moment. I thought I'd seen her fragility, but then, in the way one does, I'd chosen to make little of it, told myself it would pass. But this day of travel and walking around Laramie had sucked the blood from her face. Her lips had no colour. The skin of her cheeks was sallow and thin, stretched tightly over her bones. The flesh around her eyes was swollen and the whites had a slightly yellowish tinge.

She asked me not to behave any differently with her when at her home. There was time before she had to tell the boys. And when I, again, urged her to see a doctor, saying we'd find someone of reputation in a larger city, I'd go with her, she moved her face close to mine across the table and looked me in the eye.

'I am at home with this, Sarah. I have lived according to my faith, as you well know. You must allow me to die in my own way.'

We sat back. There was nothing more to say. She smiled.

'I think I've had enough of this City of Laramie,' she said. 'Let's go home.'

I have no idea what we talked about on the ride home, but we did talk. Laughed, too, at this and that, at nothing. I wonder if we would have been able to do that if the last two years had been anything other than what they'd been. We were like soldiers from very different backgrounds who had come through extraordinary times together, now riding side by side, making small talk about the weather.

I might have mentioned the air that was surprisingly mild. I might have noted how the late sun lit the heavy tops of the grasses so they looked made of gold. I'd probably have pointed to the shimmer of lush colour in the sky as the sun slid lower. I hadn't been looking when it dropped behind the edge of the earth and was sorry I'd missed it. I hoped Lizzie had seen it. There'll be other sunsets, I said to myself, as one does, and the words felt empty. The stain of colour in the west lasted a while, but the air had changed and Lizzie felt cold. She said she'd put a blanket under the seat. She held the reins as I tucked it around her.

It was dusk when we reached her house, the lamps were lit, and William was sitting on the porch, playing his guitar. We watched him lay it down and stand up. He waved to welcome us home. When he came to help her down, he saw how she was, and he and I exchanged a look over her shoulder. Juan and Maria had been just about to head home, so Juan said he'd take care of the horse and buggy, as the barn was on the way.

I handed Lizzie's packages to William, then climbed down. I pulled her to me and we hugged long and close. I kissed her forehead, then wished them all goodnight and turned to walk towards the cabin. William asked if I wanted a lantern, but there was still enough light to find my way. He turned then, put his arm around his wife and led her into their home.

CHAPTER 7

'You girls picked the right day to go to the big bad City of Laramie!' William said. He had a story to tell and was excited about it.

'I heard that the day after you were there — *the very next day!* — the county sheriff, Boswell, led that bunch of vigilantes he'd collected into the The Bucket of Blood and got the best of that gang — the town marshall and his brothers — dragged them down the street to an empty house and *hung them all!* How about that!'

'Good Heavens, William! Where have you taken me!'

She didn't mean anything by it, but poor, dear William took it to heart. Shortly after this, one afternoon, after Lizzie had finally fallen to sleep following a bad bout of coughing, he came downstairs into the kitchen as I was helping Maria clean up after having fed the boys. They were lying on the parlour floor in front of the fire, reading something I'd told them to study.

He stood around a minute, looking lost, then took out two glasses and the bottle and poured us both a couple of fingers of whiskey. Maria wiped her hands, said she'd go on up to their house to fix dinner for herself and her father. We sat down at the table. William drank fast and poured another.

'I shouldn't have made her come out here. The trip out was hard on her, though she'd never tell you that. Terribly hard to leave her folks. That whole family was crying when we set out. Hurt my heart to see it. But she seemed to have fallen in love with the idea. And then, she fell in love with this country, and threw herself into our life here. It was *hard* out here at first. Early on, losing those baby girls was just dreadful. I thought she was dying back then. Then that long time with the Indians. And now... If we'd stayed home in New York, I'd have done alright, and she'd have been with her family, she'd have stayed healthy. I shouldn't have made her come out here.'

He put his head in his hands.

'William, during our year with the Indians, all she talked of was coming home to you and the boys. She loves you so very much, and knowing how you love her gave her strength then, as I'm sure it gives her strength now. Please don't punish yourself. This sickness could have been lying in wait inside her for a long time.'

'But, if I hadn't...'

'Don't William. There's no point.'

'No, there's not.'

Whatever it was that had been waiting to kill her, came on fast.

One day, I was reading some Herodotus to the boys after their lessons. It was cold outside, so they were happy to stay in by the fire. Lizzie was on the couch under blankets, her head on some pillows. She enjoyed hearing the stories. William had just returned from Laramie with some supplies and Maria had come into the parlour to help him put things away. Suddenly the two of them and both boys looked at Lizzie in shock. I turned around and saw that she was bleeding profusely from her nose.

She looked at us curiously, apparently unaware of the bleeding, though it had run over her cheek, onto the collar of her nightgown and the pillows. I grabbed the napkin in my lap — I'd brought out sweets for us — and put it against her nose then Maria took the pillow from under her head and put it under her chest so her head hung backward and she was looking at the ceiling.

William had told the boys it was nothing to worry about, a little nose-bleed, it happens sometimes, to take their schoolwork upstairs. Maria had rushed to wet a towel with cold water, she handed it to me and I kept it pressed on her nose. None of us really knew what to do so we did everything we could think of. She started coughing and choking, spitting blood, so we helped her to sit up. It took a bit for the bleeding to stop. William had pulled up a chair and was stroking her forehead.

'That was a bad one, sweetheart. How do you feel?'

'I have a terrible headache, I always seem to have a headache. And I'm *tired!* I'm so tired of pain... I'm sorry to complain, William, forgive me...'

'Hush now. Let's just get you to bed.'

I moved my chair back out of the way, so William could take her in his arms. He carried her upstairs to bed. Maria and I looked at one another. Then, because it was getting late in the afternoon, we went into the kitchen to pull together something for dinner.

'Does this happen often?' I asked her, as she spent more time with Lizzie than I did.

'It does, but this time was very bad.'

'And does she often say she is in pain?'

'No, but I can see it in her face. And she will hold herself here.' She placed her hand just under her ribs on her right side. Remembering her injuries when we were captured, I wondered if perhaps some part of her had never properly healed. But that was two years ago.

'I wish she would see a doctor.'

'So does William. And me too, and my father. But she will not. I am thinking... Maybe she will speak to a priest.'

'She isn't Catholic.'

'Maybe someone of her own faith?'

'I will ask her. But, I don't want her to think… Besides, Maria, I believe there's time yet for that.'

She looked at me and, with her eyes, said the thing she knew was true and that I did not yet want to believe.

A bit later, William, Maria, Juan, the boys and I ate a meal in which our entire purpose was to pretend there was nothing serious happening in that house. Afterwards, William walked me to the door. It was dark, the clouds had hung low all day, so there was no light from the sky. As he handed me a lit lantern, he said,

'From now on, one of us must be with her all the time. Maria is still so young and will be doing all the housework and all the cooking. Juan is busy. I'm always busy. Will you do this?'

'Yes, of course. She cannot be alone.'

CHAPTER 8

I could not sleep that night. I was sick with fear that, in spite of my promise, I would not be able to do what William needed me to do. What Lizzie needed. How on earth should I talk with my dying friend? What do I say? How long will it take? How horrible will it be? I decided I'd get some laudanum in case the pain became unbearable for her. Or for me. But I didn't.

I hoped she would die soon. That would be horribly sad, but better that it be quick and soon. I berated myself — *selfish! coward!* — but I was terrified. I wanted to pack a bag that night, ride away. Ashamed, I slammed that thought down hard. Enough. I'd told William I'd stay, so I'd stay. I'd give myself over to whatever would come with Lizzie. I'd do whatever needed to be done, for whatever time it took.

In the morning, I had a bit of coffee and walked up to the house. Lizzie was still in bed. Maria had made her some tea with bread to dip in it, and I told her I'd bring it to her. She lifted the covers on

William's side and asked me to get in beside her. She put her head next to mine. 'It's hard,' she whispered. I held her. After a bit she reached for a handkerchief on the bedside table and wiped her eyes and nose. She lay back on her pillows, turned to me.

'But this is how God meant it to be. I am here with my husband and children, in the middle of this life of ours, with all God's blessings.'

I could not help but admire her, and I could not help but hate the choice she'd made.

'And *you're* here, Sarah! You're so good to be here with me. Like a sister.'

She reached a foot over to touch mine and I remembered my mother doing the same thing when she'd sometimes come into bed with me. Lizzie *was* my sister.

So, we began a habit. I would get into bed with her either sometime in the morning, or in the dark winter afternoons. Sometimes I'd read to her, sometimes we talked until she was ready to sleep. When she had to relieve herself, while she could still walk a bit, I helped her to a small commode behind a screen, and held her so she could do what she needed to do. When she became too weak to walk even with my help, I put a pan under her. Then I'd wipe her clean.

With this intimacy, time spun backward and we were once again as we'd been when with the Indians. Especially after Mary Small Wing's death, when we were left with only one another to depend on. Even after I'd fallen in love with Far Cry, and through times of anger, I believe we both understood that we were only angry because we were frightened, we needed one another badly. We always found our way back to one another.

Maria would bring us tea and sweets, sometimes she'd sit with us a bit and chat. We talked about how the boys were growing, how good they were, how funny they were when they were *not* being good. But when it was just the two of us, Lizzie talked about the past.

As she couldn't be there, it seemed important for her to bring her family into the room. She wanted me to know her people.

She told me about her three brothers, two older, one younger, and the rambunctious, loving way they had with one another. But her mother's next pregnancy had been hard. Lizzie said it seemed as if the midwife had moved in with them.

'And a woman from the church came to stay for a bit, too. Everyone tiptoed around, saying they didn't know if the baby would be born dead or alive. I think they feared for Mama, too, though no one said so in front of me. Mama told me this story many times, as if I might not remember it otherwise. Finally, she'd say, "*And then, there she was! Our angel straight from God's Heaven. So tiny! So perfect!*" Her name was Anne, but we all called her Baby.

'We loved one another so much, Sarah. Our life was blessed and we knew how to enjoy it. We were gifted in that way. And this little family of mine, here, also has this gift, it's why I had to get back to them. Nothing is as good as this. Only God's love is as good, and the love for one's family comes from God, so it's all one.

'Sometimes I think I should have tried to go back for a visit, but this dying would then have happened away from William and my boys and I hate to imagine how sad that would have been. And my father would have had to watch it. I couldn't have that, I'm glad he will only read of it. I've told William not to write to him until after I'm gone. He's had too much of death.'

She told me about two tragedies one after another than had hit him hard.

'One cold spring, Daddy and my oldest brother were repairing a bad leak in the roof of one of the barns, and my brother slipped and fell. He broke his neck and was dead by the time my father reached him. It had been raining and the rain had turned to sleet, yet they kept working. My father blamed himself.

'Then in the late summer, less than half-a-year later, we all got sick. Influenza. Mama, my youngest brother and Baby were the sickest. A doctor came by with concoctions to drink and poultices to put on throats and chests, and Daddy and I took care of the others as well as we could, being pretty sick ourselves. Mama and my brothers started getting well. But Baby didn't.

'My father never got over those two deaths. He sometimes couldn't get out of bed which was not like him. Work was not getting done and winter was coming. Mama got men from the church to come by, knowing he wouldn't stay in bed then, and they pitched in to help.

They'd bring their wives and children, stay over a few days. In the evenings, when it was nice out, we all sat around and played music and sang. Old songs, hymns. You know, the songs I love to sing with William. That helped. But he was never who he'd been before. I've done the right thing, Sarah. I could not have had him watch me die. It would have been cruel.'

I asked how she'd met William. It was at a church dance.

'Oh, I loved him the minute I laid eyes on him! Loved his funny bashful ways, loved watching him play music, loved everything about him, but I would not show it. My brothers would have teased me without mercy. I flirted with him at a few dances, but he was too shy. Finally, one time, when he'd sat out a dance and was re-stringing his guitar, I gathered up my courage, went up to him and asked would he please he join me in that reel. He did, and he was a terrible dancer! He said he'd rather play for others to dance. So we got some cider, sat down, started talking and we haven't ever stopped. He's not only my husband, Sarah, he's my best friend.'

She was quiet for a moment. Then she adjusted herself so she was looking directly into my eyes.

'You and I, we are a special sort of friends, aren't we, Sarah.'

'Yes, Lizzie. A very special sort.'

'If we had met anywhere else, someplace like the sutler's store at Fort Laramie, or waiting for mail to come, we'd have chatted a bit, I'd have invited you to the house for supper, but I don't think we would have become such close friends. Do you?'

'I don't know, Lizzie, it's hard to say.'

'I think we would not have. Our lives were so different then. Now, too. We see things so differently.'

'Well, let's not think about that, we are dear friends now...'

'Yes. We are. We were thrown into a world neither of us had ever imagined. I'd thought all the time about the possibility of getting captured, was scared to death of it. Then, it happened. We thought we'd die together, you and I, so we clung to one another. But we lived. We lived and we each became more deeply *ourselves*, I think. Yet we held to our friendship. That's sort of a miracle, isn't it? I am so grateful. So grateful.

'Ah! But here is my husband! Just look at him! Isn't he the hand-somest? *Ha!* I can still make him blush! Oh, my darling! Come here. I happen to know that Sarah wants to go home now, and I want *your* company.'

CHAPTER 9

A string of pretty good days for Lizzie came to an end around the first week of December. She slept most of the time. Sometimes she was wracked by a deep cough, sometimes there was fever, some-times pain would make her moan in her sleep, or it would wake her. Then she'd somehow rally and would eat a little soup, but only if we begged her to.

William came down to the cabin one morning early. I'd moved a chair in front of the stove and was drinking my coffee. The weather had turned suddenly frigid and there was snow on the ground. He was tired, he told me he stayed awake most nights listening to her breathe.

'Lizzie and I are going have that talk with the boys in a bit. Would you come?'

I told him I was very uncomfortable with that idea, I believed it should be the family only. I'd wait downstairs, and would read to the boys afterwards, if they wanted me to. I'd ask Maria to make something special for them. He nodded.

'This is horrible, Sarah.'

I poured him some coffee. How would they take it? They would take it hard. How could they not? I held his hand and we sat that way for a bit, then walked back up to the house together.

When William went upstairs, I joined Maria in the kitchen. She heated some chocolate in milk for the boys and poured it into their mugs. She put cookies on a plate. We didn't talk, not wanting to intrude even with the muted sound of our voices. We pulled out chairs as quietly as we could and sat down at the kitchen table.

Drank coffee. Waited.

In a little while, William came down alone looking stricken. He said the boys wanted to stay with their mother, they'd come down later. I remember thinking, Oh, the chocolate will get cold. Odd, what you think of when you can't bear to think of the larger thing. William stood around for a moment and then said he was going back upstairs. Maria asked him to wait one minute. She put the chocolate in a pot, put it and the mugs on a tray with the cookies so William could bring it up with him. I told Maria I'd be back at the cabin if I was needed.

I don't know what I did with that day. I hope I had something good to read. William came down later that night after the boys had gone to bed and Lizzy seemed to be sleeping soundly. I'd gotten a bottle of whiskey on one of my solitary outings and poured us both a bit. He rarely came down in the evenings now, not wanting to leave her.

'I've seen death, a few up close in my family. We're surrounded by it out here, always a possibility. But nothing prepares you, does it? This is way too soon.'

I could think of nothing useful to say, so said nothing. He said he was worried about Christmas.

'I hope she makes it, for the boys.'

I'd also thought about this and the germ of an idea had come to me, so I told it to William, to see what he thought. I suggested that we should make the day come to meet her, begin celebrating early. We'd decorate the house. Make the atmosphere as festive as we could, starting the very next day. This would help keep the boys occupied. When we felt it was time — whether the twenty-fifth of December or sooner — we'd make a feast. He liked the idea. He knocked back the rest of the whiskey and went home.

I liked the idea, too. Every year of my life before I'd left home, my mother had done all the work of making the holiday, or directing it, at least. I would make Christmas for Lizzy.

The boys hadn't yet finished breakfast when I came into their kitchen the following morning. Their faces were blotched red and it was clear they'd not slept much.

'Charles, Joey, I have an idea. There are about three weeks until Christmas. Let's make this the most beautiful Christmas ever. For your mother. Yes? We'll forget about lessons until after the holiday, but I have work for you to do. Important work.'

They looked at me, curious, a bit cautious.

'I want you to make presents for your mother, little things, so she has a surprise from you every single day until Christmas. We'll get a basket for them, and every morning, when she wakes up, there will be something in it from you two. You can make things together.'

'What sorts of things?'

'Well... Maria could help you to bake special cookies, tiny ones. They could do that, couldn't they, Maria? And I thought we could string some ribbon across the window in your mother's bedroom and hang little ornaments on it, something new every day. You might find things outside that you can decorate. Your mother has a box full of yarn and ribbon, buttons, beads, all sorts of things you can use. You have paint. I think that would lift her spirits, don't you? To decorate her room?

'And start making ornaments for the tree. You and your father will cut one soon. Ah! Charles! You write very well now, you could write poems for her, that would be a fine thing for you to do. And Joey, you draw so, so beautifully. We'll get you more paper in different colours, and more paints.

'So. Let's start today. Maria, do you have a basket you could give them to use? Wonderful. We'll keep it down here, and you can put in it what you make today. Tonight, after your mother has gone to sleep, your father will put it by her bed. Imagine how happy she'll be when she wakes up and finds her surprises!'

I was nervous. Words had tumbled out as if I'd emptied a bowlful of half-baked ideas onto the table in front of them. The boys were wide eyed, but I could see their minds working with each suggestion: *Yes, we can do this. Yes, we can do this, too. Yes, we will do this.* I told them I would help them in any way they needed.

I should have said that I would *try* to help them. I'd seen Maria put her hand gently on Charles' shoulder, hug Joey to her and kiss

325

his head. But I wasn't able to freely express the affection I'd come to feel for them. I sat close when I read to them, I looked them in the eye when they spoke, I answered honestly, compassionately. I hoped that if they needed more from me in this time of great difficulty, they'd ask. I hoped they would *not* need more.

Lizzie was dying. The most natural thing in the world, when you come to think of it, yet none of us knew what to do with ourselves or with one another.

The boys cut paper in the shapes of stars and angels and animals, and painted them. They tied bows on small sprays of evergreens. Painted pine cones. Maria taught them how to make what she called *cartonería*, like papier-mâché, out of which the boys began sculpting figures for a crèche. She also helped them make tiny butter cookies with little pieces of dried fruit in them. Charles wrote poems — he'd clearly worked hard to make rhymes — on sheets of paper that he folded in the shape of tiny boxes. Joey drew pictures of birds, animals, trees, the barn, the house during a snowstorm, the family at dinner, Maria amid a jumble of pots and pans, Juan and his father with their instruments, mouths open in song. There was one of me sitting with them in front of the fire, a book in my hands. Joey would grow up to be a fine artist.

One day I asked Lizzie what she thought the boys needed in clothing, I'd go to Laramie to get them gifts to put under the tree. She told me and had me write down their measurements. I'd already ordered more books and hoped they'd arrive on time.

On a bitterly cold but clear day, I borrowed the buggy and went alone to the City of Laramie. I got money out of the bank, picked up my mail — the books had come! — and bought sweaters and shirts and trousers and socks and coats and boots for the boys. I bought new candles in rich colours, and pewter candlesticks. A new dress shop had opened. The clothing was fancy, I wondered who in that rough town would buy such things. The whores! Of course! There I found a pale lavender bed-jacket of padded silk that I bought for Lizzie. I bought a plaid wool-flannel shirt for William, and a dress I hoped would fit Maria and that she would like. I bought a plum pudding in a tin and two bottles of Cognac. As I was walking back to the livery stable, leaning against the front wall of the hardware store was a magnificent sled, curved wood and red-painted metal. I bought that, too.

Lizzie was asleep when I got home, but the next morning, while the boys were helping in the barn, I showed her my purchases. While we talked, I wrapped the gifts with paper I'd bought. We were the happiest conspirators. I told her about the sled and she reached up and put her arms around my neck.

Lizzie's bedside table was soon a riot of First-Thing-in-the-Morning-Mama gifts. The wall above it was festooned with pictures and poems. A braided ribbon over the window directly across from where she lay gathered new ornaments daily. William and the boys went into the woods and cut a fine little tree they began to decorate. Supper every evening was a picnic in the bedroom. To our great relief, Lizzie ate. Not much, but more than she had been. Juan and Maria joined us, and often the men brought up their instruments and played.

I made another trip to Laramie, this time with the boys. I realised they should have an opportunity to pick out something special for their parents. I gave them each a small wallet with enough money to buy these gifts. I told them it was a reward for the hard work they'd done on their lessons in the last weeks. They were serious in their choices, asking what I thought. I had them help me pick out a good shirt for Juan, I'd forgotten about him on my last trip. Before leaving to go home, we had lunch in the hotel restaurant. People treated them as if they were grown men, which made them proud and happy.

William and Juan went hunting one day, determined to bring home meat for the feast. In case they weren't lucky, Maria and I had our eyes on a big, friendly hen who was in her prime. Maria had already begun to gather things together for some special dishes. She said she'd try to make some Mexican Christmas foods her family back home had loved, but that it would be a little hard because there were too many ingredients she would not be able to get. The men were gone overnight, as they'd said they would be, but they came back with packets of venison. There'd be a fine roast for Christmas

Eve dinner.

We were in a race with Death, and Death would take her, but we would not let it ruin her last Christmas. The air in the house was bright, ringing, defiant, joyful, it swirled up and down the stairs, filled our bodies with vigour, as if we all had a bit of a fever, enough to make us giddy. The house itself seemed an eager participant in our endeavours. It enhanced every gesture we made, enlivened everything we tried. It had a heart, a generous spirit of its own. It embraced Lizzie, and she responded.

'Help me to put on that light blue velvet dress you gave me last year, Sarah, I will be on the couch for Christmas Eve. I will not miss it.'

And she did not.

In late morning, William carried his wife downstairs in the velvet dress. I'd fixed her hair, and tied the opal pendent — William's gift from last Christmas — around her neck. It was a dark, cold day outside which made the house feel even more festive with all the candles lit, even those on the tree, and the lamps were lit and a fire blazed in the hearth. So many evergreen garlands had been placed around the room, it smelled like a pine forest. As soon as they were far enough down the stairs for her to see everything, Lizzie exclaimed with delight. Charles grinned so hard it looked like his cheeks would crack, and Joey jumped up and down.

We adjusted her pillows and tucked the green silk quilt, another gift from last year, around Lizzie's legs. Her eyes were bright as a child's. When the boys showed her the crèche they'd made, set up on its own small table with their *cartoneria* figures and William's intricately carved animals, she clapped her hands. William brought down the old wooden box that held, still in cottonwool, the six glass ornaments I'd brought them last year. He'd saved it for last so Lizzie could tell them where they should go on the tree.

Maria brought a tray to the low table by the couch with bread, butter, plum preserves and cheese. I brought a pot of coffee and a pot of hot chocolate. After breakfast, Maria served us a holiday eggnog similar to one she'd enjoyed while growing up. William, Juan and I doused ours with a bit of Cognac and, to our great surprise, Lizzie asked for a bit as well. I imagined it might do her good. She'd even eaten a little breakfast, which pleased us all.

Suddenly, William said, 'I almost forgot!' He put his hand in his pocket, brought out a white silk pouch and handed it to Lizzie. She carefully took from it a tiny gold cross on a fine chain. I moved out of the way so he could fasten it around her neck.

William had made the boys new snowshoes. He'd made shelves to put in their room for all their new books. He'd made me a wooden box with an exquisitely carved lid, a dove on a flowering branch, in which the boys had placed poems and pictures. Maria had knitted gloves for all of us.

But William and Juan had kept the best thing hidden under a blanket behind the tree to be brought out last. They'd carved and painted a train with many cars, people looking out the windows or staring straight ahead, and they'd built tiny buildings for a station remarkably like Laramie's. The boys were clearly delighted with all their gifts and said so, they were good boys, but the train captivated them utterly.

Maria and I spent a lot of time in the kitchen for the rest of the day. She did most of the cooking, as she was better able to concentrate. I could not stay away from the family for long. Lizzie slept intermittently, but lightly. When William or one of the boys laughed, she'd smile. Suddenly, it was dark out, and Maria told me it was time for the last of the dinner preparations.

We had our feast in the parlour and because there wasn't much room on the small table, Maria and I served dinner one platter at a time. First the meat, sliced and drenched in gravy. Then came mashed turnips and potatoes, a compote of canned peaches and cherries, beans Lizzie had canned at the end of summer, chicken in what Maria said was a sort-of-mole sauce, mushrooms sautéed in butter, fresh bread. We let everyone fill their plates, then we sat down. The rest of the family had waited for us. Lizzie asked William to say grace, and then we tucked into the food that looked so beautiful on the plates and smelled so good.

While Maria and I cleared up, Juan added wood to the fire and William put new candles on the tree. We brought out desserts and coffee. The boys quickly gobbled some pie and then returned to their train, while we five talked softly. After a bit, William picked up his guitar and Juan, his mandolin. Lizzie said, 'Oh, yes! Wonderful!' We started singing carols. Maria began a lovely, fast carol in Spanish while her father played, and William joined him.

The boys asked what it meant, and Maria told them it was a song about fishes in a river and how they kept swimming away and back again to be right near the place where the baby Jesus would be born. Lizzie remembered I'd sung a carol in French last Christmas and asked if I'd sing it again. After the first couple of phrases, William and Juan picked out an accompaniment. By the last bit, '*King of angels, sleep*', sung softly and slowly, it was as if they'd always known it.

A quiet followed. We looked at one another, breathed deeply, and then looked at Lizzie. Her head was back against the pillows, her mouth was open and slack, her eyes were closed. All of us must have had the same horrible thought at the same moment and I'm certain that's what wakened her. She took a deep, loud breath, coughed a bit, then turned her head.

'I fell asleep! Play, sing, more.'

So we did. We added wood to the fire. We sang. The boys got up on the couch and fell asleep on Lizzie's legs. Lizzie slept. William, Juan, Maria and I drank Cognac and sang. We sang deep into the night for all the reasons human creatures have always sung. We sang to keep the dark at bay a little longer.

CHAPTER 10

The cold slammed down hard in early January. It was impossible to get warm. Most days, the sky was low and dark, always ready to drop snow, and it snowed often. Sometimes, it would come down so thick that, if I was at Lizzie's house, I could not see my way back to my cabin and would spend the night on their couch. Or if a storm came up when I was home, I could not get to Lizzie. A reprieve, yet horrible.

For a while, she still wanted me to lie down with her, so I would.

She'd nestle her head in my neck. Her body had become small, with bones like a bird's. Sometimes, when she spoke, her voice seemed to come from a distance.

'Sarah?'

'I'm here.'

'What day is it?'

'Tuesday, I think.'

'What month?'

'January.'

'Who are all these people?'

'What people, Lizzie?'

'Yes.'

'Is there anything you need?'

'My dress... '

'Which one?'

'*Oh? So...*'

Sometimes, when I'd try to leave the bed thinking she was asleep, she'd reach for me. She might not open her eyes, she might only open her hand. Her need for me and my need to please her had became one thing. No separation existed, no call and response. I knew if she wanted me to stroke her arm, I knew if she did not want to be touched. I knew if she wanted me to speak, or be silent.

Increasingly, I felt she was not entirely in her body. Sleep seemed like a current she was caught in, sometimes deep under, sometimes closer to the surface. One day, lying with her as she slept, the wind carried down from the barn the sound of a hammer on wood. I knew what it meant and was afraid Lizzie would too. I kept my eyes on her, ready to distract her. But on that afternoon, she was deep enough under not to hear anything of this world.

Pain would jolt her suddenly and shockingly awake. She'd gasp, 'Oh, God! Oh, God!' The boys would run into the room and stand helpless. Maria would race to get William if he wasn't in the house. She'd apologise. 'So, so sorry.' William would hold her hand, lift her head so she could drink some water. More than once, I pleaded with her to let Juan ride fast to Laramie get laudanum. But she said she wouldn't take it. She said she prayed through the pain. She'd say, 'It will be beautiful. I must be awake.'

In the last few days, she wanted only William and her boys. They stroked her head with cool cloths as she moaned and pulled at the covers. Her lips were cracking. They tried to get her to suck on the wetted corner of a cloth but she turned her head away. Sometimes I thought she saw me, standing a bit apart, but probably not. Silently, I begged her to go ahead and die. 'Die, dear friend, go now, please go now.'

Directly across from me, on the other side of the room, over the bed with its rumpled counterpane, this boat of grief and love, was Death. I'd felt his presence, and now, with increasing frequency, I could see him. Waiting. We were all waiting.

I'd done all I could think of to do. I'd done what I'd known she'd have done for me. It did not any of it come naturally, but I had done it. I knew we could not cheat Death, although, I have no doubt that the Christmas we'd made had held him back for a bit. But there was no justice in the cruelty of her dying. I remember thinking that her god, whom she had loved and trusted without equivocation her entire life, could at least have sent her a damn angel.

It was not beautiful. It was hard.

When it was over, William took her in his arms and stood up, holding her tight against him, the bedclothes streaming. He wept into her hair. I began to gather the boys and take them outside, but he said, 'No. They need to be here. This is their mother.' He walked over to the rocking chair and sat down holding her like a child in his lap. He gestured for the boys to come close and they did.

I walked downstairs and out onto the porch and was furious that after so many days of snow and dark, the sun was daring to rise, that the eastern sky was pink and gold with it, that Life seemed not to notice this horrible thing that had happened to these good people.

They buried her up by her still-born twin girls and my still-born daughter. The tree that had been a slight thing when my girl was buried — had that really only been two years ago? — seemed taller. William and Juan had been afraid the ground would be too hard, but there'd been a freak thaw that week in late January, and they were able to make the grave deep enough.

There was a service. A minister intoned, 'in the midst of life, we are in death...earth to earth, ashes to ashes, dust to dust... Thanks be to God.' The boys tried not to cry as William and some other men lowered their mother into the ground, but they cried. William cried. Maria cried. Lizzie's two favourites among the assimilationist women cried. Others, too. People I didn't know. I couldn't cry.

After hymns, everyone walked down to the house. The parlour filled quickly. I was surprised at how many people had learned of her death and had come to pay their respects and to console William and the boys. How did they know her? How did they know when to come? I had no idea how word got around. Maria and I served coffee and things she'd baked. People had brought food, as they do at a death. For those who stayed late, William brought out the whiskey.

For several days afterward, I remained in the cabin. I drank a lot, slept a lot during the day, very little at night, and then I made my decision. Late one morning, no doubt wondering where I'd been, William came down as I was packing my bags.

'Where are you going?'

'I need to get away, William.'

'The boys need to get back to their lessons.'

'I'm sorry.'

'When will you be back?'

I just shook my head.

'I don't understand this. Why now?'

I told him I had to leave, and I had decided to leave that day. He again asked where I was going and I said it didn't matter. The boys had plenty of books they hadn't read yet; they should read the Shakespeare aloud together. Charles was fairly good at math, but Joey was hopeless and I was of no use in that regard, he should take over that part of their lessons. Charlie should write essays, Joey should draw and paint. I'd heard a school was just getting started in Laramie. He should look into it.

'I asked you when you plan to come back.'

'I don't know, William. Don't count on me.'

I'd been jamming things into my bag as I spoke. I turned to see him studying me, his face dark.

'How can you be so cold?'

He asked it as if it was the kind of question for which there might be an answer. There wasn't. We stood facing one another. It was the second time I'd seen him angry, and both times, it was at me.

'*You're family*, damn it! That might not mean much to you, but it means a lot to us. Besides, the weather is only going to get worse. It's no time to light out for who-knows-where.'

He turned away, took a breath, turned back and said,

'*Please*. Stay through the winter, at least. My boys are shattered by this, Sarah. Can't you see this? They need you. *I* need you. I need your help with the boys. And, you know? Whether you realise it or not — you *stubborn* woman! — you need *us* now, too."

His voice was hoarse with feeling, I couldn't bear it. I said I'd stay until spring. He could tell the boys that lessons would resume the next day.

Something in me had cracked open during Elizabeth's long dying. The pain was intolerable. It wasn't only losing Elizabeth, there was much else, but it was too deep in me to name. Moving fast would help. Strange vistas. When William came to the cabin, I was packing to escape. I had no plan other than to head for the train station. I'd actually hoped to sneak out unseen.

William essentially demanding that I not go was a relief. He saved us both an awful scene, and the price I'd have paid in guilt would have done me in. He'd said we were a family. Lizzie had often told me that I was part of their family. Her *sister*. I'd begun to believe in this, but with her gone, the centre had fallen away. I no longer felt it. I again felt like a stranger.

But I'd promised to stay until spring. So I did.

PART FIVE
THE LEDGE

I met Bell in Laramie by accident. He'd been expecting a man from Boston who'd wanted a guide for buffalo hunting, but when Bell wired him saying there were too few of the animals left and these were wary, he'd agreed to hunt elk. But the man had apparently changed his mind, he wasn't on the train. I'd been thinking I'd board that very train heading west, but I, too, had changed my mind. I'd not replaced that plan with an alternative other than lunch.

I'd told William and the boys I was taking the train to New York, that I wanted to see my half-brother, Ezekiel, and that I'd only be gone a few weeks. I hugged them all, hoping this demonstration of affection would leave an impression stronger than my leaving. William had looked me in the eye as if he'd suspected I was lying. I was. I'd made no plans about where I was going — west or east — or when I'd come back. I didn't know if I'd come back at all.

Bell saw me through the window of the restaurant, the one that was part of a respectable hotel, the same place at which Elizabeth had told me she was dying, and where the boys and I had eaten lunch before Christmas. I'd ordered food but couldn't eat. I motioned Bell to come in and sit down. He did. He sat back in his chair, looking at me.

'You don't look so good.'

'I've got to get away from here.'

'Where to?'

'Doesn't matter.'

'I heard about your friend. I'm sorry. You still living with them?'

'Can't talk about it.'

He kept glancing at my beef steak, so I pushed the plate to him. After he'd eaten, we walked down the street to one of the several saloons. I have an image in mind of the two of us at a table, leaning towards one another over glasses that seemed to refill themselves, talking with great intensity, but I have no idea what it might have been about. It would not have been about Elizabeth. Then it was night and we went back to the hotel with the restaurant downstairs. I paid for the room, but told him I did not want to fuck him. He said he'd sleep on the floor. It was chilly, though, so I told him he could sleep in the bed.

I fucked him and was glad I did. The drinking and the fucking allowed a different Sarah to emerge, one I recognised from way back. This Sarah was better able to take a quick turn, get dirt under her nails, be disliked. Besides, and more simply, the fucking *felt* good. It felt good down to my bones, a fine anodyne. Raw pain got burned away in sweaty, mindless pleasure.

We kept the room for a couple of days, eating downstairs, drinking at a bar we liked — I can't recall its name; it was *not* The Bucket of Blood! — and rolling into one another in the dark. Lying in bed with him one night, talking, I suddenly remembered how sometimes when drinking with him and Garrett at Fort Laramie, he'd get itchy and have to disappear for a bit. If he was still using, I wanted some. Oh, how I wanted some. So, I asked.

'I stopped all that. Wasn't doing me any real good. Kept me weak and sick.'

My reaction was to break down in sobs that I couldn't control. Bell sat up, lit the lamp on the table by the bed, and looked at me.

'You need to meet a woman I know. Cheyenne medicine woman. To my great honour she's a relative of mine and the best human being this earth. She'd help you. If you really want to be helped.'

Without asking any questions, I said, 'Yes. Take me to her.'

'It'll be a long, hard ride, and April is a tricky month, but worth the trouble. Up for it?'

'Yes.'

Then I told him that I did not want to fuck for a while. Or drink.

'I won't be good company, Bell, and I'd understand if you want to back out.'

He laughed and asked when this abstinence was going to begin, because there was a bit of whiskey left in the bottle right there on the floor, within easy reach of his hand. I thought we might as well finish it.

In the morning I told him I wanted to pay him to be my guide into that country and he said he wouldn't take my money. He considered me a friend. He would, however, allow me to cover expenses. He suggested I buy a pair of men's pants and long johns and a better coat. I did, and bought him a new coat as well. He also pointed out a hat he said I might find useful, a broad-brimmed leather hat that would help keep the weather off my face. I liked it. He asked about my blanket roll and I said I didn't have one.

'No hotels where we're going, darlin'.'

He helped me outfit myself for sleeping outside in rough weather. At a trading post he knew that was on our way, we'd get good cold-weather moccasins which we'd need, he said, as we were going a good distance north and west, into high country. That's where we'd find the Northern Cheyenne and the medicine woman, his relative. Though it was late in the month, it would still be cold up there. Snow would still be on the ground, and unless we were absurdly lucky, we could expect a heavy squall or two when we hit the mountains.

We set out early in the morning, provisioned well enough with full canteens, a pot, a frying pan, a bowl and a cup each, cutlery, dried foods, and a few other edibles. We both considered coffee and a pot to make it in an absolute necessity. I'd taken my revolver, he had one, too, and also a good rifle, so we got plenty of ammunition. He said things could get touchy with Indians along the way because what had happened on the Washita River at the end of November. I hadn't heard of it.

'You know about that massacre at Sand Creek, don't you? A few hundred Cheyenne killed, mostly women and children? About five years ago, I think, sometime in 1864.'

'I heard of it when I was still with Far Cry and his people.'

'Well, Black Kettle, the chief of that clan, and his wife barely escaped Sand Creek alive. But they had the misfortune to meet Custer down in Indian Territory...'

'*George Armstrong Custer?*'

'The same. He'd just come back from being court-martialled...'

'*Ha!* Why?'

'Wild disobedience, what else. He does whatever he fucking wants to do and, this time, it cost him his command. He'd gone back east to deal with all this. Word is that Sheridan told Grant how bad he needed him back out here, so he got re-instated. Just in time to raise hell down on the Washita.

'So, here's Custer looking to truss up his reputation as the Great Indian Fighter, and here's Black Kettle, who saw absolutely no percentage in fighting whites, who wanted to stay on the good side of the government. But ever since Sand Creek, a lot of young Cheyenne believed all out war was the only way to deal with whites, so there'd been a fair amount of raiding. Black Kettle did his best to restrain them, but they had no ears for that.

'Sherman and Sheridan were also hungry for all out war, and President Grant was behind it. They'd start by making an example with the Southern Cheyenne. And they'd do it in the winter, when the Indians usually counted on hunkering down.

'Sheridan had ordered all friendlies in the area to make their winter camps along the Washita. There were a few thousand Indians, not all of them Cheyenne, some Kiowa and Arapaho, a few Sioux, too, in different camps all along the river. And a big herd of ponies. Black Kettle and his people had set their camp some miles west, apart from from the big group.

'There was about two feet of snow on the ground. Thick fog. Black Kettle and his people were staying put, keeping warm. Then some Kiowa came through and told him they'd seen tracks of many soldiers heading right towards them. Black Kettle said they had to be mistaken.

'He decided they'd wait until the snow melted down a bit and then find the soldiers and explain that there were only friendlies down along the Washita. They'd done what they'd been told to do. A lot of people didn't like this idea, including Black Kettle's wife. She had a bad feeling about it. She told some of their grown children what she thought and they took their families and left.

'Custer attacked at dawn when the people were still under their sleeping robes. Came at them from all sides, band playing. Black Kettle and his wife jumped on a pony and tried to cross the river but were shot in the back. Custer and his soldiers rode over their bodies. Some Osage scouts took their scalps.

'Sheridan had given orders that Custer was to kill all the men and take the women and children prisoner, so he took some fifty or so women and children. Used them as shields, so his men could get away. Knowing he needed a count, Custer asked each of his officers how many dead Indians they'd seen. The total came to about a hundred. Not good enough. Custer said it was about three-hundred. But the women captives said only about twenty braves were killed and about forty women and children, most of these were shot as they ran, some as they lay on the ground.

'Then, in a final gesture, the soldiers shot about six hundred ponies. That was Custer's big win at the Washita.'

He let that sit for a minute then told me that, while there'd not been any signs of retaliation up in these parts, we'd be smart to keep our eyes open.

'The same stories, over and over. There has to be a better way.'

Bell looked at me as if I were a child. I persisted.

'Elizabeth and some friends were talking about assimilation. I hated the idea, but maybe they were right. Maybe it's better than murdering them. Again and again and again.'

'Fuck no. It ain't better. Not one bit. The end result's the same. Whites just want to make the Indian disappear. Those who don't want to kill 'em outright, want to turn 'em into whites.'

'Did I ever tell you I used to imagine killing Custer myself?'

He didn't say anything.

'Looks like we're in for some rain. Let's see if we can find a clump of trees and make camp.'

We did, and after a bit, there came a steady cold rain. I was glad for my hat. There was no building a fire, so we chewed on some jerky and ate a couple of dry biscuits, then rolled up in our blankets. I was tired to the bone, but could not sleep. All my many unkindnesses towards Elizabeth had become one heavy, wet, stinking beast that sat on my chest all night, made it hard to breathe. It was still raining when we got going again in the morning.

'By the way, Sarah. You don't need to worry about killing Custer. The Indians'll do it if his own men don't do it first. There's a lot of bad blood about everything having to do with that bastard. He's got

his hangers-on, young, stupid, ambitious types, but on the whole...'
He spat.

CHAPTER 2

Dense clouds pressed down on us. There was rain or mist or fog or all of it. One afternoon the rain turned to sleet, then snow, then icy rain again, and for days the wet and cold were constant. Bell told me that we'd been moving into higher and higher country. He was usually able to find a place where we could arrange branches for some shelter at night, but conditions were pretty much a thorough misery. Finally, the sleet and snow stopped, though the sun stayed hidden. Ahead of us, a thick cloud bank obscured any glimpse of the horizon.

One day, I opened my eyes after some few hours of sleep — as usual, curled into a tight ball against the cold — and was surprised by a solitary star in the paling eastern sky. As I watched, a few small clouds that had at first been grey turned to pink-gold. The snow reflected this tender colour, and I could see that it lay in patches, with tufts of grass sticking up here and there. There was even bird-song, when for days there'd been only the hiss of icy snow and the crunch of our horses' hooves.

I shook myself from my blankets, stood up and turned around. The cloud bank was gone. In its place, the Shining Mountains rose from the plain as if they'd thrust themselves up overnight in triumph, in jubilation. With the sun on their white shoulders it was clear how they'd gotten their name.

'Pretty, aren't they,' Bell said. He'd built a fire and was making coffee.

He said that in about three more days, we'd be well into the folds of the mountains and would find the Cheyenne camp.

'How will you know where to look for it?'

'I'll know.'

Something shifted in me. My horse felt it. Or perhaps he too smelled something different in the sun-warmed air and earth, he was more alert, he danced a bit. Life came out of hiding. Bell pointed out, a good way off, a large brown bear, a female with two young cubs. I saw many deer. I watched a fox dive into a patch of snow after some small creature. Hawks circled.

I felt the shape of the earth and was reminded of my journey with Far Cry that summer of our running away. We'd traveled in sight of these mountains. He'd offered them to me with a sweeping gesture and pounded his fist over his heart. I remembered the thrill of being with him in this place he loved.

It was slow going, but the air was good. Astringent with pine and the mineral smell of wet rock, all was sharper and clearer. Following Bell along steep, stony paths, my horse picked his way carefully and I sat him respectfully.

By the third night, there was enough moon on the snow to see where we were going, so we continued into the night. We went over a rise, smelled the smoke and then saw the fires of the village below us in a narrow valley. The fires made the walls of the tipis glow like lanterns and their lights were reflected in a meandering stream. Knowing our approach had been observed, Bell called out a greeting, and a greeting came back in answer. I put on the eye-patch I'd been keeping in my pocket.

Riding in, people came up to meet us and welcomed him as a dear friend or relation. At first, they looked at me warily, then he said something and they were warm towards me as well. We dismounted and a boy took our horses. As we walked through the village, I asked what he'd said. 'I told them you're my woman.' I side-eyed him, but he laughed. The phrase he'd used meant an honorary kins-woman or an old friend.

The sights, sounds and smells of a friendly Indian camp during a time of what appeared to be relative plenty, carried me back. I looked into the faces of these people, meeting their curious, kind eyes with a surprising upwelling of emotion.

We arrived in front of a large, beautifully painted tipi just as an old woman was coming outside, followed by a couple of shy children. She was short and solid, her broad face dominated by a smile that crinkled the skin of her cheeks up to her eyes. She opened her arms wide and embraced Bell, then pulled back to look at him, stroking his face. Everyone was happy to see what was clearly a reunion. And I'd never seen Bell look as he did at that moment, full of honest joy. He presented me to her, I heard my name spoken, and she took my hands in hers and said something with great sweetness. He then introduced me to the woman, speaking her name in Cheyenne and then in English.

'Sarah, this is Bright Eyes. She is the sister of my wife's mother. Cheyenne custom wouldn't have let me speak to her directly, but when my wife and children were killed, she made an exception. She can decide such things. Like I told you, she's got powerful medicine, is famous for it. Her spirit animal is the otter. Look.'

He waved towards her tipi and I saw that the nearly faded paintings were of otters sliding in graceful curves all along the sides of the skins. Their eyes looked straight at us and were as full of life as Bright Eyes' own.

'Her husband was the painter, but she's been a widow a long time now. She kept those skins. No one's come along who could paint like he could. You can see here how they're sewed to newer skins underneath.'

There was to be no serious talking that night. Bell had come! There was eating and singing and dancing. I wanted to join them when Bright Eyes and many of the women got up to dance, but was not sure if it would have been right. I was happy enough to watch. It must have been clear that I was very tired, because a young woman came after a bit and led me back to Bright Eyes' tipi where sleeping robes had already been put in place for me. I slept well that night for the first time in a long time.

There was no talking the next day, either, because the men went out to hunt so there could be more eating, and Bell went with them. It was sunny and surprisingly mild. We'd given what was left of our coffee and sugar to Bright Eyes, so after I'd bathed in the stream with some of the other women, she and I sat outside sipping the hot brew and watching the camp. Women went about doing the things I'd done — gathering firewood, cleaning up the lodges, talking and laughing as they repaired torn clothing and moccasins and performed the million other needs of the camp, as the children played.

Bright Eyes moved around to sit behind me. She worked her fingers through my still wet hair, making *tsk tsk tsk* sounds at the mess of snarls. Then she went at it with a variety of brushes and combs made from bunches of stiff sticks, quills, and finally some sort of animal hair. Girls of several ages came over to watch, all of them giggling at the faces I made. It hurt! Then Bright Eyes unwrapped the leather from the top of a pot and I recognised the smell of bear grease. I recalled how Lizzy had hated that smell, had never gotten used to it.

After she massaged my scalp and worked the thick stuff through my hair, crown to the ragged ends where it breaks off just below my shoulders, she opened a second, smaller pot and from this one, came the scent of some flower. She rubbed this fragrant oil into both her hands, then placed her palms on the crown of my head. She intoned something in a low, sweet voice, very different from her slightly rough speaking voice. It was a song. The girls became quiet, respectful. Bright Eyes stroked my hair, over and over, braiding it loosely.

Then, still singing, she turned me to face her and pulled down my eye patch. After putting fresh oil on her hands, she began to stroke my naked face, going gently over my scars, even over my eye, singing as she did it. Her gentleness quieted me and the heat of her hands comforted me. I was being given a blessing. That's what it felt like, so I chose to imagine that's what it was. I did not wear the eye patch again while I was with these people.

When the men came home, there was yet more cooking and eating and drumming and singing and dancing. This time, Bright Eyes took my hand and had me join her and the other women. Again, I retired early, long before Bright Eyes, and, again, I slept well. A good thing, as the next day started before dawn and was the beginning of a different sort of journey.

CHAPTER 3

The eastern sky was just a shade past absolute dark and there were still plenty of stars when I joined Bright Eyes and Bell at the fire. Bright Eyes filled a bowl with stew for me and poured a cup of coffee. Bell said he'd told her all about me.

'All?'

I couldn't remember what he knew, what I'd told him. The gossip at Fort Laramie might have filled in a few blanks, though very little of that was likely to have been true.

'I told her you'd been a captive of the Lakota, Far Cry's clan. With them for a year. She knows of him and had heard about you and Elizabeth. She knew you'd been his woman and that things had gone bad when the cavalry came to get you.'

'Does she know about our child? That I lost the baby?'

Before Bell could answer, Bright Eyes turned to me, reached over, took the spirit pouch, my daughter's bones, from under the neck of my shirt and, smiling, gently cradled it for a moment in her hand.

'She answered the question before you translated it. Does she understand some English?'

'A word or two, but she understands people. She watches and listens. And she's been watching you close, if you didn't notice. Besides, like I said, she's one of the holy ones.'

'Does she know that Elizabeth is dead? That I am... '

While I stumbled with how to say something I still didn't understand, Bright Eyes reached over and stroked my face. Then, for a long moment, she looked at me. No one in my life had ever before looked at me that way, and no one's done so since. I wished in that moment I could tell her everything. I wanted her to know about my childhood, my ugly marriage to Byrd, my passion for Far Cry, my despair over our child, my love for Elizabeth, my shame, about Ruth and Zeke, my mother, my guilt, my evil father, my anger. I wanted her to put all the pieces together, and hand me something whole and sensible. I wanted her to tell me who I was.

I turned to Bell.

'What exactly are we going to do, she and I?'

'She's going to take you to a high place, a place where people go to wait for visions, then she'll leave. You'll stay there alone for four days, fasting and praying, and then she'll come bring you back here.'

'Praying. I'm not especially godly, you know.'

'Ask for help. See who comes. Be *serious* about it.'

'What if no one comes?'

'It's very possible no one will. You're a *wasichu*. You're kind of disdainful about religion, and this is religion. Your kind of defiance could get in the way of what might happen.'

'What can I do about that?'

'Keep your eyes and ears open. Try to shut down your mind. For you, that'll be the hardest part. Helpers can be animals, birds, angels, stones, anything. If nothing comes, you're on your own. And that can bring on some good strong learning. Assuming you survive it.'

'Good god. What do you mean by that?'

'I mean, assuming you don't get eaten by a wild animal or jump off the edge of the cliff.'

'Thanks, Bell.'

He tipped his hat.

'So, you know this place?'

'Yes, ma'am. Sure do.'

'Do you have... helpers?'

Bright Eyes laughed as if she'd understood the question, and knew the answer. I wondered what the story might be. Then she became suddenly serious and spoke to me, spreading her arms to bring close the sky and the earth, the camp, the mountains, everything. She signalled Bell to translate.

'When you're on the mountain, you must let the helpers know that you're ready, and then, like I told you, ask for their help. She said you must never forget that we *all* are friends and relations. And when she says "we all", she means all living things between the earth and the sky and under the earth and coming from the sky, including things your kind don't usually think of as being alive.'

My kind. Right then, a boy arrived with two Indian ponies, one with a large pack strapped to it. Bell told me that the path was too rough and steep for my big American horse, this one was better. He said I should put on all my clothing, it would be pretty chilly up there. I did so, and put an extra shirt and my revolver in a pack and brought it to the pony I'd be riding. Bright Eyes was already mounted. I turned to Bell, still sipping his coffee.

'Aren't you coming?'

'Nope. I'll wait for you here.'

The pony was a surefooted girl, and I was glad to be riding her. As Bell had warned, the going was as tricky. I followed Bright Eyes in the grey dawn up a narrow path that switched around so many times, I lost my sense of direction.

As the light increased, I could see more of this mountain. Sometimes, I could reach way out to my side and run my right hand along a rock face going up and up with here and there, green lichen, and here and there, small gnarled evergreens sprouting from the cracks. On the other side, I could see by the look of the air through the trees, many of which were still pretty bare, that we were not far from the edge of a ravine. Sometimes, I'd hear water and once, where the trees were thinly spaced and the path closer to the edge, I saw across the ravine to a narrow stream of falling water coming out of an opening in the rocks on the other side.

Winter was melting. Snow remained on the ground among the trees, shrubs and rocks, more as we climbed higher, and frost glittered in the early morning sun. But the path was dappled gold, and pushing up from the dirt was here and there the green of new things rising. Occasionally, there was the rustle of an animal moving in the brush.

Bright Eyes, who sang bits of songs as we went along, would greet those creatures. Sometimes, she'd point, wanting me to notice, though I rarely saw what she could see. As we approached some dense shrubs, I heard the chattering of chickadees. Bright Eyes stopped her pony and looked back at me, her face lit with delight. She then had a conversation with the birds. This is true: it was a *conversation*, a give and take in both Cheyenne and a perfect imitation of the birds, a conversation that must have involved humour, as she chuckled a lot. When she stopped talking and we continued on our way, the birds flew off.

Sometime before high noon, we emerged from the trees, the path having stopped at a clearing. Before us, was a very broad flat rock, a big ledge that jutted out from the side of the mountain. I could see the path continuing across from us, on the other side of the ledge, but it appeared to be narrower and overgrown. To the right of where we'd stopped, and back a bit, was a rise of giant boulders sticking out of the mountain, haphazardly piled, rising to a summit that I couldn't see.

Across from this, to our left, the flat rock table of the ledge hung over an abyss. On the other side was another mountain, not quite as high as the one we were on. I could hear water far below. I stared at that edge. Bell had said, 'assuming you don't jump off the edge of the cliff.' The bastard.

Bright Eyes dismounted and began to unpack, carrying things towards the opening of a cave I hadn't seen. The cave was neither small nor large, I could easily stand in it, though the ceiling was not far above my head. It was about thirty feet wide, and maybe twenty feet deep. In its centre was a round pit, maybe a yard across and about a hand deep in the middle, in which fires had been built.

She took me through a low opening in one side of the back wall into another room, narrower than the first and with a lower ceiling. It was much darker here, but light enough that I could see there was an underground stream close to the entrance that appeared to run through it from and to rooms on either side. She filled a large bladder with water. It was cold and damp in there and I was glad to get back to the first room.

She went outside, stood in the middle of the ledge, hands on her hips, looking at the sky. The sun had slipped a bit past the meridian and was on its way towards our mountain. The cave opening would get the morning sun. Bright Eyes turned and looked at me. I felt she was assessing whether or not I'd be able to do this. So was I.

She led me into the brush opposite from where we'd come, and moving quickly, we gathered deadwood for a fire, a lot of it, breaking it into the right size. We put it on one side of the cave. This took several trips. Satisfied with this pile, Bright Eyes began to gather kindling. We made several trips back and forth and put that by the other pile. Next we collected dried pine cones, dried pine branches with dead needles, dead leaves. She went a bit deeper, searching the ground, and let out a *Ho!* She'd found some dried deer dung, gathered it in her skirt and brought that inside as well. I followed her everywhere like a pup, gathering stuff.

She went out, took a large knife from a pack still strapped to her pony, and cut green pine boughs with plenty of soft needles. She lay these down on the opposite side of the cave from the firewood. My bed. Over this, she spread a buffalo skin with the fur side up. Then came a couple of woollen blankets — among which she'd rolled bunches of sweet grass — then another buffalo skin, the fur side down.

Then she went out again to her pony, put the knife back in the pack and pulled out a flat board with a stick tied to it. Both were about the length of her forearm. She brought these to the fire pit. Then she carried over some of the small dried stuff, including a bit of the dung, some of the kindling, and a few of the larger pieces of wood. She sat down and had me sit next to her.

She gathered the little stuff into what looked like a bird's nest on the ground, then placed the board so the opening of a round hole on its edge was over the nest. She anchored it with one foot, fitted one end of the stick into the hole and began moving her hands fast, back and forth and up and down, turning the stick. Smoke started pretty quickly and I was excited as a child. Bright Eyes immediately sped up her movements and very soon there was more smoke. Sparks had fallen into the dried stuff and when she blew gently on it, a fine little flame started. I thought she'd add kindling then, but she let it go out. She grinned at my expression. Then she refreshed the nest, moved things over and gave me the stick and board.

My efforts amused her. She kept saying something that I was sure meant, *Keep at it! Keep at it! Keep at it!* My hands, arms, and back hurt, I was out of breath and sweating like mad in that cold place when, finally, some tiny bit of smoke started. I whooped with joy and stopped working the stick, and it went away. Just like that. I must have looked pathetic.

She laughed so hard it almost made me mad. Then she got up, went back to her pack, and brought me a tin box tied with a leather cord. It was full of matches that she showed me would light when struck anywhere on the box. Why hadn't we simply used a match? I was embarrassed and a bit irritated.

As she built a proper fire in the pit, her demeanour changed. She sang softly to the fire. Still singing, she got up and took an object wrapped in soft deer skin from her pack, holding it as if it were a holy relic. A pipe. It was not as long as many I'd seen and was very plain. From a pouch on her belt, she filled the clay bowl with tobacco and lit it, waving the smoke over both our heads. She invited me to smoke. Then she stood and had me follow her outside.

The colour of the light on the cliffs across from us, on the other side of the ravine, had warmed as the sun had moved. Bright Eyes' singing increased in intensity, became a chant. She offered the pipe to the four directions, to the sky and the earth. Then we re-entered the cave and sat again by the fire.

She carefully put the pipe down on its wrapping, and took a small pot of white paste from her pouch and painted my face. Her chanting rose and rose, then softly fell and came to an end. She sat looking at me for a long moment. Then she took the pipe and the deerskin it had been wrapped in, a small pouch of tobacco, placed these in my lap and rose to her feet. She motioned for me to remain sitting. She stood straight, said a phrase that sounded like a benediction, then she turned and walked out. She tied my pony to hers and rode away. I listened to the ponies' hooves recede down the path.

CHAPTER 4

I sat for a long time where she'd told me to sit. I decided that on this first day, I'd watch and listen and do nothing else. Besides, there was nothing else to do and no place to go. This was where whatever might happen would happen, if anything were to happen.

I watched the light change on the cliffs opposite me as the sun passed behind my mountain and shadows rose from the ravine. The wood hissed and, occasionally, there was the small crunch of something settling. I watched the fire and its amber reflection moving on the walls. The sky darkened. A couple of stars came out.

I'm here to ask for help. What if no one or nothing comes? Bell said that would likely be the case. What if someone or something *does* come? I would be overwhelmed.

I was cold and suddenly very tired, so I burrowed into my bed. Elizabeth's voice, from the other side of the cave, startled me awake. The fire had gotten low and it was dark. I waited, wondering if I'd hear her again, wondering what I might actually have heard.

The cliffs were lit by a blue-white light, I could see every sharp edge, every crack on the rock face. The moon must have risen from behind my mountain. I told myself, Don't go back to sleep, wait until the moon is overhead, shining down on the ledge, then go out. I wanted to see this bright moon. But I fell asleep.

The morning of my second day was cold and dark. I longed for coffee. I longed for a pot in which to heat water. I longed for too much else to name, I was a thing defined by longings and was sick of it. I announced to myself, and whoever else might be listening, Today I will do what I've come to do. I built up a good fire and sat until it got a bit lighter outside. Then I couldn't sit any longer.

On the ledge just outside the cave, the sky, low and leaden, bears down on me. I sit. I hear the water in the ravine. The wind.

Mama had the Book of Common Prayer by her bed. When I was little, she'd read to me from it. '*Oh, Lord hear our prayer. Let our cry come unto thee.*' My mother used to say she believed in God, but not in the Devil, nor in any Hell except that which we make for ourselves in this life. She said she had faith. I wonder how much good it did her.

It's time. I stand, walk to the centre of the ledge to offer the pipe to the four directions. Which first? Does it matter? I face the cliffs across the ravine. East. I hold the pipe in both hands and extend my arms with what I hope is the proper feeling. Then I turn to my right, south, and do the same thing. Turn again, facing the cave mouth, west. *I do not at all like having my back to the abyss.* I turn quickly from the west to the north. The clouds are darker and roiling. The wind's picking up. I again face East. Sky, I lift my arms, looking up. Earth, I lower them, looking down. Now I hold the pipe out in front of me, a suppliant.

Hear me. I am a woman alone asking for help. How am I to live?

Silence. Not complete silence, the trees off to my left are agitated. The north wind is suddenly sharper. Boreas. The Greeks found gods and goddesses in everything. 'We are all friends and relations,' said Bright Eyes. Bell said this 'we' includes things *my kind* doesn't think of as being alive.

This wind is very much alive and is gathering force. I lean into it. It's driving something through the trees and suddenly there's a torrent of rain beating down on the rock and splashing up, coming towards me, then lashing me, cold and hard. I stand in it a moment, amazed by the ferocity, then hurry back inside, soaked to the skin, my moccasins slipping on the wet rock.

I add some wood to the fire and urge up a good blaze. Outside, the wind blows the rain sideways. I take off my wet things and wrap myself in a blanket. I walk in bare feet over to the opening, bend down and find a place where, with my finger, I can make a small hole. I empty the pipe into my hand, and push that pinch of tobacco in there, a small tribute to whatever gods might be at the threshold. Someone had taught me to do that, I can't recall who.

I'd asked for help, I'd accepted a drenching, I'd offered a gift. What more?

I stand and watch the storm. Listen to it. It has business with me. It wants to penetrate me, get under my skin. What does it want to tell me? Perhaps it means to mete out punishment, that mild lashing having been only a taste. I'll take the punishment for what it might have to say. Maybe this is what I came for. I put down the pipe, drop the blanket and step outside.

The rain has turned to sleet. I take a few steps towards the centre of the ledge and both feet shoot out in front of me. My skull slams the rock. I'm looking up, stunned a bit, head towards the cave, feet towards the edge. Needles of ice beat the entire front of my body. I roll onto my belly and struggle to my knees, my eyes on the cave opening, the fire. Hands flat on the rock, I put one foot under me, then the other, and slowly straighten. Then I do something inexplicable. I turn around to look at the ravine's edge. I can't see it for the sleet. The world tilts and I am shot through with terror. My feet slide wildly as I try to turn back, they fly out from beneath me and my body, twisting and flailing, goes down. Again I'm on my back, but this time, my head is towards the abyss.

Lightning and a crash of thunder right above me, wind from all directions at once, sleet now mixed with snow, and I am slowly sliding towards the ravine. I scramble to turn myself around but can't get purchase and every move brings me closer to the edge, as if something wants me over and down and gone. I manage to roll onto my belly, spread my arms and legs and make movements like a bug on the surface of a pond. I *will not* be swept into the abyss. Not this day.

I crawl like this, belly to the rock, fingernails grasping at tiny cracks, toes pushing, until I am through the entrance. I don't try to stand until I'm completely inside, then I rush into my bed, shivering convulsively. I need the weight of the buffalo robe on me as much as I need the warmth. I curl up tight, sobbing.

I was sliding into the ravine. Perhaps, if the ravine, wanting a sacrifice, beckons again, I should go. Maybe that's why I'm here. I feel the sin in me, iron-hard, fist-shaped, just below my breast bone. It swells, crowding my lungs, my belly. A vicious legacy, like the curse of the House of Atreus. I also have the gift of violence. In violence, I had found a fundamental part of who I am and celebrated the discovery.

I was awakened by birdsong. The storm had passed and sunshine dazzled the ledge. I was about to get up, when Elizabeth appeared outside the cave opening, naked and made of light. I tried to call to her but no sound came. I couldn't lift my hand to greet her, nor lift my head to see her better. Just as I was forming words to speak, she smiled and disappeared.

I told myself, You were sleeping, it was a dream. But it wasn't exactly a dream. I'd been sleeping, yes, but then I heard the birds. I opened my eyes to see the light and its reflection on the wet stone. Then I saw her, then she left. The light remained brilliant but Elizabeth had gone. I'd been awake. She'd given no instructions. She'd smiled.

The sun was so warm on the wet rock that steam rose. The birds were ecstatic. I'd forgotten it was spring. I'd try again. I loaded the pipe, lit it with a stick from the fire, then, still naked, went outside, walked carefully to the middle of the ledge and stood still. I held out the pipe in front of me, reaching out, arms straight. In a moment, I lowered my arms.

I am a *wasichu*. I can't cleanse myself of who I am by offering Bright Eyes' tobacco in Bright Eyes' pipe to Bright Eyes' gods.

I looked towards the edge. The damn thing still pulled at me — some trickster spirit, amusing itself at my expense — but I wanted to look into the ravine, see what there was to see. I got down, put aside the pipe, and crawled forward. I lay on the rock, my feet reaching back towards the cave, my finger tips grasping the edge. The sun felt like a warm animal lying on my back. I slowly pulled myself until I could see down to the narrow river that ran through the valley, not nearly as far below as I'd imagined.

To the south, the valley widened into grasslands. Patches of snow gave way to green, gave way to a haze of colour. Wildflowers. I believe I was looking towards the westernmost part of the Powder River country through which Far Cry and I had traveled.

The sun shone down on the sparkling surface of the river and lit the fish as they swam. I know, I know, but I do believe I could see them — flashes of movement, a bright flick at the surface. A red-tailed hawk swooped past below me. And in the brush, creatures feeling my presence looked up. Nature in its perfection was observing me. I will never be good enough, but I can be better.

I inched back until I was in the centre of the ledge before I stood up. A rock caught my eye, small and pale, smooth as an egg. I picked it up. I picked up the pipe on my way back into the cave. My clothes were dry enough, so I dressed.

I figured it was just a bit past noon. Of what day? I'd lost track, but it didn't matter. Bright Eyes would come today or tomorrow. I'd stopped feeling hungry after the first day. There was enough wood. I sat in front of the fire and fed it from time to time, smoked Bright Eyes' tobacco without guilt. After all, I'd offered some to whatever gods might be pleased by it.

I settled myself. At some point, I looked down and saw that my hands had come to rest in my lap, holding one another. I felt a springing of love for my own two hands.

Then I heard the ponies coming up the path, and Bright Eyes called out a greeting.

CHAPTER 5

Back at the village, I was neither as hungry as I'd thought I might be, nor as tired. Bell never did ask me how it had been and I never spoke of it. Bright Eyes gave me a set of fresh clothing to put on, so I could wash what I'd been wearing. Smiling, she handed me a new pair of tall moccasins, beautifully beaded, that Bell told me were a gift. She'd done the beading.

There was drumming and singing that night, but I'm not sure what was being celebrated. Bell told me that in a bit, this group would move to a different camp. Very soon the pretty stream running past the tipis would become a roaring torrent from snow melt, nearly filling the narrow valley. Already, after only four days, it appeared quite a bit faster and wider than when I'd first seen it. These people would join with others in a more open place lower down the range.

A young Cheyenne who knew Bell from somewhere else had come to the camp while I was gone. He was related to the chief and to Bright Eyes, and he was very anxious to speak with me. Bell said he had many questions for 'the *wasichu* woman who came from the east, who'd lived with the Indians, who is wise and knows both worlds.' My mouth dropped and Bell made a subtle expression of amused sympathy. He'd translate for the boy, who appeared barely out of his teens. They came to my tipi and he, Bell and I ate some stew Bright Eyes had brought. As usual, she did not stop in one place, but went among the many cook fires, visiting, adding to the pots, taking a bite here and there, blessing the food and the people. The boy turned to look at me, smiled shyly, then spoke to Bell in a soft voice. From time to time, Bell asked him for what I assumed was clarification, the boy would respond and then continue. This went on for what felt like a long time. Finally Bell turned to me, took a deep breath, and told me what the boy wanted of me.

'He wants to know how many of you whites there are back in the east. More and more keep coming. He also wants to know how it is that you always have newer, better guns, many different kinds of guns, many of which are not for hunting, but are for killing people, especially for killing Indians. Indians cannot make guns, but have to bargain for them or steal them. Why is this? Did white leaders decide to keep this knowledge away from them? He knows you want all the land for yourselves, and not only the surface of it, but what's under the land as well, gold and other riches. The Indian is told he has to give up this land in exchange for things he doesn't want. If he doesn't agree to this, he will be killed. When the Indian agrees, you give only a small part of what was promised, and then kill the Indian anyway and take back the land. The buffalo are nearly all gone, and the Indians are forced to live on bad land. Their holy places are ruined. When they fight, as *anyone* would fight, you call them savages and punish them severely. He does not understand why all this is so, and he hopes that you can explain it.'

Bell looked briefly into my eyes, smiled inscrutably, then looked down, reached into his belt pouch and brought out tobacco and papers. He very intently watched his hands roll a cigarette. 'Good god', I said. The boy broke the silence, saying something else to Bell.

'He also wants to know how it is that you whites could build such a thing as a train, how you could even *imagine* such a thing, and the Indians could not.'

Bell continued to smile his damn smile as he worked in his

tobacco pouch. Was there anyone on earth who could answer these questions? I wondered if this boy had ever put the question to any of the wise ones of his people. As if she'd felt herself called, Bright Eyes walked up smiling. She joined us around the fire but would have no food, having eaten with others. She saw our grave faces and looked to Bell for an explanation. I asked him to tell her what the boy had wanted to know. I needed to know her answer as badly as the boy did. Bright Eyes listened carefully, then answered in one sentence. Bell translated.

'She told him we clash the way we do because our gods are so different.'

Bright Eyes and Bell smiled at one another. I marvelled at the elegance of her answer, the obvious truth of it. But it wasn't enough. The boy asked another question that seemed more urgent than the first. Bright Eyes' response, longer than the last, came without hesitation. Again, Bell translated.

'He wanted to know if a time would come when we whites would manage to kill all the Indians, and there would be no more. She told him such a thing could never happen. She said of the whites that our hatred, this evil, will turn against itself over and over again, and finally, after a long time, it will lose its power. She also said that all the Indians who had ever lived on this earth were still here. If you listen closely, she said, you will hear them singing. They will always be among us and new Indians are born every day. She told him they *must* stay alive, so they *will* stay alive. They will be strong again.'

Bright Eyes placed her hand on the crown of the boy's head as she left to go on about her rounds.

Days passed, I'm not sure how many. I ate heartily and slept well. I helped Bright Eyes and some of the other women with their work, enjoying the labor, enjoying their company. I sat at Bright Eyes' fire at night. When the women danced, I danced too. I liked the strong rhythms and the powerful way they used their voices.

I wanted to stay. I told Bell and he just cocked his head and looked at me. He didn't have to say it. I knew the danger this would bring them. Yet I still held a yearning for that life, and for the man who'd evoked in me such powerful love, a love that was beginning to feel like a story I'd been told a long time ago and that I was beginning to lose.

Then, on a warm and bright morning, as the people were packing their travois to move camp, Bell and I left for Laramie. As I was about to mount up, Bright Eyes emerged from the swirl of activity, and, smiling beatifically, took my face in her hands. She looked deep into my eyes for a long moment, then patted my cheek before she turned and went back to her people.

PART SIX

BEAUTIFUL SWIMMERS

Bell rode with me part way, but then turned off to head for Fort Laramie while I continued on to the house. It was late afternoon when I went over the small rise and saw William sitting on the porch with his guitar. He stood up. I waved so he'd know it was me and he turned, went into the house and shut the door. I rode up to the barn, took care of my horse, and then debated about going directly to see him or cleaning myself up first. I thought it would be better to see him right away and let him vent his anger. I'd been gone longer than I'd thought I'd be.

I knocked on the door. When he opened it, I saw the boys on their way upstairs. William, politely, coldly, invited me to sit. Maria brought glasses of water and asked if I wanted tea, I declined, trying to catch her eye, but she averted her gaze and went into the kitchen. We each had a sip of water, then sat back, and only then did William look me full in the face. I was dirty from the long trip, wearing my man's pants that badly needed a soaking wash, tucked into the rough, stained moccasins I'd gotten on the way west (I'd carefully packed the beautiful pair Bright Eyes had given me), and a calico shirt that was so faded and dirty it was hard to tell what the colours had been. There was dirt under my nails, I put my hands in my pockets to hide them, and felt the little rock from the ledge. My hands and forearms were grimy and I was sure my neck and face were similarly streaked. I stank. William's face was twisted in anger. I'd said I'd be gone about two weeks, it'd been longer. But I'd returned. Here I was. I'll apologise, I thought. That will have to be enough.

'Where is your eye-patch?'

I'd completely forgotten about it, not having felt the need with Bright Eyes and her people. They seemed not to notice the damage so much, or upon noticing it, forgot about it. William seemed offended that I'd apparently chosen not to shield him from it.

There was much else he could have said. I'd promised the boys I would write to them as soon as I got to New York and tell them all about the trains. I promised I'd bring presents from that city and other places where I stopped along the way. But I was empty handed and had no stories of trains. I could not tell William and his sons about my time in the Laramie hotel with Bell in search of oblivion, or why, instead of going east, I'd gone west. Could I tell them that a Cheyenne medicine woman had taken me to a high place where I'd stayed alone for four days, terrified of the darkness in my soul? Or that their mother had appeared before me naked as a newborn, shining with a rare and glorious light? I wanted them to know she was alive to me. I could *not* tell William and the boys that I'd not wanted to return to them, but had wanted to continue going deeper into Indian country.

But he needed to hear something, so, I cleaned it up. I said I'd missed the east-bound train and run into Bell. William narrowed his eyes at this and I wasn't sure why, I thought he'd gotten along with him. I said that, once there, at the station, I realised I was not ready to go back east. I needed to come to terms with my grief at the loss of Elizabeth and with the other losses that weighed on me. I needed to finally make a plan for my future and was sure that the distractions of New York City would not be conducive to this effort.

I said I had needed to go back to the Powder River valley and the foothills of the Big Horns, the name the whites gave to the Shining Mountains. I'd last been in that country when I was with the Lakota and remembered how beautiful it was. I'd paid Bell to guide me and for protection. I knew he'd respect my need for quiet. I told William I was very sorry that I'd disappointed him and the boys.

'*Disappointed* us? You were gone a long time with no word. We were all worried sick, damn it! It's turned June!'

I hadn't known. It was a bit of a shock. I apologised honestly and then begged his leave, saying that I needed to clean myself up, I felt bad about sitting on the furniture. He told me that he'd put wood in the cabin a bit ago, I'd have plenty to heat a few buckets-full of hot water. He also said that, coincidentally, just that morning, seeing the day would be fine, he'd opened the windows to air out the place. 'In case you decided to come back anytime soon.' I thanked him and left quickly. Shamed.

That evening, he knocked on my door. I'd washed and put on clean clothes. found an eye-patch, and quickly put it on so I'd not appear such a hideous gorgon. He'd brought a bottle of whiskey and a plate of the supper Maria had made. Peace offering, I'd assumed. Wrongly.

'She insisted I feed you.'

He put the dish on the table carelessly, it clattered against the wood. I got two glasses from the shelf and poured us each a stiff drink. I asked if he intended to stay standing. He sat. We tossed down the whiskey and I poured another. William cleared his throat.

'Someone at the fort told me you'd taken off with that Bell character. I didn't know what to think. Some say he's got a couple of Indian wives here and there and a whole bunch of children. I heard he steals guns from the Army and sells them cheap to Indians. Why on earth would you go off with someone like that? I'd thought better of you.'

I was affronted. Very much affronted.

'*Who the hell do you think you are!*'

I got up from the table, walked away, walked back, sat down, finished my drink, poured another and downed it. I took a deep breath. The surprise on his face pleased me.

I did feel sorry for the distress I'd caused the boys by being gone so long and said so again. Then I told him that whomever I chose to 'go off with', should I choose to do such a thing again, *which I might well do*, was none of his goddamn business. He finished his drink, and I poured us both another shot. He looked a bit chastened, and agreed that some of what he'd said might have been out of line.

'*Much* of what you said was dead wrong! Bell's a good man. You met him at the fort. I thought you liked him.'

'I did, but that was before I heard about the kind of man he is.'

'And you believe the shit you hear at the fort? He had a wife whom he dearly loved, a Cheyenne woman, and they had a daughter. Both his wife and the child were killed by drunken US soldiers who got clean away with it.'

A thing I'd always liked about William was that he could recognise the truth when he heard it, and was quite willing to change his mind accordingly. He was as transparent as his boys, and I could tell that he believed me and that he felt bad. He mumbled something to the effect that he'd not known this, that I was right, that he should not have believed the gossip, should have known better. He said he was *very* sorry.

I told him that Bell had a good many reasons to want to even out the matter of guns. I also told him that I thought — and I still hold to this — that if one good white man chooses to offset in some small way how the Indians are cheated over and over and over again by whites, even by stealing from whites to do it, I will salute that man. William simply nodded.

'Now, though I shouldn't have to do this, I will set you straight about my time with Bell. It's not what you were so obviously thinking.'

Of course I left out the part that was exactly what he'd been thinking. I said that Bell, seeing how I was suffering, had suggested that he take me to the Cheyenne camp in the Big Horns, the medicine woman there was his aunt, his late wife's mother's sister. I told him that she'd taken me to a place sacred to those people and left me there to fast, to smoke a ceremonial pipe she'd given me and to pray to the spirits for help. Elizabeth had come to me and wasn't that a wonderful thing.

He was so clearly uncomfortable, I stopped speaking and asked him what was troubling him.

'Sarah, I'd rather you don't tell the boys about this.'

'Why not?'

'Just please don't tell them. You *saw* their mother? No. This would be too hard for them. And about that Indian woman's pipe, and spirits, they don't need to hear this now. I'm reading to them from the Bible, like she used to do. I know you don't believe in God and that's your business. But *they* don't know this. I'm afraid all this would be... confusing.'

So, he was filling her place in their spiritual lives. Of course he would. My experience of *seeing* Elizabeth probably would be too much, I agreed with him there. It was almost too much for me. But I'd looked forward to showing the boys the pipe, telling them about

Bright Eyes, telling them something of the beauty of Lakota religion, how we're related to everything and other bits and pieces I'd gathered and that had enriched my life, but I would honour his request. Perhaps, he'd soften in time and those stories could come later. (He did, and they have.)

I poured us both another drink. Together, we had settled the air between us. We'd gotten drunk. We truly liked one another, in fact, we loved one another. We each took a few swallows and several deep breaths. I asked William how things were with the farm.

'*Farm?* This isn't a *farm!* We're a *ranch*, now, woman! I got big plans for this operation!'

We laughed. I ate a bit of Maria's good food and asked that my appreciation be conveyed. We talked. We nearly finished that bottle, which made us laugh. I told William to tell the boys that we'd resume lessons day after tomorrow in the late morning. They should be ready to read aloud to me some of whatever it was they'd most recently read and talk about it. We'd go on from there.

As he was leaving, William said, 'I'm truly sorry I spoke ill of your friend. I should have trusted you to be reasonable about the company you keep.'

I smiled. Good god, if he'd ever met Jake Byrd... Then he said, 'Welcome home, Sarah.'

The weeks leading into high summer rolled by fast, as they always seem to do. I suspended lessons after a bit, as William and Juan needed the boys' help, and the boys wanted increasingly to be outside with the men, moving their bodies in the good heat. Charlie especially. Joey would sometimes have to be called away from something he was drawing or painting. He could be obsessive about it, which I loved to see. They were intelligent and talented boys and were growing into good men. Like their father.

I grew increasingly fond of Maria. She, like Lizzie, had a lovely capacity for finding joy in small things. We added to Lizzie's garden with seeds from Mexico. I helped with some of the cooking. She, like Lizzie, loved to sing. She taught me a few songs and, mostly through them, a bit of Spanish. A very little bit.

I began to notice a growing warmth between Maria and William. I wondered if William missed not only the person of Lizzie, his dear love for so much of his life, but missed the presence of someone who loved him and took care of him, kept his home a sweet haven. I wondered if he missed the habits of loving. It seemed reasonable.

I made trips to the City of Laramie for mail and banking and an occasional meal in the hotel restaurant. Maria's cooking was far better, of course, but I liked sitting alone over a meal, watching people and eavesdropping on their conversations. When you put together fragments of talk, you can learn a lot about what people are thinking, you can get a sense of how things are shaping up. I didn't like what I was hearing.

'Damn redskins. Most of 'em is barely halter broke. Job ain't done yet.'

'Now's the time. Sioux don't have enough ammunition to fight off serious action.'

'They're saying "go easy" on the vermin. Quakers don't know shit about how it is out here.'

'We can beat 'em. Them Sioux, all them fucking Indians, no talent for tactics. I say take 'em down now!'

'You know what needs to happen, don't you.'

'Yes, sir. No question.'

CHAPTER 2

I've found that how we measure time doesn't necessarily have anything to do with how we live it.

You can move place to place, living fast and hard. There can be days and nights of being done to and doing to others in ways you'd never imagined. You can know a wild surfeit of joy and think, *Oh! This is Life!* And suddenly get axed down by despair, realise you've been a fool, and say, *Oh. This is Life.* And you're shocked to realise that all this happened in a single season.

Then, too, time can move like the water in the pond in Virginia where Ruth and I swam. So slow, it might as well have been still. It can be hard to keep track of what happened when.

So it was with the years leading up to The Event on the banks of that river the Indians called The Greasy Grass and the whites called The Little Big Horn.

I went to New York, as I'd planned to do, and then went south to visit Ruth. I left in September, but I'm not sure of the year. I think it was around 1872.

Ezekiel met me at the Grand Central station, a palatial train depot, and I almost didn't recognise him. He'd grown so tall and become so handsome. But that wasn't entirely it. His new situation had allowed him to become himself more fully, it showed in his posture and I heard it in his voice. Language rolled from him without the least stutter or hesitation. My brother had left that shy mulatto boy, and Virginia plantation life, way behind him.

His employer, Mr. Herzog, and his wife had a fine house in a part of the city called Union Square. We walked there from the station. The buildings! The shops! I was agape with amazement. Zeke laughed at me.

He had rooms on the very top floor of the house, fixed up for him by the Herzogs, that he was proud to show me. He had a bedroom that was small but certainly sufficient for one young man, but the main room was of a good size and filled with light from windows that looked out over a park. There were plush chairs and a couch, worn but inviting, small tables with lamps, and a long table at which he could have entertained several people for dinner under a chandelier.

But I did not get the impression that he'd served any dinners at this table. It was covered with books, some stacked, some opened to a particular section, sometimes held there with a weight such as an unopened ink bottle, or in one case, a small bronze sculpture. There were several notebooks, stacks of documents, many loose papers strewn about. I had imagined I'd take him to a bookstore, perhaps buy him some Greek myths or other stories. He was far beyond that. Far beyond me. My brother was a serious scholar.

After leaving my things in the room I was given, I expressed my desire to see a little more of the city, so Zeke took me for a walk. We wandered about in a nearby park — maybe part of the park we could see from his rooms, I don't remember — where there was a huge statue of George Washington on his horse. I watched for how my dark-skinned brother and I might be perceived, walking together. No one seemed to notice.

My visit would be short, three days or so. That first night, Zeke and I were invited to share a light supper with Mrs. Herzog, and she told me a dinner party was planned for the following night. I said I would have to go shopping in the morning, as I had nothing to wear that would be appropriate. She laughed and said that their dinner parties were far from fancy affairs, I should wear whatever was most comfortable. She mentioned that 'our mutual friend, Mr. Sands', was traveling and would be unable to join us for dinner, but would call on me the following day.

At the dinner party, the story of my time with the Indians was, as to be expected, of great interest, and once the ten or a dozen guests were assembled around the table, I was asked to tell it.

'Oh, yes!' 'Please do!' 'How fascinating!' 'We want to hear all about it!'

I had no idea how to to distill that story into something to tell as people were passing platters of potatoes and beef in gravy, vegetables and bread, and pouring wine into glasses. I don't remember what I said, but when I was done, everyone toasted my bravery. I was embarrassed. I'd never thought I was being 'brave', I was simply staying alive. Someone said I should write about the experience, I should lecture, I should do something with what I'd learned. I was utterly intimidated and could only stammer that I still had much to think about.

Everyone seemed free to express themselves and did so with verve, the women no less than the men, the young no less than the mature. Even the two girls helping Mrs. Herzog — white girls who spoke with accents; students, apparently — were often asked their opinion and gave it freely.

I knew nothing about most of what was being discussed. *Nothing.* One of the major topics was a set of laws called Enforcement Acts (I had to write this down later, so I wouldn't forget) intended to stop the Ku Klux Klan from keeping Negroes from voting, from working for pay, from generally participating in the rights and duties of citizens. Mr. Herzog and the others believed these new statutes, if properly enforced, would be effective in putting down that hideous organisation. Yet they seemed not to trust the states, especially the former Confederate states, to interpret them properly. This was the crux of it, and I remember thinking, *Yes, you're right not to trust the south.* I kept imagining the derisive laughter, the rude comments my father and his friends would make hearing this talk.

Zeke acquitted himself so impressively I was amazed, yet none of the others seemed to be. At one point he quoted language from the Bill of Rights (he announced this, otherwise I would not have known the source) and when he was done, all lifted their glasses, saying, 'Here! Here!' I noticed Mrs. Herzog watching me watch Ezekiel. There were tears in my eyes. We smiled at one another.

Someone quoted a man named Frederick Douglass who'd been born into slavery but had escaped and achieved an education and was, apparently, a brilliant thinker and orator. He lived in Washington, the District of Columbia. A woman at the table who'd not said much, entered the conversation in a strong voice.

'Mr. Douglass is undeniably admirable in his efforts regarding the rights of Negroes but he has also spoken a good deal about the rights of women. He's said he supports woman suffrage. But he has made enemies of both Elizabeth Stanton and Susan Anthony. He says they're mistaken in calling for the fight for women's suffrage to be linked with that of the black man's right to vote. He insists that the Negro's rights must come first. Well, I don't agree. It's one fight, as I see it. A fight for the rights of all citizens.'

General sounds of agreement. Then my brother spoke.

'You will not like to hear this, but I am of the opinion that those two women are not terribly interested in the plight of the Negro. And, I believe that class is overly important to them. They have said that an *educated* white woman is more qualified to choose our leaders than is *any* black man.'

The woman who'd spoken was apparently affronted and began to interrupt, but Zeke continued.

'Mr. Douglass argues that the persecution of people entirely on the basis of race must be attended to *now*, or the moment might pass. The violence perpetrated against Negros, and Negro men in particular, must be stopped. This *must* have precedence.'

All the guests at once looked to Mr. Herzog. He said that he agreed with Douglass and Ezekiel.

'If one's resources are limited, one must make hard decisions regarding how to spend them. Philosophically, yes, of course, this is one fight. But practically, we can only manage one battle at a time. Negroes are being killed simply for trying to live reasonably. Women will get the right to vote before long.'

My brother — I believe he was not quite fifteen, at the time — had more to say.

'When women do get the vote, that legislation must include black women, as well. Women like my mother. This must be guaranteed.'

'Nothing can be guaranteed in a war, Ezekiel, and our current situation is nothing less,' said Mr. Herzog, 'but you continue your studies, lad, and join that fight and I have no doubt that in time you will be on a dais with Mr. Douglass and he'll be endorsing your run for the legislature!'

More cheering and raising of glasses.

These people were having a wonderful time arguing with one another; I'd never witnessed anything like it. But throughout the discussion concerning when and how to get white women the vote and defend the rights of Negros, I kept thinking, *What about the Indian?* Why does no one speak to the wrongs being done the Indian? Surely they know. They must know. At one point I thought I should raise the matter, but was too insecure. I knew I'd be unable to answer intelligently all the questions they were certain to ask.

The conversation became more philosophical, the names Emerson and Walt Whitman were mentioned. I was asked if I knew them. I shook my head. Other writers and intellectuals were discussed. I was mortified by my ignorance. I decided that at the next opportunity I would ask my young half-brother for a list and I would go to a bookstore for myself.

Because I could quote a bit from Shakespeare and a few ancient Greeks and Romans, could speak a little French, I'd considered myself educated. I could play the piano forte, though not well, and could sing some art songs in my thin soprano. My parents' set had considered me *well* educated. What a laugh. As if I were a doll, they'd dressed me prettily and done up my hair, Mama had draped her pearls around my neck. She'd whisper, 'Sing the Scarlatti tonight.' My 'education' was nothing more than grooming for display before potential husbands.

The day after the dinner, I was indisposed. Possibly fatigued, I don't remember. I woke quite early and then returned to bed. I woke again in the late morning and someone had placed a pitcher of fresh water with lemon slices in it, and a plate of buttered bread on a table. There was also a card from Sands. He'd called on me earlier, but wrote that he'd call again at about two that afternoon and take me out for a stroll if I was so inclined. I was.

A steady drizzle did not deter us. We walked downtown under Sands' large black umbrella, going down one street after another, walking and talking until it began to get dark. Off a narrow street where the buildings were shabbier and the people more colourful, we went into a club. The place was small, dark, smokey, crowded and the atmosphere felt friendly. He said he liked the place for its lack of pretension and because he was treated well enough. They welcomed Jews. Many public places did not. Most didn't allow Negroes. Many were closed to women.

'They'd bar the cream of the city's intelligentsia, the fools! And the most attractive human specimens, as well.'

Here were whites, Negroes, mixed-blood people, women and men in different configurations at small tables, avidly engaged in conversation in a variety of accents. Sands said that late on most nights there was music. Sometimes Irish, sometimes Negro songs, 'or all of it together,' he said. 'People break out singing and dancing, it gets lively.'

We drank large goblets of a dark beer and were served some sort of sausage with it. I recall I got rather drunk rather quickly. Sands began to talk about my portfolio, an economic downturn was coming, I'd lose a bit of money. I was bored by this talk. I was thinking about the Indians.

'The Herzogs, and correct me if I'm wrong, with all their involvement with the Negro and with women's rights, do they give *any* thought to what's happening to the Indians? They should, you know. They could do something, speak to people in Washington.'

'They know. But resources must be husbanded and the Negro question is their primary concern. There are others haranguing Grant to de-fang Sheridan and Sherman, as if Grant isn't at the root of the matter. The Quakers are very active...'

'But they want assimilation of some sort.'

'Yes. They believe...'

'I know all about what they believe would be best for the Indians. But that's the *last* thing the Indians want. To be made to live like whites? To give up their ancestral lands? Their religion? *To farm?* Good god!'

'Which Indians are you referring to? From what I understand, some farm quite successfully, and live well enough on reservations.'

'"Well enough?" No one lives "well enough" on a reservation. Certainly not the Sioux and other plains tribes.'

'There may be no other way, Sarah.'

'There *must* be. Whites don't need the whole damn...'

'Have you heard the plans for the Northern Pacific Railroad?'

'Yes, I have. And it must not go where they intend to put it. They need to make a different plan. Game animals must be able to roam freely, and the Indians must be able to follow the game. Besides, what do we need with more trains? One line across the country should be enough.'

'Sarah. Dear girl. Listen. This is an industrial economy, a growing economy...'

'I know, I know. But there has to be a better solution.' Sands signalled for more beer. 'Why are they so powerfully hated?'

'You're asking *me* to explain the hatred of one race for another? My people have always been despised. We survive. We *assimilate.*'

'You're white, for one thing, and you don't threaten the progress of this "growing industrial economy". '

'Don't make speeches at me, Sarah. The Indian needs to adjust. Learn to live differently.'

'That's exactly what Elizabeth said. They must learn to live like whites. I *hate* this idea, it's wrong in so many ways...'

'I'll put it another way. They need to learn to live enough like whites so whites are less inclined to kill them. If they would move on to the reservations...'

'They'll starve. Most of the land carved out for reservations on the plains isn't farm land, you can't grow anything on it, and hunting is prohibited. And there are places holy to them that... Ah, goddamnit.'

I wasn't getting through, and the fault was mine. I was insufficiently educated, insufficiently connected to people who understood the underlying politics. But I understood the underlying hatred. None of this was to me any sort of abstraction to be tossed around in conversation. I took several large swallows of my beer. The taste was bitter, but I wanted to be more drunk.

'Sands, I'm not an intellectual or a speechmaker like the Herzogs and their friends. Like my half-brother. But please tell me how those people who care so much about injustice can put the Indians out of mind. They could fight for them. Those people who are fighting for the Negros, for women, for Jews...'

'No one cares about the Jews, my dear, except other Jews. We're on our own.'

We'd been talking across the table, practically butting one another in the head as the noise in the club had got quite loud. I looked around. Cheeks were ruddy, mouths wide in laughter, in spontaneous hoots and shouts. A fellow began to play the piano and sing, some people joined him.

'That's a Stephen Foster song. Foster sometimes played in clubs farther downtown, around Five Points. What a place that was! Minstrel sorts of songs. Very popular. Bad drunkard, though. Fell in his hotel room, broke the sink, they found him lying in a pool of blood, and...'

'Answer my question, Sands. Explain to me why people like the Herzogs can't make their arguments big enough to include the Indians. Why don't they gather the best minds together, put them in a room and tell them they have to solve this problem. Why can't this happen?'

'No *idea*, no policy conceived by a bunch of radical intellectuals in a closed room, or by anyone else, is going to make people who hate, stop hating. Especially haters in high places, who lust after the votes of large numbers of other people who hate. You're asking for rationality, my dear, and there is none to be found here.'

'But it's happening for the Negros. They were talking about a set of laws that recently passed, Acts of...'

'Enforcement Acts.'

'Yes! They're working to make things better for the Negro, *why not work at the same time for the Indian?* And don't roll your eyes at me! I will keep asking until I get an answer that makes sense.'

'Don't mistake good intentions or even good laws for victory. It'll be a *long* time before blacks are dealt with honourably in this country. Mostly people want all four million of them to go back to Africa. And the problems are not identical. The Indian's story of how the Indian must live in this country, and the white man's story of how the Indian must live are utterly irreconcilable. They intersect in a way that can only be bad for the Indian. That's simply how it is. It's bad luck.'

'*Bad luck?*'

'Yes. On a very large scale. To God, looking down at the sweep of it all, considering all the history of all the nations of the world, these people on this part of the earth, *at this time*, are not among the lucky.'

'So, are they just to fucking die?'

'That's melodramatic, Sarah...'

'Someone once told me it was a problem of different gods.'

'Isn't it always.'

The din was fantastic, now, and a few people were dancing, leaping up and down on chairs and tables. I heard the crash of glass breaking and a raucous burst of laughter.

'You leave tomorrow, to visit Ruth?'

'Yes. In mid-morning.'

'I'll come by earlier for coffee, I know the Herzogs will be home to see you off and I'll take you to your train. There are a couple of things to talk about. The economy may experience a bit of a hiccup in a couple of years and I have some suggestions. And I know Herzog has something to put to you having to do with Ezekiel. Oh, here. I got you some reading material when I was out this this morning. Zeke gave me a list. He's quite a fine boy, quite fine. Incredibly intelligent.'

He reached into a satchel he was carrying and pulled out a sack containing several books that he smacked down on the table one after the other. Walt Whitman's 'Leaves of Grass', two or three slim books by Ralph Waldo Emerson, something called the 'Bhagavad Gita' — 'Hindu stories, like your Greek stories, Emerson read them, you'll like them', Sands explained — stories by Alexander Pushkin, and a novel, 'Jane Eyre', by Charlotte Brontë.

'Read any of these?'

'No, I haven't. Thank you. Thank you very much.'

'You must *read*, Sarah. It's more important than having things to say at dinner parties. Don't make that face, there's no need to be embarrassed. You lived through a cultural cataclysm in the south, and another is shaping up in the west. You must read history. Philosophy. You must read and read and read.'

'The Indians might surprise you.'

'They can't *win*, if that's what you're thinking. They'll move onto those reservations and make the best of it or they'll die. Or a lot of them will. There are too many of us and most don't care one whit for honour. There has never been a time in the history of this world that some group of people was not intent on annihilating some other group of people whom they'd decided was inferior in order to justify getting them out of the way. But it's only rarely been entirely successful.'

'Good god! I wish you could sound a bit more optimistic.'

'But I am! I am! The Indian will survive, my dear, one way or another.'

Bright Eyes had said much the same thing. We stepped outside. The rain hadn't stopped and Sands was displeased.

'Let's get one of those Hansom cabs, it's too wet to walk.'

'We have your umbrella. Look how the lights reflect on the pavement. It's beautiful, this city. I want to get another look before I go.'

On the way to Grand Central the following day, I asked him what on earth he had been doing, working for my father. He shook his head.

'I was a junior clerk at a disreputable but effective — and very rich — Richmond firm. Your father's solicitor was embroiled with him in some criminal matter, but had an unfortunate accident. Someone killed him, as I recall, and I had to take over the case. It was only to be for a short time.'

But apparently my father soon discovered that the young man with the accent was smarter than any of the others and offered him a generous retainer to manage his accounts.

'There was only one reason I agreed. Well, two. I needed money as quickly as possible to bring the remnants of my family over. And the second reason was that I would be in a position to protect your mother, to create income for her of which your father would remain ignorant. She could go to Paris. Do whatever she wanted to do to escape. And yes, she was dying to escape that life. I so wish she'd found it in herself to do so.

'Her money, in addition to your father's, is now yours, and there's plenty of it. I'm good at what I do. I fucking hated your father. But I'd have done *anything* for your mother. I was devoted to Jane. I loved her.'

'Did she know?'

'She did not. Convey my warm wishes to Ruth.'

CHAPTER 3

She was standing on the ferry landing, a yellow dress swirling around her legs. Her hair was long and breeze-blown under a straw bonnet, her face was shining with joy. She came up to meet me with long strides, her arms flung wide to embrace me.

'You look a bit peaked, girl, let's get some food into you!'

Ruth showed me into the small cabin where I'd sleep — the owners, a young couple, were off somewhere and would be happy for me to stay in it. She was in a hurry to feed me, but I could not wait to tell her the substance of the conversation I'd had with Mr. Herzog and Sands before going to the train station.

'It's about Ezekiel, Ruth, you'll want to hear this. It is such good news.'

So we sat at the table while I told her that Mr. Herzog was so impressed with Ezekiel's intelligence and diligence as a scholar that he wanted to invest in him and would pay for his formal education. In a year or two, Mr. Herzog said he would have him at Harvard, his own alma mater, where he'd study law. He said he had the instincts of a fine solicitor and the industry to work hard. He had a fire in him to right wrongs. If he were ever to be so inclined, he would make a valuable legislator.

Mr. Herzog had said he'd be honoured to undertake this shaping of her son's future, if Ruth approved. The Herzogs had spoken about it with Ezekiel and he was eager to get started. Mr. Herzog told me he'd written a letter detailing it all but knowing that the mail can be slow, had counted on me to convey their ideas to Ruth. They'd make no plans until they heard from her.

Ruth pulled the letter from her pocket, said she'd just gotten it that morning. She handed it to me. It was signed by both Mr. Herzog and Zeke. Ruth said she'd taken her time reading it, had been pondering the thing, but that writing was harder than reading. I suggested that to save time, she could tell me her thoughts and I'd do the writing on her behalf.

'What would you like me to say to him?'

Ruth thought a moment before answering me.

'Tell him, Yes. Educate my boy. But tell him we don't want to be beholden to him in no way. He wants to do it, good. "Investment" he says? If my son wants to change his mind, do somethin' else, or wants free of this arrangement, well, that's the kind of thing can happen with a *investment*. My boy gotta be free in every way there is. Do you hear what I'm saying?'

I did. I wrote the letter and mailed it the following day.

My short time on Chincoteague with Ruth and her friends was mostly one long banquet.

This constant feast tended to take place at a long wooden table on the side porch of Ruth's uncle's store that was also a restaurant. He sold fish, his own catch and that of a few friends — his boat was docked just around the corner — dried beans, canned goods, flower, corn meal, tinned biscuits, hard candy, coffee, tea, I'm not sure what else. Ruth baked pies that were also for sale, and they were quite popular. 'Can't keep up with 'em!'

She'd said he was her uncle, his name was Arthur, I don't know if he was an actual relative or not. He was a widower and seemed sweet on Ruth, though when I mentioned it, she shook her head as if I were being ridiculous. It didn't take long for me to see that all the men seemed a bit sweet on her. But then, the women and children were also sweet on Ruth.

Somehow there always seemed to be enough chairs at dinner, and if another two or three were needed, someone would fetch them. The table always had a cloth on it and it always got spilled on and a new one always appeared. There'd be flowers on the table in jars or pitchers, cut from one of the beds that grew around most of the houses along the narrow dirt road. In the evenings someone would bring out a lamp or two.

Bright red tomatoes; green and yellow peppers; little brown potatoes; yellow corn on the cob, corn chowder, corn fritters; egg salad flecked with pale green celery and dill and sweet red pepper; greens of all sorts; Ruth's buttermilk biscuits. And the fruits of the sea, cooked outside in the yard, boiled in big pots, or battered and cooked in fat, or thrown in a hot pan, seared black and pulled right out again. Butter and lemon. Lots of salt.

'Sarah, remember when we couldn't get enough salt to make food taste right?'

'Your food was always delicious, Ruth.'

'Ah! G'wan, girl! See why I love this child?'

I was offered a platter full of crabs by the man who'd taken them from his traps that morning and cooked them right as we were eating.

'Are these the blue crabs you showed me earlier?'

'Yes'm, these are the ones. Wait till you taste 'em.'

'They've turned red!'

'That's how they do. College teacher was through here a couple o' years ago told me the Latin name for 'em. Can't remember it, but it means 'beautiful swimmers'. Beautiful swimmers! Don't you just love that?'

I did. They were delicious. And I loved the oysters. The raw ones shucked right then, platters and platters kept coming. They showed me to squeeze some lemon on them. I couldn't get enough. In one, there was a tiny pearl. A little girl came running up to see.

'Here,' I said, 'You can have it. It's pretty as you are.'

'No'm. You keep it. That happens all the time. Just wanted to see if it was BIG! It ain't.'

And off she ran to re-join her friends.

A gentle languor prevailed on those long, soft blue evenings. People stretched out their legs, tilting back their chairs. 'Son, you gwine ruin that chair for me.' 'Well, then I'll fix it for you.' A serving platter never stayed empty, more would get added to it, and people kept eating, though they slowed down a bit as it got later. Then a woman might appear with a big sweet potato pie. 'Oh, Lordy! I can't eat another bite!' 'They's some liquor in it, so y'all watch out!' 'Well, might as well have a taste...'

Children came and went and no one seemed to worry about where they were. I remember leaning over to Ruth to tell her how much Elizabeth would have loved this. She squeezed my hand.

Then between chair legs and children running, I saw her.

'Sally?' She stopped, turned her speckled face to see who it was, and came right up to me, wagging her long, feathered tail. I stroked her ears, then she ran back to be with the kids. The sweet girl that Zeke had rescued from the woods near the Virginia house, was now a happy island dog. I was glad to see her.

After a while, the children were put to bed and the mothers of the youngest ones said good night. Finally, it was Ruth, one or two of her women friends and me at the table with Arthur and a couple of men, one of whom would produce a jar of homemade spirits, strong and sharp.

The atmosphere on the island between the free Negros and the whites was polite, though separate. The papers were delivered regularly, and I think there might have been one printed on the island. But no one talked about what was going on, the continuing depredations against Negroes — the insane laws, the lynchings, the torturing, the murders — on the Virginia mainland and elsewhere in the south. No one talked about the Enforcement Acts, about the KKK. No one talked any kind of politics after dinner. Maybe it was because they wanted to keep things nice for Ruth's white guest, the daughter of the family that had owned her. Or maybe they'd just had enough and wanted to enjoy their evenings.

The night before my last full day on the island, right after supper, Ruth asked me to come to the cottage she shared with a widowed woman. She had me sit next to her on the bed, she reached under it and placed on my lap a parcel wrapped in tissue paper. I unfolded the paper and lifted out a lovely half-bonnet of golden straw with light green velvet ties. Then, from her pocket, she pulled something small, also wrapped in tissue. 'Now, don't you laugh', she said. It was an eyepatch made from the same soft linen as the yellow dress of hers I'd so admired.

'I thought you might be needin' somethin' pretty to wear on your head for church tomorrow. You'll want to come with me,' she said. 'We got a fine preacher, but it's the singin' draws people. We get people from all over the island come for the singin'. After, we'll have some coffee and sweet things like we always do, then we'll go to Arthur's. He's gonna let us use his little buggy. Where I want to take you, it's too far to walk. We'll take a picnic and set ourselves down and spend the afternoon. You gonna swim in the sea, girl.'

Ruth and I were among the first to arrive in the small, clapboard church. People poured into the pews, greeting one another as if they hadn't just been together not many hours before. They'd dressed up, it was Sunday and the sun was shining.

The preacher read from the Bible, and the reading brought

occasional murmurs in response. He prayed a long prayer, stretching out the vowels with the congregation coming in softly with *Mm Hm,* or, *Yes, yes,* and, *Hear us, Jesus.* The *Amen!* was said with gusto, to send the prayer on its way.

Women were fanning themselves. The preacher stood up straight, intoned a line and the congregation answered in unison — everyone knew this conversation — then another line and another response and another again until the whole congregation was moving, swaying, clapping, and shouting out, *Yes, Lord! Tell it, brother! Amen!*

The preacher danced down from the dais so he could get closer to the people. I was worried he might come to me, look at me strangely, wonder why I was there. I got over it quickly. His face was open and joyous as he sang out his exhortations and the congregation sang back their answers.

Soon the voices of the preacher and the congregation came together and people went into the aisles, dancing and singing and clapping. Someone had started playing an organ. Occasionally, one voice would rise above the others, a man or a woman, and people would say, *Oh, yes, my sister! Praise him, my brother!* I wanted to sing but didn't know the song until there was *Hallelujah!,* the word repeated with voices harmonising and taking off. That, I could do. Finally the last syllable made its way to a major chord that the congregation held out long enough for several voices to ornament until everyone agreed the thing had been accomplished and had came to its natural end.

During coffee in the preacher's small house next door, people came up to me and shook my sweaty hand, sometimes in both of their own sweaty hands, saying, 'Welcome!', and 'Wasn't this a fine service!' The preacher's wife had put out a nice spread. I was hungry, and would have stayed, but Ruth took my arm.

'We got someplace to go, girl, and you gonna want to spend *time* there.'

Ruth had an extra swimming costume that she lent me, bloomers and a shift, we put shawls over our shoulders and packed other clothes, though Ruth said it didn't really matter, no one was ever bothered much about how anybody else dressed as long as they were decent. She packed a basket with things to eat and a bottle of fresh water, and we walked over to Arthur's. He had the trap ready.

''Nother pretty day. You ladies been real lucky with weather.'

On the way, Ruth said, 'You liked our singin' and praisin', didn't you.'

'Oh! I liked it very much!'

I told her it sort of reminded me of the Indians' singing, how the spirit of it built upon itself. One of the women's voices was high, sometimes sounding like a baby's wail. I said I wondered if our first sounds were singing. I was warming to my subject when Ruth held up her hand and said I needed to be quiet.

'You gotta hush, now. Listen.'

The narrow road, more like a path, was strewn with pine straw, so the pony's hooves barely made a sound. I heard the wind in the reeds and marsh grass, and in the low, wind-bent pines along our way. The path stopped in a tangle of brush, so we got out and tied up the pony. 'Stand still now. *Listen.*' The wind. Birds. Then I became aware of a pulse, like the blood in my veins, the swoosh of a coming and going, coming and going. The sea.

I followed Ruth through some scrubby growth, the sound filling all the air around us now. Ahead, between the spindly trunks and branches of the stunted pines, I could see a gold strip and just above it, a line of blue. When we came out into the open, I ran to reach the top of a sand dune. And then I ran down to meet the sea.

As I write these words, I can still feel how it thrilled me to come near that great rolling blue body with the white foam where the waves broke, one wave after another, curling in a line and breaking into white froth, and how the froth rolled over and over, licking at the hard packed sand, and then rolled back again. As it had done forever.

I turned around to see Ruth smiling broadly at me.

'That's how I was when I first saw it.'

She'd spread a blanket on the sand, taken off her shoes, taken the pins out of her hair, shaken it loose, and was replacing her bonnet, a wide brimmed one. She'd lent me a similar bonnet and I could now see why. We were specks on a long, wide strip of sand and the sun came down on us directly and with force, as it came down on the sea where it glittered like hot diamonds.

'We're gonna walk out into it, up to where you can feel it take hold o' you. Ain't rough today, it's nice an' easy, nothin' to worry about. But if you want to come back up here and just look at it, that's fine.'

We walked into the lacy water at the edge. It was not cold, not as warm as the pond, but, oh, how I loved that effervescence on my feet and ankles. I wanted to go in deeper right away. Ruth held my arm, and looked up and down the beach.

'I'm usually alone here, families like the Bay side better, but I'm checkin'... No one. What you gotta do is to walk out with me 'til you're about waist deep, then scootch yourself down, slip off them bloomers and that shift and give 'em to me. It's a shame not to feel this water on your whole body. Anytime you wanna get out, wave and I'll come with a wrap. Swim around much as you want, but don't you forget for a single minute that *this*' — and she spread her arms to include the whole of the ocean — 'ain't like that pond. Respect it like it's God.'

After I gave Ruth my costume, I lowered myself so just my head was above water and paddled out a bit. I pushed up against the bottom to lift above a wave about to break over me, but missed the next one and got slapped in the face. I hooted with surprise and could hear Ruth laugh. I pulled the pins out of my hair and leaned back. I could float without much effort at all, but the waves kept washing over my face. I rolled over and swam out to where it looked smooth. Smooth it wasn't. Waves were gathering below the surface, this body was muscular, yet full of play. So I played.

I turned on my back and floated, looking up at the few small puffs of white cloud. I was carried towards the shore, bobbing on the surface, and when I reached where I could touch the bottom, I turned and dove into a wave and the next after that, each time rising like a sea creature, swimming further out. I turned and arched and coiled, twisting and curling, making shapes my body had never before made. Boundaries dissolved. This ocean knew me, yet I understood its absolute implacability.

When I was ready, I waved and Ruth brought out a blanket. I changed into the set of dry clothes I'd packed. I was glad she'd brought fresh water, I was thirsty, and there was a bite of lunch. As we finished the buttered biscuits stuffed with sliced cucumber, Ruth pointed out to sea.

'My mama came from somewhere over there. Her people, whoever they were, if there are any left, might still be there. I might have family in Africa. Ain't that something to think about.'

'I must have relatives across that water, too, in England and maybe elsewhere. I wish I'd asked more questions about who we were and where we'd come from.'

'Only ones didn't come from somewhere's else is your Indian husband's people.'

'Yes. And now...'

But I couldn't bring myself to talk about it. I was pleased that she'd referred to Far Cry as my 'Indian husband'.

Then she suggested I walk down the beach a ways, look for some shells to bring to the boys. She'd stay with our things. She was a better 'auntie' to these boys she'd never met than I was. A day or so earlier, she'd taken me to the home of an old white man on the island who carved and painted ducks, gulls, and other shore birds. They were exquisite in their detail. He'd also done some dolphins, a couple of ponies, and had one or two replicas of fishing boats. He was working on one such when we visited, but he was generous with his time, happy to show his work. I picked out several gifts for the boys.

I found a number of beautiful shells along that beach. A few I'd keep for myself, one beauty I planned to give to Maria, and the rest would be for the boys. 'Too bad we didn't see the wild ponies.' Ruth said that sometimes, in other places on the island, you'd see the descendants of horses escaped from wrecked Spanish galleons. 'Another time,' I said.

We sat for a bit in silence. The sun was getting low in the sky behind us and the colours were changing. The sand was a richer gold, the sea a deeper blue and the white froth topping the waves was gold-tinged. The few floating clouds were now pale gold, with here and there a brush of coral. The horizon looked as if it had been drawn in deep indigo straight across the visible world.

As we were watching, way out along that line, a huge silvery-white fish threw itself out of the water. It seemed to hang in the air a second, its body a perfect arch, and when it started down again, it turned gold before it disappeared. And then there was another. And another. And another. Four or five, at least.

On the way back in the buggy, I mentioned how the sight of those fish had moved me, and went on a bit about some sort of metaphor of hope. Ruth chuckled.

'And I was wondering how big was the thing that was chasin' 'em, to make 'em leap like that.'

Arthur and three of his friends, men whose company I'd enjoyed over many dinners drifting into late evenings of conversation, met me before dawn to take me to Richmond in the same sturdy conveyance in which I'd arrived on the island. They'd packed water and food — Ruth had seen to that, of course — and guns.

Ruth and I held one another a good long moment. I promised I'd come back at the first possible opportunity, and invited her to visit me, I'd pay her fare. She stroked my face.

I didn't really think Ruth would come west. She'd told me how blessed she felt having found a place where she feels safe for the first time in her life. Besides, though she never said so, and neither of them betrayed anything like this, I had a strong sense that she and Arthur were very close.

When I got back to the cabin, a telegram from Zeke was waiting for me in an envelope on my table. Arthur and his friends had left me at the train station and then, rather than stay over in Richmond, they'd decided to turn around and head right back to Chincoteague. They never made it. When it was clear to Ruth and others that something had happened, people went looking for them. The four had been hung and their bodies set on fire. The murderers had even shot the horses.

C H A P T E R   4

Summer, 1876. Charles and Joey were going to a school in Laramie. William had bought more land for his increasing cattle herd and occasionally had to hire extra hands. Yolanda, one of Juan's sisters, had come to live with him and Maria. Every now and then Yolanda and Maria would let me make a meal, but most often they ruled the kitchen and I was happy to let them. William had gotten to know Bell. They'd learned to respect one another and that had grown into friendship.

Bell brought a Danish friend named Theo Jensen, a talented woodworker, to meet William. While William's cabinet-making skills were impressive, Theo's were far better. The house — all the buildings — needed work, so he came by fairly frequently. Theo played flute, so when he visited, there was a new sound added to the music on the porch after dinner. Theo had lived in Cape Breton, Canada, for a while and could play the dance tunes of the place. William and Juan picked them up easily.

A small concern in Illinois had begun making wire with barbs, and William was among the first around Laramie to start using it. I hated this idea, knew how the Indians would see it, but he needed to keep his cattle contained. Besides, there hadn't been buffalo roaming in our part of Wyoming for some time. There were still some up in Montana and Dakota, and Indians were hunting them, but I knew, sorrowfully, this wouldn't last for long. South of us, hide men, a vicious lot, were fast killing off the southern herd, leaving rotting carcasses wherever they'd been. The bones were gathered up and put on trains to Chicago to be made into fertiliser.

The dying buffalo, the arguing over where the Indians could and couldn't hunt, impossible rules about where they had to live and how, the relentless flood of white settlers, the desecration of their holy places, the Army's continual raiding of their villages, all stoked the Indians' desperation and fury.

This fury had come to seem an end in itself, conceived in

Washington, and perpetrated by the Army. Attack an Indian camp and the Indians would retaliate. They'd attack settlers on the trail, burn down a house, cut telegraph lines, harass railroad workers. Then the whites would yell at their legislators. *See what they do? Want our vote? Protect us from these savages!* So the cavalry would mount up and raid an Indian village, kill a lot of innocent people, for which the Indians must then take revenge. And so it would go, on and on.

I'm not really sure what I did with my time, other than just live it. I was neither very happy nor very unhappy. I was in good company when I wanted to be, and I had plenty of time to myself. I read a great deal.

July fourth of 1876, America turned a hundred years old. I'd turned thirty that January.

A bit after the holiday, I thought I was asleep in my bed having a nightmare about people pounding at my door. Then I realised there was still some daylight and that I was lying in the dirt of the street, and someone was kicking me hard in the ribs. I heard Bell and Theo, 'Get the fuck away from her!' 'Swear to god I'll kill you!' I heard shots.

The next thing I remember is being in bed with a doctor turning me this way and that, wrapping bandages around my body.

'She's got some broken ribs but I'm pretty sure no lung's been punctured or anything else of importance. She's breathing fine. She needs to lie still for at least a week. Looks like she might have got knocked in the head, too. Either of you with her? Or know her people?'

Bell said he would ride to the house to tell William what had happened, and come right back the next day. He asked Theo if he'd stay with me until then. Theo said he would. The doctor gave me something he said would help me sleep. I recognised the taste of laudanum.

In the morning, Theo told me that, on a few occasions that night, I'd awakened and asked, 'Is he really dead?' Once assured this was the case, I'd go back to sleep, to do it again in a little while. But by the time Bell came back late the next day, I was fully awake and making sense. The doctor came to see how I was breathing. I was breathing, but everything hurt like hell. He asked if I wanted something for the pain and, though tempted, as I always am, I said I did not.

Bell said he'd told William the whole story, assured him and the boys that I was okay and would be back in about a week. William said to tell me he'd have the cabin ready for me whenever I came home. I did think I'd rather recover in my own bed, but Bell and Theo urged me not to rush things. The ride would be an unnecessary discomfort. I thought about it, and agreed. I could barely sit up. The hotel would be fine, they said I could pay them for the room and meals any time.

Bell said he wanted to ride out the following morning, visit some Indian friends who would be able to tell him more about what had happened. Again he asked if Theo would mind staying with me until he got back. Though I argued that it wasn't necessary, Theo said he'd be glad to. I thanked them both. Then I asked them why the hell I'd been attacked.

'You laughed,' Bell said.

As he and Theo told me the story, it began to come back.

I'd gone into Laramie for mail and to speak with the banker. I'd seen Bell and we'd decided to meet a bit later at the hotel restaurant, my usual place — then, briefly, his and mine — for an early supper. The place had gotten cleaner, the decorating more tasteful and the food better. The owners knew me pretty well, and I liked that familiarity.

When I left the bank, there were a lot of people walking in the same direction I was, some were running. As I got closer to the hotel, I could see people — mostly men — crowding around the door, leaning in, straining to see and hear what was going on.

The place looked packed, and, from the little I could see, everyone was facing a table more or less in the centre where a man was gesturing dramatically and talking in a loud voice. When I got a bit closer, I saw Bell and Theo standing outside. Theo had seen a crowd gathering, been curious, and found Bell already there.

'Custer's been killed in a fight with the Sioux,' said Bell, 'that man is reading the newspaper reports. It happened on the twenty-fifth of June, twelve days ago. He called it "a day of odious infamy", apparently the battlefield looked like "a slaughter pen", and he said we should never forget it.'

My mouth flew open wide, my fists were on their way above my head, I was about to whoop in exultation, but both Bell and Theo pulled my arms down, shaking their heads vigorously. Bell hissed in my ear, 'Don't be stupid.' I looked around me at the people who were staring at the reader, gulping in every syllable, and I saw shock and grief. But the strongest emotion, the one making the air in the room thick and ugly, was anger that seemed to be feeding on itself as I watched. A kid passed by the door with a tray of shots. We each grabbed two and tossed them down fast.

They told me he'd been reading from a big stack of papers for about fifteen minutes or so. Custer's 7th Cavalry had attacked a big encampment on the banks of the Little Big Horn, a river the Indians knew as the Greasy Grass. It seemed the Army hadn't surveilled adequately. They were met by about four thousand Indians, mostly Sioux. All the great chiefs were there, and Crazy Horse had led much of the action. Custer and all his men, about three-hundred or so, had been killed, their bodies stripped of clothing and mutilated, their weapons taken. The man read that it had been impossible to estimate the numbers of Indian dead.

I wanted badly to go inside, to hear better, get more details, but my friends wouldn't have it. The crowd was turning into a drunken mob. Just then, the man reading was interrupted by angry shouting. He held up his hand, waited a second, and then picked up where'd he'd left off. We leaned in a bit.

'"*Indians kept up galling fire until nightfall ... suffering was heartrending ... Forty-eight hours' fighting, no word from Custer ... twenty-four more hours ... officer rushes into camp ... found Custer, dead, stripped naked but he'd not been mutilated... seventeen commissioned officers killed, Mack Kellogg, the Bismarck Tribune correspondent, and 190 other men and scouts ... one Crow scout remained to tell the tale ... Custer was among the last who fell, but when his cheering voice was no longer heard...*"'

Another eruption of fury and grief. Some men were weeping openly. 'Fucking devils!' 'Savages!' 'A true hero! Murdered!' 'Best of 'em all!' 'Our finest!'

Bell put his hand on my shoulder. The reader continued.

'Listen to this from yesterday's Salt Lake paper: "*Citizens very much excited over the Custer massacre, and several offers have been made to the Secretary of War to raise a regiment of frontiersmen in ten days for Indian service…'*

The crowd took this as a call to action.

'Where do I sign up!' 'Yessir!' 'Let us at 'em!' 'Why wait, boys? Let's go hunting!'

The kid came by with more drinks.

'"…*the campaign as currently prosecuted is an utter failure, and there must follow a general Indian war…'*

'Goddamn right!' 'About fucking time!' 'Kill 'em!' 'Women and children, kill 'em!'

The reader went on, stoking what he'd stirred up. His audience was shaking with rage and so was I.

'"*The Sioux live by the chase and feed chiefly upon flesh…'"*

'Like fucking wolves!' 'Kill 'em all!' 'Revenge!' 'Revenge for Custer!'

Before they could stop me, I'd pushed my way in and shouted:

'*That arrogant bastard got what he deserved!'*

Oh, the roar! And rising out of it, someone in a filthy blue uniform stood up, pointed at me and shouted, 'I know that one-eyed bitch! Lives at Fort Laramie. *She was fucking Crazy Horse!'*

I was told later that I laughed very loud and hard at this. Bell and Theo grabbed me and got me outside, but they had to fight off a crowd of idiots who'd followed them.

Lying in the street, I looked up to see glaring down at me a ring of white masks of hatred. I'll never forget that sight. When it comes to mind, I think of Ruth and Ezekiel. Of Arthur and his friends. Of Sand Creek. The Washita. Of the Indian counting coup on the train. Of Far Cry. If I'd been an Indian or a Negro on the street that night, defaming their hero, they'd have ripped me apart.

When Bell came back, we all three went to William's house. We rode slowly, as I was still in a fair amount of pain. I was glad to get home, and everyone was glad to see I wasn't too badly hurt. After dinner, Bell asked if we wanted to hear some of the Indian side of the story. We did and moved out onto the porch. William brought out a bottle of whiskey, chairs were arranged, and Maria placed a pillow on a small table so I could put my legs up. She and Yolanda brought out trays with glasses and food. Charles and Joey were allowed to stay.

I was never entirely certain of how William felt about the Indians in general — there was definitely some ambivalence — so I was gratified that he'd thought it important that his sons hear what Bell had learned. They'd get an earful about it from their white friends.

CHAPTER 5

The night was warm. Not much breeze. Starry. We sat in quiet for a bit. Then from a good long distance away, we heard wolves. We all lifted our heads in that direction. I immediately thought of those men in Laramie. To malign the Indians as cruelly as possible, they called them wolves. Ranchers hate wolves, their wives are terrified of them. They feel the same way about Indians. When I hear wolves, something feral in me rises, the hairs on my neck prickle. Yet I love to hear them. While the Indians' customs and gods are quite different from ours, we are more alike than many care to admit. We're all wolves, in one way or another.

Bell rolled a cigarette for himself and one for me when I asked, and then offered around his tobacco pouch and papers. He briefly described the scene at the restaurant, leaving out details that the boys didn't need to hear.

'As Sarah and Theo can tell you, everyone in the place that day was saying — and you'll probably hear people say it now — the Indians camped along the Greasy Grass, the Little Big Horn, were getting ready to make war. Not true. It was a *big* camp, maybe twelve thousand people, maybe more, but it was whole families there, women and children, and it was set up where there were any number of easy places to ford. Not the way it'd be done if you were planning a battle. Besides, a big group of them were recovering from a bad fight back in March.

'Colonel Reynolds had attacked the camp of Chief Two Moons

of the Northern Cheyenne before dawn one day. These were *friend-lies*, they'd been about to head to the reservation, like they'd been ordered to do by January, but had just heard about it. Reynolds killed a lot of people and started burning all the tipis, destroying blankets and warm clothes, everything they'd put up for the winter.

'Well, those people turned *un*-friendly right fast. They put up a good fight and Reynolds retreated. But among the other dead were eleven Cheyenne babies who froze to death that night. So, Two Moons' people went up to Crazy Horse's camp, a few miles away, near the Greasy Grass. They were most definitely not looking for another fight any time soon.

'A good number of other tribes moved into the valley right around then and joined up with Crazy Horse, Sitting Bull, and other chiefs the Army calls "the wild Sioux". They'd refused to touch the pen to that '68 Treaty. The village along the river got bigger and bigger. But let me say again: *no one was planning to go to war.* The hunting was good and it was a good place for the people to be together for a while before moving on west, which was what they all wanted to do.

'But on June seventeenth, General Crook with about thirteen hundred men made camp along the banks of the Rosebud Creek, about a hundred miles east of the Greasy Grass village. He kept telling his scouts to go out, but they'd refuse, they'd seen too many signs. Finally, Crook had to force them. They came racing back, yelling, "Many Sioux! Many Sioux!"

'Crazy Horse was advancing on Crook's camp with maybe fifteen hundred warriors. He *played* with them, diverting them, dividing them, taunting them. Then he yelled, "Come on Lakotas, it's a good day to die!" What followed was ferocious fighting, a lot of it hand-to-hand, until about mid-afternoon when the Sioux just rode off. They said they were "tired and hungry". Crook decided not to go after Crazy Horse right then, he'd wait for reinforcements. None ever came. So, Crazy Horse's fighters kept him sitting there, firing at them, setting fire to the grass, harassing the horse and mule herds.

'Now listen to this. Sometime around the twentieth of June, the solstice, Sitting Bull woke up from a dream in which he'd been told that a vision was on its way to him. So he quick got together a sun dance, not far from the village. He had fifty pieces of flesh cut from his arms and another fifty from his chest and went into a trance. He had that vision. He saw blue-coated soldiers falling and falling out of the sky right down into their camp. Everyone was excited. Crazy Horse was still tormenting Reynolds' men, but this had to mean that a bigger fight was coming to them, and that the Indians would win.

'Now, how did Custer come into it? He'd lost his command but had recently got it back. Well, that "arrogant bastard" — as Sarah called him, and she's got good reason to, and she got beat up for it — was put in command of the largest Indian fighting force the US had ever brought together.'

Bell had a good voice for story-telling. I looked at the boys and their eyes were huge, waiting for what would come next. Custer was a hero. So was Crazy Horse. Bell continued.

'I think Custer had some kind of notion how things would go. You all know how he liked to ride into battle with his yellow hair flying? Well, the day before the fight, he had it all cut off, right down to his scalp. And instead of wearing his fancy blues with the stripes and all, he wore buckskins. It was like he didn't want to be seen.

'Now, the Indian camp was spread out along three or four miles down the west bank of the Greasy Grass. Sitting Bull's people, the Hunkpapas, a whole lot of them, were protecting the entrance to the north. Some Blackfeet were there, too. Then there were Mniconjous, Oglalas — Crazy Horse's people — then back a bit from the river were Brulés and Sans Arcs. Arapahoes, too. A big group of Cheyenne led by Two Moons and Gall held the southern end of the camp. All the greatest of the Indian leaders were there, and more than four-thousand warriors.

'But Custer had no idea, he couldn't see all this. The banks on the east side of the river are cut up into ridges with trees, deep ravines and thick brush, making it nearly impossible to see the other side. But the Indians could see them. The chiefs had decided to wait, see what the whites wanted. If it was talk, they'd talk. But if they wanted a fight, they'd get one.

'Well, as you know now, it was a fight. That whole battle lasted only about two hours on the afternoon of June twenty-fifth.'

Bell paused for a sip and a bite of pie. Then rolled a cigarette as he began to tell the rest of his story.

'It was hot that day, so people went swimming in the river, the water was good and cold. Crazy Horse was in swimming. Other people were just sitting around. Men were smoking and joking. Everyone had been up most of the night singing.

'Then suddenly, in the middle of the afternoon, there's gunfire and shouts. "*Soldiers are here! Soldiers!*" The Army had crossed the river down in the southern part of the village where the Cheyenne were, and were riding through the camp, shooting into tipis. Chief Gall's two wives got killed right away, along with their children.

'A lot of very angry Indians leapt on ponies and went after these soldiers. Crazy Horse took his time, doing his medicine, rubbing dust over his body and his horse's, painting a lightening bolt on his face. Some of his men were getting restless, but when he was ready, he was ready, and the fight was on. Women were doing the tremolo, people sang braveheart songs. Some women jumped on ponies and rode out with the men, singing and shouting taunts.

'Gunfire, powder and dust was so thick you could hardly see through it. Thousands of arrows were in the air. And flowers! They said plums and wild crabapples were in bloom and the petals were swirling around in all that dust and smoke.

'They attacked the soldiers as they tried to go back across the river and killed a good number of them. Their commander — the Indians didn't know who it was — and others made it back across the river and up a hill into the cover of trees. The Indians didn't go after them because people had seen another group of soldiers, a larger group, all on grey horses, up on a ridge across from the middle of the camp. These had tried to come down to cross the river but the bank was bad there, so they went back up. A bunch of Indians went after them, killing soldiers as they came to them. These men tried again to get down to the river but were chased back up.

'From then on it was up and down the steep hills, sometimes scrambling on foot, sometimes on horseback, with Indians pulling soldiers off their horses, stabbing them with knives, beating them with clubs. The fighting went in and out and around the bends on that side of the river, with Crazy Horse riding back and forth across the river urging his fighters to get in closer. It was hard to see or hear anything for the dust and gunfire, and the screaming of horses and men.

'At the end, the Indians said that the soldiers who were left knew they were going to die. A few had shot themselves, but most fought hard right to the end. One man said he'd always thought the whites were cowards but now he had more respect for them. Most hadn't tried to run, he said, but died where they'd knelt to shoot.

'The Indians went all over the hills and gullies, making sure all the white soldiers were dead. They took their guns and cartridges, took things from their pockets, tobacco, silver coins, whatever they found. They stripped them naked.

'Scalps were taken, at least one soldier lost half of his beard, too. And a lot of the men were cut up. People had lost relatives at Sand Creek, at the Washita, just recently at the Rosebud, and in other fights. Still a lot of the damage to those soldiers' bodies was from the close fighting.

'Because he didn't have his long hair, people weren't sure which body was Custer's. But whoever stripped off his clothes, found written notes and a map in his pockets, and so they thought he must be the chief, must be Custer, and should not be cut up. A Cheyenne woman told me someone she knew recognised him. He'd met him in a Cheyenne camp a while back as the lover of a girl named Monasetah, so he was sort of a relative. I don't know about that story, but for whatever reason, they didn't cut up his body. One other body was left alone. This man was wearing a medal on a chain around his neck. An Indian who'd been taught by priests knew it was a Lamb of God. Strong medicine, they decided, so no one bothered him either.

'Custer never made it into the river, he was killed pretty early in the fighting, on a little rise in a tight knot of men and grey horses.

'There was mourning in the Indian camp that night, they'd lost a fair number of people including many women and children, nobody yet knows how many. But louder than the lamenting, was the drumming and cheering and singing. It went on for a long time.

"So, that's it, friends. That's everything I could piece together from what people told me. More will come out and a lot of it'll be lies. There'll be all kinds of stories, now you'll know this one, too. But I believe these people, they're good people. I can't mention any of them by name, or even tell you what tribe they're from. Everyone's afraid of what might happen to them now, and I don't blame them. Whites are gonna want some terrible kind of revenge. There'll be no stopping them.'

The boys were quiet. Joey had his head in Maria's lap. Charles was looking out over the dark prairie. I was curious about their feelings.

'What do you two think of all this?'

Joey wanted to know about the horses. He asked why that one bunch of soldiers were all riding grey horses. Bell told him that Custer 'coloured' his horses, had different companies riding horses of different colours. Just to be fancy. This company rode greys.

William then figured the boys had had enough and sent them in to bed. But as they were on their way inside, Charles stopped, turned around, and looked at me with a serious expression.

'Why did you call him "arrogant bastard"?'

'Because he believed he could do whatever he wanted to do. He never considered the consequences of his actions, who would suffer as a result. He was a completely selfish man.'

'Do you think he was a bad man?'

'I think he did some bad things, Charlie.'

'But he was the one who rescued you and Mama from the Indians. That was a good thing.'

'Yes. It was a very good thing that your mother was able to come home to you. Most people have some good them, and some bad. We are complicated creatures, we humans.'

William put the period at the end of the sentence.

'Yes, we are. And you two are very tired people. It's been a long night. Bed! I'll be up in a bit to hear your prayers.'

They said their good nights and went in. Maria, Yolanda and Juan also said goodnight and walked up towards their house.

There was whiskey left in the bottle, so I poured another drink for the four of us: William, Bell, Theo and me. None of us had much to say. After a bit, William said good night and went into the house and closed the door after him.

So. He was dead. I remember wondering why I didn't feel more jubilant. I did feel some justice had been done.

'It's good they got him, and got him good. Such a victory has to have turned a corner in this war.'

Bell shook his head.

'No. They fought well. But nothing's changed.'

'How can that be?'

'Think about it, Sarah. Think about those men in Laramie. How could their hero get done in by a bunch of savages! That anger, fed by drink and hate and ugly talk, will foul the air in every saloon in the west. They're gonna tear down doors, all the way up to the White House. There will be reprisals.

'Besides, there's gold in Paha Sapa. Indian country up here in the northern plains is some of the best grazing land there is. There'll be more railroads, more roads. More and more of us whites are coming. The old men know this, have known it for a long time. Spotted Tail, Sitting Bull and Red Cloud have all been to Washington. Indians who have been east and seen the cities, the big buildings and everything lit up at night so bright you can't see the stars, those who have seen the vast numbers of us, know how things will end. Custer's dead. That's all. Nothing has changed. In fact, things will more than likely get worse.'

PART SEVEN

YOU WILL HEAR THEM SINGING

1877, August.

All the days and days of cooking were done and the wedding feast was being set out in William's house and on tables outside. Children had to be kept from the sweets. Cisneros family members had been in residence for about a week, most of them staying up in Juan's house. Other guests had begun to arrive in the morning, had been coming all day, and it was now mid-afternoon. Someone said there might be more, but I couldn't imagine who they'd be or where we'd put them. Both barns had become hotels and there were several tipis. Bell had arrived a few days earlier with some Cheyenne, four men, two of them with their wives. It did my heart good to see them.

But the guest whose presence most thrilled me was Ezekiel. I'd sent him a first class ticket but he'd been forced to ride third class (I assured him he'd ride more comfortably on the return trip). We'd both hoped that Ruth might come, and we'd both known that she would not. She was still in mourning for Arthur, whom she'd loved, and the others, and nothing had changed down south. She'd stay on the island, within sight and sound of the sea.

But *he* had come, and I was beyond happy to see his face when I met him at the train, a man of about twenty, a brilliant scholar, my brother. I was proud to introduce him to my other family. I looked down from the window at Juan's house where I was helping Maria get ready and saw him sitting on the ground with Theo, deeply involved in conversation.

People who'd brought instruments were tuning up. Many of these were part of the Cisneros contingent. They were excellent players of what was called *son Mexicano*. Just about every evening since their arrival, they'd joined William, Juan, and Theo on the porch to play. It was fine music. Today they were dressed in all white and had set chairs for themselves at far end of a large rectangular wooden platform, almost as broad as it was long, and it was quite long, that William and Juan had finished building the day before. I'd asked Juan if it was for dancing and he'd said, 'Sí! Claro que sí!', as if it was the silliest of all questions. A sort of trellis had been placed at one end, with flowers woven through ribbons and a rug laid down under it. Posts supported a frame around the entire thing from which hung lanterns for when it turned dark.

The Cheyenne had sung a song to ward off rain and it had worked. After several overcast days, not unusual for mid-August, this day had dawned pretty clear. There were a few clouds around but they didn't come together and the sun was rarely blocked for more than a minute or two.

The plan had been to have the ceremony at three, and it was almost four o'clock. The light was getting richer by the minute, the air moved gently. People were sitting on blankets clustered in front of the trellis. The priest in his vestments was turning the pages in a prayer book, Bell had met him in Laramie and convinced him to officiate. Children and a few dogs were running around.

Everyone was waiting for Maria.

Dressing her in the various layers, each of which had meaning that was cried and laughed over, had taken time. The pale yellow blouse with the full sleeves had been worn by her mother when she married her father. The many tiered green silk skirt had been made by her aunts, each of whom had contributed to the embroidery, and each motif had a story. The sash, deep red with long fringes, was pulled twice around her waist. Arranging her long thick hair had been a complicated affair, with the silver comb several generations old, and the white lace mantilla that had also seen a number of the family's brides to the altar. The shoes were Spanish, of soft white leather, from one of the aunts.

Once she was dressed, Maria and her two sisters and the sisters of her dead mother — Yolanda and two more of Juan's sisters and their husbands and children were down in William's house — came close and said a prayer for Maria's mother. Maria suddenly had a flare of regret that she was not to be married in a Catholic church in Mexico as her mother would have wanted. She turned to me, tears welling, repeating this in English. But the women assured her that this was a new life in a new world and that the missionary father seemed a perfectly pious man. One of them held up the *lazo*, the string of ribbon and flowers that would be looped around her and William as they repeated their vows, and they all laughed. She'd soon be quite thoroughly and suitably married.

I stood a bit back from these exchanges. Though Maria had asked me to be with her, an honour, and she translated much of what was said, and these women were more than lovely to me, I felt awkward. Yet I was glad to be with this beautiful, kind young woman who would be William's wife. I thought of Lizzie, of course. How could I not?

William had come to me before speaking to Juan or even to Maria. I'd watched their love deepen and in recent months had seen his face — both their faces — when they looked at one another. So when he knocked on my door that winter night and asked to come in, even though it was late and he was already 'a *tiny* bit drunk', for which I would not let him apologise, I pretty much knew why he'd come.

I put two glasses on the table, he'd brought the whiskey, and we sat across from one another in the arrangement that had seen so many conversations over our long friendship. I poured. He lifted the glass to his mouth, then put it down. He cleared his throat and took several deep breaths before saying what I'd known he would say. If he'd not been so terribly serious, I might have laughed.

'I want to marry that girl, Sarah. I want to marry Maria. I will, of course, ask for Juan's blessing, but I want your blessing too. I know you loved Lizzy and she loved you like a sister. She had a heart... I am having one *hell* of hard time finding the right words. Our love was... Damn it! For me to want to marry someone new...'

'Dear friend! Listen for a moment.'

I told him that of course I'd loved Lizzie, still did. We had, indeed, confided in one another as sisters do. I knew how much she loved him. She'd want him to be happy. And, of course, he had my unreserved blessing.

Then I asked why the hell it had taken him so long. We laughed, clinked our glasses and I said 'L'chaim' as Sands had taught me to do and I'd taught William. We were about to toss down the shot, but William paused.

'Sarah, I love Maria dearly, and so do the boys, and I've respected her... chastity, I hope that goes without saying, but I cannot get over a feeling of guilt. As if I'm... sinning against Lizzie. I loved her for so damn long, and when I married her, I vowed...'

'William! Stop! If I remember correctly, when you get married you promise to honour your husband or wife "till death us do part". Remember?'

'Ah! Yes, of course. That was the vow. And I *will* always love her. Always.'

Then before he had a chance to think about it any more, I said she was probably leaning over the edge of Heaven, looking down at him, shaking her head and laughing at how silly he's being. He nodded, said, 'Yes. She would be doing just that. That's my girl.'

So, we drank to what had been and to what was soon to come. To Life.

Maria had been about to walk out the door of Juan's house with her sisters and the aunts and me clustered beside and behind her when she put her hand to her throat and gasped. '*Dónde está?* Elizabeth's bird! *Dónde está!*' I knew what she was talking about, a tiny blue enamel bird, wings spread, that Lizzie had given her before she died. Maria was feeling around her neck and down her blouse, then she shook her skirts and was down on her knees feeling all around on the floor, crying, '*Debo encontrarlo! I must find it!*'

I walked up the stairs, looking in the corners of each step, examining the coils of the rug at the top of the stairs. As soon as I entered the room, I saw it on the floor. The ribbon must have come undone while they were fixing her hair. I called out that I'd found it and came quickly down the stairs.

As I tied it around her neck, I whispered into her ear, 'Lizzie loves you, dear girl. Be happy.'

William's hand had shook so that he couldn't put the ring on Maria's finger and she had to do it. They laughed, so did we, so did the priest. When he pronounced them married, William just stared at her and, again, Maria took over. She raised herself on her toes, took William's face and pulled it down to hers for a good strong kiss. We all clapped and cheered.

All that love made us hungry, so there was a rush of eating and drinking, talking and laughing, rising to get more food, moving to another group, introductions, helping one another to yet more food. There was so much food, of such different varieties, and all of us were greedy for more and more of that good food and, most especially, the good will that came with it.

The sun went down, and as soon as the lanterns were lit, the players from the Cisneros clan began a waltz. The accordion player was inspired. They all were. Maria pulled William onto the platform. He held to her so tightly, they couldn't do a proper waltz — I remembered Lizzie speaking of William's shyness on the dance floor — so several other couples joined them and soon the floor was swirling with dancers. Theo asked if I could waltz, I said I could, so I danced that lovely dance for the first time in many, many years, with this man who'd become a dear friend. He danced well.

We turned round and round in the lanterns' light. Skin glowed, eyes were bright. Juan had joined the *son* players with his guitar, and the next time we passed by, I saw that William had picked up his fiddle. Another kind of music started, fast music. One of the Cheyenne had a drum and a Cisneros brother urged him to join them. The heartbeat of the music got stronger. Theo and I sat down. Zeke joined us and after a bit, Theo went to get us some punch.

Zeke was shouting, we were close to the music and it was loud, trying to tell me I should read Kant. 'Who?' '*KANT!*' He and Theo, who'd read him at university in Copenhagen, had been talking about his work. 'You'd like him,' he yelled, and he was about to try to tell me why, when I was distracted by a new sound in the music. Theo had joined the musicians and was playing clarinet, a rare thing. He usually played his flute, mostly tunes from Cape Breton where he'd lived several years.

He'd come from within what the others were doing, twining around their melodies, harmonising, and then he'd taken off on a wild, high-flying descant, his horn sounding like a human voice. The others followed and the players taunted one another with dissonance then joyful resolutions followed by another tease, then all the players would somehow agree on something and rise together, higher and richer. It was lusty music, everyone was in motion. Zeke clapped his hands in amazement. 'I've heard that music! Sands took me, it's a kind of Jewish music! Where'd he learn this?' I had no idea. Theo had been everywhere and learned the music in all those places.

The dancing changed, people couldn't help themselves. No more couples, no more doing steps, they took hands and made a circle that grew and spiralled. Children came to the centre and leaped up and down. One of the Cisneros women stood and curled her strong voice around Theo's clarinet, and the Cheyenne added their voices. Were there words? I don't recall. Yolanda passed by me and reached out, I took her hand, grabbed my brother's and pulled him onto the dancing floor. We were all singing, laughing, and dancing in a way that I imagine we humans have always danced, it came so naturally.

Much, much later that night, I looked around. The newly married pair had disappeared. Juan and some of the musicians remained, playing softly as they talked, a little drunk. Yolanda and other women were clearing up, but they weren't in a hurry about it. A few people were sitting here and there in quiet conversation. Zeke was with Bell and one of the Cheyenne, engaged in a serious discussion. A few people had fallen asleep on the ground. Theo and I were lying on the blanket I'd brought.

We were a bit removed from where the party had been, and were looking at the stars — two had shot across the dark field of the sky as we watched and we were hoping for more. We were holding hands. It was the only intimacy I'd allowed myself with him, though we known each other for a few years. We were always glad to see one another, and our pleasure in these accidental meetings had increased.

He kept a room in Laramie, but came often to work with William and Juan outside and inside the houses, the barns, and various outbuildings, often staying a few weeks. He'd built me an armoire and a beautiful book shelf, and he'd rearranged things in the wall that was my 'kitchen' and put in a window. When he was here at the *ranch*, as William laughingly insisted we now call the farm, he'd sleep in the barn. We'd all eat meals together, and nearly always afterward, there'd be music. Often he'd walk me to my cabin. Often, he'd reach for my hand. I'd give it, and then I'd take it back when we approached my door.

The stars seemed to have stopped flying, a waxing half-moon had risen. We got up. He took the leather case in which he carried his instruments, and I folded the blanket under my arm. Only those who'd decided to sleep outside remained. We walked slowly to my cabin. I don't recall if we spoke, I think we did not. There were fire-flies down in the hollow by the stream. We sat on my porch for a bit, listening to the song of some nightbird neither of us knew the name of. I said I'd get us some whiskey and he followed me into the cabin. I was about to light the lantern when he turned me to face him. The moon reached in through the window he'd built for me, touching both our faces.

He gently pulled down my eyepatch and kissed my ruined, naked eye.

CHAPTER 2

The year before Maria and William got married, when we were sitting on William's porch listening to Bell tell us what he'd learned from several Indians who'd fought at the Greasy Grass and participated in Custer's defeat, I'd said that such a victory ought to turn things around for them. Bell had said he expected things to get worse. As usual, he was right.

Months before the wedding, in February of '77, the US government took the Black Hills, Paha Sapa, perhaps the Sioux's holiest place. They were told to turn it over or starve. Spotted Tail, Red Cloud and the other reservation chiefs had no choice. The remaining 'wild Sioux', those who had refused to sign the '68 treaty, those powerful men and their people, were being hunted mercilessly. Sitting Bull escaped to Canada with more than three hundred people sometime in early May of '77.

Right around the same time, on May sixth, Crazy Horse, the deeply admired Oglala Lakota chief, surrendered at Fort Robinson. But he did so riding at the head of eight hundred people, his men armed and in full war regalia. I can see this clearly, hear their horses' hooves. It was said they were singing, and I wish I'd been there to watch them pass and do the tremolo for them. General Crook had lured him in with the promise of a reservation in the Powder River country, on the Tongue River, exclusively for him and his people.

Crook *might* actually have intended to do this, he might have *wanted* to do this. Crazy Horse had driven him back in the battle at the Rosebud a month or so before Custer's defeat and Crook respected him, one military leader to another. But Washington was not going to hand this famous war chief any gifts. Crazy Horse and his men were quickly disarmed and they set up camp near what is now called the Pine Ridge Agency.

During William and Maria's wedding, Bell had come up to me and we spoke briefly about these events. He said word was that Crazy Horse was being treated pretty deferentially. He saw me sigh in relief and said this had its difficult aspects. A few prominent Indians were not just a little envious that Crazy Horse was being doted on as if he were some sort of hero — which, of course, he was to many — while they were being generally ignored. I wondered who was talking about him in this way, and he said that Spotted Tail and Red Cloud had been mentioned.

This surprised and disappointed me, but at that moment I could not think about what it might mean. I didn't *want* to think about it then. I wanted to revel in my dear friends' joy, in the music and the dancing, in everything about The Night of the Shooting Stars, the name Theo and I later gave to that night when we first slept together, when we realised we were in love and had been for a while.

Neither did I think about Crazy Horse the following day. Beginning early in the morning, Theo and I began to draw plans on scraps of paper. We would make the cabin into a real house, still small but a house to accommodate our two lives. We'd build a second story, and planned how we'd rearrange the first. Theo went to work on it with the help of Juan and William when they could spare the time, and he hired men in Laramie when they couldn't.

Things happened pretty fast. I bought a new bed. Theo built good sized work tables for each of us that went in what had been my bedroom downstairs. He lined most of the walls down there with shelves. I told him to leave room for paintings. 'We don't have any,' he said, 'just that one.' He meant the Corot I'd brought from Virginia. I told him I intended to buy more.

In mid-September, Theo and William had gone to Laramie for building supplies and paint, other needed items. While there, they'd heard some bad news.

Bell had spoken of the possibility that Crazy Horse's elevated status might cause some problems. Rumours had spread that he was planning to escape. When he was questioned, a stupid mis-translation made Crook fear that Crazy Horse planned to kill him. He ordered him arrested and taken back to Fort Robinson, and then Crook had business elsewhere. I suspect he knew what was coming and didn't want to get caught up in it. Coward.

When Crazy Horse realised he was about to be put in the guard house, he struggled to break away from the soldiers holding him. One of his own people, Little Big Man, grabbed and held him and a soldier stabbed him in the back with his bayonet. Crazy Horse died around midnight of September fifth, 1877.

When Theo told me, I felt as if I'd been struck in the gut and had to sit down.

'I had a feeling this would hit you hard. Did you know him?'

'No. I never met him. But Far Cry admired him very much. All the Indians I knew admired him. He was a true hero. And a *good* man. Not like that yellow-haired fucker...'

I couldn't talk any more. I got up and silently resumed what I'd been doing when he came in. It was getting on towards evening,

Theo said he'd put together something for us to eat. I told him to first pour us a drink. He did, and brought mine to me. I was putting my books on the shelves he'd built, and among them, my talismans — Bright Eyes' pipe, shells from Chincoteague, the egg-shaped rock that had called to me from the ledge in the Shining Mountains, a couple of Joey's small paintings that I'd framed with twigs, a poem of Charles', other things I'd gathered over time, the way a crow gathers pretty things.

'I got paint today for those shelves, why don't you wait...'

'No. I want to put these things in place now. Don't paint anything. Leave it all raw. Like it is.'

I could not help imagining how Far Cry would have received this news. I wondered if he was alive, and if so, what hearing of this death would do to him. I hoped he was dead. Or, if he wasn't, I hoped he'd long since gathered up whoever was with him and taken them to Canada. I hoped he'd never hear of it. I hoped he closed his ears to any news of the horrors the *wasichu* continued to heap on his people down in the territories and states. I entertained fantasies of him living the old life in some remote, Arcadian paradise rich in game. I knew how stupid this was. All the good ones were dead or dying, or they'd given up. Finally I broke down, and Theo came to hold me.

I told him I wanted to leave the country. The weather was good, and between us, we had enough money to go and stay gone for a while. He looked around at the unfinished work, I knew he didn't want to leave right then, but he said yes. We were ready in about a week. Before closing up the cabin, I took the spirit pouch from around my neck and put it in the little box William had made for me the first Christmas I'd spent with him and Elizabeth. The deerskin had become too fragile, the beadwork was fraying. I didn't want to lose it.

William took us to the train station. We were gone for about five years.

C H A P T E R   3

First we went to Copenhagen to meet Theo's family. They all looked like him — tall, handsome, fair-haired people. Most of the men were merchant seamen. Others, including many of the women, were scholars or artists of different sorts. He hadn't seen them in a long time and they were thrilled to have him back. They were friendly and welcoming, yet I could not wait to be on the move again. The dislocation of travel suited me, and this long journey promised several journeys, by land and rivers and sea.

We made our way down through the heart of Old Europe to the Black Sea, then through the Dardanelles — our ship passed where Troy had flourished and was then sacked by the Greeks, as Homer told it in 'The Iliad' — and into the Aegean. We island hopped our way to the mainland of Greece. That landscape seemed as familiar to me as if I'd lived there, though I only knew it through its writers and artists. I could admire the culture yet feel no responsibility for it. We stayed for a couple of years in the Peloponnese, then sailed to Crete. We lived in Rethymno, a beautiful old port town on the northern coast, for another couple of years.

Theo found musicians, as he always does, and was learning to play new instruments. He began composing. He'd written a bit of music now and then, but never seriously. It was good to sit on our balcony, watching the light change on the Aegean, and listen to the music grow phrase by graceful phrase. I loved him for this gift, and for the hard work he gave to it. I was a bit envious of it. I wrote poems and threw them away, sketched in a pad, and threw those pages away as well. Though I often liked doing these things, just for the sake of *doing,* nothing was quite good enough. I was in a more or less constant state of dissatisfaction with myself. One thing alone brought relief. Whenever I felt the need, I swam in the sea.

One morning, drinking coffee and looking out to sea, we both understood it was time to return. We stayed with the Herzog's and visited with my dear, brilliant Ezekiel when we arrived in New York. He told me Ruth was feeling her age. She was only about forty-five, but Zeke said she was plagued with rheumatism and had some lung problems. He also suspected she wasn't very happy, although, of course, she never complained. I was tempted to go down and spend time with her, but Theo and I both wanted to get back to the west. We both needed to be home.

Nevertheless, we stayed a bit longer than anticipated in New York City. I'd been feeling half-sick on the trip, and we took advantage of the Herzog's generous hospitality to rest a bit. I'd wondered if I was pregnant, but wasn't, and was relieved. Theo, to my surprise, was a bit disappointed, but we agreed that we did not want to bring a child into the world as it was then.

Mr. Herzog knew a good surgeon and suggested I see him about possible removal of my eye. The man examined me, a procedure I didn't care for one bit, and was rather excited about the prospect of a glass eye for me to be made by a colleague in Germany. I'd have to live at the Herzog's place for several weeks at least — for fittings and check-ups and such — and there would be some pain after the surgery. When I asked how long I could expect the pain to continue, he couldn't tell me. Some people stay in pain, he said, but the look of the beautiful new eye compensates. When I asked what would happen if I just let things be, he shrugged.

I said no thank you. I'd get myself a beautiful new eyepatch. I'd get several. I like my patch. When I go out among strangers, it makes makes me feel safe in an odd way.

We listened to music played by the New York Philharmonic Symphony Orchestra. I can't remember what we heard, but the effect of sitting in the middle of all that sound was astonishing. Theo said we had to make a point of coming to New York to listen to music at least once a year, more often, if possible. He wanted to meet and get to know composers, conductors, players. I agreed heartily.

In a gallery with which Mrs. Herzog was connected, I bought a painting by an American artist named Winslow Homer. Theo teased me about the man's name, saying that was the attraction. But the image was two young women, their hair and clothing blowing in a stiff wind, that reminded me of Elizabeth and myself when we were young.

We arrived home — I believe it was the spring of 1883 or '84 — to a new family member. William and Maria had named their little girl Elizabeth Angelita, Angelita being Maria's mother's name. She was a bright three-year old with Maria's dark hair and William's blue eyes, a wild little thing running barefoot outside all day. My daughter would have been about sixteen.

Yolanda had never gone back to Mexico, she shared Juan's house with him, so was able to give Maria help and companionship during the pregnancy. It was a good thing. Maria had carried an earlier baby, a boy, through about six very difficult months and then lost him. They buried him up under the cottonwood tree, now tall and leafy, above the barn. William had put a wooden fence, painted white, around this graveyard. He left room, 'for the rest of us to lie down when we get good and ready.'

Theo resumed his old rhythms, rearranged to include his new passion for writing music. We continued to work on the house and I helped Maria in the vegetable garden we shared. I'd told Theo about Mama's roses, and one summer, he planted some for me. He somehow made them flourish when so many had said they'd not do well in Wyoming.

He could wrangle and train horses, play a number of different instruments and compose all kinds of music, build houses and do fine carpentry. He was well educated, widely read, a lovely conversationalist, a kind and generous friend. He could make roses grow. I asked him once if there was anything he could *not* do. He thought a moment, a serious expression on his face.

'You forgot to mention that I am a superb lover.'

'I have to admit that you're not bad.'

'Then, no. There is nothing I cannot do. So you'd best treat me with proper respect.'

I may have thrown something at him.

The ranch was growing and Charles had come home from university in Columbia, Missouri, to help William run it. He and his brother sort of crossed one another in their coming and going. Joey went to New York to study painting at a school called The Art Students League. He wanted to live in Paris, continue his studies there. My finances were in good shape, thanks to Sands' talents, and the fact that, aside from our magnificent journey back in the late seventies, early eighties, Theo and I lived simply. He'd come into some family money that he added to our pot. We invested in the ranch on a regular basis — not caring how the funds were used; this was William's affair — and I planned to set Joey up in Paris.

For my birthday one year, Theo and William gave me an upright pianoforte made by Steinway and Sons in New York. Theo said they were the masters. It arrived by train, and to get it from the station, finally, into our house was a great effort. I did not have the heart or guts to confess that I'd forgotten most of what I'd learned and that hadn't been all that much, but I suspected the instrument was as much for him as for me. It didn't matter. I loved having it in the house, hearing him working out an melody on it. And I began to learn all over again how to play. It gave me more pleasure than I'd anticipated.

We started dealing in quarter horses. One of Theo's musical compositions won a prize. We traveled to New York from time to time. We got a dog. Part wolf, or so we liked to think. From a head-strong pup, she grew into an extraordinary dog, one of the best I've ever known. We appeared to be people who'd made a good life and were living it fully. This was mostly true.

But, often, it seemed to me that this 'good life' had been painted on a canvas behind which was a very different truth. I was not at ease. I was waiting, but could not say for what. My predilection for dire imaginings, for which I was roundly teased by both Theo and William, had plenty to back it up, past and present, but I mostly kept my sense of foreboding to myself. I thought it interesting that the men teased me, while Maria and Yolanda took me seriously. They felt it, too. Women often feel currents in life that men can't.

Sitting Bull had started performing with Buffalo Bill's Wild West Show sometime in 1885. *Sitting Bull!* One of the 'wild Sioux'. The man who'd had a vision of blue-coats falling into his camp before the battle with Custer, this famous war-chief, was living on the Standing Rock Reservation and was performing in a goddamn circus. What the hell is one to think of that! But Theo said, 'How else is he to live?' Yes, of course, how else, in these hideous times. He had people to feed.

One prevails, if one can, often in defiance of the odds, and the odds against the Indians were getting worse and worse. The government's degradations were relentless. Over a couple of years, through the passing of a handful of rotten laws and the coercion to sign yet another fucking treaty, the large Sioux reservation — bad enough as it had been — was broken into small pieces. The US government believed the Indian could only be turned into a true American by owning and having responsibility for a piece of land, working it, making it produce according to the government's terms. The rest of the reservation, land that the Sioux had been told in 1868 would forever belong to them alone, was opened up to settlers. This was in 1889.

We were killing them bite by bite by bite.

One morning, in the early fall of 1890, after not seeing him for a long time, Bell surprised us, calling out, 'Hello, the house!' He'd been spending most of his time with a group of Cheyenne up in the mountains, near where I'd met Bright Eyes and her people. She'd gone to Canada with a small bunch not long ago. In an odd coincidence, when Bell came, I was painting designs on the pipe she'd given me.

Sitting next to him in his buggy was a young Indian woman whom he introduced as his wife. I forget her name. She was Cheyenne, very pretty, visibly pregnant, quite shy. She spoke only a little English. They'd been to Laramie for supplies and had wanted to say goodbye to us before leaving the country. He'd brought some venison and hoped to feast one last time with me and Theo, William, Maria and Anglelita, Juan, Yolanda, whomever else was about.

Maria, Yolanda and I cooked. It was a fine feast. Afterwards, we moved outside to the porch. Angelita took Bell's wife by the hand, she wanted to bring her to one of the barns to see twin calves that had recently been born. Bell rolled cigarettes as he spoke in his low voice.

Things were bad. The Indians on the reservations were hungry and sick. Hunting was prohibited — those who ignored this and went out found hardly any game — and the annuities they'd been promised were nearly always late and usually short. People were dying. He repeated: 'They are *dying*.' None of this came as a surprise, it had been like this for a while. But there was now a bizarre addition to this story.

A new religion was coursing through Indian country like a contagion. A Paiute had started it. This man, Wovoka, who called himself a messiah, said he'd come down to earth to bring back to life all the Indians killed by the *wasichus* from the time of their first arrival to the present day. And he'd bring back all the dead buffalo, so the plains would be thick with them again, the people would hear their thundering hooves and ride out to hunt them.

While he was at it, he'd cause all the whites who were in Indian country now to be killed, and no more would come from the east. The Indians would rise to their former glory, once again they'd live the life of their fathers and grandfathers. He mixed the old religion with the new one, brought by missionaries. According to some who claimed they'd met him, he showed them wounds in his hands and feet. He'd been crucified, he claimed, and had risen like Jesus. They said he'd performed miracles.

'He's teaching people a dance they have to do until they fall, five nights in a row. They chant songs, go into trances and talk with dead relatives. He tells them that the more often they do this "Ghost Dance", as he calls it, the sooner their dead and the buffalo will come back. It's happening on a lot of reservations, many different tribes. I'm told that thousands of Indians are doing it. *Thousands*. Sioux are wearing Ghost Shirts that are supposed to protect them from bullets fired by any white man's gun. And I just heard that Red Cloud gave this new religion his blessing. Poor, good old fool. He's old as Moses now, but still respected. The Army's just waiting for a reason.

'So we're getting out of this country, my friends. Something is going to tip over any day now and all hell's going to break loose. I don't want her to see it, she's been through enough. And I don't want our baby getting born in the middle of it. We're going to Canada.'

They slept in the barn that night and we saw them off in the morning.

Vindicated in my Cassandra-like fears, I told Theo I felt exactly as Bell did. Something bad was coming. I'd felt it coming for a while, I could smell it, taste it. Vaporous and rank, it was poisoning the air.

'We should leave, too, and we should do it soon. Maybe go back to Crete, where we were happy.'

'Sarah. We can't keep running.'

'Why the hell not? I can't watch this, what's coming.'

But he was working on several short pieces using an eclectic assortment of instruments. 'We'd spoken of you writing lyrics,' he said. Besides, William and Maria wanted more children and they were drawing plans to expand the house. He didn't want to stop everything, pack up and take off because of something that *might* happen, *sometime*.

'*Will* happen. *Soon*. I'll go alone, then. I can't stay and just wait.'

'Do what you have to do. Nothing will make any difference. You know this. If something's going to happen, it will happen.'

I did know it. It made me sick to know it.

CHAPTER 4

It's now close to the end of January, 1891, and it's snowing. It's coming down hard, as it did a few weeks ago, on the twenty-ninth of December, when it turned the bodies of more than three hundred Indian women, children and men into grotesque frozen statuary on the ground near Wounded Knee Creek.

When I heard about it, I ran outside and vomited. I screamed over and over, '*Where were their gods?*' Theo and William ran out after me. It was William who'd brought the news.

Afraid that Sitting Bull would leave the reservation to join the Ghost Dancers, the Indian agent ordered him arrested. It went wrong and the old man was shot on December fifteenth. What was left of his hungry, cold, sick people rushed to join another camp not far away. With the atmosphere agitated by the new religion, the sudden increase in numbers made the authorities nervous.

On the twenty-ninth, troops of the 7th Cavalry who'd been dispatched to handle the situation, began to take away the Indians' weapons, tearing up tipis, treating the women roughly. A medicine man ran back and forth blowing an eagle whistle, urging the Lakota to fight, reminding them that their Ghost Shirts would protect them.

As the shoving and shouting accelerated, a deaf Indian, probably confused, who had hidden a gun under his blanket as a few others also had done, fired it, possibly by accident. He didn't hit anyone, but it didn't matter. At the sound, the soldiers — as if they'd been waiting for a signal — turned rabid. Some, no doubt, were wild to finally avenge Custer. Most — I have no doubt about this — were taken over by their hatred, their lust to kill Indians, and a blood feast ensued. The Lakota men, having only a few guns among them, and though they fought hard with whatever else they could grab, were killed quickly. Children and women trying to run away were chased down and slaughtered.

On New Year's Day, the three hundred or so frozen bodies were shovelled into a long pit. Many were half-naked. Guessing they might be worth money, Ghost Shirts had been stripped off. No missionary bothered to pray over these people, and the one Catholic priest who would have, had been stabbed during the butchery and was near death.

William left and Theo held me until I was screamed out. He helped me back inside, took off my wet clothes and wrapped a blanket around me, settled me on the couch. He put wood on the fire, poured whiskey for us both and came to sit beside me. He waited for me to speak. It took a bit, as I was shaking so hard.

'What will we do?'

'We will live our lives, Sarah.'

'It's not enough.'

'No. But it may be all we can do. Live honourably.'

'What does *that* mean? How are we to do that?'

'I don't really know. We'll have to figure it out day to day.'

I stayed on the couch that night and kept the dog with me. Together we went outside many times to see if the stars were speaking of this atrocity, or the trees, or the night creatures. Were they howling with particular fervour? But all was as it always is. Nature watches us, and is unmoved.

Theo came down in the early morning to make coffee. He put out some bread and butter. I couldn't eat, but joined him at the table.

'I can't do this any more,' I told him.

'Do what?'

'Live this life. Be comfortable. Be rich. Be in love. How dare I? The injustice! Why do I deserve this, and they…'

'Punishing yourself for the luck of your birth will not make it just. We must live our lives as well as we can.'

'*Honourably*, I think you said.'

My tone was derisive, but he ignored this.

'Yes. Honourably.'

'That's not enough. We must *do* something. *I* must do something. Or I will not be able to live with myself.'

'A bit ago, you wanted to run away. Now, you want to be a hero. This country is going to be at war with itself for a long time. There'll be a few heroes, but my love, you will not be one of them. And neither will I. Your brother, your Zeke, of whom I think the world, may well become a hero for his people, and heroes will arise among the Indians, and *for* them, but it will not be you or me. Sometimes, it must be enough just to live an honest life. To be simple. To be *kind*. To reach for the small goodnesses…'

I could not listen to his philosophising. His words — any words — seemed useless. And *ideas*? An indulgence of the well fed. I rose from the table angrily, put on boots and a buffalo coat, told him to keep the dog inside and went through the deep snow down to the stream. There was ice on the surface but I could hear the water moving under it.

Bright Eyes had told me — and I'd taken it as a promise — that death would not vanquish them.

'You will hear them singing,' she'd said.

That had been many years ago. She'd been a sweet old woman, probably dead now. She'd also said that evil would in time succumb to its own poison, but I'd seen no sign of this. No sign at all.

I sat, scoured hollow, emptied of emotion. I wondered if I was dying, my senses were shutting down. Fine, I said to myself, die. The world was too white — the irony of that! — and I couldn't see clearly. I'd lost feeling in parts of my body. I could do nothing but sit there. And listen. So, I listened.

And I heard them. I didn't believe it. I thought I was going mad, so I made myself breathe slowly, slowly. Still, I heard them. My heart leapt and I made it quiet for fear the miracle would evaporate.

I heard them in the water running under the ice, in the small sounds of the winter morning, in my heartbeat. It was all of a piece. I could hear them singing. The sound of their singing grew, as if they were passing through the air above me — I could hear the flying hooves and the bells on their caparisoned ponies, muffled by unearthly distance, yet clear — until it faded back into the sounds of the creek bed in snow and ice, and my own breathing.

I heard them. I might have heard them because I needed to so very badly, but it didn't matter. It doesn't matter. Bright Eyes had never spoken despairingly of the Indians' future, she'd trusted in their vigour. There'd be terrible hardship, terrible cruelty, it would seem relentless, but there was also resilience and profound courage.

Theo was right. I had wanted want to be a hero, an avenging goddess. I am only a witness, so, I shall be a witness. That will be my work. It's not enough, but it's the best I can do.

I went back into the cabin. Theo put on another pot of coffee as I washed and dressed. It was still quite early. I took down a jar of preserves from the plums I'd gathered in the fall. I cut us each a slice of bread. Theo poured the coffee. We ate breakfast.

A C K N O W L E D G M E N T S

This project took a long time and was often a personal battleground. The love of family and friends sustained me.

Carol Zaloom did the art work for the cover and interior title pages. It's as if she pulled images from my imagination; she understands me well enough to have done this very thing. A number of other people who are accomplished writers, editors, artists in various disciplines gave me invaluable help.

My brilliant friend, Mary Gallagher, novelist-screenwriter-playwright, read drafts of early chapters and urged me to persist when all I wanted to do was go swimming. Nina Shengold, Laura Shaine Cunningham, and other members of Actors and Writers with whom I had a crazy lot of profound fun for about ten years in Olivebridge, NY, gave me the courage to try new directions in my writing.

George Crane, Melanie Byres, Tad Wise all gave me notes at various stages that helped me clarify my vision, sharpen my attack. Steve Gorn, acclaimed bansuri flute master, gave me unexpected support for the book at a critical time. Many dear friends continue to keep me going simply by being part of my life. Gioia Timpanelli, master storyteller and novelist, has given generous friendship and inspiration for many decades. I am grateful.

Since 2009, I've lived on Paros, one of Greece's Cycladic islands, where every day I experience the ancient ethos of filoxenia — friendship extended to foreigners. Also in Greece, on the island of Tinos, in July of 2018, I participated in a literary festival, eighteen writers from eight countries. The only American, I felt welcomed into a global community of writers and my life changed.

I'd also like to acknowledge the sense of collaboration I've experienced with Colin Rolfe and Paul Cohen at Epigraph Publishing in Rhinebeck, N.Y. Thank you.

Note: My father, Maj. James H. Wallace, served in the U. S. Air Force for twenty years. A relative of his, Capt. George D. Wallace, rode with the 7th Cavalry during the Indian Wars. He'd been deployed to the Little Big Horn, and was near the site of Custer's defeat. Fourteen years later, he was one of the twenty-five white soldiers killed at Wounded Knee, December 29, 1890. He was commended for 'conspicuous gallantry'. I learned about this well into my research, and it's not easy to live with. I hope that my relative was a coward. I hope that when he fired his rifle to keep up appearances, he fired high.

www.ingramcontent.com/pod-product-compliance
Lightning Source LLC
Chambersburg PA
CBHW020412030726
47495CB00006B/1483